ALEXANDRIA LEE

Seducing Danger

Star-Crossed Series: Book Two

First edition

Editing by L. Mariani
Cover art by Darla Cassic
Illustration by Sara Beeksma

This book was professionally typeset on Reedsy.
Find out more at reedsy.com

Contents

Acknowledgement

To all of my readers, old and new, thank you for giving my characters and their world a chance to live and be seen and be loved. I am nothing without all of you.

And to my mom. Aside from, you know, giving me life, she took every single phone call of mine when I had questions about police procedures or anything in that realm. She's hands down the best mom in the world, I swear.

I love you to the moon and back, Mom.

Seducing Danger

Book Two of the Star-Crossed Series

Happily ever afters don't come for the wicked...

ONE

"State your full name, please."

"Katerina Reigh Sanders."

"And you're aware that this conversation is being recorded?"

Stiffly, I nodded.

"Can you give a verbal response for the tape recorder?"

Rage fumed, burning holes through my mostly non-existent patience as I eyed the police officer conducting the interview across the table.

My upper lip twitched. "I'm aware."

This guy. This fucking guy was every single stereotype a cop could be, and it put my gag reflex to work. He was overweight. He was balding. He even had dustings of what looked like a powdered donut clinging to the collar of his olive green shirt.

His appearance, the smugness to his face, his tinge of body odor, all of it—*all of it*—was shredding through my last goddamn nerve.

"All right, start from the beginning of what happened and don't leave nothin' out."

The officer righted his legal pad notebook on the cold metal table between us, a number two pencil in hand and hovering over the lined yellow paper. The notebook had his eyes' focus instead of me, and I pinched my sharp tongue between my teeth until blood seeped through so I didn't scream at him to look at me when he was talking to me.

I unlocked my stiff jaw, barely breathing. "We were sitting on the—"

"Who's we? We need you to be specific."

Red flashed around my vision as he interrupted me, haloing the pudge-faced officer in a ring of lightning fire. "*Layla* and I. Layla Irene Montez. The entire fucking reason we're here at two in the morning."

He finally flickered a look up at me, unkempt eyebrows driving together.

"Young lady, there's no reason to get mad at me, so watch your mouth and watch your attitude, okay?"

The condescending pet name narrowed my eyes to slits, and the temperature dropped several degrees in the tiny four-walled interrogation room. Hair on my arms prickled, ice exchanged out the blood in my veins, and my voice wielded the same frozen and deadly potential as an icicle.

"Where's Dominic?"

I hadn't seen him since we got to the police station. I wasn't *allowed* to see him.

The officer shifted in these god awful plastic chairs we both sat in. "Detective Reed is finishing up giving his own statement."

"He barely saw anything," I argued, indignant and pissy. "He heard me scream, but in the ten fucking seconds it took for him to get to us, she was already gone."

Gone.

Layla was gone.

It had only been a few hours, but I felt her loss like it had been years already. Years of missing her, agonizing about her, and drowning in the blame of her loss. I was breathing guilt instead of oxygen, the heaviness coating my lungs until they were drenched in self-loathing.

This was my fault.

Whatever happened to her would be my fault too.

"Tell me about how you got to Detective Locklin's residence," he pressed to continue.

I handed him a look like he was really fucking stupid. "Is that Ryan?"

He rolled his heavy-lidded eyes rather indiscreetly. "Yes."

"Layla took me there."

"Why?"

"Because I wasn't supposed to be out tonight, but I didn't *listen,* so Ryan and Dominic got her to trick me into thinking we were going to some house party, when really we were going there."

"How does she know Detective Locklin?"

"They're fucking." Officer Stereotype blinked extra hard like I'd slapped him with the information. "They met at the hotel last week or whatever, and they're kind of together. I think. They had a date planned."

A date that now was ruined.

Ryan was a mess. I was a mess. Everything was a fucking mess.

"Are you currently seeing anyone?"

I rolled my eyes back to him, drawling, "Why? You asking me out?"

"*What*? Lord, no." His fat cheeks pinked as he blustered. "You're the same age as my daughter."

"Then it doesn't matter if I have a regular dick to fuck or not. What *matters* is finding Layla, so how do you plan to do that?"

"By getting as much information—important or not—as we can." His murky-colored eyes needled to a fine point on me. "Such *as,* did you notice anyone following you while you were out tonight? Why'd you go out when you weren't supposed to? *And* are you dating anyone or not?"

A growl climbing up the back of my throat, I bared all my teeth and snapped. "*No,* we didn't notice anyone following us. I went out because I'm a fucking *idiot,* and it's none of your goddamn business, but I'm *single.*"

Technically.

Couldn't exactly date someone who's married. Or separated. Whatever.

Dominic and I couldn't go out on dates or kiss or touch in public. All we had were stolen moments behind closed doors and feelings that could kill us.

Feelings that could kill Layla now that she was caught in the middle of them.

If I had never gone out…

If I had never tried so hard to avoid Dominic because of all these *feelings.*

"Did the man who took your friend say anything to you?" The officer brought me back, keeping my sanity spiral balancing on the edge, like toes dangling over a cliffside one wrong step away from tumbling over.

"All he said was that she was the 'wrong one' but that she'd do," I spat, disgust rolling off my tongue.

I was the right one for whatever fucking reason, and it should have been me.

It should be me. I should be gone. I should be—

"Why do you think they didn't take you if you're the gal they went there for?"

I passed my hands over my face to block out the aggressive fluorescent lighting above us, digging fingers into my eye sockets as I sighed and tried to keep my voice from cracking. "Because I fought back, and Layla..." I swallowed, my throat parched and swollen. "She didn't."

A beat.

"You didn't help her?"

My fingers rubbing into my eyes froze. Oxygen refused to pull back into my heavy lungs.

Slowly—so fucking slow you'd have thought my muscles turned to sludge— I moved my hands away to meet the officer's eye. He flinched, the heat in my glare nipping him from across the table.

"I don't know if you've ever been punched in the face before," I started *real* low, but my temper caught up fast, chomping at the syllables as they left my mouth. "But it's not a fucking picnic."

Displeasure flushed the officers cheeks, and he gripped his pencil harder. "I've had my fair share of tussles. I know it can be scary, and it's common for people to freeze up."

A second screamed between us.

"I didn't freeze."

"We don't have to call it that if you don't want—"

"I *don't* want because it's not true." The stiffness in my jaw protested as my teeth knocked together, grinding in fury. I hadn't seen a mirror yet, but I imagined the left side of my face was splashed in ugly purple colors, imprints of knuckles nearly black.

I'd been given a bag of ice by the paramedic that came with the cavalry to Ryan's place right after it happened, a bag of ice that sat next to me now, deflated into a pointless puddle of water.

"*People* may freeze up. *You* may freeze up." My temper canted me forward. "I don't fucking freeze."

He pushed a light scoff, pointing a chubby finger my way on the table. "I said to watch your language, did I not? Young ladies like you shouldn't be using that type of language anyway."

Frenetic, fiery energy piled together inexplicably fast in my chest—a bomb setting itself in ready. "Are you serious? Are you actually serious right now?"

"I am." He set his pencil down and folded his arms over his stomach. "Do you think I let my daughters use that kind of language?"

The lightning energy glitched a flash of hot white over my vision and down my body, sending tingles like fire ants all over my flesh, biting and burning. I wanted to scratch at my skin, claw it right off to make the needling sensations stop.

"Do I fucking *care*? All I care about is you doing your job and finding my best friend!"

"*Hey*." He thrust a warning hand my way, and I realized then that I'd come forward to the table, pressing myself against it like I was trying to merge into the metal. "Lower your voice, rein back that attitude, and don't be telling me how to do my job, okay? I've been doing it for thirteen years just fine."

"Your job does not consist of telling me if I should say *fuck* or not," I seethed venom. "Your job is to find Layla!"

"Don't you think I know that?" His voice rose.

Mine rose higher. "If you know that, then do it!"

His whole face boiled beet red, blotchy spots rising up the slopes of his neck. "You're upset about your friend, and I get that, but you need to *watch* how you speak to a man of the law."

Man of the law. Man of law. Man. Men. All men.

All men thought they were *special* when, in fact, they were the *problem*. Men took Layla. This man was doing nothing to help find her. A man named Tommy targeted me for a reason no one could figure out. All men were the fucking worst.

All men except Dominic.

He was the exception to every rule I'd ever learned, and he could fix this.

"I want Dominic," I started, voice teetering a dangerous line.

"Detective Reed is busy."

My top lip caught on a sneer. "I don't believe you."

Officer whatthefuckever streamlined an exhale, his patience leaving his body in the breath. The sides of his cheeks started to pulse, his anger taking over. "You don't have to believe me. Can we get back to your statement?"

"What, so you can keep shitting on how I speak or asking me if I'm fucking anyone?" I shoved myself back from the table, shooting up on my feet. My sanity dangling over that cliffside bowed nearer to the free-fall. "*No.* I want someone I know is going to do the job and help Layla. I want *Dominic*!"

"You don't get to make demands, missy." He slapped his hands down on the table, metal vibrating back. "Or have you forgotten why we're all here tonight?"

His question sucked all the air out of the room.

It was oxygenless. It even dried out my eyes that were glued on his, wide and daring him to say more. The lack of air soured the room, the taste on my tongue, the feel of my own skin against my body. It all felt… wrong. It all felt like my body had become something strange. Something uninhabitable.

Something not human at all.

Like I didn't need oxygen to survive, but *fire* to give me life.

Lightning.

"Why?" I asked him, stretching my fingers around the energy buzzing through them.

Say it. Say it. Please say it. Let me explode. Let me ignite. Let me lose my goddamn mind for good.

He lowered the angle of his double chin, stretching my sanity cord down with it. "Because you didn't fight for your friend and they took her when they were there to get *you*."

And the cord snapped.

My lightning ruptured beneath my red-hot skin and ricocheted around the room, breaking loose and striking any and everything in its path. It was loud.

It was screeching in a pain it didn't know how to handle and kept zapping at any shadow that moved. I couldn't see anything but the lightning, didn't know where I was going or what I was doing.

My control was as blind as my vision.

I saw nothing but searing white. Boiling heat imprisoned my body and put shards of glass in my words and anyone who got in their way were my victims. My hearing melted to slow cries and booming shouts. Something clanked—*slammed*—and I jerked at the noise.

Then something touched my arm, and I jerked at the foreign grip.

I bucked the touch from my body and tried to turn, tried to run from it, but my eyes were too blurred over to see where I was trying to go. I spun around, fire burning in my lungs, a whirling pit of thousands of colors following me in circles, bursting so suddenly from everywhere and capturing me in the eye of its color storm.

Blues, greens, oranges, reds, yellows exploded around me, splattering the once white canvas of anger with more color than I knew even existed.

Something grabbed at me again, something powerful and strong, and this time, it wrapped around my back, pinning my lightning-fast arms at my side. A cry retched out of me, body thrashing in the confines of whatever force had me.

"Kat."

Thunder crackled across my rainbow-colored skies.

My fight stalled for a second—a split familiarizing second—to hear the thunder speak. My sick heart wanted its sound; my lightning *needed* it. That quick second was used against me in the very next, a force locking around the back of my neck and pinching it *hard*.

"Kat, look at me."

A gasp sliced up my throat, distraught and desperate for the thunder reigning right above me. I could hear it, rumbling and shaking my world, but I couldn't see it. I blinked and I blinked until tears leaked down the sides of my face like rainfall.

Where is it, where is it, where is it?

"I'm here," the thunder rolled, gently and sweetly, encouraging the rain to clear my eyes. "I'm right here."

A dry sob spilled between my lips at the sound of him and nothing more. There were still too many glitching colors orchestrating my emotions, but the force holding the back of my neck didn't give up.

It slid up into my hair, delivering a stroke so soft, it wiped away one of the rainbow layers. Relief so sought-after it *hurt* braided up my spine, and a breath rattled down my throat as the force played the same motion again and again. It held me and cured me of my blindness, sweeping all the colors away until only one was left.

Gray, the same shade of the sky after a brutal storm, hovered over me. A pair of thunderclouds hoping to cool off the lightning still running hot in my veins.

"Dominic," I breathed, because my voice had gone into hiding.

He was here.

He was here, and he'd never looked closer to shattered. Every beautiful line of his face had been fractured, exposed fear glinting beneath the cracks. Tonight hadn't been easy on him either.

A noise clattered through the small room, jumping my stare over to see the fat-faced officer being ushered out by nameless uniforms.

"She's *crazy*. Did you see her? Reed, she's—"

"Get out," Dominic cut him off, talking to the officer but staring at me. The pitch of his voice tracked chills down my arms, the threat of it rumbling in his chest. The asshole apparently didn't hear it as I did, though.

"Reed, you can't be—"

"I said get *out*," he snarled, snapping his head towards the door.

I couldn't see the look he was giving him, but I imagined it to be a murderous one by the way words died out on Officer Stereotype's tongue and his face paled. Quickly, I cut my eyes back to Dominic who was still delivering death with his glare to the other players in the room.

I took a moment to clock everything about him. The stringent hold he had over the muscles in his face, each one taut down to the cords in his thick neck, straining beneath smooth skin. Also, the way he was hunched over me, hiding me in his broad chest so no one but him could touch me, let alone see me.

His protection over me radiated out of him in waves that screamed louder than they should, and if he wasn't careful, anyone who bothered to listen would be able to hear our dirty secret.

Eventually, everyone left the room to just me and Dominic.

The effects of my outburst slammed into me as soon as we were left to our silence. Exhaustion slumped my shoulders and dragged my eyelids down, pouring a heaviness over my mind that tempted me to fall into Dominic and rest.

I wouldn't though. Not until I either found Layla or I died trying.

Through the film of exhaustion, I hadn't seen that Dominic had been staring at me since we'd been left alone. I didn't realize it until the undeniable burn of his gaze simmered over my stiff cheek where the muscles throbbed the most.

Voice cracking, I asked, "Is it bad?"

He filled his chest slow, filtering the air through his lungs to breathe out the lie. "No."

I could tell by his face it was though. He looked like he was the one who'd been sucker punched instead of me, agony breaking his stony eyes to rubble as they traced the side of my face.

"Were you listening to the interview?"

He nodded with trouble, the cords in his neck still tense.

"He's not wrong," I said, hollow and shameful.

Dominic's nostrils flared with a sharp breath like he expected me to say exactly that and had his argument prepped. "He *is* wrong. He never should have made you feel guilty. You did exactly as I taught you. You did…" Poorly timed pride backlit his stormy eyes, and he exhaled sharply, chewing back on his bottom lip. "You did *exactly* as you should have," he asserted, the rich notes of his voice strangely thick. "And that's why you're still here."

"Yeah. And why Layla's not."

The truth spilled out thoughtlessly and dragged a broken piece of my heart up with it. It razored the sides of my throat, cutting reminders into my flesh so every time I breathed, I remembered Layla might stop at any moment.

I pinched my eyes shut fast, trying to squeeze out images of what might be happening to her right now. She was probably crying for me, her parents, anyone to help her. Her heart-shaped face flashed behind my eyes despite me trying to block it out, and all I saw were her tears rolling down her cheeks, big and fat and all my fault.

What if she's already—

Dominic caught my spiral in his knowing hands, squeezing one around my body and the other at the nape of my neck. My eyes fluttered back to his, blurry with all the salty tears I imagined in Layla's.

He brushed the rough patch of his thumb beneath one of the tears, catching it as it spilled. "We'll get her back."

"Do you know that?" Weakness shook my vocal cords, and I didn't care. I was weak. I was a weak goddamn person, and that's why Layla was gone. "Tell me you know that for sure and don't lie."

Tell me you're positive. Tell me I have nothing to worry about. Tell me I didn't just get one of the only people in the world who loves me killed because I was too scared of falling in love with you.

Silver-ringed eyes looked between mine, steadying on my swollen tears. "I know that this is different than the other abductions, and different is good. We have more to work with than we ever have." His hand gathering my tears settled on my shoulder, a less suspicious place to be. "I'll get her back. I promise."

My heart squeezed, the suffocation familiar and welcomed.

"Don't promise."

Dominic pulled back, asking a question that proved his soul was pure. Maybe a little naive. "Why not?"

Painfully, I muttered, "Because I don't wanna hate you if you break it."

And I would. I'd hate him if he broke a promise to save her life. It was the only way I think I *could* hate him. I tried so many other ways to hate him to save myself from him, and it never worked, but that would do it.

In the middle of staring up at him like I was scared to hate him and him staring at me as if he was terrified of the exact same thing, my phone rang.

The number on the screen was unknown.

I went to shove it back in my pocket when long fingers clasped my wrist. Confusion brought my stare up, but Dominic wasn't looking at me.

He was looking at my vibrating phone.

Glaring at it as if it had fangs.

"Answer it."

Two words, and the fire ants from before broke out beneath my skin again. Nibbling. Scratching. Poisoning my body with tension. My heartbeat *thunk, thunk, thunked* up my throat, the severity of Dominic's tone driving it up.

Did he think—

"Kat, *now*," Dominic clipped, pushing my phone towards me.

It buzzed and buzzed, taunting me and scoring my blood in fire-hot terror with every pulse. Terror. I was *terrified*. I was exhausted and terrified and heartbroken and not at all me. Layla being taken had confused my wiring, and I couldn't find the switch to work my confident spitfire mouth right now.

All I wanted was to chuck the phone across the room and watch it shatter into a million pieces, whoever was on the other end shattering with it.

Instead, I pulled it to my ear and tried like hell not to let my voice crack.

"Hello?"

A pause hung over the line, and I died a hundred deaths waiting for it to be over.

A husky laugh trickled through the other end. Then an unfamiliar voice. "There she is."

Even though I only knew three words by this voice so far, I knew immediately it was a voice that would narrate nightmares for the rest of my life. It was… empty. A shadow's voice.

It spoke again.

"You're a hard girl to get face time with, you know that?"

The gravel in the voice scraped along my spine, like nails on a fucking chalkboard, tearing a shiver through my bones. They all clashed and clanked until my body seized in a uniformed cringe.

I spun away from Dominic, hiding my phone between my palm and cheek. "Who is this?"

The voice taunted me with silence, already manipulating the things I hated most against me. I waited and I waited, eyes jumping from side to side and focusing on nothing.

"Come on. You're a smart girl. Or at least, that's what your high school papers said, Catnip."

Tension in my jaw slacked, and his name slipped out on a dry breath.

"Tommy."

A groan came through the phone, the satisfaction oozing through the line. "My name sounds like heaven in your mouth. Say it again."

The texture of his satisfaction was so slimy, so greasy, it slipped between my ears and dripped down my faulty wiring, squeezing between all the cracks until it reached my temper's switch…

And fritzed the thing into override.

My spearing tongue unlocked, my temperature ignited, and I went from terrified to a terror in a lightning flash.

"What the *fuck* do you want from me?" I growled into the phone, strangling it hard. "*Where's* Layla?"

And he chuckled. He actually *laughed*.

Except it didn't sound like real laughter. It sounded like echoes of footsteps in a haunted graveyard.

"Your little friend is right here next to me. We're having a nice time, aren't we?"

In desperation, I willed the world around me to shut the fuck up in hopes that I could hear Layla reply, hear even a whisper for proof of life. I got nothing but Tommy's yapping. "She says hello. Well, she would if she weren't gagged. Which is a *very* nice look on her. Those big, beautiful eyes and a stuffed mouth? She'd be sold in a finger snap."

Sweat sprouted cold beads on my hairline.

"*Sold?*"

Dominic crowded in behind me, his body heat sweltering against my back. He was too hot. Everything in this room was too goddamn hot.

"And I'm talking *big* money," Tommy went on. "Maybe even more than we'd get for you."

Big hands—*hot* hands—grabbed my waist and turned me around. Dominic clustered my vision, the closeness frightening my limbs and I stumbled back into the wall. He caught me by the shoulders, directing my frazzled attention to his lips as he mouthed, *'It's Tommy?'*

Wide-eyed, I nodded, trying to find the train back to where this conversation was going.

"So this is about money? Does my mom owe you money? If that's all this is about, I can *pay* you."

Dominic nodded for me to keep going before showing me his strong back as he bolted for the door, jamming it open and leaving me alone with Tommy.

"You're asking the wrong questions, gorgeous."

"Then what are the *right* questions?" I sneered, blood flaming.

"How about you meet me and find out?"

I didn't think. I just asked, "When?"

Tommy clicked his tongue on the other end, the noise like a gunshot. "Right down to it. No theatrics. I knew I'd like you."

"Yeah, I'm a fucking treat. Now tell me *when*, asshole."

"Jesus, Mary, and *Joseph*, you have a wicked tongue," he exclaimed, excitement vibrating his hollow voice. Then he said something that snatched the fight right out of mine.

"Do you kiss your cop with that filthy tongue?" Tommy's voice drew lower, grating my rotten secret against his vocal cords. Like rocks in a blender. "I bet he can't get enough of it, can he? Is he there right now? Put *Detective Reed* on so I can ask him myself how much he loves that mouth of yours."

Dominic's name went from Tommy's vile throat to my dry tongue, sitting a steel brick on it so I couldn't talk. I could barely breathe.

How did he...

"Don't tell me. Cat got your tongue?" Tommy purred in place of my silence, mockery painting the words.

Mockery that hit my blood like gasoline, drenching me from the crown of my head down to my toes, sparking my brain back to focus and lit my temper full of fresh fire.

I didn't even *know* this guy, and he'd already fucked with my best friend, *took* my best friend away from me. Now, he wanted to go after Dominic?

He wouldn't touch a goddamn hair on Dominic's head without me there to put my foot through his throat first.

"I don't know where you get your gossip, but your information's faulty, jackass."

"Lying?" Tommy grunted. "That's a disappointment. I guess you can't be completely perfect, can you?"

Lightning burned up my throat as I screamed. "Can you just shut the fuck up and tell me when to meet you? I'll do it, okay? I'll meet you, and I'll pay you however much money it is my mom owes you, do a nice little tap dance for you, and then you give Layla back and get the fuck out of my life!"

"You know that's not how this goes, Catnip. You've seen the movies."

"Yeah, but I don't remember auditioning to be *in* one."

"You did that just by being you. You're a *star*, and you caught everyone's eye burning as bright as you do."

"What, now you're reciting me poetry?" I spat. "I'm flattered, really, but I don't wanna be a star. I just want Layla back."

The voice Tommy spoke in next was the vocal equivalent of the dirtiest smirk you could imagine, rotten with devious intent.

"You're gonna have to come and get her."

The door to the interview room burst back open at that very second, worried eyes and a tightly wound man coming through. Dominic and I locked eyes, a beat of energy crackling the air between us and freezing him in his tracks.

Gaze still trapped on the man who would hate me for saying it, I forced the three damning words anyway.

"I'll do it."

Panic speared from all sides of Dominic's steely eyes, and I watched his jaw constrict *so* hard, even mine felt sore.

"Peachy," Tommy crooned inside my ear like an earwig. Yeah, that's what he was. He was a fucking earwig of a human being. "I'll call back later with details."

"Fine."

"You gonna miss me until then, Catnip?"

My lip curled up. "Like I'll miss an STD."

Dominic stalked towards me, closing in until my head bowed back beneath his. It was with the man I'd equated to a god countless times reigning over me, swearing he'd protect me with all he had using that glint in his burning eyes, that the devil himself signed off.

"I'll be seeing you."

And the line went dead.

TWO

"What time are we expecting her?"

My neck twisted towards the buzzing road sitting at the edge of the small slope we were on, gaze traveling down the street to the vacant bus stop. "The bus she took should drop her off any minute."

"Mom—"

"I know, I know." Dominic's mother waved him off, patting his hand lying on the picnic bench all five of us sat around. The Lakeside park only had two picnic tables, and somehow, we'd nabbed the one sheltered beneath a monstrous oak tree. "Maya, Charlotte, and I are going to go check out that jungle gym when she gets here. Maybe even get some ice cream if we're feeling reckless."

"Yes, please!" Maya nearly fell over as she shot up on the wooden seat of the picnic table, Dominic wrapping a quick hand around her arm to keep her upright. She barely registered the near topple, landing those big bright blues down on her father. "Can I get the birthday cake flavored one?"

Dominic parted his mouth, a soft laugh rolling through his fatherly bravado. "You can get whatever flavor you want, so long as it's small so you don't fill up before dinner."

"Katty?"

The sweet little sound of my nickname pulled my attention over the table with an easy smile. Charlotte's chocolate eyes were on me, scribbled in worry.

Her bottom lip protruded to a pout, and my easy smile became difficult to hold.

"Can I get ice cream *and* say hi to Mommy?"

Goosebumps that had nothing to do with the passing breeze stirred with purpose on my arms. That purpose being to remind me how *much* Charlotte loved our mother, and how important it was for them to see each other today.

Despite how I felt about our mother, Charlotte's heart was swollen with nothing but unconditional love for her, and I had to remember that when she got here.

"Yeah. Yeah, of course you can." My cheeks dented with love just for Bugs, and she gave me a half-lipped attempt back, dropping her attention to the grooves on the well-worn cedar table. That mismanaged organ in my chest protested at the sight of her half crescent smile and spewed my next words fast and aiming to soothe.

"She's really excited to see you. She told me on the phone last night."

Blonde pigtails bounced as she snapped her head up. "She did?"

"*Oh* yeah. Big time. She's gonna want a huge hug when she gets here."

Excitement glittered across her eyes as she grinned a thoroughly toothy grin, just how I liked. Her attention jumped behind me for a split second, and that glittering excitement exploded in a bomb of tinsel happiness.

"She's here!"

Charlotte took off in the direction she pointed, ignoring my calls for her to be careful and slow down. She didn't listen at all. She just kept barreling her tiny legs all the way down the sweeping field of nearly neon green grass until she ran right into the narrow legs of a woman.

Of our mother.

Who was out of bed and out of the house at two in the afternoon, which left me to stand completely and staggeringly corrected on one of my strongest beliefs.

Miracles really did exist.

And one was walking this way on surprisingly sturdy feet. Charlotte had locked herself around our mother's hip, head tipped back to her and mouth running a mile a minute with all the things she'd wanted to tell her since we left our house less than a week ago.

Maya and Meredith made themselves scarce, and Dominic straightened his already perfect posture next to me as Kathy and Charlotte got close. The wood beneath my thighs creaked and warped as Dominic shifted himself to fill the gap where Maya had been between us. His arm pressed against mine, the long-sleeved shirt he wore refusing me direct skin contact, but his body warmth fed through in heady doses, and it was enough to stroke down my frazzled nerves.

It had been less than twenty-four hours since Layla had been taken, and I wasn't… *handling* well, some might say.

Some might say I'd officially kicked the crazy bucket. I might even say that. I hadn't eaten much, but I wasn't really hungry. Plus, I couldn't help but wonder if Layla had food wherever she was, and if she didn't get to eat, then it didn't seem fair that I could.

I didn't sleep last night either. Not a wink, and maybe that's why my mother looked different as she approached.

Her skin wasn't quite so translucent, her hair not quite as ratty and creased in unwashed oil. The bags under her eyes were still heavy, but the red-rim outlining them was gone.

And when she put her gaze on mine, it was purposeful, and it was lucid for a change.

Or maybe I was just sleep-deprived and lucidity wasn't a thing I had myself at the moment. Whatever. Bottom line, she looked all right. Not like walking death like she had been for the last three years.

She even dared to peek the end of her pale pink mouth up at me as she and Charlotte reached us.

"Hi."

Hi. Fucking hi. Great opener, Mom.

"Katty, Mommy brought me a flower!" Charlotte detangled herself from our mother to show me her flower—an origami rose, water-colored in reds and pinks, folded neatly and precisely.

I swallowed hard, my throat suddenly stuffed full.

"It's beautiful, Bugs." *It's just like the ones she used to make me.*

"Can you hold onto it while I play?"

I pocketed the triggering memory, nodding. "Sure. Give her a hug and go ahead."

She did, squeezing our mother's waist that was so tiny, Charlotte's arms could wrap around her with hands overlapping. Surprise lit a map over Kathy's not-so-sunken-in face, and I watched her ride the trail from shocked to delighted to melancholy guilt at her youngest daughter's blind affection.

She didn't deserve it, and she knew it.

Charlotte skipped away to meet Maya, who was currently hanging off the monkey bars, and Dominic's mother, who was snapping a photo on her phone of her granddaughter's hyjinx.

"Is the curly-haired one yours?" my mother asked, skirting a glance to Dominic next to me as she rounded to the open side of the table.

Dominic's reply was brief and polite. "She is."

Kathy struggled only slightly slipping her legs over the bench seat, her arms wobbly and noticeably frail. She managed, eventually, sitting down and nodding in Maya's direction. "She's a cutie."

Again, Dominic spoke in clipped tones. "Thank you."

He wasn't happy to be here. He wasn't happy we *had* to be here. It had been my idea, and he'd fought me through every iteration of the plan until we settled on one he approved of and had me nowhere near when it went down.

Kathy was our only connection to Tommy, meaning she was the only one who could help us get Layla back, and that wasn't an opportunity we could pass up just because I couldn't stand to be around her.

I already lost Layla once because of my insane emotions.

It wouldn't happen a second time.

The three of us sat for a moment, nothing but the elements of nature talking around us. Water rustled from the lake as the wind blew its gusts all over it, the leaves making just as much noise if not more, crinkling like wrapping paper on Christmas morning.

Children laughed, car horns honked, and the world rotated with life all around us. Our stiff triangle was the only thing dead about it, and I just wanted to get this the fuck over with.

"Your pal Tommy tried to pay me a visit last night."

Now *that* was an opener.

Kathy's eyes cracked wide open. "*What?*"

"Yup. One of his buddies gave me this," I angled my head so she could see, tracing my thumb down the edge of my sensitive jaw. "as a gift to remember him by, which was sweet of him."

What could have been misconstrued as worry streaked a blurry line through her stare, and she made a move to reach across the table. "Oh, *god*. Baby—"

"*Don't.*" All my muscles jerked me back like I was heading for a car crash, airbags deploying to keep me safe. Head down, the thought of her bony fingers on my face twitched my lip up and back. "Don't touch me."

A sigh left her body with enough weight in it to deflate her shoulders. Her collarbone stretched beneath her pale, moonlight skin as she hunched into herself. I wondered if she'd been eating since we left.

"He called Kat last night on a burner phone after trying and failing to abduct her," Dominic interjected, my mother's sharp gasp filling the fresh air. "His men took another woman in her place, and we believe it's Tommy's intention to have Kat trade places with the abducted woman later this week."

"*Layla.*" I threw the name in my mother's face and watched it splash horror all over.

She knew Layla. Vaguely. She knew her as someone I cared about. Someone who had been around for the last three years when she wasn't.

Her horror infused with confusion that weaved together her darkly-colored eyebrows.

"This doesn't make any *sense*," she said, scratching at her scalp with fingernails chewed down to the buds. "I-I've been going over it and thinking about it and…" My mother sunk her fingernails into the dead skin clinging to her lips and began to pull. All my teeth dusted against one another as I watched her worry her lips with our nasty nervous tick. "I can't-I can't think of anything. I haven't done anything to him. I-"

She heaved a heavy breath, stress pouring through. "I haven't even bought from his people in over two weeks."

"The why doesn't really matter at this point," Dominic interjected, leaving the last thing Kathy said to float in the back of my brain. *Two weeks?* "Last night all but confirms Tommy's involvement in a series of abductions in the area, and we think you can help lock him down long enough for us to find Layla."

Kathy blinked, eyes fluttering. "Me?"

"Yeah, since you're so buddy buddy with him."

She flicked me a look that said my words hurt, but she never confessed the pain out loud. She just moved on, passing her crinkled stare to Dominic. "If he told you he had this girl, why can't you arrest him?"

"Because it would be my word against his," I answered. "I say he called me, he says no he didn't."

"We couldn't track the call either. I ran out to see if we were getting anything, but—"

"He's too smart for that," Kathy finished for Dominic.

"Yeah…" I trailed off, an awkwardness hanging in the air that not even the slap of wind or lapping ripples in the lake could erase. The severity of Tommy and what he could and would do sustained us all in silence, and I didn't know any other way to break it than to just spit it out.

"We want you to meet with him."

Terror inflamed Kathy's stare, burning it wide and glistening the lens of it. Tiny droplets of sweat even dampened her hairline from the scalding degree of fear.

She shook her head vehemently, flitting her gaze down to the table.

"I can't do that."

Her fear, her answer, her refusing to look me in the damn eye when she denied me, provided all the kindling I needed to snap like firewood left in the flame too long.

"Since we're only in this mess *because* of you, I think you can."

"No, Katerina, he's-" Her panicked stare slid to Dominic. "He's dangerous. Tell her he's dangerous."

I cut a glance over to Dominic to see him giving her nothing but his stern silence.

Good.

"Yeah, well that dangerous man has my best friend, and he's coming after me next, so do you wanna maybe think about someone other than yourself for once?" Still, Kathy wouldn't look me in the eye. Her focus was on Dominic, on begging him with her pathetic gaze to help her, to fucking help *her* instead of me.

Lightning fizzled, bunching my hands to fists that shook. They trembled until all of me followed suit, my body charging up with too much energy, too much hatred, too much fucking electric fire to contain beneath my flaying skin.

"God*dammit!*"

A crash struck the happy park, emanating from under my fists that smashed into the tabletop. Heavy, unabated breathing wrecked my lungs, chest rising and falling as I realized I'd have to play my ace in the hole.

I would use it shamelessly even though I never should have had to.

She just should have said fucking yes in the first place.

"You owe me, okay? You *owe* me."

The vicious vibration distilling my voice nabbed her beady-eyed attention finally, her pale lips cracked in awe and sucking up every bit of truth I spit her way.

"For every parent/teacher conference you missed my senior year, for every time I cleaned up your puke and put you to bed, for every time Charlotte got a scrape and wanted her mom to kiss it better and you weren't there, and I did it and made up some lie about why you couldn't. You owe me for the childhood I gave up for *you*. I stepped in when you couldn't deal, and now you owe me."

A heated hand covered my knee beneath the table and squeezed. It squeezed support into me, lending me his compassion and affection and said that he was *here*. A rock wedged in my throat, choking me and my emotions. I tried to breathe through it, cleared my throat to dislodge it, but nothing worked.

So I just kept speaking, a hoarseness to my words that wasn't there before.

"For every date I missed, for the education I don't have, for having to watch you turn into something I *hate...* you owe me this. One meeting." I swallowed thickly. "I think I've earned that."

Kathy didn't look away from me this time.

She kept my eye contact, stringing a tension between the two of us that was its own thing of energy. It was ripe and raw, sensitive and simmering. It had the familiar feeling of lightning, but the birth of it rather than the execution.

And then, she soothed the binding of electric energy we created with three words.

"I'll do it."

Air suffused back into my lungs, and I hadn't realized I'd been holding my breath. I huffed outwardly like I'd run a small marathon sitting right here on this picnic bench. Dominic stroked a thumb over my knee, reminding me he was there and encouraging my anxiety to take a breath too.

While I caught my breath, Dominic explained the plan.

"You'll be completely safe. You'll be wearing a wire, and we'll have a team set up around the perimeter to move in the second we get him on tape saying or doing anything illegal. The goal is to lure him in with the intention of buying from him and arrest him the moment we have proof of a crime being committed."

My mother risked a glance Dominic's way. "You think that'll work?"

"We do." And he was nothing but confident as he said it.

His confidence instilled a batch in me too, letting me find my voice and tenacity again. "Then they can hold him and question him or beat the shit out of him until he tells us where Layla is."

Dominic's pointed gaze pushed into the side of my face as I suggested violence, but I didn't really care. In fact, I hoped they turned Tommy's insides to outsides to teach him his lesson.

Don't *fuck* with Kat Sanders.

"One condition," Kathy said suddenly, and I swear, I felt my heart stop. Just *stop.*

Of course. Of-fucking-course she had a condition. I wanted to laugh at myself, a real disgusted laugh that I so quickly accepted she would do this out of the goodness of her soiled heart.

Man, I really *was* out of it today.

Almost like I was expecting her to tell me the funniest joke, I asked, "And what would that be?"

"You can't be anywhere near the meeting."

Any bitter laughter prepped on my tongue dissipated.

I blinked hard at her. "What?"

"He's already tried to hurt you once, and I don't want you near him. If he gets even a whiff that something's up, he'll know it's to do with you, and I want you as far away as possible if that happens."

"We—"

"This is non-negotiable, Katerina," she cut me off, eyes like granite that wouldn't crack.

I sat back where I was, the breeze running its fingers through my hair and over my parted lips, drying them out with the taste of fall and sunshine. For the longest time, I just stared at her as something impossible happened.

Time and years blended, a smearing of colors, bright emotions, and dirty memories too. In that glitch, the last three years with this weed of a woman sitting across from me blurred like it had never been more than a terrible nightmare. In that faint miracle of a second, the nightmare melted away, and I saw a glimpse of a dream.

My mom. My *real* mom.

She was here, and she was even *better* than a dream. She was everything she used to be: protective, a little frazzled, and a lot messy, but loving above all else. She was the woman who put me to bed with stories of knights and castles, and the one who crafted origami flowers for me when she was feeling her best and let me paint them any color I wanted.

I hadn't seen this person in three years, and my chest fucking ached like someone had carved a bleeding heart on the outside to mirror the one on the inside.

It was only a glimpse of a ghost, of someone I used to love and cherish and who used to love and cherish me, but it hurt to an unspeakable degree to see her again. Even if it was only a mirage or my heart playing tricks on me.

She moved her strangely sturdy gaze from me over to Dominic. "You promise you'll keep her protected?"

"I do."

"Say you promise."

The demand shocked and mortified me. "*Kathy.*"

"I promise," Dominic swooped in with no reservations, and of course, went the extra mile. "I won't let anything happen to her. Ever."

My rounded eyes jumped back and forth between the two of them, confusion growing over my face like the spontaneous daisies in the grass beneath my feet.

"What the fuck is happening?" I asked, voice trilling higher than I planned.

Mom fidgeted with her fingers on the cedar tabletop, filling her chest with fresh air that I imagined sweeping her lungs like a cleansing, filtering out the smoke and soot caked in them.

"I've never met one of your, um, boyfriends?" She sent the question to Dominic for clarification.

Oh my god. No.

Heat flushed hot and fast up my chest, and I wanted to crawl into the inferno and die. We hadn't even had that talk yet, but Dominic tweaked his first smile of the conversation, the corner of his mouth curving softly.

"Sure."

God, could he sound *more* happy agreeing to that label?

My mother nodded slightly, dropping her gaze back to her folded fingers. "The first couple times we met weren't my... best."

No, I'd say drug dealers, home invasions, and unloading your emotional trauma weren't the best first impressions. But hey, Dominic's first impressions of me were back-talking, over-the-line jokes, and slapping him in the face with pizza, so maybe it ran in the family.

"But I'm sober," she said forcibly—*pridefully*—shocking my lips to a part. "Two weeks. I've been going to these, um, meetings and they help."

Next to me, Dominic stood, and as he did, lowered his face to my ear. "I'm going to check on the girls."

I craned my head back as he towered over me, wearing that devastating smile of his where even his dimples dared to peek through. A noise cracked between my lips that said without words I didn't want him to go, and his gorgeous smile deepened, his hand twitching like he wanted to grab my face and kiss me.

He couldn't, and we both knew it.

He settled for a squeeze of my shoulder before stepping out of the bench, walking around to the edge of the table.

Mom tilted her head up at him, morphing her eyes to slits that pretended to be menacing. "The next time we meet, I've got some questions for you."

Dominic being Dominic, grinned at the challenge.

"I look forward to answering them."

He rested those eyes like diamonds on me once more and smiled sweetly. The sight of it—of him—eased in my first full, belly-button-deep breath of the day.

I needed it. I hadn't breathed properly since last night.

Dominic's smile was a momentary relief however, and I hated to say that I missed him before he was gone, so I wouldn't.

I'd just think it and pretend it wasn't true.

As soon as Dominic was out of earshot and at the playground with the girls and his mom, Kathy asked, "How old is he, Katerina?"

Old enough that we're not having this conversation right now.

The wind blew my hair, strands flying in my eyes that I pushed away, sweeping them back over my head so I could keep my squinting eyes on my mother. We had other things to talk about than the ten year age gap between me and my still technically married ex-boss.

Lord, what a fucked up sentence.

"You're going to meetings?"

I didn't mean it, but a heavy coat of disbelief tainted my question. She didn't seem affected by it though. She just nodded.

"Down at the rec center. I take the bus there and back every day."

The information digested slowly, and my head shook back and forth at the same speed. "Why? Why now?"

Shame stole her focus to her hands, down to her chewed on, ripped at cuticles that now made sense if she'd been going through withdrawals. "Because of everything that's happening. I tried after the break in but… it didn't stick," she admitted, keeping her voice low. A murmured confession.

"I've, um," She stopped, pinching the space between her scrunched eyebrows and squeezing her eyes shut. My attention on her was fastened tight as she shook her head like she was trying to shake the words right out. "I haven't been *right* for you. I haven't been fair to you or your sister and… I've known it and I've seen it, but I didn't think I had to do anything to fix it because…"

A rattling breath inflated her sunken chest, her hand falling from her face and eyes flashing wide open. A gasp speared between my ribs, a needled pain to follow as she showed me so vividly the open breaks in her eyes, right down to her withered soul.

"Your dad leaving felt so unfair to *me*, and I didn't see how it affected you or your sister. I couldn't see anything but how *mad* I was at him for leaving after eighteen years and everything I—*we*—put up with from him… It cut into my view of everything and—"

"Your heartbreak blinded you."

Another side effect of the sickness.

"It did." She nodded in quick motions, running her hand up and down her arm, squeezing the pale flesh periodically. "It did, but that wasn't right. I shouldn't have let it. I-I should have been strong. Like you."

A pathetic laugh pushed past my lips. "I'm not strong."

I wouldn't be here if I was. In this situation where I was holding my sick little heart in one hand and searching for Layla with the other.

"Baby, you are." She scooted forward, arms reaching across the table to me but faltering at the last second, falling limp in front of her. We both stared at them—the offering—as my threat from earlier not to touch me permeated tension in the air.

She listened. She remembered and she listened.

And now my hands felt cold and lonely hidden beneath the table.

"You are strong. You're *so* strong," she pressed on, balling her hands up. "You carried this family when I couldn't, and you've raised your sister so beautifully, and I…" Her voice cracked and she dropped her chin to her chest, noticeable tremors shaking her pointed shoulders.

Soft sobs poured from her lips, and I sat there watching as she cried to herself. I just sat and *watched* like I'd been shoved into a state of shock. Tears rolled down cheeks that had gone blotchy with high emotions, and I'd seen those tears before. I *knew* I had.

But somehow they were different.

Something moved inside my chest, shifting and sort of aching but sort of not.

Her breathing shook in stutters as she inhaled sharply, putting those tear-stained eyes on mine that fucking shined like they never had before. "I'm just so proud of you and *so* sorry I let it get this bad," she sobbed, and that thing in my chest gripped itself *hard*. "I'm so sorry, baby. So so so sorry."

Her tears must have been twofold in purpose, washing shame down her face but also washing a flood through my head. I struggled for fragments of thoughts to put together into a coherent sentence, but they were all drowning. *I* was drowning.

My mom was proud of me.

Proud of me for everything I'd done for her and Charlotte. Maybe she was even proud of me as a daughter, and that *gripping* thing in my chest wanted so badly for it to mean something. Her pride.

I didn't need her to be proud of me, I kept thinking. I didn't need her tears that I'd been given too many times before. I didn't need her apologies that had somehow never sounded more like diamonds before, clear cut and pure.

I didn't *need* her. I'd been *fine* without her for years. I was absolutely fucking fine without a mom for *three years*. I had *myself*. I'd been there for *myself*.

But...

Why then did I want more? Why did I feel that stupid organ in my chest wheezing and begging for *her*?

"I know better than to trust you," I said out loud to remind myself it was true. "One good day, or two good weeks, isn't enough to make me trust you."

She started nodding, running her fingertips along the grooves in the wooden table. "I know. I know, but..." She blinked up at me, her eyelashes gathering away all her tears. "I'm gonna work on it. I'm gonna get better. For you and for your sister."

I hope so, I almost said.

"That'd be nice," I went with, knowing it was a smarter choice of words.

Hope was what got us here in the first place. Hoping for that fairytale ending, hoping for a life that didn't totally suck. So I wouldn't be naïve enough to hope for anything better with Kathy than what she'd given me to work with over the last three years.

Instead…

I'd just think about how nice it would be if my mom came back.

THREE

A few days later, and still no word from Tommy about Layla.

It was now Wednesday. She'd been taken Saturday night. That was four days of God knows what happening to her, four days of blind wondering what she was going through, where she was, if she knew I was out here trying to find her. Had Tommy even told her about the meetup we agreed to?

Why the fuck hadn't he called to set it up?

The plan with my mom had been set in motion already, her arrangement with Tommy planned for Friday. That meant all we could do until then was twiddle our fucking fingers or hope Tommy called before then to confirm Layla was still alive and our deal was still on.

The wait was nauseating, so I hadn't been eating much. The not knowing was pure torture, the pain clawing gruesome images at the backs of my eyes so I couldn't sleep much either.

As of this moment, Charlotte and Maya were sprawled out on blankets, watching a movie on the living room floor. I didn't know what movie. I hadn't been listening when they picked it. I hadn't been listening to much of what was going on around me the last few days, just sort of suspended in this deafening unknown.

It took a lot to jar me out of it and get my attention; both Dominic and Charlotte had been victim to my lack of presence.

But at that very second, the slam of the front door that shook the house to its bones and shrill scream that followed—yup, that did it.

"Dominic!"

Both of the girls' heads popped up high, snapping in the same direction as mine as clicks of stilettos punctuated the next venomous screech. "Dominic, what the *fuck* is this? Tell me what the fuck this is!"

The double f-bombs dropped hard on the two five-year-olds sitting in front of me. Their eyes rounded, innocence holding them wide as they looked back to me. Clacks of furious heels echoed closer, searching for Dominic—who wasn't home yet.

They came close enough that my posture righted back, locking tight in defense. The girls' attention was snatched from me to her as she barreled into the room, a wild viper chasing down her next kill.

Her diamond blue eyes landed on me first, her target switching over in a deadly flash.

"*You*," Heather hissed, chilling the temperature in the room with a word. "*You* did this."

The moment was more than awkward with the girls watching, and I replied through clenched teeth. "Did what?"

"This!" She ripped her hand up from the side of her sleek obsidian pants suit, holding a fisted, thick yellow envelope high in the air.

My head tilted up to the apparently criminal envelope and then back down to her.

"I don't know what that is."

"You really expect me to believe that you had no idea about this?" Her pretty eyes morphed into bladed slits. "You're moronic, but you're not *that* moronic."

On the couch, my fingers curled around the stuffing until I heard thick threads pop. Electricity thrummed from the shallow of my skin, easily plucked and provoked.

The air in the room got very, very stiff.

Maybe it was because I was both sleep and food deprived, or maybe because I'd been living on the brink of an emotional breakdown for months. *Maybe* it was because I'd had just about enough of Heather fucking Reed.

Whatever the reason, it didn't matter.

I was going to skewer this woman until her blood dressed my arms in sleeves up to my elbows. I could feel it—the snap, the lightning strike brewing. I just needed to move Heather outside so the bloodshed didn't get on either of the girls.

"You know what?" I snapped my fingers, shooting up so I was standing. "I think we should continue this scene outside."

I swiveled an arched look down at the girls and their confusion. "We're rehearsing a play. Your mom's the villain," I told Maya with a wink that should have awarded me the part.

Heather barked at me from behind like the yappy fucking bitch she was, and I ignored her. Spinning on my heel towards the backyard, eager fire simmering beneath my feet, I called back to her, "You're a good villain, but you could be great! Really lock into that natural *heinous* vibe you have going for you."

My feet didn't stop their pursuit to get out of earshot of the girls, and threatening clicks of fast-walking heels followed behind me just like I knew she would.

I spilled outside onto the back patio, putting my back to the yard and my front towards our leading villain as she made her way outside with me. She didn't close the door behind her like I would have preferred, but it was better than letting this ugly mess spill out right in front of the girls.

Heather's dark, pin-straight hair dared to bounce out of place as she huffed wildly, gritting her perfect teeth at me.

"How dare you act so disrespectful, so *audacious,* in my house."

"Which time are we talking about?" I asked, provoking with my words.

And she took the bait, cheek twitching. "Every single time you've opened your big mouth."

I took a beat, amusement catching the corner of my lips. My gaze curved to the ground, to the chipped nail polish on my toes as I lingered a step closer.

"You know, I was nice to you when we first met. I admit, a few crass comments made their way out, but I was polite for the most part. Then, every time I saw you after, I was nice, I minded myself, and I let you scoff under your breath when you saw me and pretended I didn't hear."

My lightning *flashed,* eyes snapped up to hers, hooded under my heavy, threat-lined brows. "You're not my boss anymore, Heather. I don't have to be *nice* to you. I don't have to let you walk all over me and bite my tongue so I don't bite your fucking head off instead. You had me on a leash for months in this house, but now I'm unchained, and I've been *dying* to show you just how sharp my teeth are."

I wanted to do this woman *damage.* For all the snide remarks, for all her bigotry, for all the pain she'd caused Maya and Dominic, I wanted to rip chunks out of her rich bitch exterior and watch her apology bleed from her.

"You're pathetic," she spat at me. "You know that, right?"

"You have mentioned it, yes. I've filed it away as '*Things hypocrites say'* in my brain."

Fine lines cracked in her porcelain forehead from her disgust. "You think *I'm* pathetic? I'm not the one who moved myself in with my previous employers despite the fact that she is most certainly *not* welcome."

"Do you think that I want to be here? Around you and your *sunny* personality all the time?"

She tapered a step closer, clenching the large envelope still in her hand. "Then why don't you go?"

"Because your husband doesn't want me to," I countered with a cock of my head.

Careful.

Dangerous suspicion zig-zagged through Heather's fire-blue stare, her pupils turning charcoal. My stomach flipped in fast-acting regret.

Roll it back, roll it back, roll it back.

"He feels partially responsible for me being targeted by this Tommy guy, and he doesn't want me dead," I recovered, tagging on a bite of sarcasm to seal the sale. "Which is, like, basic human compassion. You should take notes."

She erased another step between us, her perfume overpowering the sweet fall air and hooking a whiff up my nose. Gardenias. She smelled like gardenias. She didn't deserve to smell like something so pretty.

Even her pretty scent couldn't disguise her ugly sneer. "I don't need compassion for you, Ms. Sanders. I need nothing but you out of my house and out of my life for good. *Forever.*"

"Well, you'll get your wish as soon as we arrest Tommy on Friday during the setup."

For the first time since she got home, Heather looked unsure. Vague divots chiseled in her forehead. "What setup?"

I gave her a look like she was stupid for once and enjoyed the fuck out of the irritation that burned a red line across her cheeks.

"The one with my mom? I assumed Dominic would have told you."

She took a moment to absorb the information behind her arctic eyes. A long moment. "His name has no business being in your arrogant mouth, so *wash* it out. He is Mr. Reed to you."

"Actually," My shoulders rolled all the way back, confidence inflating my lungs. "I can call him whatever I want now that I'm fired. Dominic, Mr. Reed, *Dom.*" Like she called him.

The one syllable nickname exploded behind her eyes, shockwaves of its intensity rippling over her smooth skin. Her viper-like features narrowed, sharpened as she bared her thirsty fangs.

"I warned you, Ms. Sanders. I *warned* you to stay in your lane or else I would own and destroy your entire world."

"Listen, I know money can buy you a lot, but it can't buy you my *world.*"

Her nostrils flared. "You'd be surprised."

"Oh, I love surprises."

"Then keep coming at me, Ms. Sanders," she challenged, excitement sparking fireworks across her eyes like she really, *really* wanted me to. "I'll give you a surprise."

"Is it gonna be a pony? I hear rich ladies like those."

"And I hear poor little girls like married men."

Finally she said it. The real reason she hated me. The real reason she targeted her venom at me today when she couldn't sink her fangs into Dominic. Her jealousy. Her paranoia.

Which was completely justified, but she was still a cunt. So.

Any guilt I felt in the beginning had been completely squashed by now. Now that I'd seen her reduce her daughter to tears and dismiss her existence, take for granted and demolish Dominic's good heart, and straight up wish me dead.

Heather wasn't a good person. Now, I was a far cry from saintly, but I sure as shit was better than her.

"Why'd you come home so pissed off today?" I asked, curiosity bubbling in my gut.

Something about the mention of that cranked up the flames in her hot blue stare. "I'm assuming because of *you*. You've been putting ideas into Dom's head, I know it."

"He's a grown ass man. He can think for himself."

Heather poised her head down, chin pointing to the ground to chide me like an insolent child. "You know as well as I do that all men have the same stupid weakness. They're idiots when it comes down to it, and you've attempted to execute that very weakness in my husband."

Three months ago, I would have agreed with her. Three months ago, I believed all men ran with hot blood in their veins willing to hurt, steal, and lie to quench that heat. Then Dominic, the beautiful exception to every rule that he was, proved that there are other weaknesses more potent than lust.

Like me.

Dominic's weakness wasn't sex. It was his heart. His good, pure, thunderous heart and how much it roared for mine.

And Heather, being someone Dominic had dedicated that unapologetic heart to for over a decade, should know that. She should know him better than I did, and yet—

"It's pretty shitty how little you actually know about him, you know that?"

Heather canted her head at the poorly lidded offense that I felt very personally on Dominic's behalf vibrating in my tone.

"And you know him so well, is that it?"

I held my ground in front of her, lightning stirring in my veins. "I know he's different. I know he's nice. I know it could have been anyone targeted by Tommy, and he would have done everything he could to keep them safe because he cares about people."

Because his heart is so fucking big, it was taking over mine and trying to make them into one, love-struck vessel.

Her snake eyes slitted. "But it just had to be you, didn't it?"

"I was the best one for the job."

She did not like that. The proverbial steam shooting out of her ears and turning her heat red-hot said she didn't like that at all.

"You *seduced* my husband," she snarled, pupils blazing.

Yes, I 100% did.

But secrets are secrets, and I'd lie to this bitch all day long to keep her from hurting Dominic anymore.

"You keep implying that, but you don't have any proof, do you? It's just easier to tell yourself that your marriage failed because of me and not because *you* failed."

"I have the proof!" The conspicuous yellow envelope was thrust up in the air again, shaking in Heather's tight fist. "I have it right fucking here!"

Suddenly, to the side of us both, thunder rolled in from the open back door, booming and tumultuous.

"*Hey.*"

Dominic earned both of our attention with one word, one casual word dressed like a pointed threat. Silence sliced the air and waited for him, all of his contorted, furious, gorgeous focus aimed at Heather. "Why are you screaming?"

Like she didn't even hear him, she did it again. The screaming.

"What the hell is this?!"

The heavy envelope smacked Dominic square in the chest, his quick reflexes grabbing it and holding it to him as a strange realization scrambled his face. My eyes dropped to the piece of thick mail.

What was in there?

"Heather, I—"

"You are taking this *one* step too far, don't you think?" Her hands balled up at her sides now that they were free. "This is insane. You've lost your goddamn mind, Dominic. You've lost it in this *slut* over here!"

"That's *enough*." Thunder cracked and rippled across his face, stare blackening and jaw sharpening. "That's too far. I won't have you throwing blame and vile insults just because I hurt you. You're mad, you take it out on me. Not on anyone else."

"Oh, can you not be so *noble* right now, Dom?" she spewed, face pinched. "I'm sick of it. I'm sick of all of this! I just want our lives back!"

She came forward with both hands, pounding her fists against Dominic's chest. It happened so fast, and the second I saw her body hit his, a bolt of electric fire hit mine.

"Hey!" My lightning charged me right up in her face, loving the surprise that widened her eyes. "What did I say about *hitting*?"

She blinked, and that surprise disappeared behind her eyelids, malice taking its place. "Are you really idiotic enough to try and tell me how I can and cannot touch my husband *again*?"

"You touch him, I touch you back, and I won't be fucking *nice* about it," I snarled, showing her all my sharpest teeth.

Her thin, nearly black eyebrows lifted. "Is that a threat?"

A smirk, bold and rebellious, trembled my lips as I remembered the words she'd given to me way back when. I came in close, her gardenia scent burning up in my lightning like a garden set on fire.

"It's a warning, and you'll only get one."

Venom flooded in from all sides of Heather's stare, soiling it in seconds flat.

"All right. That's *enough*."

A wall of crisp white and the muscles straining beneath it cut in between my view of Heather. I tipped my chin back at the wall, finding it staring down at me with winter eyes—*frostbite* eyes.

"You need to go inside."

His chill dried out my lips, freezing my tongue in place. I hadn't seen that look in his eyes in weeks…

I parted my lips to breathe in some warmth.

"*Now*," Dominic cut me off. "I'll be there in a minute."

A slap of icy wind pushed me back from him, piercing my heart. My crippled heart that used to crave the burning freeze of his winter stare, but now preferred them warmer, like summer, instead.

I looked between those frostbitten eyes, waiting for the warmth. The familiarity.

And when it stayed hidden, I stomped off just as he told me to, going up to my bedroom and slamming the door.

FOUR

I wasn't in my bedroom for more than ten minutes before there was a curt knock at the door.

A sigh heaved my chest as I laid flat on the bed, staring up at the ceiling fan, getting lost in its rotations and enjoying the zone out. Fatigue creaked in my bones as I sat up, a head rush sweeping in quick and threatening to bring me sinking back down.

Blinking out tiny white dots poking into my vision, I rose and made my way to the door.

Dominic stood on the other side of it unsurprisingly, an appropriate distance away and a pre-packaged protein shake in his hand. My stare tracked up from the shake to the black leather belt wrapped around his hips, jumping up each button holding together his stark white shirt, to the loosened collar around his neck.

But that's where I stopped.

I didn't wanna see the bite in his eyes, the brutal cut of winter when all I wanted was to roll around in summer afternoon rain clouds.

So instead I jutted my chin towards the shake. "Peace offering?"

His hand tightened around the packaged drink, veins flexing in his forearm. "Have you eaten today?"

I thought for a moment, checking in with the hollow pit in my stomach. He knew I hadn't been eating much just like he knew I hadn't been sleeping

41

much.

"Some toast," I answered. Dry, cardboard toast.

"Then it's lunch." Dominic held the shake out to me, and I stared at it, knowing I'd have to take it eventually or else he might force feed it to me like I really *was* a child.

Sighing audibly, I snatched the thing between my fingers, cold condensation rubbing over my fingertips as I turned it over in my palm to read the flavor.

"Salted caramel?"

His hands vanished inside his pants pockets. "They're for after my workouts."

I nodded slowly, uncapping the shake and bringing it to my lips. Sweet, almost milk-like texture goodness poured back into my mouth, and immediately, my taste buds gasped for more. I pulled back another and another drink of the shake, filling that ache in my stomach I hadn't realized was so bad until now.

I finished it. Actually finished it on the spot, and Dominic watched me with approving eyes.

Which I only saw by accident. I hadn't meant to look at him, but as I was tipping the last of the salted caramel back, my eyes naturally flickered to his without even thinking.

But once I was there—once I'd *seen* him—there wasn't a chance of looking away. Not when the sun had broken through and melted all the ice, uncovering all that beautiful warmth and silvery affection.

A tightness pulled between my ribs, and I imagined it was my heart gasping in relief. It didn't like thinking I'd hurt him or upset him, adding another layer to the goddamn sickness.

"You don't look mad at me anymore," I spoke quietly, licking my sweet lips.

To his credit, he didn't pretend to act like he didn't know what I was talking about—that *bitter* look he gave me, sending me away.

He simply clarified.

"I was never mad at you. I was mad at Heather." He tucked his chin low into his chest, muttering. "I'm always mad at her."

Defeat trampled his usually strong voice, diving his gaze to the floor. His wide-set shoulders were visibly tense too, taut with the strain of holding up all that anger and sadness his marriage had caused.

And I believed him. I believed he wasn't mad at me as easily as I blinked. Honestly, I didn't have the energy to waste fighting him or denying him, nor did I have any good reason to. As he made sure to point out on Saturday night, I… *trusted* him.

I super stupidly, bound-to-bite-me-in-the-ass, pathetically trusted him.

And I didn't know how to stop.

"Well, I wasn't completely innocent," I said, trying to lighten the mood and his burden.

The rise of his lips was slow and lazy, but it eventually reached his glowing eyes.

"Are you ever?"

I smiled too. Half-assed, but a genuine half-assed.

"The girls said you told them you and Heather were rehearsing a *play?*" Dominic leaned his shoulder against my door frame with an amused gleam, lingering a breadth closer. His body heat teased, like fingernails scraping gently against my skin. That crisp cologne he wore, all musky and manly, danced underneath my nose too. It tripped up my thoughts with ones of having him closer.

So close he consumed me and my anxious little heart.

"Yeah, well. She came in screaming at me, and it was the first excuse that popped in my head." I shrugged, shaking my head and skirting my gaze down to the floor.

"It was quick thinking," he commended, voice a velvet blanket wrapping up my tired mind. "Except, now both girls have asked what part they can play and cast me as the prince who slays the villain."

My eyes rolled back up to him. "Type casting at its best."

"How do you mean?"

I drew an eyebrow up, cocked high and incredulous. "The strikingly handsome man with a hero complex? Come on, now."

Dominic breathed a short laugh, slight curves holding to the corners of his mouth. Hands still shoved deep in his pants pockets, he drifted closer yet again, talking lower and sweeter than he should have.

"What does that make you?"

I paused to think, sinking my stare down to the center of his chest as my brain provided the obvious answer. My heart sunk with it.

"The damsel who's really goddamn tired of being in distress," I whispered, too over it to bother using my full voice.

Unwrinkled material rustled in front of me, and I realized too late that Dominic was moving in, the quiet click of his wingtip shoes tapping the hardwood hallway floor as he came up to me.

My head jumped up and then arched back in shock at how close he was, at the fact that I could count the shades of gray in his monochrome eyes and taste the sweet mint from his breath on the tip of my tongue. Almost looking helpless—almost looking *desperate*—he took his eyes back and forth between mine.

"Can I take you somewhere?"

"Where?" I breathed, resigned to say yes wherever it was.

His voice got real low, secretive and intimate. Just for me. "Somewhere I can kiss that frown off your lips."

I think I started nodding before he finished speaking, fast and needy for him to do just that.

* * *

Within a half hour, we were parked in the driveway of a townhome.

Its neighborhood was quaint and precious, two-story buildings stacked side by side with red painted doors the centerpiece of them all. Flowerbeds of crimson roses flourished the lawns and accented the doors, charcoal gray window shutters flanking both sides of the large first story windows.

The home we were sitting in front of in particular had nothing distinguishable about it. Some had welcome mats or wreaths on the fronts, maybe even children's bikes parked outside on the driveway, but this one was barren.

"Are we meeting someone here?" I asked, unlocking my seatbelt.

Dominic cast me a side glance, smiling a smile so dastardly and devastating that whatever I'd just asked got lost in the curves of that perfect mouth. Legitimately, I forgot what I was saying, and before I could remember, he was opening his driver's side door and motioning me to follow him.

So I did, pushing the passenger door of his Explorer open and stepping out onto the pavement. The impending chill of fall breezed past me as I came around to Dominic, to where he stood peering up at the townhouse with one of his impossible-to-discern looks.

He held his keys in the palm of his hand, bouncing them once, twice, three times before folding his fingers around them, clenching.

Next to him, I shifted on awkward feet, moving my attention from him to the house. "Are we, like, breaking in to makeout in there?" I asked, staring at his masculine profile. "Because I'm not judging you if we are."

He swept a sweetened gaze down at me and chuckled. "I have a key."

And he showed me that very key, bronze and glinting in this sinking sunlight. Before I could say anymore, he was moving up the fresh green lawn, up the two steps of the front porch, and pushing the key inside the lock.

The red painted door tiptoed open, and I scurried up behind Dominic to see inside.

My palms brushed the sides of his waist, not thinking if I should or shouldn't before gripping onto the smooth fabric of his work shirt and clinging to it as I peered around him. Dominic let me. He let me hold onto him, sealing my front to his back as we walked inside, my heart thumping a strangely intune beat with our unison footfall.

"Um…" I trailed off, not finding any words to say as I took it in.

As I took in… nothing.

Not really, anyway. The place was empty save for a few cardboard boxes against the far corner of a wall with a built-in, brick-faced fireplace and what looked like a tool bag dropped in the middle of a hardwood living room.

The walls were a blank, white slab screaming for some color or decorations to play with. My eyes followed the vacant walls up to their vaulted ceilings, poised high to make room for the second level of the house. My focus trailed back down the staircase that zigzagged only once before finding the landing of the first story again, dropping off in the living room.

Dominic folded a hand over mine at his side, drawing it up with his to point forward together. "The kitchen is just down that hallway. There's a little backyard patio too just outside of it."

Okay?

"There's a spare bedroom behind the staircase. Nothing big, but would work well as a home office I think," he continued, walking us further inside. "Upstairs is the master bedroom and second bedroom, plus the guest bathroom."

Was this his idea of a date? A do-it-yourself HGTV tour of a deserted home?

I leaned around him, trying to catch a glimpse of his face as I asked, "Do you know the people that live here?"

Craning his head down at me, he nodded once. "I do. They just signed their lease and moved in today."

Dominic adjusted our position, pulling me by the hand from behind him until I was glued to his front, all small and fragile huddled up in his big chest with his breath-stealing beauty towering over me. Silver flecks stood out in his eyes as he gazed down at me, and something pulled *tight* in my chest.

Dead center of my heart.

I tried to swallow past it.

"It's why they were late getting home from work today," he said, curving his thumb down the small of my back with a knowing smile. "Because they were here, getting things ready for when they brought someone over later."

Buzzing began in my belly, humming at the smile turning up his eyes, the familiarity of his words…

And then it all clicked in one unbelievable second.

My lips dried out. The usually caked on strawberry chapstick sucked dry as a gasp escaped me and left my mouth ajar.

"You…"

And there were no more words. None at all.

Dominic grinned at my speechlessness. "This place fell into my lap fairly quickly, so I didn't get a chance to tell you with everything else going on. Then I decided it could be a surprise. Something to erase that frown."

Which it did.

It really did.

"This… is yours?" I asked, scanning all around the naked home that suddenly had so much potential, so much future bursting from its walls that it hurt. It actually *hurt* that tightness already in my chest, squeezing it until I thought it might pop. "You're moving out?"

"I am." Dominic watched me closely, collecting every reaction I gave him at the news. "I spoke to my lawyer and once the time comes, once you and Charlotte are safe to move back with your mom, I'm moving here. I can't…"

His words held on his tongue, strapped down by the shame and torment that rearranged his handsome face. His stare fell, a frown worrying between his thick brows, mouth parted in wordless defeat.

I didn't think about it before I put my palm to his cheek, working out the lines of stress breaking his smooth skin. I didn't even realize I was stroking my thumb in mollifying circles over his cheekbone until Dominic shut his eyes and breathed hard, washing my lips with the taste of his relief.

"I can't stay in that house any longer. It's draining."

"What about Maya?"

"She'll come with me. Heather and I haven't talked about custody yet, and I'll give her the option for joint, but…"

But he wasn't sure she'd take it.

He didn't say it, but he didn't have to either. Even in the few months I'd known the Reed Family, it was easy to tell Heather didn't love Maya like a mother should. She didn't want to be around her if she didn't have to.

I think that was half of what broke Dominic's heart the most.

Again, my body reacted before my mind had a say, squeezing him like I was trying to hug the sorrow right out of him. Dominic's eyes went all smoky with adoration as he stared down at me, and he squeezed my waist in return.

"It's all really in her court now that she has the papers," he said quietly.

My brain paused, blanking as I tilted myself back.

"Papers?"

He began to nod before realizing I was *not* on the same page, his eyebrows scrunching. "Did you not know that's what was in the envelope she was holding?"

No.

No, I had no idea she was holding the very divorce papers that were the *only* thing suctioned between us. The papers that were basically a contract to the only rule Dominic enacted in our relationship.

The papers I'd been waiting to be signed so Dominic could finally take me to bed and demolish every last boundary between us.

"No wonder she came home so pissed…" I breathed, still reeling from the news.

"I had no idea she'd get them that fast or else I would have made sure to be there when she got home."

I nodded though his words barely digested, pulling through one ear and out the other. I couldn't hear anything but what this meant, but the thumping of hot blood pulsing in my neck, my heart, between my legs.

"So…" I swallowed, desire thickening my voice. "Papers are signed."

The profound meaning of that fact didn't miss him either. It smouldered his eyes and thickened his husky voice like mine.

"They are."

The confirmation clenched my core, body aching and hollow and wanting something that *finally* was mine.

"Kat—"

"You never kissed my frown away," I said to stop him from whatever he was going to say.

Whatever it was had dragged a serious film over his smoking eyes, and I didn't want it. I didn't want serious talks or rationale.

All I wanted was him. I wanted him all over me, inside of me, fucking away the pain of everything going on and consuming me until I forgot it all. Until all I remembered was Dominic and how he felt buried between my legs.

"You're not frowning anymore," he commented.

And so I corrected that, pushing my bottom lip out and catching his shaded gaze falling to it. His focus turned heavy-lidded, lust charring over that serious film of his until it was ashes to help darken his eyes.

"That would be pouting, Ms. Sanders."

"You don't like it when I pout?"

His grip around my waist tightened, pressing his punishment into me and making me squirm. "I didn't say that."

"So you do?" I panted, bringing my face up to his, kissing the corner of his mouth. "You like when I pout for you, Mr. Reed?"

"*Kat,*" he growled in warning, the sound vibrating in my lower stomach, sensations popping and whining for more.

"Why don't you show me upstairs? The bedroom."

A delicious burn scratched along my face as Dominic moved his bristled jawline over it, turning his face down to catch my heavy stare. His was just as heavy, loaded down with smoke and sin as he burned down the last boundary between us.

"Now, that I can do."

FIVE

Dominic led me upstairs, holding my hand as I followed behind him. The walk up to the master bedroom was riotous even though neither of us spoke. The particles in the air chanted for us and the moment we'd been mounting to; the oxygen around us vibrated in anticipation like a crowd of thousands stomping their feet all at once.

Everything—*everything*—in the atmosphere was ours, cheering for us and our moment that was finally here.

This was *exactly* what I needed.

This would be the perfect way to forget, to lose myself somewhere between the lines of pleasure and pain and drown beneath them both. Dominic could kiss away my fears of Tommy, bite out perfect distractions along my neck and shoulders that helped overshadow the way I fucking *ached* for Layla and her return.

He could fuck his name into my walls and leave fingerprint bruises all over my body so I could shove it in Heather's face that he was *mine*, and that he knew what I felt like inside and out.

Dominic brought us to stand in front of a plain white bedroom door, positioning me in front of him before he turned the knob.

And my breath left my body.

Rose petals as red as the blood rushing to my cheeks littered the entire space, spilling across a bed that was the only furniture set up in the whole room. In the whole house, for that matter. It loomed in the center, propped together by an iron rod bed frame and headboard, neat pillows and a fluffy blanket dressing the mattress.

In the corner, sitting on the floor was a lamp no taller than my knee, and it was the only source of light. It stretched this dim glow over everything, painting the walls an amber yellow and making shadows out of everything.

"What…"

Dominic pressed in behind me, stopping the words that, let's be real, probably weren't coming out anyway.

"I want to make it very clear that I don't expect anything," he said, dropping a soft kiss between my shoulder and neck. "I didn't know they had served the divorce papers today, honestly. I just wanted to be able to give you a night away from everything and some good news in a place we didn't have to look over our shoulder."

His lips brushed the slope of my neck, painting my skin in his deep voice and dreamy words. "There are snacks and wine in the fridge, and I brought a few movies we could set up and watch. Or we could just hang out and relax together. You could take a nap, and I could get out of your hair entirely."

He let a small breath of a laugh wash against my body before nosing the crook of my neck and kissing it again. Another honeyed peck of affection.

Followed by a twist up my spine.

"You didn't have to do this," I tried, the words coming out all pathetic and unconvincing. "This is…"

Too much.

This was way, way, way too much.

"My mom agreed to put the girls to bed tonight, so I'd say we have until around midnight before we have to be back."

That should have been great news. That should have made me happy. Instead, it made me want to vomit. It made my toes prickle and my blood run cold, encasing me in a block of ice skin with a quickening heart.

"And if Heather asks where we were?" I asked, still dumbstruck, staring at each innocent rose petal that burned *criminal* red in the amber hue.

Dominic caressed a hand down my arm. "I already told her I was taking you out to see your mom, and that it might be late."

His touch. It was hot. *Melting*.

It would melt my icy skin and brittle bones, but I couldn't move away. I couldn't move at all. A night alone with Dominic should be amazing. It should be everything I wanted right now. Which is why it didn't make sense when the air in the room turned fucking toxic with every breath I took, filling my lungs with poison that made my head spin.

My chest… my goddamn *heart* was already struggling for oxygen, panic nipping at the corners of my mind. I needed space. I needed air. I needed out of this orchestrated fairytale room.

So I spun around to tell Dominic just that.

Except, I didn't get the words out. In fact, I didn't get *anything* out. Words, oxygen, sputters. Nothing. Not when I saw what Dominic was holding in his hand, wrapped neatly in a red bow.

His eyes were on me, this picture-perfect snapshot of a man both bashful and unshakable. "You didn't tell me when your birthday was, so this is admittedly late. I picked it out last week, but there hasn't been a good time to give it to you."

"You didn't ha—"

Dominic shushed me with a tilted smile, pushing the small gift into my hands. My trembling hands.

"Just open it."

My fingers latched on somehow, someway, folding around the edges of the thin, rectangle box. I brushed the coarse fabric of rich ribbon tied around it, wondering how long I could admire the gift without actually opening it.

I didn't want whatever was inside.

I didn't want to see whatever it was he had picked out for me.

For *me*.

But I had no choice.

"Don't forget to read the note."

My head jerked up at Dominic's voice to see him pointing with his sculpted chin to the square of folded paper tied gingerly to the ribbon.

"Oh." I picked it up between my fingers, not at all convinced that it wouldn't slice me open with one of its sharp edges and I'd bleed out. Most might be naïve enough to think this was just a safe little card, but I knew better. I knew it could be deadly.

On the front written in cursive were the words *'Happy Birthday, Kitten!'* with a smiling cartoon cat holding a pink balloon in its paw. Inside, his beautiful penmanship read simply. One word and one name.

'Yours, Dominic.'

Mine.

"I couldn't believe the store had a cat themed card." A lopsided grin peeled up his face, and it was deadly just like the card. "It was fate."

Fate.

Sadistic fucking fate.

"I also think it means I have to start calling you Kitten."

He arched an audacious, playful, sexy-as-fuck eyebrow at me, and I forced a weak chuckle in response.

I tugged at the wrapped ribbon, slowly undoing it as if I was undoing my sensibilities at the same tortured pace. My heartbeat was crashing, pulse thumping in my neck; I wasn't sure how Dominic didn't hear it.

It was just a present, right? Just a present. Maybe it was a gag gift. Yeah, maybe that was it. It was a gag gift. A funny present to make me laugh and not one that would kill my heart for good.

I hoped and I dared to pray for a joke, a rubber chicken, a whoopee cushion, *anything*.

Anything except exactly what it was.

Placed gingerly against the backdrop of a tiny ivory silk pillow was a necklace.

A thoughtful, stunning, silver necklace with a glinting emerald at the center.

"It's called a Claddagh," Dominic spoke, steady and soft. "It usually comes as a ring, but I saw this at the store. The emerald…"

Risking a careless glance up, I found Dominic already staring at me, his irises of sterling silver refined and brighter than ever, moving between mine.

"It reminded me of your eyes."

My eyes.

The same eyes that were stretched wide, showing off just how round they could get as Dominic told me tales of things that didn't make sense. Like how one glance at this deep green gem, and he was reminded of me.

Of a *part* of me.

And he liked that part of me so much, he wanted to wrap it up and gift it to me so I'd always know that he thought of me even when I wasn't around. That I was *with* him even when I wasn't.

He shifted closer, lifting the necklace out of its box like he was lifting a baby bird. "Do you know the meaning behind a Claddagh?"

Dumbly, I shook my head no.

A speck of a smile never waning from his mouth, he draped the delicate chain behind his fingers, settling the centerpiece of the necklace in his palm facing me.

"My dad taught me growing up. He's something like 40% Irish and very proud of it."

He laughed faintly, and so I tried too, but the flavor of his laughter reached me before I could and tangled my lungs with his sweet breath. It strangled until I couldn't breathe, and if I couldn't breathe, then I couldn't laugh, and so I just stayed silent as the feeling of suffocation grew and scratched at my chest.

"Each symbol means something different. The hands represent friendship." He passed his thumb over the two silver hands, running up next to touch the crown sitting on top of them. "The crown represents loyalty."

He then drew the chain out wide between his two pinched fingers, reaching around either side of my neck and pushing past my mass of hair. The chain bit my neck, its touch colder than dry ice, colder than death sinking its teeth in and piercing my rushing blood.

Then, I wasn't suffocating anymore.

I was drowning.

I was fucking drowning in that roaring, soul-stealing ocean I'd been fighting through this whole time as warm lips caressed the shell of my ear, his voice of thunder rumbling against it.

"And the heart means love," he murmured. "It means the person giving it to you thinks you're extraordinary and is grateful for every day you're with them."

The ghost of his words lingered on my neck, haunting the space between my ears as Dominic clasped the necklace in place, draping it right over my wheezing heart.

Skin to metal. Hot to cold. Life to death.

Holy fuck.

My heart spasmed beneath the silver one, exploding, deflating, choking out its last breath. I choked on mine too, noxious air clogging up my throat with fumes as my eyes flared in terror.

Terror that it was happening, that it *had* happened already.

Dominic pulled back with the strangled sound, sharp eyes cutting a scan down my face.

"Are you all right?"

No.

No, I wanted to say. *No*, I *tried* to say, but nothing came out.

Our heroin chemistry burned so hot in my veins, scorching, flooding my blood full of flames that licked with razored tongues until the chemistry became something else entirely.

It wasn't a drug anymore. It had gone past addiction and straight to something *worse*, something truly and utterly inescapable.

Something that I was made up of down to the marrow in my bones.

"Kat," Dominic tried again. "Talk to me."

Panic snapped my eyes up to his, collecting all of his concern, all of his caring, his special brand of affection that was born in his thunderous eyes just for me. I collected it all until I was full of it, stretching apart at the seams with all his devotion and the realization that kept smacking my dying heart again and again.

Oh my god, oh my god, oh my fucking god.

I needed to get out of here. I needed to think. I needed to—

"I need to use your bathroom," I mumbled, eyes darting back across the room and not waiting for him to respond before I bolted for the first door I saw.

"Kat—"

I shook his fingertips from my elbow as he reached for me, yelling back to him, "I just need a minute, okay?"

A minute to process. A minute to scream.

A minute to cry my heart out that had lost to the sickness.

Oh holy *fuck*, I lost. I lost. I lost. I lost.

My legs were all but numb as they carried me towards the closed door on the far side of the bedroom, hearing Dominic call out as I gripped the doorknob of it.

"That's not the—"

I threw myself in the dark room and wretched the door shut, expecting to fall to the floor of the bathroom. Instead, I ran my nose into some shelves.

"Kat, that's the closet," Dominic's voice muffled through the door.

In the darkness, I huffed loudly. "I see that."

At least I was alone.

Only a thin crack of light spilled in between the edge of the door, showing me the closet was wide but not terribly deep. I blinked against the darkness, pupils adjusting to the absence of light as my heart grappled to adjust to the absence of life as we'd known it.

The sickness…

It got me. It swallowed my whole heart up before I was ready and killed it. Whatever was beating in my chest now wasn't the heart I'd been born with. It was new. It was layered differently, it *beat* differently—double time.

A pulse for me and a pulse for him.

A solemn pause passed between us and the thickly wooded door.

"I'm sorry," Dominic lamented. "The necklace was too much, and I should have known that."

His apology hit me square in the chest, rage vibrating down to my toes. "*No*, no. *You* shouldn't be apologizing because you got me a thoughtful and beautiful present. *I* should be apologizing for panicking about it."

Dominic sighed so heavily, I swore it shook the closet door.

"I can take it back—"

"No, no!" I cried, pain sparking beneath my knuckles as I hit the wood in front of me. "I don't *want* you to take it back. I don't want you to feel like you have to apologize just because I'm... *broken*."

The ugly word rolled off my tongue like sludge, my forehead meeting the cool wood of the door.

"You are *not* broken."

"Then why am I in a fucking closet right now?" I shot back, eyes pinched.

"Because I overwhelmed you," Dominic said as if it was logic, as if his blame for my freak out was fact.

"*No*." My retort was bulleted, but followed up by, "I mean, *yes*, but that's not it." I sighed aloud, sliding my hands up over my face, the heel of my palms buried in my eye sockets to block everything out. "That's not why..."

The wood creaked, and I imagined Dominic leaning his shoulder against it. "Then why?"

Pressure mounted behind my eyes as I dug the heel of my hands into them harder, fingers gripping my head like spikes on a crown until both my hands and head shook from the effort, until I wondered if my fingernails might draw blood.

A noise creaked out of me, whimpered and repressed, getting all tangled up in the isolation and heavy panting. Keeping my hands over my eyes, I squeezed them tight.

"Because I didn't get the fucking memo."

My jaw pulsed and ached as I chewed my teeth together, sawing them back and forth as I waited for his voice in the darkness.

"You're going to have to help me out with that one."

I growled out, "The *memo*. The one about *feelings* and falling in love, and how it's all one giant clusterfuck."

He held a pause, his rich voice coming through steady. "Meaning?"

I squeezed and squeezed and squeezed my head until it felt like it would pop, all my crazy feelings bursting out and splattering neon warning signs in the darkness. Signs telling me to stop talking, stop confessing, stop admitting to the insanity born inside my heart the second he put that necklace around my neck.

But I couldn't. The words were knocking behind my teeth, falling out like the haphazard truth bombs they were.

"They're supposed to be different steps, right? Falling in love and being in love? I thought you *fell* for a long while before you *loved*, but that's bullshit, isn't it?" I snapped my eyes open to stare at blackness, flattening my shaking hands against the door. "Why do they even call it falling when it's jumping? It's jumping from one death-defying stunt to the next and just *praying* you land on your feet."

Stupid fucking prayer and the magic cure it had been made out to be.

My head drooped, fingertips curling into the door as if I could claw my feelings—my *failures*—into it.

"I thought I could do this at my own pace so I wouldn't fuck everything up, but even *that* was out of my control. Everything is..." *Out of my control.*

On my feet, I started rocking back and forth, unstable in mind and body and the proof of it everywhere. The burn of something awful, something weak and pitiful, touched the backs of my eyes, and I pinched them shut to squeeze out the feeling.

My hands coiled to fists against the wood, trying to hold onto the strength I could feel depleting from my system in cause of the sickness.

It was taking it all from me—everything I'd depended on to stay standing—and my ability to stop it had passed me by days ago, and I hadn't even known it.

I'd lost the battle *days* ago in that tiny back bedroom at Ryan's house, and I was too caught up in everything to realize it. I thought I was just *falling* then, but I wasn't, was I?

I'd already taken the deadly plunge.

"Do you know what I was thinking right before Layla was taken?" I asked, laying my cheek against the door.

Dominic replied a somber, "What?" sounding as if he was laying his own cheek right against mine on the other side.

I pictured that he was, visualized him pressed up against the door right over me, listening to me with that wholehearted, quiet focus of his.

"I thought... that I might actually get a happily ever after kind of love story," I murmured, embarrassment thieving my voice.

"I was stupidly hoping for the whole fairytale shabang. Princes, and true love, and happy endings. I completely forgot that every fairytale needs a villain, and that's when they showed up. They showed up and reminded me why it's *stupid* to hope and wish on shooting stars and love the prince."

The burn was back behind my eyes, trickling down to my throat and constricting it tight.

"It's safer hating the villain than falling for the hero," I whispered to no one.

Silence ticked on, and I swallowed the burn thickening my throat, flames settling in my stomach. The door I was leaning my face on creaked, wood warping as weight shifted on the other side of it.

I wondered if he was leaving. If he'd finally had enough of all my crazy and was getting out before the sickness swallowed his heart whole too. It had to be close, right?

The necklace he put around my neck grew heavy as I wondered, the weight telling me I already had my answer.

"You've called me a hero, or a wannabe hero, many times." Somehow, his velvet voice resonated through the wood, warming my cheek against it as if he was holding it, holding me. "But I'm not a hero, Kat. I'm just like you. I fall down, I get up. I make mistakes, and I do my best to right them. I'm not perfect or anybody's hero."

Something incredibly cheesy popped into my brain and tumbled right out of my mouth.

"You're mine."

My lip twitched up as I said the words like I'd tasted something truly revolting. The fucking cliche of what I'd said *was* revolting, and so was how true it was and had been from the very start. I hated that it was true and sounded almost offended as I admitted, "You swooped in, and you saved me when I didn't have a job, when people came after me, when I needed a place to stay. You said all the right things to make me swoon and fall, and I did, and now I'm *here*. In a closet."

A break in the conversation heightened my sappy fucking feelings, heightened the tension coiling in the air between us until I couldn't breathe.

"Because you love me?" he asked.

And the fire burning in my gut reached up and *twisted* around my throat... until tears poured out.

They spilled over my cheeks, running down my face in hot shame as the first sob tried to punch through my chest. I clamped my fingers over my mouth, screwing my lips tight to shut down anymore humiliating cries from breaking through. I squeezed my lips and I pinched my nose between my thumb and pointer finger, suffocating back any sounds that would give me away.

My chest convulsed and caved in, wet tears sliding over knuckles and drenching my fingers at a pace I couldn't stop. I couldn't stop any of it.

Just like I couldn't stop my loving Dominic Reed.

My knees wobbled and shook, everything inside of me breaking down and shivering at the nakedness. All I wanted was to collapse to the ground and curl into a ball, sobbing about how I couldn't stop it and how fucking scared I was of this sickness.

Of this power he had over me now.

Quiet beats of nothing but the occasional squeak as my sobs gasped for breath strung between us and the door.

"Do you want to know the first time I fell in love with you?"

My head snapped up to the slab of wood between us, staring at it wide-eyed. That reborn organ in my chest stuttered, water petals still dripping from my eyes.

Did he just...?

I curled my free arm into my chest, peeling my fingers away from my mouth and righting my breath just enough to ask...

"The first time?"

There was barely a hesitation between responses.

"I've fallen in love with you several times since I met you, Ms. Sanders," he spoke, tender and *so* sure.

A sob broke through my unclamped lips, spilling out before I could slap my hand over the noise and swallow it back. Horror exploded a frigid gust inside my chest as I scrambled to lock down anymore embarrassing noises, but it was too late. It happened again and again, sobs wracking my chest and soaking my neck down to the collar of my shirt.

Dominic could hear them now; I knew he could.

He went on like my cries fueled him, a welcomed flood for him to swim through to get to me so he could rescue my stupid self.

"The first time was the Monday after you ran out of the garage." After our first kiss. "And I found you asleep with Maya on the couch. I don't know how long I sat there and watched you two, but that was the first time I knew. It was more of a slow-burn realization than a jump like you mentioned."

Desperately, I flattened my palms to the door as if I could feel the words coming through before he said them.

"Since I'd been falling in love with you from that very first day you walked through my door."

I collapsed against the closet door, elbows going limp, sniffling and swiping the backs of my hands at tears as they shed themselves free. My born-again heart *ached* so fucking good, overflowing and singing and priding in the confessions Dominic was writing out in inspired words.

It loved it. *I* loved it.

"The second time was when you frosted my beard with pink icing. Third time was the water fight later that night. Fourth, when you fearlessly called Heather out after she hit me. And then about a hundred times after that."

I couldn't take it anymore. My hands were shaking. My *heart* was shaking, needing to be with him, and so I twisted the doorknob and spilled out, the shaking needy thing I was.

Dominic was there waiting for me, smiling and perfect and in love with me.

The flawless sight of him blurred behind new tears as they sprung and slipped free, some tragic noise between a sob and a laugh choking in my throat. I was entirely unequipped and undeserving of love—of *his* love—but here he was, setting his heart at my feet despite all the times I tried to throw it back in his face.

Despite the terror of his love, I moved up to him in a teary-eyed daze, a doe on newborn feet, and somehow made it against his warm chest. He grabbed my waist in one hand, brushing a thumb beneath my eye sweetly with the other.

"Sometimes I fall in love with you when I'm just thinking about you. Sometimes you're standing right next to me when it happens."

I sniffled, blinking water from my eyelashes. "What about now when I'm all weepy and pathetic?"

He turned his face down at me to scold. "You're not pathetic."

His well-worked thumbs swept over my wet cheeks, ridding the evidence of my weakness for me. When he was done, he grabbed my face in both hands, tilting my head back so he could properly tower over me and show me all the love shining in his lucent eyes.

"And yes, right now."

He was falling in love with me *right now.*

More salty drops of water flowed down the sides of my face, and Dominic caught those too. He wiped away the tears my body simply didn't have any room leftover for. It was too full of love and terror to hold on to the tears created by both.

"What about earlier when I was screaming at Heather and crazy?"

His smile widened so deep, dimples winked at me.

"Definitely. I love how hot your fire burns when you're protecting someone." His thumb skimmed my bottom lip, petting me as he softly admired, "My little spitfire that could burn down worlds if she wanted."

I anchored myself to him, fisting my hands in his shirt. "I'll burn down anyone who tries to hurt you."

"Maybe you've got it backwards," he heartened, face lowering to mine. "Maybe you're my hero."

"I hate maybes."

"And I love you," he hummed. "Deeply and wildly out of my control."

The most pitiable breath squeezed from my lungs, painting his mouth above mine in all my disbelief. He was stupid enough to love me, and I was stupid enough to love him back. We were stupidly in love, and the perfect storm we forged roared with life in my new heart.

Thunder crashed. Lightning snapped. My entire body vibrated with its ferocity, its *intensity,* my skin a casing of buzzing electricity needing to ignite and explode.

Dominic brushed his mouth against mine, nudging my awaiting lips with his. "I never stood a chance against you, Ms. Sanders."

"I think you should kiss me now," I breathed, eyelids falling heavy and focus narrowing.

His full lips with all my attention gave a wicked grin.

"You got it, Kitten."

SIX

My back hit the mattress, Dominic covering me in his power and sweet mint kisses.

Rose petals floated up and back down around us as we bounced on the bed, but I only caught red flashes of them as I threw my head back, a moan screwing my eyes shut. Silk-soft hair tickled the underneath of my chin as Dominic laid fervent kisses down the arch of my throat, his tongue swirling in the dip of my collarbone.

Blood rushed to every nerve-ending in my body, lighting me up from the inside out until I felt like I was glowing red with need for him. The blanket beneath us got strangled in my fingers, soft fibers splitting between knuckles as I fisted it to death while Dominic scraped his teeth over the throbbing pulse in my neck.

I panted hard, wiggling my body beneath his until he was between my legs, square hips right over my heated core. My feet locked behind his ass, dragging his hips into me, a cry popping off my lips at the feel of his thickening cock pressing *right* at my center.

We were both wearing too many clothes.

My leggings, his pants, our shirts needed to go.

It all needed to go.

"Kat." Dominic kissed my name against my jawline, my lips chasing his as they came nearer. He gave me a peck, a chaste and unsatisfying one, pulling a whine from me as he leaned back.

"We don't have to do this tonight," he spoke, smooth and barely out of breath when I was heaving like a prepubescent boy who'd just seen their first pair of tits.

"This wasn't what tonight was about. We can wait."

I stared back and forth between his sincere eyes, doubt snagging my reborn heart in a tremor.

"Do you not want to?"

The lowering of Dominic's chin alone was an admonishment. It shadowed his sharp features, darkened his eyes, and hitched my breath in my throat.

"This has nothing to do with me not wanting to. I've thought about you like this more times than I care to admit." An amorous glance down my curves didn't go unnoticed. "But you have a lot going on right now if you want to wait."

"I know, and I admit that when I tried to jump your bones downstairs, it was as a distraction from all the fucked upness in my head, but now," I swallowed, licking my lips. "I feel like if we don't, I'll cry or explode or both. I don't know. This is all new to me."

Again, I was breathing way heavier than was called for. All these freaking emotions were haywiring my system, providing me with too much oxygen and too little sense. I was all out of that, nothing but needy and in love and scared as fuck about it all.

Aw, fuck. In *love*. I was so sick in love with him.

Dominic canted back some, a tempered gleam curving around his gaze like a shooting star crossing the night sky. The look he was giving cowered me into the mattress, shoulders curling in to bow my chest—my heart—back and away.

"Why're you looking at me like that?"

Knowing in his brilliant eyes, he asked, "Like how?"

I searched his face, all adoring and gorgeous, brain and tongue working together to try and form a definition of the look coming in from above.

"Like you…"

"Love you?" he finished, the words an affectionate murmur he passed over my parted lips.

I sucked them down with a startled and tiny gasp, feeling his *love* for me wash my mouth and fill my lungs. It was so unapologetic in its existence and power, flooding my body like the ocean it was, salt threatening to burn my eyes and its lethal current threatening to take my head under.

"I guess," was all I could say, was all I could think.

Dominic dared to look prideful above me, beautifully arrogant and victorious.

"Because I can, and because I do." Pillowy lips ghosted mine again, pulling air from my stinging lungs. "And because this torture to be with me that you're feeling?"

"Uh huh?"

Words. I had no more left. Only *feelings,* and I was drowning in them.

Formidable, sticky, hot, desperate feelings.

"I've been feeling that for a *very* long time."

He kissed my chin, slow and sweet, dragging his lips down the column of my neck and rumbling against it. "Wanting to touch you and knowing I couldn't. Wanting to kiss all of those smart remarks off your strawberry lips and not being able to."

Warm hands found and encased my slim waist, pushing my shirt up and up until it hit the bottom of my bra. He squeezed around my ribcage with his big hands, reminding me how small I was to him, and how completely he could and would dominate me.

Lips made of fire grazed the skin right beneath my bra, slow and fucking torturous. "Wanting to bend you over my knee and make you say sorry for all those times you flirted with me when you knew there was nothing I could do about it."

"Ah," I gasped sharply, his teeth nipping at my exposed stomach. The gasp quick-changed into a moan as he smoothed his wet tongue over the bite, his mouth finishing off with a dirty kiss in the same spot.

My hands were in his hair before I realized it, gripping the thick strands and pulling in greed for more. More kisses, more sucking at my skin, more of everything Dominic could give me tonight.

A grunt ripped his gaze back up to me, flashing bright with hunger and something darker.

Something entirely dominating.

"Hands, Ms. Sanders," he nearly growled.

In surprise, I retracted my hands from his hair, holding them up in surrender in front of me. Dark eyes tracked between them both, ideas forming in dangerous swirls around his dilating pupils. His focus switched back to me, the connection between us a promise of punishment being made without words.

Oh shit.

"Put your hands behind your head and grab onto the rails of the headboard."

And you can be damn sure I followed orders in seconds flat.

I waited to see approval or satisfaction flourish in those deep-seated eyes as I gripped the railing behind my head, but nothing. He didn't look like he was happy I followed his rules.

He looked like he'd expected nothing less of me when he had me spread out on his bed for him like prey begging to be slaughtered.

He sat back on his haunches, reaching around his belt.

A silver flash bounced off the dim lighting as he produced them, striking a bolt of feverish excitement straight through my body. They dangled in his fingers like a prized treat, taunting me with the deviant pleasures just out of reach.

"Do you remember these?"

I jerked out a nod.

"Do you remember why I had to use them on you that night?"

The memory of them tingled the skin around my wrists. "Because I was touching things you told me not to."

He even said that on Saturday night. That I was always touching things I shouldn't be. Buttons in his patrol car, papers in his office, *him*. My hands were as rebellious as I was, magnets to things they shouldn't want but were attracted to anyway.

He angled his chin down. "You think it's fun to disobey me, don't you?"

Another nod. "I love it."

I loved watching his eyes thunder and his jaw tick; I reveled in how he tried not to enjoy my misbehaving as much as he did. Like right now.

"You love it?" he hummed, rolling my answer around his tongue. He nodded slightly, casting a glance down to where I'd split my body in half for him, legs spread and pussy waiting to be touched by him.

He was kneeling between my legs, handcuffs clenched in his palm as he observed how completely I'd displayed myself for him, how *desperate* I was to have all of him. Slowly, he came forward, hovering over me and leading a flash of silver cuffs over my vision before disappearing somewhere over my head.

"You've loved breaking my rules and driving me mad, have you?"

Cold metal clasped hard around my first wrist.

I jerked my hand, finding it locked to the iron-rod headboard. Excitement swelled inside me, parching my mouth and working my chest up and down.

Suddenly, a hand grabbed for my chin and tugged my head to attention.

Thunderous eyes waited for me, exacting and storming. "I asked you a question, Ms. Sanders."

"Um…" I quested through every section in my brain for what he'd just asked, tripping over my own tongue as I shook my head up at him. "What was it?"

"I asked if you've loved breaking my rules and driving me mad."

Oh. Right. "Yes."

He paused, reaching his thumb up and petting my pouty bottom lip. "Yes, what?"

Desire pooled between my legs as I watched him and he watched my mouth, realizing what he wanted. What he finally wasn't afraid to admit he liked.

The corner of my mouth inched.

"Yes, sir."

Clouds clustered over his stare, darkening it impossibly fast as his sharp jaw clicked. His fingers grabbing my face bit down just a *little* harder, making me squirm for more as he breathed over my lips, hot and feeding me his taste, his fucking addicting sweet mint taste.

"Good girl," he commended, pressing a hard kiss to my mouth.

He was gone before I could reciprocate, fastening my second wrist in the biting lock of the handcuffs. I pulled both hands, arching my head back to glimpse the chain weaved around the iron-rods, my wrists imprisoned right where Dominic wanted them.

He leaned back again, still kneeling between my legs, hands circling either side of my waist and making me look so goddamn small against him.

"You loved teasing me with what I couldn't have, didn't you?"

"Yes, sir."

One of his hands slid beneath my thigh, splaying out and squeezing until I moaned, until I twisted my hips to get closer to him. His firm grip kept me in place, and he bent my leg at the knee and guided it across his body to lie with the other. Both of my legs now on one side of his body, deft fingers found the waistband of my leggings and pulled.

Down my thighs, over my knees, lifting my legs up straight to peel the clothing off my body.

"What do *you* want, Ms. Sanders?"

Warm lips pressed to the sensitive underneath of my ankle.

A whimper squeaked into the heady air as I watched him paint my bare legs in feather-light kisses, each pass of his full lips thoughtful and intensifying the hollow ache growing inside me.

"You," I huffed. "I want you."

Never parting his mouth from my leg, he asked, "How badly?"

"*So* badly."

"Do you ache for me?"

I nodded vehemently against the pillow.

"*Out loud*, Ms. Sanders."

"Yes," I panted, squirming against the bed. "Yes, sir. I ache. I ache so fucking badly, it hurts."

"It hurts how much you want me?"

"Yes, sir."

Predatory eyes flashed up to me. "Where do you want me?"

I yanked my hands to grab where I throbbed, where heat was building, when cold restraints cut into my skin, holding me in place. Dominic observed me struggle and whimper, jerking my hips up towards him.

"Inside of me."

I *needed* him inside of me, the pressure compiling into actual pain the longer he went without touching me. It was bordering on agony, and Dominic seemed to watch my torment with ease.

Ease and quiet enjoyment.

The exquisite structure of his face had never been more pointed and angular, severe and intimidating. His hair remained neat despite my efforts, portraying him as put together and *beyond* controlled when I was a whimpering mess beneath him. And his eyes.

God, his fucking eyes were carnality embodied.

Gently, he eased my legs down but left his heavy hand sitting on my lower stomach *just* above my heat. Anticipation suffused my lungs as he lowered himself next to me, his manicured five o'clock shadow scratching my shoulder, his molten lips cusping my earlobe.

"How you're feeling right now, that ache? That's how you made me feel every day for *weeks*." His voice rolled up my neck, throaty and domineering, and I arched myself to get closer to his unadulterated power.

"Every time you gave me your wicked smile or got closer than you should have and forced me to smell that goddamn coconut shampoo you use, it got worse."

He nosed my neck where my hair fell, inhaling a hit of the addiction he was lamenting about. "It got so bad, I was in pain whenever you were around and in agony whenever you weren't."

His voice dug deeper, sinking its teeth into the frenzy I inspired in him and burning hotter, turning torrid.

"I have never in my life been reduced so completely to such a primal state before. I wanted you so madly, I felt it with every part of me. Every fiber, every molecule I possess, *you* possessed until you were all I thought about. You turned me into a man of *want* and *need* for something I couldn't have… and you had fun with it."

Shivers shook the nerves in my stomach at his tone, punching up at his palm laying over it. There was *undeniable* danger lurking in Dominic's words.

An undeniable threat to make me pay for all I'd put him through.

Exhilaration and fear spliced together into one sensation, circulating my blood and heightening all of my senses, my aches, my emotions that were already on the fritz. It rose everything to the shallow of my skin like flowers blooming, and Dominic was the rainstorm sent to water it all until he fucking drowned me in my own need for him.

My rainstorm left the crook of my neck, thundercloud eyes coming front and center. "Now it's my turn to have fun, Ms. Sanders."

Except 'fun' sounded a hell of a lot like 'payback is gonna be a kinky bitch.'

"Are you gonna be mean to me?" I asked, tracking my eyes over his sculpted face.

"Extremely."

"Are you gonna let me come?"

He held his answer back like he was really, truly considering it.

"Eventually."

The torment hadn't even begun yet, and I was already squirming with the thought of it. Dominic's hooded eyes absorbed my wriggling against him, the whispered pleas as they dropped from my lips. He lingered in close, nose brushing mine.

"You have no idea what I've imagined doing to you to make up for what you put me through, Ms. Sanders." Soft lips warmed mine with a teasing graze. "What I'm going to do to you tonight."

"What're you gonna do?"

My voice was far off, a distant sound in the face of the tease Dominic had started between our lips, nuzzling just barely, caressing our open mouths together and fanning my tongue with his breath, but never quite kissing me. Not even a peck.

He dripped his husky tone all over my aching lips. "You want to know what I'm going to do?"

I nodded fast, tilting my chin up to beg for a kiss.

He denied me. *Again.* Instead, doing something much worse.

"I'm going to put my mouth right here," I gasped as he cupped my core, grabbing it like he owned it and washing my lips in his rough voice, "and I'm going to spell out my name and listen as you scream it."

My head dropped back into the pillow, moans clawing their way out as he squeezed my mound, sensations sparking and tightening.

"And I'll do it again and again, slowing down when you beg me to go faster. Giving you less when you beg for more. I'll take you to the peak over and over again, but you won't fall until I let you."

Teeth nabbed onto my bottom lip, bleeding out a strangled cry. Dominic bit at and sucked my flesh until it was swollen from his effort and pouty just how he liked it. My lip popped out of his bite, the wet smack sound hitting right between my thighs and making me pant.

"I'll keep going until you're so frazzled, so worked up, so desperate to come that you'll cry real tears for it." A cry like he spoke of ripped from my throat as he removed the pressure of his hand over my core, taking away the delicious friction and leaving me *more* than aching.

Dominic caught my pleading stare in his, satisfaction in his burning eyes. "And I'll kiss each one away because I can. Because you're *mine* tonight, Ms. Sanders."

Oh, fuck me.

His.

I was his, and he was going to ruin me and make me beg for more.

Already pulling on my restraints, I whined when Dominic started down my body, trailing smooth kisses down my stomach. He *completely* skipped my tits, ignoring them and my nipples that were perked and growing raw for attention still under this bra and shirt.

With a feral groan, I jerked my head up off the pillow.

"Was I really that much of a tease?"

Wet mouth curving the edge of my hip bone, he answered simply. "Oh yes."

"I didn't mean to be!" I tried, fighting down the corner of my mouth that knew I was lying.

Gunmetal eyes flashed up, his pink tongue finishing a tantalizing circle above the band of my thong. The sight alone clenched my walls around nothing, arousal soaking through.

"You and I both know you're a terrible liar," Dominic chided, authority thrumming his timbre. He dropped his focus down to my pussy, to the lace red thong I just so happened to be wearing.

"And a *brat*."

Oh, he was *mad* at the thong. Mad at me for wearing it. Maybe he would tear it off with his teeth like the animal I knew he could be? The one thriving under his hero skin that I brought out of hiding.

"Was I wearing something like this all those times you pictured punishing me?"

He stared at the crimson garment really, *really* hard, jaw locked tight.

"Actually, yes."

My eyebrows strung together, and Dominic gave me every ounce of his intense focus. "You were wearing something similar the night I picked you up at that party. Your shirt got pulled down when you tried to run from me, and you had on this vixen red bra that started to show."

Memories sparked in the back of my brain, and I wanted to smile. A real *devilish* smile. I remembered that night. I remembered wondering if he'd noticed me like that, wondering if he was seeing my peeking bra and if he would have ripped it off of me if he wasn't married.

"So, you were looking," I confirmed.

His razor-cut jaw ticked to the side. "Against every better judgement in my body screaming at me not to."

Prideful fireworks went off inside my chest, setting my need aflame for more. I wanted to know more. I wanted to know all the ways and times Dominic had been turned bad when he was trying *so* hard to be good.

I blinked slowly in the amber lighting, holding his gaze.

"Did you get off thinking about me?"

And if I thought his stare was intense before, it had nothing against the severe cut of his silver eyes now. They were so sharp, I inhaled a gasp like his gaze actually pierced me.

"Would that make you happy if I did?"

Chest heaving, I nodded despite his voice equaling a warning not to.

I was testing him, pushing him, doing exactly what got me chained to this headboard in the first place, and I couldn't help it. The punishment promised to me in his searing gaze was too good to resist. It was like its own addiction.

I *had* to push, I *had* to play, and Dominic had to teach me what happened when I broke his precious rules.

It started as he hooked both hands beneath my thighs and tugged—a brusque, gasp-igniting tug—until my torso was pulled straight and my arms pulled tight against the cuffs. My head jumped up to find Dominic settling his face between my legs, flaming eyes catching mine.

"It would make you happy to know that sometimes I took an extra shower during the day so I could get myself off thinking about you?"

A pass of his silk tongue over my inner thigh shook my breath and dropped my head back into the pillow. Hot breath washed over my bundle of tense nerves, a gruff voice unfurling after it. "That I'd make sure the bathroom door was locked so I could stroke myself thinking about my nanny and her bottle green eyes and pouty fucking mouth?"

"You love my pouty mouth," I breathed, writhing against his mouth kissing my inner thigh.

"I do love it," he hummed, nosing the front of my panties and breathing deep. "I love every single inch of you."

He paused and I risked a hazy glance up, finding wicked eyes waiting for me.

"Inside and out, Ms. Sanders."

A gasp punctuated the very next second, tearing up my throat as Dominic sucked my clit into his mouth through my underwear. I bucked against him as much as I could before his hands still latched around my thighs anchored them flat to the bed, holding me open for him to devour.

My heart arched towards the ceiling, his name falling out on repeat in a song of worship as he built my pleasure to the high heavens. He rolled his tongue over my thong again and again, flicking my clit and sucking back on it, daring to fucking nibble it through the fabric.

"Can you," I panted, eyes squeezing. "Can you take off the thong? Please?"

Against me, he rumbled, "You want it off?"

"Yes." My voice was a squeak. A pathetic, wanton squeak. "Fuck, *yes*."

"Then it stays on."

My eyes snapped open. "What?!"

"You want it too badly." He laid a kiss on my mound much sweeter than the cruel punishment he was delivering to it. "You don't get what you want until I want to give it to you, Ms. Sanders."

"But—" *Think, think, think.* "You can't really…"

Oh shit, what's the word?

"Taste you?" Dominic filled in.

Yeah, that!

"There are other ways I can taste you without taking these off."

A sting slapped the air and my thighs as Dominic snapped the band of my thong.

Frustration ground the back of my head into the pillow, my pussy crying to be properly and thoroughly touched, licked, fucked by Dominic's tongue. Even with the over-the-clothes example he'd given me so far, he was clearly an expert, and I wanted him to give me an exhaustive lesson.

Cool air swept suddenly across my heated center, and my breath hitched, eyes widening. I waited, anticipation bubbling as Dominic stretched my underwear to the side, exposing only part of me. I held my breath—actually held it completely still—as I felt Dominic taking me in, his stare like sunbeams heating me up from the outside in.

Pressure pressed at my core, pressure and then—

"*Oh*- oh…"

Dominic and I groaned in unison as his two fingers sunk into the middle of me, stretching me out something delicious and widening the ache of pleasure building within me.

He cursed under his breath, pumping his fingers slowly. "Kat, you're small. You're so small."

Genuine worry gripped his voice. I was tight, and he was afraid he was going to hurt me now that he planned to have sex with me.

"I'll be fine," I reassured, wrapping my fingers around the thin rod railing over my head and holding on tight. "Plus, I like when it hurts a little."

His fingers stopped moving inside of me, bringing my gaze down to him between my legs.

He'd gone from hungry and deliciously vengeful to serious in a flash.

"It's not right to hurt you like that."

My heart that loved so newly and so profoundly squeezed at his concern, and somehow even *that* made the walls of my core flutter.

Dear lord, did emotional intimacy turn me on now?

Being in love was so fucking weird.

"Dominic, I'll be fine. It's not like I'm a virgin."

"Yeah, but you're tight like one," he hissed, testing a third finger inside of me and looking like *he* was in pain trying to work it in.

The feeling of being so full swallowed me up, stuffing hot air down my throat so I could barely get words out. It was a miracle I said, "We can cross that bridge when we get to it, but for now," I locked my eyes to his and pleaded, "please don't stop."

Dominic tracked his dark eyes between mine, collecting my reactions and pleas, assessing how to move forward in that dissecting mind of his. I huffed and whimpered as he weighed his options, three fingers still stuffed inside of me.

Then—

"No!"

I cried out as he removed his fingers, leaving me emptier than I'd ever been in my life.

My brain rushed together strings of words to implore, beg, and bargain for him to put his fingers back where I wanted them, but all those words dried up on my tongue the second I saw him.

Shadows played along the hollow of Dominic's high cheekbones as he opened his mouth and placed two fingers behind his lips. Two that had glistened in the singular lamp lighting with my arousal.

My *taste*.

His eyes rolled in ecstasy and then closed as he sucked on his fingers, savoring the flavor of me and what he did to me. My lips split ajar watching him, memorizing how he drank down what he took from me, his swarthy eyebrows curved in tight as he enjoyed every fucking second of tasting me.

Eventually his heavy eyelids peeled back open, his sucked-on fingers retracting from his mouth. The craving in his pupils had eaten up almost every dash of color in his eyes, and Dominic Reed had never before looked more like the animal I knew he could be.

"That's cheating," I breathed on a wisp.

Predatory eyes on mine, he spoke like he was pissed off. "And you're addicting."

And then he grabbed at my thong the same way, tearing the flimsy fabric down my legs with the same combustible anger, growling. "What's cheating is tasting that fucking good."

Wild breaths fueled my lungs as he folded my legs together to peel the underwear off, tossing them to the side before crushing my thighs apart on the mattress again, splitting me down the middle for him to feast.

And *fuck*, did he ever.

His mouth covered me, wet and hot and so goddamn greedy. A cry pierced the air as he dipped his tongue inside of me, fucking me and lapping at me like he really was trying to spell his name out. He was writing his name inside of me to make me his, and I screamed out his name to prove it was true.

"Dominic."

Strong fingers tightened their grip around my thighs, and I had a feeling it was his name falling from my lips that made Dominic grab me like he'd never let me go. I didn't want him to either.

This was the only place I wanted to be right now, strapped to his bed with his mouth fucking me like he was trying to lick every last drop I had to give.

Electricity coiled in the pit of my stomach, each suck of his lips and rotations of his tongue cinching the searing sensations tighter. My thighs twitched beneath Dominic's grip, incoherent sounds dragging from my tongue as my gut dipped, and I swore I glimpsed a beam from Heaven.

Air compacted. Lungs swelled. Eyes squeezed at the radiating light peeling in from all sides.

And then it was gone.

That heavenly beam was sucked back up into the ceiling, and Dominic's mouth left me cold and *sorely* unsatisfied.

My temper and my lightning exploded in place of my stolen orgasm, head snapping up. "What the *fuck?*"

A mouth that glistened down to his stubborn chin caressed up the inside of my thigh, kissing hard and then kissing soft, lips stroking in wide passes, tongue sweeping in circles. He ignored my question just like he ignored my climax that was *right* there, instead skipping over to my other thigh and staining my flesh with his kisses.

On the bed, I thrashed my arms locked above my head, stretching my fingers out in some blind attempt to get my hands back. The metal bracelets latched around them both only scraped at my skin and bones, crushing them all together and I cried out.

"You'll only hurt yourself trying," Dominic murmured over the bend of my knees.

Groaning deeply, I arched myself against the mattress. "I don't care. I don't *care*. I'll break the fucking bed if I have to."

"Please don't," he replied casually. "It's new."

"Dominic, I—"

My vocal cords froze, hot breath steaming over my weeping center… and then lips. Aw fuck, lips. Tongue. Teeth. It was all back, kissing and biting and sucking at my clit that fucking stung in relief.

My fingers curled back around the iron rods, gripping until the metal peeled my skin as Dominic spread me apart with his tongue, licking me up and down like I was liquid sugar and he had a sweet tooth.

The electric sensations were back in my stomach, my legs shaking again under his firm hands. A strangled mewl stretched out of me, heady air compacting in my head, my chest, that delicious pinch tightening between my legs—

And then nothing. *Again.*

"Oh my *god*, I'm gonna throw you down the stairs," I groaned viciously.

Dominic let out a husky laugh over my crying core, bristles from his beard scraping my thigh. Yeah, he actually fucking *laughed*.

"I thought you said you'd burn down anyone who tried to hurt me?"

"Except me. *I* can hurt you if you don't stop being so mean," I whined out the last word, stretching it into like four syllables instead of one as he blew cool air against me, tingles spreading like wildfire that hurt like real flames.

This was pain. Actual *pain*.

"I warned you, Ms. Sanders."

"Yeah, and I didn't listen. Are either of us shocked?"

"Shocked? No." A tender kiss to my swollen center. "I'm quite enjoying myself however."

A cry needled out of the center of my chest, and its melody rang with true agony as he placed that kiss over me. It caught Dominic's sparkling eyes in the dim lighting, shadowing the slants and hills of his god-like beauty.

"I-I can't," I panted heavily. "I can't take it, Dominic. I need you. It *hurts*."

Something moved behind his dark stare.

"You need me," he rumbled, repeating and savoring the fact.

I nodded fast. "Yes."

His fingers around my thighs flexed, holding me looser and tighter somehow.

"You need me to take the pain away?"

My gut pulled back, fisting tight in the next second at the change of quality of Dominic's voice. It dropped in register, wading into intimate territories that said the pain he was speaking about wasn't the one he'd built between my legs.

That wasn't the pain of mine he was drawn to healing. He wanted my real pain, my *fucked up* pain, and he wanted to make it go away.

I couldn't deal with that right now. I couldn't even think of that right now past the splinter of need pulsing between my legs. I needed him to make that pain go away before we tackled anything else.

"Please," I begged, pitiable and not even caring.

The gray of his eyes smoked to burnt charcoal, recording my every reaction. "Does this mean you're sorry for all the fun you had while I couldn't have you?"

"No," I breathed, nose crinkling. "Not even a little."

He leaned back, head tilting. "No?"

"*No*. We're here right now because I was a tease and you liked it."

The retort refocused Dominic's stare sharper, so I kept going. "I drove you crazy, and you liked my brand of crazy. We're here because I didn't follow your rules and you couldn't get enough of it."

Slowly, Dominic began crawling over top of my body, his bright eyes on me and scorching my oxygen to wisps.

"You liked seeing what I would say next or do next or—"

"You're wrong," he quieted me, close enough now to brush our lips together.

My heart *banged* up against my chest, wanting to reach out and touch his. A whimper traded between our breathing as he bumped our noses sweetly. "I *loved* it. I loved every single second of you turning my world inside out."

A cry to have him, to kiss him and hold him, reached out of me like it had arms and dragged him down, our lips fitting together in a way that *proved* to the cynic in my head that our lips had been created as pieces of a whole.

When we kissed, they were complete—and so were we.

The proof spurred an ache unlike the one swollen between my legs inside my chest, wrapping its bindings around my ribs and scoring my marrow, consuming me, *changing* me, and I remembered the feeling from before. It was the same feeling I had in Ryan's tiny back bedroom when Dominic laid a kiss on me after asking me if I trusted him.

That's when I became sickest, I realized.

That was the exact moment I jumped, not fell, into love with Dominic Reed.

The revelation pulsed waves of my electric butterflies through every inch of me, tingling to the tip of my tongue that slid along the seam of his lips that tasted of me. He opened up and fucking kissed me like he was dying, like we both were dying and this kiss was our only avenue for survival.

In my view, we'd both already perished and each stroke of our lips was attuned to the stroke of a pen, signing our lives away to each other and rewriting our stars for good.

The way Dominic cupped my face in his hands, then changed to squeezing the back of my neck, my hair, my everything he could touch while delivering me the taste of his love was overwhelming.

It was too much, too good, too intoxicating for my addict-prone genetics.

I still couldn't think straight, my mind as locked as my wrists by the need absolutely throbbing between my thighs. I needed it gone, vanquished, conquered by the strong tongue coasting around mine.

Tearing my lips from his, I huffed and jerked my chin down. "Pretend I can push your head back down."

A husky chuckle tickled my kiss-swollen lips, adoration infusing his deep voice.

"You have no patience."

I shook my head, panting wildly. "Not even a little."

Totally ignoring my lack of patience, Dominic laid a kiss to my mouth that started soft and grew hard, dominating and consuming every bit of me, stealing whimpers from the pit of my throat—from my *soul.* He snatched every single one of my needy noises and swallowed them down, using them as sustenance as he broke our kiss and trailed open-mouth kisses down my trembling body.

Each kiss stained my soul past the point of return and corrupted me as his for good.

I was *permanently* his and he was *permanently* mine, and it was as terrifying as anything else so unchangeable.

A cry split my lips as his face found between my legs again, burying his mouth against me and resuming his torture. It was insane how fast I reached the peak again, legs twitching, mewls dripping from parted lips, that splinter of pleasure digging deeper and deeper.

My fingers wrapped around the handcuffs and iron rods, death-gripping it as tears—*real* fucking tears just like he predicted—pinched at the backs of my eyes and leaked over.

Oxygen too heady and too big packed my lungs; my ribs felt like they might crack under the pressure. Dominic wasn't yielding this time, tongue relentless, lips sucking, teeth grazing.

Gasps of his name quilted the bedroom, the ache in my core burning hotter and wider.

Dominic wrapped his hands around my thighs, securing me to his hungry mouth and groaning against it as I cried his name and jerked in his grip.

"Are you ready for me to let you come?" His lust-gripped voice resonated inside of me, and I bucked against him.

"Yes."

"Do you think you've earned it?"

"*Yes.*"

His tongue flattened against me, licking a slow, savoring pathway up my slit as he hummed deeply. *Satisfied.*

"So do I."

"Oh *god*," I squeaked, eyes screwing shut, all muscles tightening and tensing as Dominic's mouth sought out the upcoming orgasm. It was so close, I could taste its musky flavor on the tip of my tongue as Dominic used his to flick and swipe and obliterate any expectations I might have had before this.

He wasn't using his fingers anymore, and somehow, it was awful and amazing at the same time. It was just his mouth chasing the ache crescendoing in the pit of my stomach.

He hunted it out, chased it down, and finally—*finally*—conquered it with a prevailing grunt.

Electricity crackled through my blood, tears streaming out as the tortured orgasm hit.

A screech inhuman ripped through me, white spots filling in behind my pinched eyes as heat washed up and down the entire length of my body. Dominic's hold around me anchored tighter as I tensed up the spine, his mouth almost as greedy for my climax as I was, drinking every second of it down like honey.

Bites of pain dug into my flesh as I pulled at the cuffs as I arched up, sustaining the high of the orgasm for as long as I could. I basked in it, *lived* for the blinding sensations and the man who had drawn them out until it drained me. The orgasm wiped me completely dead as it wound down, sucking every ounce of strength from my muscles as I slumped all my limbs back to the bed.

My chest rose and fell, hot breath pushing and pulling between my lips as I laid there, entirely spent and layered in sweat.

The room was a haze of passion and echoes of my cries, and my head felt the same way, all hazy and dense as the mattress dipped below me, fingers working at the handcuffs around my wrists.

My elbows hit the bed as my hands were freed, slacked of all power. Lips so feather-soft and affectionate smoothed across my jawline, telling me how good I'd done and calling me beautiful.

An angel, he said.

And suddenly, my muscles weren't so useless. They'd found power again in his words, in Dominic's worship and the nonsensical name he'd given me.

I was no angel. I was sin embodied and born straight out of hell.

I was his little devil, and he was a god. He was supposed to smite me, not love me.

I brought my devilish arms up, my hands covering his shirt and pulling apart buttons, dragging it down his arms. They tugged at his undershirt until he rose to his knees and removed it too. Then my renewed muscles helped me sit up at the waist and mirror his motions.

Smoky eyes watched me as I discarded my shirt to the side and folded my arms back around to the clasp of my bra. It fell free and joined my shirt on the floor, the hot air we'd created breezing across my bare tits that waited for Dominic's attention.

There was this evident strain holding his expression tight, his stare keeping on mine for as long as he could until whatever self-inflicted torment he'd unleashed on himself snapped, and his focus fell to my breasts.

Desire fanned up his face, his strict jawline cementing down hard. My nipples pebbled under his severe gaze, tits growing heavier as they begged to be touched like he'd touched the rest of me.

They needed it. *I* needed it.

I needed him.

His hand appeared on my shoulder instead, slowly guiding me down until my back melted to the bed and my head cradled against the feather-down soft pillow.

Dominic hovered himself above me, shirtless and breathtaking and holding himself up by his arms positioned on either side of my head.

His mouth was almost a frown it was so serious, and the lens brightening his eyes was no different.

It was the same lens from earlier, the kind that burned of starlight and made my heart stutter and cower.

Everything that had been born again inside of me twisted at the radiant look being delivered to me by a man I didn't deserve. He was a man devout and worshiping as he gazed at me, absorbing every single facet of his beloved religion he took so seriously.

A religion he looked like he'd lay down his life for.

"Stop looking at me like that," I demanded on a breath of fear.

Eyes of silver raked over me, my forehead, my neck, my bare tits, and he shook his head.

"No."

"Yes," I fought back, weakness tangling up my voice.

Again, he disagreed, gently brushing a lock of hair from my face and pushing it back into the pillow with the rest of my splaying hair.

"I can't. I won't."

His denial sounded as lost for rescue as I felt, as unable to detach himself from me as I was to him. We were fused wholeheartedly, souls clinging, hearts *loving* like idiots, our bodies the only parts of us left unclaimed.

And I couldn't stand it. I couldn't fucking stand another second of not having him inside of me, moving over me, showing me how it felt when you made love to someone instead of fucked them.

It was corny as shit, but I needed to know.

There had to be a difference, right? All the adults growing up said there was an emphatic difference, and that's why you needed to wait until you were in love before you had sex.

Actually, scratch that. They said to wait until you were married, but that was some bullshit I knew from a young age I wouldn't follow.

But being in *love* was the crux of it all, and now here I was—in love.

Would I be able to *feel* the difference everyone always talked about? Maybe it was stupid to wonder, but I couldn't help it. I needed him to show me how it felt.

My fingers dropped to Dominic's belt buckle, our eyes still locked. I undid it without fumbling—*score*—and went for the button and zipper on his slacks next. Dominic let me, watching me with severe focus that parched my throat and tousled my live-wire nerves.

The want to ask him what he was thinking weighed heavily on the tip of my tongue, but I was sure I already knew.

He was still technically a married man. Even despite the signed and served divorce papers, he was a husband and he was about to bed someone who wasn't his wife. In his too-good-for-me heart, he knew this, and maybe it was hurting him to know it.

He hadn't been inside another woman in over a decade, hadn't had another wrap their delicate fingers around his bare cock and stroke him like I planned to, and he was overthinking all of it.

Every time he and I crossed these lines before, it had always been him touching me and never the other way around. He never let me ease down the zipper of his pants before like I was now. He never let my fingertips graze the lip of his underwear, feeling how hot his skin was just above the band or how coarse the dark hairs were leading beneath it.

And he'd never let me slip my hand below the cusp of his briefs and wrap my fingers around his cock.

My desire doubled, no fucking *quadrupled* as I held him in my hand, heavy and thick and smooth. Dominic hissed through his teeth, an inspired sound as I squeezed my fingers around the shaft of him.

My fingers barely touched around him.

I let a breath go that was drenched in heat, in *need* as I stroked up, my eyes falling to my hand as I pulled him out of his underwear to watch myself do it. My eyes widened and my core pulsed.

Fuck, he was perfect.

And big. Holy shit, no wonder he was worried.

The tip of him glistened as I moved my hand around him, my palm riding over jutting veins and smooth skin as hard as fucking stone. Dominic breathed through his nose, heavy and concentrated, and a quick glance up showed he was watching my hand ride him just as I was.

"Please tell me you brought condoms."

His tight nod brought my eyes back up to him.

"I put some in my wallet right after I signed the papers a few days back."

A sharp breath sucked between his bared teeth as I squeezed him again, his thick brows furrowing together. Lust-darkened eyes snapped up to me, falling to my pouty mouth as I spoke.

"Because you knew I'd try to get you into bed the second I found out?"

His nostrils flared, the animal breaking skin.

"Because I know us, and we've never been good at staying away from each other."

Truer fucking words had never been spoken.

"Off." I pushed at the waist of his slacks, abandoning his heavy cock. "I want these off."

Dominic met my desperate demand with quickness, getting off the bed and plucking a shiny square packet from his wallet in his back pocket before letting his pants fall to the floor, stepping out of them, and next, his black underwear.

My eyes were everywhere over his naked body, drinking him in like I'd never been closer to perfection.

Because truthfully… I really didn't think I had.

This was perfection. It had to be.

Every sculpted line on his torso was art, every chiseled ridge of his abs was a masterpiece, every bulge of strong muscle in his big arms and wide-set shoulders was a paragon of beauty. Dominic's body was a carving of golden power and it *had* to be perfection.

His face was beyond it.

And his eyes. Those were the goddamn stars in heaven.

Every part of this man was beyond me. Why he wanted me, why he *loved* me, was beyond me too, but I wasn't a girl dumb enough to question that right now. Not with my heart screaming for his and my pussy throbbing for him as he rolled the condom down his entire length.

Audible breathing poorly concealed my excitement as he came back to the bed and knelt in front of me. He placed both his warm hands over my propped up knees, and they fell apart as if his touch was magic.

Gray eyes on my body, Dominic secured both his hands beneath my knees, guiding my legs to lock my ankles behind his back. Slowly, he laid himself down on top of me, warm skin to warm skin, thumping hearts going strong to the unified rhythm they brewed.

His heavy cock lay between our stomachs, one move away from being inside me.

There was nothing between us but skin tonight. Nothing and no one was going to stop us from the thing we'd been building to since that day he first kissed me in his garage.

I'd thought about this moment, even pictured this moment hundreds of times before.

But I never pictured it like this.

Soft and tender. Emotional and overwhelming.

It was supposed to be rough and careless, passion on overload as we fucked out all our forbidden affections for each other so we could move on from the heroin chemistry.

The heroin chemistry wasn't supposed to morph into *this*.

It wasn't supposed to malform into fairytale love that made this moment feel so monumental. It felt like nothing had ever felt before as I stared up at him and he stared down at me, his eyes cusping diamond-like quality they shined with a love so bright.

That all-encompassing ache welled up my throat, pinching behind my eyes as I took in all his shameless love. He was so unapologetic about showing me and telling me all about his love, and I hadn't even said the words yet.

They were there, waiting in the lump in my throat for him.

He deserved them.

He deserved to hear them and not just assume that's what my panic and tears from earlier spelled out.

Forcing clips of air down my tightening throat, I cupped my palm to his cheek, rough hairs brushing back as I scoured my thumb across his angular jawline lovingly.

Yes, *lovingly*.

I was trying, working to unstick the three little words in the back of my throat.

Dominic leaned into my touch, turning his face to place his lips on the inside of my palm in a gentle kiss. The ache *stabbed* in my chest like it had never quite done before, and I struggled for breath.

Saltwater breached my eyes, love's ocean drowning me quick and fast.

Dominic reached his own hand up and laced his fingers through mine, holding our hands together against his face. I looked over at our hands helplessly, interlocked and clinging. They looked so right holding each other, my small hand engulfed in his.

The gesture was so simple.

Holding hands *was* simple, but not to me. None of this was simple to me, and I'd made none of it simple for Dominic either, but he never gave up. He never stopped coming after me and fighting for me even when I yelled at him not to. Even when I showed him my ugliest demons and hoped they sent him running.

He stayed and he *loved* all of my ugly with all of his beauty.

He was a miracle, and he deserved to know it.

I swallowed, my throat suddenly swollen and thick. "I—"

My voice broke in half. *Audibly.*

Humiliation flushed heat waves down my chest, sweat bunching at my hairline as I fluttered my gaze back to Dominic's to see if he had heard my weakness. My stupid fucking weakness over three little words.

Diamond eyes were waiting for me, looking back and forth between my obnoxious, chicken shit tears as a tightness piled on top of my brand new heart.

My heart that *loved* him. My heart that was fighting with my terror-struck tongue to say the words.

I love you. I'm in love with you.

I'm so fucking scared to be in love with you.

Except the words didn't translate from my mind to my mouth. All that came out were creaks of nothing that sounded like everything. Everything I was afraid of, at least, rolled up into one mousy noise.

Understanding passed over Dominic's eyes, and he nodded, squeezing my hand.

"I love you too," he whispered.

The terrible ache exploded shards through my chest, cutting my salty tears free. Dominic watched them fall without a single ounce of judgement or upset distorting his perfect face.

I couldn't say the words, but he didn't mind. He just wiped them away and kissed the remnants of them gone from my cheeks.

"I don't know why I can't stop-" I hiccuped. "Stop fucking *crying*."

"Yes you do," he murmured calmly, dropping his mouth to the arch of my neck I'd sheathed for him.

Sucking down a shaking breath, I knew he was right. The mess all down my wet cheeks and seeping into the pillow beneath had a crystal clear reasoning.

"Am I gonna cry every time we have sex?" I asked, half as a joke, half out of fear that it was true.

A steady hum resonated through his chest pressed to mine. "No," he heartened, confident and deep and brushing soft lips over mine. "But I'll kiss your tears away as many times as you need me to, and I'll never get tired of it."

My new heart convulsed, struck by my frenzied lightning. "Can y-you just make it stop?"

I just wanted it all to stop. The tears. The emotions. The throbbing pain that being in love with him cast over my body.

Dominic nodded, bringing his forehead to mine and reaching down between us. He positioned himself at the center of me, and I held all my trembling breath still as the tip of him ran over me, hard and slicking himself up with my arousal.

My shallow panting and Dominic's concentrated breathing stuffed the room as the only sounds, and before I could cry another single tear, Dominic pushed himself in.

A gasp widened up my throat, a stretch piercing my walls.

My fists clenched tight, one shaking at my side and the other stealing to his shoulder where my nails bit into my palm. He wasn't even halfway in yet, and my eyes were squeezed shut to block out the painful pinch of his size.

Fuck.

A shudder wracked Dominic's body over mine, a barely controlled exhale washing my face. He'd stopped moving entirely, every muscle plastered against mine strung taut.

"Relax yourself," he told me through gritted teeth like he was in pain too.

It took a few moments, and a lot of focusing on my breathing, but eventually, I eased all of my muscles for him.

Dominic dropped his face into the crook of my neck, nuzzling there with his hot breath and silken hair tickling my skin. He hooked an arm beneath one of my thighs and hoisted it even higher for him, unlocking my ankles to fold my leg back almost to my chest.

The position opened me up, and Dominic's hips sunk deeper between me, both of us moaning at the friction. I felt him everywhere; from the crown of my head to the tips of my toes, I felt him.

Dominic filled me up like I'd never been filled before, and it wasn't just the thick as fuck cock stretching me out making me feel that way. It was all of him. Every single inch of him flooded my bloodstream with thunder. *His* thunder was inside of me, crackling and vibrating my cells with the memory of his presence so I'd always know.

I belonged to the thunder, and he belonged to the lightning.

A choked cry kicked back my head as Dominic tested a roll of his hips, pushing himself in until I couldn't take anymore. He pulled back, and I gasped for breath and for relief from the pressure he stretched me with.

Then, he did it again. Another thrust. Another cry for relief and for more at the same time.

"Am I hurting you?" Dominic's gruff question burned hot against my ear, and I shook my head.

"*No.* No, keep going."

Muffling a groan against my neck, he did. He rocked his hips into mine at a pained pace for us both, too unhurried to be more than a slow-burn tease, and I clawed at his bare back for more.

"*Kat,*" he half grunted, half sighed my name as I drew my nails down his back.

He buried himself to the hilt inside of me as punishment, breaking whimpers from my lips and proving that he was barely holding onto himself.

His good self was fraying at the edges, his animal with morals as gray as his eyes breaking loose. He wanted to fuck me hard and raw, and we were both going to get what we wanted.

"You're not gonna break me," I panted, threading my fingers up through his mass of hair. "I want *more*. I want all of you. Every single perfect bit."

He sighed hard, his controlled thrusts stumbling.

"I'm not perfect."

"I'm not so convinced," I breathed, holding onto him, feeling the powerful muscles move in his back as he fucked me long and deep.

A growl resonated down the hollow of my neck, dangerous and provoking. Cold air swept my neck as Dominic lifted himself to his elbows, gripping me head on with his stare of untapped hunger.

"Would a man so perfect want to rip into you even if it hurt you? Even if you cried out in pain?"

Excitement ignited a noisy gasp behind my lips, and the blacks of Dominic's pupils smoked. "Because that's what I want to do to you right now, Kat. I want your pain so I can turn it into pleasure, and what kind of so-called perfect man would want that?"

Searching back and forth between his shadowy eyes, I spoke sincerely. "The kind that's perfect for me."

Dominic's thick lashes fluttered fast over his charcoal eyes like he was suddenly drunk, unstable and unable to hold himself up like he had been. He had to snap. He had to break this righteous skin he'd been sewed up in all these years that constricted how he moved, talked, and even fucked.

And I was goddamn proud to be the thing sharp enough to cut him free.

A cry popped off my lips just as he predicted, blending into a moan as the sharp pain of Dominic's violent thrust sunk deeper into something so, *so* fucking good. Dark eyes watched me from up close as I rode the scale of pain and pleasure, recording every breath, every time I chewed my bottom lip, every heavy-lidded blink he unearthed from me.

He watched me and waited for me, cock still rooted inside of me.

"More," I breathed—*begged*.

Dominic's shoulders rose with untamed breaths in the silhouette of amber lighting that encased us. His browline was pinched and curious, exacting eyes fixed to mine as I pleaded for more. He *wanted* to give me more, but he still looked so unsure, so wary of hurting me past the point of pleasure.

He waited too long and worried too much.

I attacked his back with my nails once more, scraping them down like I was peeling his righteous skin right off, sheathing the thing dirty and dangerous beneath he'd locked down because he had to. He didn't *have* to anymore. I wanted his dirty. I wanted his filthy, sinful, offensive parts, and I wanted to mix them with mine.

I wanted to create a brand new color on the spectrum of filth, and I wanted to name it after us.

Dominic groaned aloud as I buried my nails in his bare back, teeth baring and cords in his thick neck pulling taut. With a teeming growl, his hips pulled back fast and penetrated forward even faster, *harder*.

A yelp tore from my chest as pain spiked, but folded over into pleasure too fast for me to care. My head rolled back into the pillow, moans falling out as Dominic shed his perfect skin for something better, something truly him and truly divine.

He speared me again and again, not caring if I screamed and going harder when I did. His thrusts were deep and brutal, the bed jerking and headboard slapping the wall in those telltale sounds of passion.

The burn was beginning to build in my core, getting hotter each time Dominic rammed himself into me like he needed to fuck me to stay alive.

No.

Like he needed to *love* me to stay alive.

This wasn't fucking. This was loving. This was loving so purely and vulnerably, I was sure of it. I understood it now. Making love and fucking? There *was* an emphatic difference.

Fucking was all lies, all selfish, and all shallow.

This? This was not that.

Dominic and I had never been as honest with each other as we were in these moments, on these sheets, and inside these walls. Our sweat was truth. Our movements were confessions. The orgasms we were chasing would be the verifiable proof of it all.

I wrapped my arms around his back as I realized the difference, as I *felt* the difference of the two acts. Dominic slipped a burly arm between my waist and the mattress, holding me tighter as if he knew the revelation going on inside my head.

I cried his name on a soft whimper and he drowned me in kisses, whispering my own. The burn in my core was becoming too much, too combustible.

I reached back, coiling both hands around the iron rod headboard to hold onto something to keep me grounded from the oncoming orgasm.

"Are you close?" Dominic huffed over my gasping lips.

I nodded fast, narrowing my focus to him and the searing sensations piling together in the pit of my stomach. Then, he was gone, out of kissable reach and sitting back on his ankles with his big hands enveloped around my slight waist.

"I need to watch." He jerked a deep thrust, breaking a yelp up my throat as I twisted my fingers around the headboard and arched up to the ceiling. Hooded eyes watched me twist and cry, sweat beading in the light on his knitted browline.

"I want to watch you come undone like this."

"You mean on your cock instead of your fingers?" I taunted, breathing heavily.

Gray eyes eclipsed nearly black, the end of his pretty mouth curving up. "Filthy mouth, Ms. Sanders."

"Maybe you should stuff it with something."

A heavy sigh took Dominic's head lower, contorting the angles of his face with shadows of promise and ruin.

"I'm still convinced you'll be the death of me."

My mouth parted to reply when a moan jammed in its place first, Dominic slamming his cock forward, driving between my legs. Back was the burn, the ache, the building need to explode. I writhed beneath the feeling, fisting the rods of the headboard as I felt my tits bounce for Dominic as he pounded into me faster, hips slapping, hearts racing.

"Oh, *fuck*." My curse was swallowed up in my tightening throat, the peak *right* in the distance. It was so close, my eyes slammed shut to hold onto it, but that move was met with an explicit command.

"Eyes on me."

Dominic's choppy breathing did nothing to hinder the authority in the request, and my eyes snapped open just like he ordered. He was waiting for me, gaze shining with approval that I'd listened and desire for me alone.

He held onto me with those eyes of starlight and passion, fucking harder and wildly, untamed in his own sweat and lust like he was always meant to be.

He was beautiful. So fucking beautiful, and he was mine.

I owned his heart. It was mine to take care of, and somewhere between the rush of terror and pride, I came undone like he wanted.

A sound I'd never made before tore between my lips, eyelids pinching shut as my climax crashed in hard, shattering my world. Waves of heat and pleasure swept my body up on a high so wonderful, I might have touched whatever was closest to heaven.

Muffled grunts strangled from Dominic as my walls pulsated and squeezed around him, his cock swelling inside of me as the feeling of my orgasm pulled him over the edge with me.

The noise he made as he came was like a goddamn roar, the ferocity of it shaking the very core of my brand new heart.

His hold on my waist turned bruising as he buried himself as deep as he could go, emptying himself out in spurts that shook his massive frame. My orgasm found a second wind as he came for me, and I lost my breath in the severity of it.

Dominic's thrusts became haggard and slow as he milked our orgasms for all they had until there was nothing left but sweat and heavy panting.

He slumped over, spent and sweat glistened, his wide chest sealing to mine. My hand was on his forehead before I could think, wiping away the line of sweat covering his hairline and taking his face in my hands. He covered my mouth with his, drowning me in slow, heated kisses.

He kissed me until my lungs burned for air, and I broke away to gulp down what I could of our passion-hazed atmosphere. Even then, he didn't stop, trailing lazy lines with his full lips up my cheek, over my nose, and finished with a kiss to my forehead.

The room was a blur as big arms wrapped around me and rolled my body so I was laying on his, both our chests rising and falling and exhausted.

Holy fuck.

We laid there for a bit, catching our breath and allowing the lust fog to evaporate from our brains. Dominic's heart was slapping against my cheek from where I laid on his chest, and I listened closely to its melody that raced because of me.

"I guess it really is true what they say," I panted.

"What's that?"

My cheek curved in a smile against his chest. "Older men really are the way to go."

His eye roll was practically audible, and I lifted my head to rest my chin on top of his sternum, catching his spirited eyes with mine.

"Thirty-one is not *old*."

"So you're saying you're up for another round?"

The corner of his thoroughly kissed mouth tipped up as I cocked my brow at him expectantly. His arms around me squeezed, his eyes warming.

"Insatiable woman," he muttered.

I nodded, humming out a mumbled, "Uh huh," while reaching my mouth up to his. He kissed me back, his big hand laying over the back of my head to hold me steady and hold me close.

"Maybe this time I'll use the handcuffs on you," I breathed over his lips.

He thumbed the edge of my jawline, his pupils sparkling onyx from up close. "There's a fat chance of that happening."

"Is that a challenge?"

"It most certainly is not."

"*Oh*, it's a challenge."

"You do know that not everything is something to be won, correct?"

"Says the man who's probably a sore loser."

Dominic's browline flattened, and a dopey grin peeled up my face.

He traced his thumb around every inch of my smile, touching me sweetly even though his pupils flamed dangerously. In a quick movement, I was flat on my back again with Dominic over me, excitement crackling in the air again.

His beauty was as wicked as his next words.

"The way I play, we'll both win, Ms. Sanders."

SEVEN

"Mommy, today I ate all my carrots like Katty told me to. Even the funny shaped ones."

Our mother's gentle laughter echoed through the phone receiver, sounding all crackled and strange on speakerphone.

"I'm proud of you, baby girl. Did your sister eat all of hers?"

"No!" Charlotte launched herself towards my phone sitting on the table in front of us, unbelievably quick to rat me out. "She said she didn't have to eat because she wasn't hungry!"

I cocked my head at my sister who wasn't paying me any mind, still nose deep in my phone. "I wasn't hungry, and *ouch*. When did you learn to drive a bus?"

And throw me right underneath it.

Charlotte didn't even blink in my direction, all of her attention honed in on my phone and our mother on the other end of it.

8pm had become Charlotte's favorite time of the day this last week. Since we met Kathy in the park the Sunday after Layla was taken, she'd promised to call and talk to us every night at 8pm sharp when she got home from her meetings.

I bitched to Dominic on the way home that I doubted she'd even remember her promise by that night. Then, I ate all my words when my phone rang at 8pm on the dot Sunday night.

She called, and she had called every night since.

Well, except for last night since I was… *otherwise engaged.*

AKA: Being fucked by my ex-boss until I couldn't even stand right.

Literally.

After the second time, I tried to stand to go to the bathroom and my knees wobbled so badly, I would have fallen over if Dominic hadn't been there to catch me. He smirked and made some cliche comment about making me weak in the knees, and I called him a corny Casanova.

He told me Casanova would have blushed at half the things he did to me, and I argued that Casanova probably wouldn't have let me leave the bed without making me come at least once more since he's, ya know, *Casanova.*

Dominic gave me a look that said I was in trouble and hoisted me over his shoulder while I screamed and laughed, taking me into the master bathroom. We spent the next hour in the spray of the shower, soaping each other up and making love in between until I got my extra orgasm… and then some.

It was by far the filthiest shower I'd ever had.

"Katerina, are you not eating?"

My mother's voice shocked me out of the gutter where my mind had been so happy to be, reminding me I wasn't with Dominic at his new place anymore. I wasn't happy and drunk on orgasms and fairytale love.

I was *here* in a nightmare, and tomorrow was approaching faster with every second.

Friday.

The *meeting.*

"I'm fine, Kathy." I sighed, rubbing the heel of my palm over my forehead. "I'll eat later."

When this is all over. I'd eat when Tommy was arrested, Layla was back home, and the thought of food didn't make me nauseous.

"Mommy, am I gonna see you tomorrow?" Charlotte cut in.

"Yeah, baby. After your sister and I have that meeting, we'll all get together and celebrate."

Charlotte bent her head, bottom lip drawing out in confusion.

"What are we celebrating?"

Kathy hesitated at her slip up, and I swooped in to help aid in a lie. "We're celebrating Mom acing her third week of classes." Classes. Narcotics anonymous. Whatever. "She'll get a button or chip or… something next week, right?"

Our mother made a noise almost bashful, and I pictured her cheeks pinking and nose wrinkling.

"I'm not sure. I think it's a chip."

Next week would mark a month of her sobriety, the longest she'd been sober in almost three years. I didn't like thinking about it, because I didn't like how easily my hope inflated about the whole thing. Ever since Dominic swooped me off my stupid feet, my hope had lost its grip on reality and become so fucking naïve.

It dreamt of happily ever afters and mothers who were present and *clean*. My hope believed in all of it coming true, and it was taking a *lot* of effort to stomp it down and deflate it back to safe standards.

"Can we go to the park and get ice cream?" Charlotte perched her chin on her elbows, staring with her whole heart down at my phone.

"We can do whatever you want, baby girl. I just can't wait to see you two," Kathy said, emotion rushing her voice and squeezing it off at the end.

She was crying.

She cried a lot during these calls, but mostly after Charlotte had gone to bed.

"All right, Bugs." I shifted my leg out from beneath my butt on the dining room chair. "It's about that time. Tell Mom goodnight and go wash up."

"Five more minutes, Katty? *Please?*"

She was giving me her best puppy dog stare tonight, all rounded and coated with an extra sheen that brightened her pleading. It was already past 8:30 though, and Maya went to bed at 9pm most nights, and I tried to keep the girls on the same schedule while we were staying here so everything was simple and fair.

"No, your sister's right," Kathy relented, sorrow clear in her wispy voice. "We'll see each other tomorrow, okay?"

Charlotte's pout was of epic proportions, but she eventually conceded.

"Okay..."

Our mother swallowed thickly over the line. "I love you, baby girl."

"I love you too, Mommy."

Charlotte bunched her sweet face together for a second, her perturbed focus aimed down at our mother's voice, and I wondered what that look meant. She was gone before I could ask her, hopping off the table she *probably* shouldn't have been sitting on in the first place, but whatever.

That just left Kathy and I.

This part of the conversation was always awkward. Most of the conversation each night was Charlotte telling our mom about her day, what she did, ate, drew, whatever string of words popped into her head. If she thought it, she told our mom about it.

I mostly just facilitated if either of them said anything too serious or Kathy got emotional.

Like now.

She sighed into the phone, and I slid mine closer to me on the dining room table.

"I'm sorry, baby. I didn't mean to cry, I—" Another sigh. Another soft sob. "It's just a... a hard day. I have a headache and just..."

I breathed in her words hard and deep, holding them in my lungs to let them brew and simmer. Pain sparked in my bottom lip, and I released the flesh I hadn't realized I'd trapped between my anxious teeth.

All of me was anxious tonight.

I pressed a fist to my mouth, holding back sharp words and upset that knocked behind my teeth without any good reason. They were just a natural response to her complaints.

But she was trying to be different, so...

I forced my jaw to unlock and the polite question to spill out. "Did your meeting help make it easier?"

"It did. It did..." She trailed off, and a force gripped my empty stomach as I waited for her to continue. "I just can't stop thinking about tomorrow. It's... I—"

"It'll be fine." It *had* to be. "Dominic offered to go over the plan with you again if you want. He's in his office now. I can go get him if you need to go over it again."

"No, no… it's not the plan I'm worried about." My hand flattened on the rich wood table, fingers flexed out tight and waiting. "It's you."

"Kathy," I sighed on a vibrating exhale, my outstretched hand turning to a fist.

"If something goes wrong, it's you who… gets *hurt*. You and your friend."

"*Layla.*"

"Yeah…"

Seconds ticked by, each one louder than the last. They screamed. They roared. They mocked me over tomorrow and just how many of their brothers and sisters I'd have to endure before this was all over.

It would be thousands of seconds. Tens of thousands of seconds of agony.

"You promise you'll be somewhere safe tomorrow?" Kathy asked quietly.

"*Yes,*" I snapped, my edge sharper than intended. Internalizing a groan, I softened the points of my temper and gave an inch. "We're staying here during it all. Dominic's partner, Ryan, will be there with you, and he'll call us when everything is said and done."

"Okay, okay…"

Kathy's not-so-steady breathing encased the staticy air between us. I thought about taking her off speaker before the sound of her breathing drove me madder than I already was.

Then she asked something that shoved my *thinking* about taking her off speaker phone into doing it faster than I'd ever done anything in my life.

"Does he make you feel safe?"

Horror slapped my fingers over my phone's screen, retching the thing up to my ear with lightning speed. My eyes darted around the empty dining room and down the expansive hallway, making sure no one with blue eyes and my name on her shit list was around to hear that.

Kathy didn't know Dominic was still technically married, or much about him at all, so she didn't know she couldn't say shit like that so flippantly, but *still.*

An exhale petered out of my tight chest. "Yes and no."

She sniffled on the other end, feeling closer to me now that I had her soft voice in my ear.

"Is the no because you love him?"

And that tightness in my chest intensified to *pain*.

Ah, panic. You sneaky bitch.

"We're not doing this," I expelled through my uneasy breath.

Quickly, my mother tried to recover. "We don't have to. I-I didn't mean to push."

Behind my eyes, I pictured her shaking her head of dark hair and plucking at her dry and broken lips. She'd hit an exposed nerve, and she knew it. "I just… I'm happy knowing you're taken care of. He… looks at you like he wants to take *care* of you, and I'm-it's good you've found that. Your dad never…"

My temper heated with the mention of our father, and like she could feel the hot blast simmering from across town, she turned to cooler topics. "I'm glad what happened between your dad and me didn't…" She paused, thinking over the right words. "Corrupt your views on, um, *love* or anything."

And the right words she did *not* find.

I barked out bitter laughter, my head jerking back with the force of it. "*Oh, it did.* Trust me, you two did a number on me. I'm a freaking headcase about love."

Poor Dominic.

Silence met my mockery.

Then a cry, muffled and quiet.

Humor based on nothing funny and everything cruel had found the curves of my mouth, but guilt snuck in and slowly pulled it off my face. I shifted in my chair, the unwelcomed feeling lodging strangely between my ribs.

My upper lip twitched.

She didn't deserve my guilt. Or at least, she hadn't for years. My body physically defied the emotion, heating up and trying to smoke the guilt out.

But the longer we sat in a silence interrupted by only her soft, hiccuping sobs, the less I could take it. Not the heat or the guilt.

Her tears.

She'd been *trying* to say something nice, however misplaced or entirely unaware it might have been. She was so out of tune to who I was or what she'd turned me into with her disease, but she was trying to learn.

She was trying. For once.

My lips peeled apart, toes tapping the hard floors in nervous beats. I lowered my head and my volume.

"But he's good."

The sobs on the other end sucked dry, and she listened to me as intently as I listened to her absence of sorrow. My reborn heart *thunked* hard against my chest as I admitted softly to my mother, "He's really good."

An appreciative beat stretched between us.

"It sounds like it."

And then more silence. How was it possible for so much silence to exist between two people? Two people who used to love each other endlessly? Maybe that's why I hated silence so much.

It was the loudest reminder of what wasn't there.

Pain splintered straight through the center of my chest, and I knew my time was up. That was enough self-realization for one night. I'd had the conversation, maybe grew a little bit.

Well done, me.

"I should go make sure Charlotte's in bed." My fingers moved around my phone, readying to hang up. "I'll see you tomorrow, Kathy."

I gave her another two or three seconds to say goodbye before resigning a goodbye wasn't coming. Then, she said, "Do you think you'll ever call me Mom again?"

And I froze.

Mind, tongue, body—it all froze. The only thing that moved was that splinter of panicked pain, twisting deeper inside my chest until it felt like a part of me.

"I-I don't know. It's just habit at this point." And when she didn't respond immediately, I gave another inch. "Maybe?"

There was a smile in my mother's voice. "I hope so."

My gut reached all the way up my throat like it had a voice, trying to warn her not to hope. But it was her life. She could hope as much as she wanted and deal with whatever did or didn't come true.

It wasn't my business until she proved it should be.

"Well, goodnight," I said, needing the conversation over before I exhausted myself on any other *feelings*.

She sounded somber about it, but cooed fondly. "Goodnight, baby. Have the sweetest dreams." A hefty pause and then, "I love you."

My lips twitched. My throat dried right out.

For the first time in so long, I didn't feel like laughing at her to make her feel bad about lying about her so-called love for me.

I just sat there in that uncomfortable dining room chair and tried to breathe through it.

"Okay," I choked out.

We ended the call there.

I went up to check on Charlotte like I said I would, dressing and washing up for sleep myself since that conversation wiped me dry of energy. I'd been surviving on the bare minimum as it was, but that conversation with my mom sucked me empty.

I didn't even remember saying goodnight to anyone before my head hit the pillow, and my mother's words echoed through my sinking subconscious.

'Have the sweetest dreams.'

A curse in four words.

Light spilled into my bedroom, the door cracking open. Brightness blinded my vision, and I squinted to see who it was, but it was just a body silhouetted by the light.

A large body.

I opened my mouth to ask if it was Dominic, but words and voice failed. I tried to breathe, tried to clear my throat, but no sound came out. Confusion worried my brows together.

The familiar thump of panic slapped my chest.

My heart started to race.

The door opened wider, more light, more rays that deafened my eyes, and still, no words. I tried and I tried, but my voice was hollow. Someone was coming in. Someone was there at my door, slinking in like a burglar in the night.

Oh my god. Was it a burglar? A murderer?

The face. There still wasn't a goddamn face. There was nothing but moving limbs, stalking closer and light pouring through where a face should be. I jerked to sit up in bed, but my body didn't move.

My body didn't work just like my voice didn't work.

My heartbeat tripled in pace. I still tried to move, thrashing and getting no more than an inch in either direction. What the fuck was wrong with me?

I was paralyzed, frozen in fear.

I didn't freeze. I didn't freeze. Everyone else froze, but I didn't freeze.

Oh my god.

Blood pumped in my ears, rushing and filling my whole head as the faceless body came closer. It reached out, long arms and claws for fingers. Sharp and drenched in blood.

Blood already?

Whose blood was that? Charlotte? Dominic?

Where were they?

Where was anyone?

The person stalked until they were over me, and I screamed a soundless scream, begging for help, for Dominic, for whoever they were to stop. My throat burned, scratching with the effort of my nothing screams.

The faceless man was coming in closer, his teeth like spikes, and I saw myself in them.

I saw my terror, my open mouth yelling for help, my emerald eyes that cried because my voice couldn't.

It was here. Closer. Here. I pushed my head back into the pillow. Nothing helped. No one helped. I was alone and dead even before the face of light, teeth of spikes, and claws of blood got me.

I'd been left to be taken. To die.

Alone and helpless.

Alone, alone, alone.

Dominic!

"Kat!"

A gasp widened up my throat, shock ripping my eyes open.

The first thing I saw was a ceiling fan, blades cutting through air, spinning round and round. Air sputtered through my lungs, panic a tight fist around my throat that refused to release.

Then something shook me. Some*one.*

Hands were on my arms, shaking, gripping, *bruising.* I shrieked and jerked, tears finally spilling free, and I heard my voice too. I heard *me.* My tears were wet, my voice was piercing and raw, and my legs were moving. Kicking.

The hands had a voice.

"Kat-*Kat!* You're *okay.*"

The hands had *thunder* in their voice.

Lightning zapped my panic, my lungs, my screams to a halt.

I blinked, wide-eyed and searching and fucking desperate as I'd ever been until I found him in front of me. Until I didn't see the ceiling fan or the blur of tears or the man without a face.

All I saw was storm cloud gray.

His eyes of thunder were alert and prominent, scouring every inch from my forehead to my dripping-with-tears chin. His hold on my arms left to grab both sides of my face, his big hands covering from my cheekbones to my neck. He was maybe holding me harder than he meant to, but I didn't care.

Rough calluses scraped my damp cheeks as he wiped my tears gone, the graze of hard skin a stabilizing feeling. I clung to his forearms, both of them, still catching my breath.

"You're okay," Dominic soothed, still catching thoughtless saltwater petals as they dripped over. I wasn't even thinking about crying anymore. I wasn't even meaning to.

It was just all the adrenaline pouring through me as I heaved and scrambled to focus on where I was and what was real.

Dominic was real. His *touch* was real.

The faceless man who came into my room tonight was not.

The full on click in my brain that it was all a nightmare crushed my eyes closed, sighing in exhaustion and relief. Dominic brushed fallen hair back from my face, touching me like he shouldn't have with the door still open, but fuck it.

I needed him to touch me.

His fingers shelved back more waves of my hair behind my ear.

"I'm here. I'm right here."

He was. He was here, and I swallowed down the knowledge and felt how it settled the jostling nerves in my stomach. I gripped his forearms harder.

Dominic sat on the bed next to me, and I realized in the hysteria of it all, I'd sat straight up and kicked all the sheets off my legs. My sleep shorts had bunched all the way up in my struggle.

It was as I was staring at the glimpse of white cotton underwear peeking beneath my shorts, just trying to *breathe,* that my brain thought of something.

Something that trickled horror through my stomach, slow and dry ice cold with each drop.

My head wrenched up, fastening my blurry sight on Dominic.

"Was I really screaming?" I whispered, switching focus between his dark eyes.

How else would he be here? How else would he *know*?

Dominic's jaw clenched hard, emotion pulsing in his back cheeks. The shadows of the room played despondent tricks on his eyes, making him look miserable. Making him look like the epitome of heartache as he nodded only once.

"For me," he rumbled, voice full of gravel. "Over and over again."

A gasp hit the back of my throat, but not for Dominic.

"*Charlotte.*"

I was scurrying off the bed before I even finished her name.

Oh god, she must have heard me too. She must have heard me crying and screaming and she was probably crying too. Scared and confused and, *fuck*, I had to see her.

"Kat," Dominic whispered, calling after me as I stumbled out of the guestroom. "She's fine-*Kat.*"

I ignored him, my bare feet meeting hard floors as I padded down the dark hallway on legs that must have still been half asleep. They were wobbling and so was I, back and forth and nearly crashing into a wall as I made it closer to Maya's bedroom where Charlotte slept.

"*Kat.*"

The quiet voice chasing behind me was an explicit command to stop and turn around, but I didn't. Maya's bedroom door was right there, and I had to see Charlotte. My heart was belting out for her, to make sure she was okay, that she wasn't crying, that she was *safe*.

A hand, big and warm, clutched around my wrist and jerked me away from the door at the last second.

I toppled into Dominic's broad chest, my palms pushing back immediately, trying to wrestle my wrist away. His fingers tightened, and protest dropped my jaw and swelled hot in my lungs.

I ripped my eyes up to his to slice him with words, but Dominic spoke first.

"Your sister is *fine*. She's sleeping and will continue to sleep unless you go in there and wake her up."

"But—"

"I was in my office when you started screaming, and it maybe only lasted fifteen seconds before I was able to wake you up. If anyone else had heard, we'd know it by now."

"But what if she needs me?" I pushed back, trying my hardest to keep my voice down.

At that, Dominic took his sorrowed stare back and forth between my eyes, a frown marring the middle of his forehead. I held myself firm, but not so strong as he came in closer than he should have when we were so out in the open.

Both my back and neck bowed as he came so near, towering over me with all his thunder and protection. Gentle fingers slipped from my wrist to grab my hand, folding our fingers together.

"Let me take you back to your room."

I shook my head beneath his, whispering, "I have to see her. I need to know she's safe."

"She's safe." Lips pressed to my forehead, warm and unexpected. They feathered lightly, promised deeply. "And so are you."

Even in a hushed tone, his words had the impact of a swinging hammer, coming down with a swift hit to my chest, caving it in and cracking all my defenses down the middle. I shuddered against him, going limp and let him lead me back to the guest bedroom.

Away from Charlotte and back to the room of nightmares.

EIGHT

ominic shut the door behind us, a soft click to pierce the silence. I walked a few feet into the bedroom, arms wrapped around my waist. "I'm sorry I woke you."

"You didn't, honestly. I was up here working."

Swiveling around to face him, I arched a brow. "Couldn't sleep?"

He didn't answer. Just bypassed the question and smiled slightly.

"I'm glad I was awake."

"So you could witness all my crazy spill out for the billionth time?"

My eyes rolled away from him, sitting my stare in the dark corner of the room. I remembered that corner from when I saw his wing-tip shoes sitting there a little over a month ago, telling me truths about his marriage that Dominic hadn't yet.

I was so focused on the corner stuffed with memories, I didn't recognize Dominic was closing our distance until he'd already done it. He was right there, black t-shirt stretched over his arms and wide chest, those godforsaken sweatpants hanging low on his hips.

Fingers appeared beneath my chin, tipping my head back for him.

"Night terrors don't make you crazy."

I took all I could handle from those hard-hitting eyes before ducking my face back down, hiding my chin in my chest.

"I've never had one before."

110

Dominic's chest moved in front of me, rising steadily and falling the same way.

"What was it about?"

The faceless man glitched behind my eyes.

I wasn't a dream expert or anything, but given that I'd never seen Tommy, and the man in the dream was coming to take me and kill me, it wasn't hard to guess who inspired the nightmare.

I wouldn't tell Dominic that, though.

He'd been doing so much to make sure I felt protected, it wouldn't be right to tell him none of it mattered. Apparently, I was still just as afraid as any other little girl was of the bogeyman.

My teeth skated against each other, pain pulsing up my temples as I lied.

"I don't remember."

I kept my gaze on the floor even though it didn't matter. I was lying, he knew it, and I knew he knew it.

Black socks shifted in my dropped line of sight. My eyes jumped up to watch the hem of his shirt rise as he inhaled deeply, a glimpse of tan stomach flashing for only a second.

"Will you be able to fall asleep tonight?" he asked, ignoring my lie.

My stare peeked up. "Will you?"

The quality of his eyes tonight was like cool gray granite. Calm at first glance, but hard and sharp beneath the surface.

"I've got work to do before tomorrow."

I hummed, moving towards the edge of the bed. "I don't have a fancy excuse like that."

The mattress squished beneath my weight as I sat. Dominic followed, sitting next to me on the edge, his thigh flush to mine. I looked at our touching body parts, his clothed and mine bare.

Memories of when they were both naked like every other part of us, intertwined and writhing, rolled past my mind, muddling it all up for just a few seconds.

A few seconds where I wasn't thinking about Tommy or tomorrow or Layla or feeling like my heart was being burned alive in my chest.

A need for more of those seconds, thousands of them, thickened in my throat and started a racing in my pulse.

I pressed my thigh into his, enjoying the scratch of his sweatpants over my skin and how Dominic pressed back with his thigh too.

A small move. A simple move, but to me, it felt like he'd grabbed right between my legs.

Heat pulsed inside of me, my stomach dipping fast and hard. I cut a glance up to him, to his strict profile backlit by the moonlight that poured in through the bedroom's double window.

He was staring right back at me, tension fabricating between us as if a spell had been cast.

A dark and dirty spell, and our eyes were the culprits.

I'd never quite felt like I was being fucked by eye contact before, but this was doing it. The potency of his concentrated gaze felt like he was already inside of me, penetrating up to my stomach and undoing me slowly.

A breath of desire parted my lips, and Dominic's steel-cut stare dropped to that next.

And it was all I could take.

Moving in the same second I decided what I wanted, I flung one of my legs over both of his, straddling his hips and sitting my core right over top of his already half-hard cock.

Even the slightest friction between us tangled our breathing harder and hotter, and Dominic's hands down came on either side of my waist.

"Kat," he exhaled on a warning, holding me in place.

"We both need it." I flexed my hips over his as I argued. "We're both tense and stressed and can't sleep."

Delicious pressure compounded around my waist as fingers with the potential to leave imprints tightened and punished. Despite the move, Dominic shook his head.

"I'm not comfortable with that. Not here."

"I can be quiet."

He slanted his chin down, skeptical eyes chiding me from below.

"I have serious doubts about that."

My eyes rolled, but an amused smirk blossomed at the accusation.

I *had* been loud at his new place yesterday, but that was because I could be and he liked it. Every time I cried out or yelped his name, desire flurried a storm across his eyes and he went harder.

"I *obviously* won't be that loud here." My arms slipped around his neck, fingers playing with the soft hair curling at the back of his neck. "Or you could just put your hands around my throat to keep my volume in check."

His cock spasmed beneath me, loving that idea and thickening to its full length. My breathing stumbled against the feeling, dropping my head back to pant.

Dominic stuck to his determination despite the disagreement in his pants.

"I already said no. Not here. Not with everyone in this house."

Not with *Heather* in the house, was what he meant to say.

A thrill zipped through me, one I would deny if anyone asked.

That would be an awful, terrible thing to get off on. A truly evil thing enjoyed by only a truly evil person.

I shifted over him, moving my hips to try and rub out the excitement brewing, the *need* to claim him in this house. In this *particular* house. Where we first met, first kissed, and first fell in love despite the wife he shared it with who slept just down the hall.

"What if I'm asking you to though?" I leaned in, flattening my tits to his hard chest. He rumbled against me, the dangerous noise running down to my core. "What if I need it to distract me, Mr. Reed?"

Resolve still stained his moon-highlighted face.

My confidence slipped as we stared at each other in the silence.

The beat of my heart thumped in my ears, knocking worry and rejection into my brain. Didn't he want to help me? Couldn't he see that I needed it? That I was drowning in tomorrow, and it wasn't even here yet?

I had a night terror for fuck's sake. I *clearly* wasn't dealing well, even if I could only admit it screaming for him in my sleep. I needed him. I—

A reminder cropped up, and all of me softened as it did.

My shoulders slumped and my heart buried itself in shame for forgetting. For acting so blindly and allowing my arrogance to bypass one of my favorite things about this man.

He didn't make decisions based off his lust.

He made decisions based off his unapologetic heart.

Both my chin and stare lowered, air fighting up my clotting throat.

"What if I just need you?" I whispered, chewing back on my bottom lip.

The moments after the admission were *painfully* devoid of sound. A fist of tightness throbbed in my chest like a heart attack, and I wanted to suck back down those six words and cure the ache.

Long enough went by that my eyes couldn't take it. They were too curious, too wandering, too desperate to lock with his as I laughed and told him my admission was a joke.

They ripped up to his face to tell him just that, but that was as far as my plan went.

No laughter. No poor lying about it being a joke.

Dominic held me and my world still with his rainstorm eyes… where my lightning had cracked a line right through his resolve.

His swarthy brows were slung down to frame his overworking mind perfectly. I'd admitted to needing him, and it was doing things to him.

Messy things.

So I tested it. I eased forward and kissed his mouth a little. Then a little more. Soft kisses, firm kisses, virgin innocent kisses to make him burn like I was.

Each pass and pull of our lips did him in a little more, chipping away at that righteous hold he had over himself. His mouth was growing greedier, tongue finding its way into my mouth, teeth joining the fun and chewing over my lips until I shivered and moaned.

He broke away, shushing me against the slope of my neck I exposed for him. My eyes slammed shut as he painted the arch of my neck with his taste, groaning softly against it like he was in pain.

"This is wrong," he breathed harshly.

Panting hard, I nodded back. "I know."

It was. I really did know it was wrong to fuck in this house, but I needed him more than I cared about how wrong it was.

"You're the only one who can help me feel better though. Only you."

A sharp breath escaped him and pierced between my ribs next. His teeth sunk into the space between my neck and shoulder, digging deep until I squeezed his biceps in surrender. He relinquished his bite, my skin gasping in relief as he scraped his teeth up to my ear instead.

"You're not playing fair, Ms. Sanders."

"I'm not playing," I breathed, shaking my head and heaving. "Do you think I'd really make a game out of being so weak for someone? Do you think that I *like* needing you?"

"There's nothing wrong with it." He planted a firm kiss beneath my ear. "I love that you need me, because I need you just as much." He held a beat against my skin, suspending us both before quietly admitting, "Maybe more."

Bullshit.

There was no way he needed me more right now. No fucking way. All my thoughts were his and my body was dying to be next. Literally, my heart was beating so fast and my blood felt like it was electrified beneath my skin.

"Dominic, *please?*"

The ache between my thighs was beginning to cry like I wanted to. I'd sealed my tear ducts shut for the night, but the urge was still there. The pressure, both physical and figurative, to be weak.

His warm forehead kissed mine, his eyes on my lips. "The condoms are in the other room."

"So go get them."

"And risk running into someone holding them?"

"Then just pull out."

He cursed below his breath, eyes pinching at the sides. "That's so juvenile."

"I know."

"That's so *stupid*.".

I nodded my forehead against his. "Yes."

But he wasn't saying no.

Since I didn't have insurance, I couldn't afford birth control, but he and I had already talked about that. He said he'd buy a year's worth of condoms the next time he was out, and I said we'd go through them in half the time.

And despite how stupid it may feel in the morning, I didn't care tonight. I needed him inside of me, and I think he needed to be inside of me just as badly because he didn't stop me when I reached between us.

He didn't stop me when I fisted his cock through his sweatpants and squeezed. He just breathed hard and let me work down to my knees in front of him and pull him out of his pants.

His cock sat in front of my face, inches away and as intimidating as I remembered it from yesterday. Thick, long shaft, ribbed with veins and strong, his tip fat and glistening as I moved my hand around it in the moonlit bedroom.

This was a perfect cock. This was a *man's* cock.

And I was a woman who'd been goddamn starving until I met him.

Starving for someone to understand me. Someone to be my center when I spun out.

Someone to pull me back when I pushed the world away.

I leaned forward, flattening my tongue to the base of him and licked up. Dominic's breathing wobbled as I covered him with my hot mouth, hollowing out my cheeks around the tip of him.

My walls clenched around nothing at this taste of him, this completely primal taste of him. A bit salty, a bit musky, all him.

Hands swept on either side of my face, clearing my hair away and holding it behind my head. I bobbed down, rolling my lips down half of his smooth length and sucking back hard.

His thigh twitched and he hissed, and I peeked my eyes up to make a good show for him: his cock halfway down my throat and my eyes that I just *knew* were hitting emerald extremes in the bask of desire and silver moonlight.

Dark eyes, cusping on sharp obsidian, were tight on me. Watching from above. Memorizing. His forehead was crinkled in concentration and his dusky pink mouth parted just so.

A hum of delight vibrated up my throat, and Dominic's grip in my hair strangled, his eyes rolling back at the feeling.

So I did it again. I hummed and hollowed my cheeks around him, keeping eyes on him so I could watch how much he enjoyed seeing his perfect cock disappear in and out of my mouth.

And I'd only gone halfway so far.

My jaw ached a little as I stretched my mouth wider, nerves bubbling up in my stomach as I tried my hardest to ignore my gag reflex and swallow as much of his cock as I could.

My lips hit my hand working around the base of him, and I choked. My throat spasmed around his cock, wet gurgles my exit music as I retreated back, gasping for clean air.

I sat back on my ankles, eyeing his spit-slicked cock and panting.

This would be my fucking Everest, and I would conquer it.

Except a hand on my chin stopped me when I went back in for seconds, tilting my focus up.

Dominic swept his thumb over my chin, cleaning away spit with a simple gesture. That messy thumb nudged between my lips, pushing inside my mouth until my lips wrapped around it, sucking back and moaning.

"Quiet," he mumbled, a command simply spoken but *explicitly* felt. My voice drained dry, and I waited on my knees for his next word.

My chin was still fixed between his fingers, and he wasn't letting go. He was eyeing me down the bridge of his nose, a darkness ringing his irises and turning his gaze severe.

"Do you like this?" His question rolled out of him like boulders clashing, startling and deadly serious.

"Sucking your cock?"

Eyes sharp, he nodded stiffly.

Astounded, I pushed myself back up to my knees so my face hung below his hard-lined beauty. "Have you met me?" I asked with humor. His eyes narrowed in confusion. "From pretty much the moment I met you, I wanted to suck you off. You're stupid hot, for one. But more than that, it's… I don't know, something I get to do for *you*?"

I paused, cringing as hot blood rushed to fill my cheeks.

"Fuck, that sounded dumb, I mean, like, I'm giving something to you, and it's something only I can give you. And I like being the only one who can do this for you, and I like feeling you in my mouth. I like your taste. I like everything about it. It's a part of you, and I want… every part."

Staring up at him from my knees, I realized that something about this conversation had made his eyes go cryptic. He'd reverted back into hiding for whatever reason. His thoughts and feelings were shadowed in darkness, scribbled over with black marker.

His mouth was sealed shut too, a strict line across much like his eyebrows.

My defenses drew me up off my knees, but not the ones for *me*. The ones I bore for Dominic, because someone had done this to him. Someone had made him feel like he had to hide about this type of pleasure, and I had a sick sort of fire burning feeling who it was.

I crawled back on his lap, propping up on my knees so I had leverage above him.

My hands came to his face, fingers drawing shapes in his facial hair. "Why do you like going down on me?"

I bypassed asking if he liked doing it. That would be like asking Pooh Bear if he liked honey. In this case, I was the honey and Dominic was the bear, mauling me every chance he could until he was full of my sweetness.

He trained his eyes still blacked out of expression on my mouth.

"All of the same reasons. Plus the control."

His honesty curled up my lips, and I breathed a soft laugh. "You were very aptly named is what I'll say to that."

My Dominant Dominic.

"And whatever's in your head telling you that I don't like it or that I shouldn't do it…" My heart tugged me lower, moving my mouth over his. "I'll suck you off as many times as I need to to shut it the hell up. Because I love it."

I love you.

Dominic tried to control the next breath coming through his nose, but it shook and gave him away. His hands told his truth next, grabbing me so hard around the waist, I knew we'd just fallen into some invisible wound from his marriage, and the invasion had stung.

I bet he'd have a lot more of those little wounds that I'd find over the next few… however long we lasted. I'd stitch them all up as best I could with the tools I'd gathered over the years from patching up my own battle scars.

I wasn't a person who healed others or even knew how, but maybe that's what this love would be.

Maybe our love would be like bandaids that became permanently sewn into our hearts. It's possible that's what love was supposed to be if you did it right, but I'd never seen or heard of anyone doing it right.

"Did you like it?" I nudged the plumpest part of my bottom lip over his, trying to encourage him out of hiding with an addiction he craved. He *craved* my pouty lips, and now he'd seen them wrapped around his cock, and I needed him to know he was allowed to like it.

He was allowed to ask me to get on my knees so he could fuck my strawberry lips until I choked, and he was allowed to like that too.

"Did you like feeling my mouth around you? Or when I started to choke because you're so big?"

A tickle traced down my arms as the straps of my tank top slipped over. The only thing holding my shirt up now was the swell of my tits pressed to Dominic's chest.

He filled that chest wide, sliding his hands to my ass. He squeezed, and I gulped down cuts of air as he kneaded my flesh in his well-worked hands.

"There are only two things that feel better than your mouth on me," he started, low and rumbling.

A dip in my stomach. A twist up my chest.

"What are they?"

Confident fingers pulled my pajama shorts and underwear to the side, cool air touching me for only a second before something hot and hard took its place. Dominic hovered me over him, lining up with my entrance, teasing the head of his cock right against me.

Anticipation inspired heavy breathing between us both, the air boiling beneath our heroin chemistry and making it bubble. I was suspended on the cusp right before the high, knowing the sensation, the crystalized *addiction* that would stock my veins full as soon as he was inside of me.

Eyes reaching up to mine, Dominic watched me close as he answered first on his list of two.

"Being inside of you."

He lowered my hips, tiny whimpers strangling up my throat as his cock sunk into me, stretching me and shooting stars behind my eyes. My mouth parted in a silent cry, hands bunching his shirt on his shoulders to hold onto something, anything, to survive the widening pressure and burning scrape of pleasure already beginning.

Sweet, hot breath fanned across my face, tasting strained and tortured. I could feel the struggle in Dominic's grip around my waist as he let me adjust to his size when all he wanted was to rip into me like he did yesterday.

Finally, two exhales tangled together in a release of tension as I reached the root of his cock, sitting on him like he was a throne and I'd conquered the king.

Warmth enveloped my cheeks on both sides, Dominic holding my face as we locked eyes. His rough thumb pet along my bottom lip, the second answer on his list shining bright in his stare.

"And being loved by you," he told me, as serious as the heart attack in my chest.

Or at least, that's what it felt like.

A goddamn heart attack of love for this exceptional man.

This love drug was too potent, tripping my brain and infusing my heart, shooting into the core of my soul as he thrust his hips up. My breathing wobbled, and so did my ability to stay quiet as a moan squeezed out of me, falling and crashing to the bedroom floor.

Dominic shushed me but didn't stop.

In fact, he shushed me *while* he dragged my hips over his, trying to turn my vocal cords into rebels like me. Except he was *so* deep inside me, I couldn't speak. He'd stuffed my body so full, there wasn't room left for words or the air to create them.

I was just breathless as he fucked me slowly, pulling my ass back and forth in his huge hands as I bowed into the pleasure, head falling back and eyes closing.

A sudden squeak cracked in the air, stiffening us both like criminals caught red-handed.

My head snapped up to find Dominic already fixed to me, silver eyes waiting under heavy brows.

"It was the bed," he answered my unasked question in a murmur.

Dread relaxed its grip over my muscles, shoulders sinking and jaw slacking as relief whooshed out of it.

Dominic, however, remained chiseled in petrified stone.

"Stand up."

His order was so fast and clipped, I blinked at his mouth to make sure I didn't imagine it moving. Shadows were funny things, you know. But he repeated himself to clear any shadow theories, lifting me up by the waist and setting me on the bed next to him.

He stood, tucking his erection into his sweats, and my disappointment exploded a bomb inside my chest. He stepped away from me and the bed, not knowing about the shrapnel currently piercing my heart from the blow of his rejection.

I...

Was he leaving me? After I'd admitted to needing him to stay?

Would I be able to let him leave without falling apart like threads of a live wire suddenly cut loose? I'd short circuit and fray all my sanity with one man's disappearance.

Like my mom did with my dad.

Jesus fuck. Was it already happening?

It had been less than a week of loving him, no more than a day of knowing it. Was I already falling into my mother's patterns? Twenty-four hours in? Was I crazy or just stressed or was I the apple who hadn't fallen as far from the tree as I hoped?

The tree I came from was poisoned, and maybe so was I. It was in me. Her addiction and weakness were my seeds, growing me into a ripe image of the apple I'd tried so hard to be nothing like.

My stomach flipped. My heart that had died to the sickness haunted the space it used to pump nothing but fear and dread, delivering a phantom pain true to its name.

"*Kat.*"

Hands squeezed my shoulders, shock hitting the back of my throat as I gasped.

Dominic towered in front of me, the aroma of earth and sex crashing over me, stinging my sinuses full of *him*.

A placating graze slid along my jawline, eyes of worry above me.

"Where did you just go?"

"What do you mean?" I asked, breathing harder than I meant to.

"You had that look like when you start to panic." Oh. *Shit*. "What were you thinking about?"

My lips peeled apart, and then I heard myself say, "Tommy."

And it sounded like the truth.

Even Dominic must have thought so too, because the worry lines of his expression softened, and before I knew it, I was being hoisted up from the edge of the bed.

My feet, they weren't so sturdy, but it didn't matter since Dominic took most of my weight onto himself, cradling me into his chest like the crescent moon cradled the lonely sky in its slope.

"He's not coming near you. Ever. I'll stay in here all night if it makes you feel safer."

My heart stuttered. "You're not leaving?"

He curled his touch over my ear thoughtfully. "I wasn't planning on it, no."

"You went to the door," I said dumbly.

"To lock it."

To lock it. Of course *that's what he was doing, dumbass.*

"So you're not leaving?" I pointed my chin down, caution in my question and in the way I kept my eyes on Dominic.

Had I gone off on an inner monologue freak out for nothing?

His thumb appeared and dug into the soft spot beneath my lowered chin, tilting it up and breaking me out of my cautionary stance. His eyes were glittering, face smooth as marble.

"You said you needed me."

Yup. I did. I was the idiot stupid enough to say that and *mean* it. The ache trapped between my legs was like the one inside my chest, agonizing and slayed only by him, proving my need for him true.

"I do."

"Then no," he murmured, his voice a quiet melody. "I'm not leaving."

To prove it, he reached behind his head and pulled his shirt over and off. My eyes watched the shirt drop to the floor, excitement in my lungs as I turned them up to his body. His naked torso, all ribbed with muscle and power that was even more finely executed in the shadows that danced over his skin as he walked us backwards.

He stalked me, a predator closing in on its wide-eyed dinner until he had me cornered.

"Instead of leaving, I'm going to push you up against this wall."

Firm hands wrapped around my upper arms and did just that, my back hitting the wall hard enough to knock a gasp from my lips. He inhaled my involuntary noise, letting me watch under him as he took a hit from my reaction, the high of our love burning his gray eyes a volcanic black.

His fingers moved next around my arms, hooking into the fallen straps of my shirt and pulling down, exposing my tits as he spoke deep and dirty over my parted mouth.

"I'm going to take off all your clothes."

He left my lips aching without a kiss, moving down my body and pulling my shirt down as he went, snagging my shorts and underwear in his grasp too.

Within five seconds, Dominic had me completely naked and heaving in front of him.

Leisurely, he stood, the scratch of calluses riding the back of my legs as he tucked his hands beneath both my thighs. Suddenly, my feet weren't on the ground anymore.

They were locked behind Dominic's back and I was sitting around his waist, back flush with the wall behind us. Dominic crowded me, filling up every space I could see, every pocket of air I could breathe.

"And I'm going to make you forget about anything that isn't me." He nibbled over my bottom lip, rumbling dangerously. "That's what you want, right?"

I was nodding before the question was out, chasing his mouth with mine for a proper kiss and whining softly when he wouldn't give it to me. He shifted my weight, lifting my body higher against the wall.

His mouth became aligned with my chin, and he gave his precious kiss there instead of my lips.

"*Dominic*," I whisper cried.

"You want me to take away the nightmares?" he encouraged, cupping one of my breasts in his masculine hand and rolling the nipple between his fingers. I bucked against him, huffing and nodding desperately.

He flattened his palm right over my thrumming heart.

"You want me to tell you how much I love you to make the pain go away in here?"

The open space between my thighs tightened and soaked at his words, pulling needy mewls from something inside of me I didn't recognize. Something that got off on his love and his all consuming devotion like it was porn.

Sweet mint buried my senses as Dominic breathed right over me, my forehead dropping to his. His eyes were right on me, blackened diamonds glinting in the heat of our passion.

"You want me to make love to you until you're so weak and spent, you fall into a dreamless sleep?"

Our heads rocked together as I nodded fervently, keeping my eyes on those black diamonds.

Then, *pressure*. Sweet fucking pressure as Dominic pried his cock inside of me, ropes in his thick neck pulling taut as he clenched hard against my tightness.

My completely bare tightness around his completely bare cock.

The feeling was unparalleled, and Dominic buried his face in the crook of my neck to muffle his groans. The sounds of his pleasure, plus the raw feel of him dominating me from the inside out was too good.

The combination was ecstasy, and I was soaring so high my thoughts were wispy clouds and my worries were the birds, flying far far away.

The guest bedroom was deafeningly quiet. Until it wasn't. Until Dominic started moving slow and carefully. In no time at all, the room was engulfed in the illicit soundtrack of secret sex, hitching breaths and suffocated moans.

Dominic sealed me up against the wall, hiding me in his bare chest as he thrust with long, penetrating strokes that tortured and provoked. He'd pull back slow, slow, slow just to bury himself with a merciless strike, penetrating as deep as he could between my heat.

Turned out, I was wrong and very *very* bad at keeping myself quiet.

Dominic would rear his hips back, sliding his slick cock almost completely out of me, edging a plea in the back of my throat. I wasn't so good at keeping that plea down when he rammed his hips forward, popping tiny squeaks out of me each time.

Dominic's thrusts picked up, my squeaks turning over into hard-to-swallow moans. I was getting close, sensations piling on top of one another to build something magnificent and explosive.

A bear paw of a hand slapped over my mouth, fingers clenching on either side to muffle my sounds. Dominic had my neck to hide himself in, and now I had his palm as he fucked us both in the dead of night while people who could never know slept around us.

"You can't follow a rule to save your life."

His dark voice steamed my neck, sticking to my hairs and muddling my brain. It was already so heady as it was, a chasm of delirious heat and addictive love unable to be put into words. All I could do was shake my head and agree. I couldn't follow any rule, and he was right to stifle me or fucking strangle me if he had to tonight.

Around Dominic's waist, my legs started to quiver, and he pushed himself harder and faster with the telltale sign. He grunted like the goddamn animal he was when he was with me, pumping deeper, grabbing tighter until he got exactly what he wanted.

My orgasm hit like the lightning in my veins, crackling heat through my blood as every electrified muscle in my body tensed up. I yelped, or my vocal cords at least tried to force the sound, but just as it traveled up my throat, a strong hand fisted around it.

Dominic choked my orgasmic cries to silence, using the hand that was previously over my mouth. He squeezed just tight enough to cut my noises off at the ankles, but the power, the goddamn *control* his big hand had around my tiny little neck exploded fireworks behind my eyes and drowned Dominic in another orgasm.

Or the same one? Who fucking knew.

All I knew were the nonstop sensations tearing through me, vibrating my skin and ringing through my ears. I couldn't see. I couldn't even see through the explosions, searing white blanketing my vision as my walls pulsed and pulsed and didn't stop.

Warmth and a lust-drenched groan got buried in my sensitive skin, and I felt Dominic slip out of me fast.

A shudder almost classifiable as violent wracked his massive frame as he found his own release, his fingers around my throat holding on tighter as he tried to survive his own climax.

Strangled cuts of air helped keep my consciousness afloat until he was finished and loosened his grip. The second he did, I slumped over, body and head wiped clean of any strength to hold themselves up any longer.

There was heavy panting and movement, but I barely registered any of it. My mind was being dragged down fast, my eyelids like bricks and my limbs useless in Dominic's arms.

All I remembered before being pulled into that dark and dreamless sleep Dominic promised was the feeling of soft sheets on my back and a gentle kiss on my forehead.

And then all was black.

NINE

Cue lights up on Friday morning.

The blackout of post-orgasmic sleep Dominic had fucked me into only lasted so long. Eventually, the sun faded its pale yellow wake up call through the double-pane window like it was any other day.

It seemed extra bright outside today for some reason.

Like the sun was mocking my nerves and trying to fry them to a crisp.

At least I'd gotten through the night. Thanks to Dominic. He came to wake me up this morning since Heather had already gone off to work but found me with my eyes already wide open and frozen in bed.

He sat next to where I laid and tried to encourage me with breakfast that waited downstairs. The sound of food shifted the emptiness in my stomach uncomfortably, but I tried to not be obvious about it.

Even though I wouldn't eat anything, I nodded and kicked my legs out of the bedsheets anyway to let him think his bribery was working and that I was okay.

Once today was over and Layla was back, I could say I was okay and actually mean it.

Charlotte and Maya were already downstairs with Dominic's mom, eating jellied toast and laughing about something to do with parrots. I had my glass of orange juice, but no toast or eggs for me.

All my body wanted was for today to be over. It couldn't stomach anything else.

I cleaned up breakfast just to have something to do.

Both Dominic and Meredith tried to push me to go sit down like I was sick or something, but I grit my teeth at them both and stayed where I was with my hands under the water that was probably too hot, caked in bubble suds and distractions.

Breakfast was over, and we still had hours to go.

Three to be exact.

The meeting was at 1pm. The team was getting there at noon to set everything up, and it was only 10am.

A fucking lifetime encased in three hours.

We managed to kill another half hour getting the girls and ourselves ready for the day. Dominic's mom was leaving back to Georgia tomorrow once everything was settled, and the girls were both super bummed about it.

Dominic, on the other hand, was super bummed about the free help leaving. He'd have to start searching for a new nanny once this was all over, and I'd have to search for a new job.

We were being real adults about it and putting it off till the last second.

Meredith had been spoiling the girls an ungodly amount this morning knowing she was leaving tomorrow, currently baking them double chocolate cookies from scratch while Dominic and I kept them busy outside.

In that blazing, mocking, spotlight-bright sun.

"My bubbles are almost empty!" Maya cried, squinting down the hole of her bright pink tube of bubbles.

"Put some water in there." Big blue eyes jumped over to me as I explained. "Not too much, but it'll give you more bubble action for longer."

Tips from my broke ass childhood coming in handy.

Except, Maya didn't look pleased by the suggestion, instead turning her pouting face towards my sister who was currently blowing bubbles up into the sky through that little yellow stick.

Maya marched right over to Charlotte and plucked her purple tube of bubbles right out of her hand.

Dominic jerked next to me, sitting up straighter. *"Maya."*

The authority in his bass deep voice zapped his daughter's attention right over to him, her expression already wide with protest.

"I don't have any left!"

"We can share what's left in my bottle," Charlotte offered, all three of us pointing our stares to her. She wasn't even the slightest bit ruffled from having her bubble bottle stolen right from her hands. She just wrapped her little hands around the nearly empty pink bottle and brought it up to the purple one Maya still held.

The burning sun highlighted the guilt showing in Maya's blue-eyed gaze as she said, "Okay. Thank you." And started pouring to split the bubbles.

And I smiled despite the world trying to break my cheeks into a permanent frown.

I caught Dominic frowning at his daughter, worry furrowed into his tight browline. Leaning over on the grass where we sat side by side, I knocked his shoulder with mine.

"It's fine. Sharing is a hard lesson to learn even for adults. Most of us are shit at it."

He blinked a few times, his bands of thick lashes creating jumping shadows over his cheekbones. Deep lines of a frown were still grooved into his face.

"I just know she knows better."

I cocked a stiff shoulder up. "She's an only child. Sharing isn't something she's had to do much."

"You were an only child for a long time," he reminded me.

"Yeah, but I was a *poor* only child. Big difference."

I didn't feel poor when I was growing up, but I learned around the time I was in middle school that that's what the holes in my sneakers and store brand snacks from the dollar store meant.

Not having a lot made you grateful for the things you did have *real* quick.

"Did your parents both work?"

Dominic's tone was stiff as a knife. Like the kind he probably was afraid I'd skewer him with for asking about my parents.

Months ago, yeah I would have taken that knife and plunged it so deep, he'd never forget the wound just like he'd never forget to not cross that line again.

Now? I didn't feel the need to be such a violent little shit just to protect myself.

Not from Dominic.

"Dad did, but he got fired a lot." I curved a glance his way. "He had a bit of a temper."

His gaze tracked down to the knowing tilt of my lips and stayed there, amusement sun-spotted in the lightest gray of his eyes. "That explains it."

Mhm. Neither of the trees I fell from were winners.

"It was a wonder I kept my job at the department store as long as I did. Probably a combination of my boss being a pushover and Layla covering for me all the time."

The space between my ribs knotted tight as her name left my tongue and hit the air.

I hadn't even thought before I said it.

The breeze sharpened against my skin, the grass prickling beneath my thighs.

"What time is it?" I asked, throat dry.

Dominic twisted the watch around his wrist to check. "About 11:30."

An hour and a half more.

Then we'd know.

In the middle of trying to unstick oxygen from my lungs, both Maya and Charlotte barreled over to us.

"Daddy! Be our jungle gym!"

And there was no saving Dominic from the attack of the five-year-olds that came next.

Poor, *poor* Dominic.

Before he could blink, the two energy-high girls flung themselves at him wearing huge smiles, limbs and happy screams going everywhere. They giggled as they knocked him onto his back on the grass, his big arms doing what they could at the last second to catch both of their little bodies.

High-pitched laughter rose like smoke through the air, the sight and sound of it all daring a hiccup of something almost like laughter to jump up my throat too. The corner of my lips twitched. The sun's scorch tapered a little friendlier.

Then, a sound not-so-happy emanated from the mosh pit.

A groan of pain that came from Dominic.

Both girls scrambled off of him, Charlotte backing up towards me and Maya big-eyed and fretting over her father who lay flat back in the neon green grass. Freshly cut, too.

His eyes were pinched shut and his handsome face screwed tight.

"Daddy, did we hurt you?" Maya asked like she was so afraid of the answer.

Despite the evident pain clutching his face, Dominic shook his head and tweaked an eye open to look at his daughter, groaning, "Daddy just needs a minute."

Charlotte latched her hands to my shoulder, twisting my spaghetti strap in her fingers. From here, I could see the tremble in Maya's bottom lip as she lowered her sorry stare to blades of grass.

"We didn't mean to…"

"Munchkin, I'm fine." Dominic reached and wrapped a comforting hand around his daughter's arm hanging limply at her side. "I'm a big man. I'll survive."

Her mouth twisted to the side. "Do you need me to kiss your booboo?"

Dominic paused, tilting his head thoughtfully against the grass. "You know what? I think that would be great."

Just like that, Maya beamed through the sadness and chased it all away with her hard grin, leaning down and pecking a chaste kiss on his forehead.

She perched back. "Better?"

"Much."

Then Maya turned her attention to me and yelled, "Ms. Kat needs to kiss it, too!"

Her shouted command jerked my head back. "What? Why?"

"Because I think you should."

For the second time today, I almost laughed. "As convincing as that is—"

"Katty, do it!" Charlotte ordered, jumping on the bandwagon and running around to stand with Maya. The two shared a funny look, mischief forming through eye contact alone.

The fuck?

Ignoring the strange look, I said, "I'm still not hearing any solid reasoning here."

"It will make him feel better."

"Yeah, Kat," a deep voice chimed in. "It will make me feel better."

My stare cut down to the deep voice, sterling eyes alight with amusement as he watched mine narrow. Dominic ticked his head, beckoning me to come closer.

I gave him a look. This was silly and I wasn't in the silly kind of mood.

"You're joking."

"I never joke when it comes to booboos."

Okay, but did he have to be *so* charming when I was trying to be miserable?

Puffing out a dramatic, "Oh my god," and rolling my eyes, I made the move over to Dominic who was still on his back, both Maya and Charlotte cheering out in victory. A quick peck to his forehead was all he got before I pulled back.

"Happy?"

He hummed in displeasure and shook his head. "I hurt my lips, too."

My head cocked to the side, a damn simper threatening to breach. "Oh, did you now?"

"Sure did."

Soft laughter finally escaped through my nostrils. *Dammit.*

Before I could reply, Meredith called out to the girls from the house that the cookies were ready, and blonde and brown curls zipped across the backyard like streamers of whipping wind.

I looked after where they'd just disappeared, feeling some type of sad as I watched the empty space.

"What about my lips?"

My head tipped down to the man who was trying his best to make me smile.

"What about them?"

"I believe I said they're hurt."

"And I believe you're a liar."

"I prefer smooth." He reached both hands up, covering the sides of my face and dragging me down. "Very, very smooth, Ms. Sanders."

His soft lips curved to mine, kissing me like we weren't in the middle of his backyard in broad daylight. Even when I tried to pull back after one kiss, he trapped me in place, one hand winding around and splaying over my back while the other gently cupped the back of my head.

My sadness stumbled a good deal as Dominic held me tight, as he held me in a way that said he was here and he wasn't going anywhere and neither was I.

He would anchor me down when I threatened to spin out. I not only understand his message, I *felt* it. I felt it when my heart began to sting in that good burn kind of way only being in love could master.

When he eventually let me go, my chest was an inferno of that pleasant love sting.

I gazed down at him, my hair falling around us and keeping the sunlight from reaching us. We were shaded in our little bliss.

"Better?" I whispered.

A sparkle lit his stare even without the sun's help. "Perfect."

A phone went off between us, deflating the momentary peace we'd created on this nervous day. It was Dominic's, and I rolled off of his chest to let him stand up and fish his phone from his pocket.

He gave it a hard look. "It's Ryan."

The pleasant sting in my heart seared to an immediate burn. My breath evaporated in the fire.

"He's calling early…"

Dominic dropped me a look that was supposed to be reassuring.

"I'm sure it's to check in."

It did *not* have the desired effect. My heart stole away on an anxious trip, running faster every second that passed. My mind ran away with it, going down rabbit holes and off deep ends as Dominic showed me his back to take the call.

He greeted Ryan.

Seconds passed in silence.

More seconds passed by until they equaled a minute, and still, nothing.

By the time Dominic said anything into the phone, it was such a deep rumble in his chest, I couldn't make it out. He hung up and lowered his phone from his ear, but didn't turn around.

Tension had wound its way through his back like vines, strangled his muscles as tight as my chest felt as I waited for him.

The silence ate away at my nerves in a starved frenzy.

It took for-fucking-ever, but eventually Dominic moved, his actions slow as he turned over his shoulder to me, keeping his eyes firmly latched on the green ground. I tried to pry his gaze up with my own, knowing he could feel the pull and burn of my focus on his face.

He was just avoiding it.

"What did he want?" That question fell from my tongue easier than the one I wanted to ask.

'Why won't you look at me?'

Dominic's lips peeled apart to speak, but empty words held his mouth open. Still, he looked at the grass and not me. What sounded like rocks garbled together in his throat as he cleared it, a thickness to his voice that wasn't there before.

"We need to go."

Something's wrong.

"Why?" I breathed, my voice already frozen in fear.

Something's wrong.

The backs of his jaw throbbed as he *still* refused to look up at me. I couldn't see what was in his eyes. Was it anger? Disappointment? Remorse? I needed to know. I needed to prepare. I needed answers *now*.

When he finally steered his heavy stare up, it was none of the three I guessed.

It was far, far worse than any of those three.

It was pity.

Dominic grabbed my racing heart with that pitying gaze, staring at me as if he was sorry I was even alive.

"Let's go."

Something's very very wrong.

TEN

The drive to my house was silent.

The worst kind. The kind that felt like its own layer of skin, it was so heavy. So weighed down by the absence of everything.

I had that feeling in my chest as we drove. Everyone knew the feeling, the one that was more knowing than feeling at all. It was a cold whisper dead center in your chest, and the whisper was saying something was wrong. The voice was gnawing, trying to draw blood from your heart that had dropped to below freezing.

Dominic turned into my neighborhood, his movements stiff as the tension between us. He hadn't said a word since we got in the car, and his absence of words scared any away from my tongue. It was too thick and dry to say anything anyway.

The familiar houses and worn down streets dragged past the passenger window. Dominic's car pulled to a slow stop at the corner of my street, the vibration of the engine humming beneath the seat.

My stomach twisted to a fist as he shifted his car to park.

We weren't at my house yet.

My fingernails drew nervous lines in the grooves of the unused seatbelt next to my window. I hadn't put it on and Dominic didn't force me. We sat in that heavy, sticky silence, neither of us moving.

I didn't want to say it, and I didn't want to hear it.

The meeting was off; I could assume that much.

Either something went wrong on Dominic's team's end or my mom had chickened out. Whatever it was, our only plan to get Layla back was in the shitter, and Dominic probably brought me here so I didn't scream myself insane in his house with the girls.

"Kat."

His voice reached over to me, stroking along my goosebumps and embedding the deep current of him beneath my skin. In my blood. The thunder was trying to get under my skin to soothe the lightning before it was struck mad with rage.

"Kat, look at me."

Already, the rage was beginning to boil and simmer. I could feel it in how my teeth clamped and ground together, how my fingers twitched and my neck stiffened. I turned that stiff neck towards Dominic like he said.

I nearly jerked back in my seat as I saw him.

The *pity* he was meeting me with was like a goddamn slap across my face. It had grown since we'd started driving, taking over his entire face. Every crease, every line, every beautiful hill of his face was spoiled with pity. It had become the only thing about him.

He was pity for me and nothing more, and my heartbeat picked up.

"I love you," he spoke *pointedly*. He drilled the words in deep with his eyes, dreary and clouded over with plumes of sorrow just for me.

Just behind his bleak gray sadness for me, I saw a different color bleeding through.

Red.

Flashing red.

The flashing crimson light snuck behind Dominic's head as it passed us, silent without its siren. My eyes followed it, confusion weeding through my brain.

"Why is there an ambulance…?"

Then, that lurking ambulance that was so seemingly out of place, turned onto my street.

It went towards *my* house.

"Wha…"

Words dried up. All feeling evaporated.

Coffee-colored eyes and hair the spitting image of mine pulsed behind my eyes.

"Kat, wait—"

My fingertips were dead of feeling as I reached for the handle of the car door. I jammed it open and stumbled out with Dominic hollering after me to stop.

I didn't.

I ran instead.

Down the street, around the corner, feet slapping the pavement, heart screaming until my ribcage shook. Then it wasn't just my heart screaming.

"Kathy!"

On my street there were even more lights, these ones flashing red *and* blue. The scene of bright strobes hit my body like a gust of stiff wind, skating my sneakers to a stop on the road. My head whipped side to side, wide eyes taking in all the faceless strangers standing around, all the police cars scattered around my street.

There were too many. Too many for this meeting. It was an *undercover* meeting for fuck's sake.

"Kat, wait!"

I snapped my head back to Dominic to see him closing our distance. My pounding heart took off again, escaping Dominic and barreling through the faceless throng of uniforms, all watching me race by with desperation screeching up my throat.

"Kathy!"

I scanned the crowd, hunting out her frail frame or tangled brown hair. "Kathy! Whe—" My neck twisted towards the line of faceless uniforms standing there like goddamn idiots.

"Where's my mom?!"

Every single one of them ignored me until someone in the crowd wasn't so faceless and couldn't ignore me when I collapsed in front of them.

"Ryan!" My hands latched to his forearms so I didn't eat pavement, my chest heaving, my voice snapping. "Where's Kathy?"

His eyes widened, touched by the same condition Dominic's had. *Pity.*

The similar quality enraged my desperation, skyrocketed my heartbeat to a full-blown nuclear explosion. "Where the fuck is she?!" I screamed.

Ryan's crystal blue eyes rounded, morphing to pools of piercing regret as they jumped behind me.

To my house.

My head jerked back to it, spotting my home—my childhood home—blown wide open, its front door broken off its hinges. Blood rushed through my ears, roaring like the goddamn ocean of love was in my head, its laughter mocking in waves as it prepared to take me under and drown me for fucking good.

My lungs squeezed and I broke away from Ryan, bolting for my house. Adrenaline pumped in my veins, fast and unrelenting as my legs pushed and pushed until my toes stomped on the pebbles of my makeshift driveway.

A body collided with mine, creating a wall in front of me and wrapping arms around my body.

"Kat, *don't.*" Dominic spoke right next to my ear, pleading and warning as I thrashed in his grip.

"Let me *go*," I grit out, fighting against his chest and shaking my shoulders to shimmy loose. His arms crushed me against him, holding me like he was trying to squeeze me to death and save me from it at the same time.

"Kat, *please.*" His voice lowered, melting so quiet and so sorry for me. "You don't want to go in there."

His sick-with-sorrow voice hit my stomach hard, rolling it over with so much strength I thought I might puke. The sickening sensation traveled up my throat until I screamed it out.

"Get off of me!"

"*No.* I won't let go," he denied, vice-locking me against his body as he begged me. "Please just let me take you back to the car. *Please?*"

"No! I just want to talk to my *mom.*"

His denial fueled my rebellion, my muscles, my fucking adrenaline until I struggled so hard, I defied logic and managed to wiggle out of his hold and break free.

"Kat!" Dominic's voice echoed behind me as I ran up my driveway, shouting for my mother.

"Kathy!"

"Kat, don't!"

But it was too late.

"Kathy!" I fell through my broken doorway, breathing hard and searching for her head of mahogany hair. "Kathy, whe—"

My voice died as I saw the couch.

She was there. My mom.

She was propped up in a seated position on the couch, sort of slumped over at the shoulders, but still sitting up. Her head had drooped to the side, bent at the neck so uncomfortably, she'd definitely have a crick in the morning when she woke up.

Her eyes were open and… so was her mouth. A thin line of dark yellow puke trickled out and dried on her pastel skin.

Her right arm was set out on the arm of the couch.

A needle was sticking out of the middle of it.

I blinked at it. At the needle and then up to her eyes just like Charlotte's. They were half-lidded but I could still see her. She wasn't seeing me though.

She wasn't seeing anything.

My lip twitched.

"Kathy."

She didn't respond. She didn't move.

My eyes dropped back to the needle piercing her vein, mouth going dry.

"Kathy?" I tried louder to get her to hear me.

She would respond. She would. She was just doped up on a high and couldn't hear me right now. This had happened before, but she would hear me soon. She'd look at me.

Her mouth… I watched it, waiting for any speck of motion around her cracked, bone pale lips. Her eyes were glazed over like a fog had come up from beneath them, and she wasn't blinking either.

She wasn't… doing anything.

A lump lodged in my throat, tightening my voice. My bottom lip quivered as I pulled it to my top.

"Mom?"

She'd wanted me to call her that. She'd said so last night.

We just spoke last night, and I told her maybe. I said I might call her mom again someday, and now I was doing it. I was calling her mom and she had to wake up and hear me say it.

"*Mom.*" Her sunken in chest stayed still, no signs of breathing. "Mom, can you—"

The floorboards to my house creaked as Dominic came inside, bringing his nauseating sorrow with him.

"Kat…"

"No," I cut him off with a jagged fucking knife in my voice, the blade chipped and ready to take chunks out of him if necessary, if he even *implied* with his grieving tone what it sounded like he was.

"Mom, wake up," I shouted, or tried to. It wobbled and broke in half as my voice cracked.

I physically jerked back with the noise, shaking my head against it and denying to myself and the room that there was a reason for it.

The weakness snuck up on me like something possessed, wrapping fingers around my throat and squeezing. Salt burned the backs of my eyes.

The burn washed down my constricting throat, dropping embers in my heart.

My hand gripped at my chest where it started to blaze, trying to claw through skin and bones and squeeze my heart to make it stop hurting.

Pain was growing, but I could make it stop. I could make it stop if she just *woke up.*

My feet went towards her but froze in place almost just as fast as pain shot up my entire front like spiderwebs of fire, a cry splitting from my mouth.

My hand clenched to a fist against my chest in a burst of fiery rage, pounding at it to stop fucking hurting. Stop producing tears like something was wrong. *Nothing* was wrong. Nothing was—

"Mom, stop!" This wasn't funny. Stinging water blurred my vision of her to the point where she looked like she might be breathing through the mirage of my tears.

"*Look* at me." Waiting and waiting and nothing. "Mom!"

Tears rolled down my cheeks despite me still trying to gouge out the thing that caused them. I scratched at my chest, digging furious lines in my flesh, hoping to peel open the skin and let the hurt pour out.

My breathing was getting louder and more panicked by the second as I pawed at my chest, needing the pain out, needing it gone, needing it not to have a reason to exist.

"Kat..." Large hands swallowed mine up, stopping my scratching with force. He tangled my hands in his, trying to pull my body into him. "Hey, hey..."

"*No.* No!" I screamed and stumbled back. "Don't look at me like that! Don't look at *her* like that! She's fine! She's—"

Another violent sob choked me, bending me over at the waist with its force.

I coughed on the sobs like I was fucking throwing them up, too much grief stuffed down my throat and making me sick to my stomach.

"She's *fine*," I cried, tears slipping down my face hot and fast as I stared at her frozen on the couch. Stiff as the dead fucking air in the room. Dead.

Dead.

"*No*," I broke down in heavy sobs, pain bleeding any and everywhere in my body. "No, no, no, no, no."

Not like this. Not today. Not because of this fucking meeting.

Not because of me.

"What about *Charlotte*?" Helpless misery mangled my voice, flaying the sides of my throat as I screamed at a corpse. "What about Charlotte?! You can't *do* this to her! You can't—"

Out of the corner of my watery eye, someone came up to our broken door.

A man. A man dressed in a white uniformed shirt and navy blue pants holding medical equipment in both hands. He flashed a glance to me hunched over at the waist as I cried myself insane, professional pity glossing his gaze.

He lifted a foot towards my mom.

"*Don't.*"

My voice vibrated deep and threatening. The paramedic cut me a cautionary stare, watching me as my back rose and fell. Heavy breaths rattled my lungs like they were packed with metal thorns. Images raced behind my eyes of his hands on her pale skin, checking her toxin-coated veins for a pulse, judging the spit-up going down her skin, lifting her like a lifeless rag doll, stuffing her in a body bag.

He took another step towards my mother.

"I said no!" I roared, upright before I could register it. That professional gaze widened with shock as I charged at him, red water-coloring my vision. "Don't fucking touch her!"

"Ma'am—"

"Get out of here! Get out!"

The man shouted as I shoved him back, getting him the fuck out of my mother's house where she wouldn't have wanted him because she hated men, she hated—

Strong arms swept around my waist, pinning my arms to my sides, Dominic's embrace a straight jacket to his little lightning gone wild. He dragged me back and pulled me away from the door as I screamed, as I hollered at the paramedic and soaked my cheeks with more tears for the dead woman across the room.

Dominic carried me away from the commotion, except I *was* the commotion. He was carrying a building imploding that was taking casualties as it fell.

And I did. I fell *hard*. I collapsed to pieces in Dominic's arms, wailing so hard I took both he and I to the ground.

Each choked cry pounded in my head, tears blasting like hail against the backs of my eyes. Dominic shushed against my hair, rocking me back and forth on the floor and whispering how sorry he was and how much he loved me.

Mom said she loved me too last night. She said she loved Charlotte, and still, she gave us both the ending that proved my life was a tragedy all along.

I wasn't living in a romance.

I wasn't living in a fairytale.

I was the star of a goddamn tragedy…

And this was only intermission.

ELEVEN

Overdose.

> *The excessive intake of something to a dangerous and sometimes fatal degree.*

Most overdoses were by choice, like my mom. She chose to put that needle in her arm yesterday, and she chose the dose of heroin that would be too much for her body to survive.

I didn't get to choose my overdose.

Mine had been injected into my veins without permission, taking years to fully alter the core of my make-up, but had been diluting my happiness over time.

Each loss—Dad, my grandparents, Mom when I lost her to the drugs, Mom when she died from the drugs—had turned the dosage up higher.

Yesterday, the cool drip, drip, drip of poison in my blood reached its limit, and the grief that lived inside me crystalized into permanence.

Grief was my overdose, and losing Mom—losing *Layla*—was my version of death.

I passed out moments after shoving that paramedic yesterday.

Something about the exhaustive trauma and low blood sugar. I woke up half delirious next to the ambulance brought there for my mother, Dominic on one side and the paramedic I screamed at on the other.

That time, I screamed at them both.

Since then, I hadn't screamed at anyone. I hadn't said much of anything to anyone that wasn't Charlotte. She'd slept in my bed last night, lots of confused tears soaking her pillow case and wetting my palm as I wiped them away until she finally fell asleep.

I didn't remember falling asleep myself. It was more like blacking out.

And I was glad for it.

It was pouring outside when I woke up and hadn't slowed down at all, and I was glad for that too. Today was a gloomy day worthy of the downpour coming down from the sky.

I liked when the weather was pissed off like I was. It felt like it was in solidarity with me and my grief, spelling out in raindrops that I was right to be upset.

Maybe later I could run outside and find comfort in one of its deepest puddles, slipping beneath its surface and never coming back up.

"Katty?"

I looked up at Charlotte in the bathroom mirror as I stood behind her and brushed knots out of her blonde hair.

"Are we going home soon?"

The idea of 'home' sunk a brick through my gut. Our 'home' was a crime scene right now, crossed out with yellow police tape over our kicked-in front door.

"Not yet, Bugs." Not with Tommy still out there and Layla still gone. "Don't you like it here?"

She nodded, lowering her face. "I just miss my toys and Mrs. Sharon. Do you think she had the baby?"

Oh shit, right. I hadn't thought about Mrs. Sharon in… days or weeks or, how long had it been since all of this bullshit started?

"I'm not sure. We can call her later if you want? See how her and Davion and the baby are doing."

She rolled her mouth together and nodded again, still staring down at the sink. That brick in my stomach moved uncomfortably at her tight-lipped nonresponse.

Charlotte was never quiet.

She didn't understand death. Not really.

Death was the real bitch of finales.

Movies, books, songs, holidays, other things with endings… they all had a beginning you could go back to or look forward to. You got to relive them as many times as you wanted—until you died.

There were no do-overs in death. No 'one more time's. There was just nothing. Infinite nothing and infinite things left unsaid. It was one of the cruelest ironies.

Death left us with nothing and everything at once: everything to say and nothing to say it to.

Charlotte would never get to list out all the things she did during her day to our mom again. She'd never get to talk to her and ask her why she wasn't there for huge chunks of her childhood or ask her about the day she was born or come home from school and gush about her first crush with her mom.

She'd never hear our mom's voice again, never see her weathered face that was once so beautiful.

And one day, I'd have to tell her it was my fault.

Her addiction wasn't my fault.

But her dying from it was.

I helped her put the needle in her arm by forcing her to agree to the meeting. I put the fear in her belly that she couldn't help but drown out with the poison.

A knock on the hallway bathroom door untangled my self-loathing thoughts.

"Come in," I called quietly.

The door creaked open, and Dominic wedged through. His eyes were like the dreary rain outside as he found me in the mirror.

"Breakfast is ready."

I dropped my attention back down to Charlotte's hair as I pulled it through a headband. "Okay."

We hadn't spoken much since yesterday.

After I passed out, he'd started watching me closely to make sure I was eating and feeding me his protein shakes when I wasn't. The eagle eye routine brewed tension between us, me snapping and him getting tired of treating me like an irate child who kept spitting out her peas.

He was *helping*. I knew that's what I was supposed to call it, but all I wanted to call it was annoying. He wouldn't leave me alone. Always checking on me, watching me, always trying to be perfect for me when I was just trying to fucking breathe.

This wasn't fair to him. This wasn't fair to me, either.

Fate had carved us out for one another, to fit, to match, to heal like stitches in an old wound. Now the flip side of fate had taken a machete to us both, and our pieces that fit so well were all out of shape.

"What, um—" Charlotte pulled attention as she spoke up, lending Dominic her sad stare. "Is it chocolate chip pancakes?"

Dominic's mouth parted just so, his eyes warming on my sister.

"I was just about to make some, actually."

He was lying, but I thanked him in my head for meaning it.

She chewed over her bottom lip, confirming for him and herself, "I want pancakes."

"Then you'll have them. As many as your sister says you can have."

She tilted her head up at Dominic, craning back as if she was staring up at a tower. "Are you going down to make them now?"

"I sure am."

"Will you carry me down?"

My eyebrows shifted up, tingles forming a cluster in my chest, poking and needling right between my ribs. She was staring up at him so innocently, so unaffected by her own blatant ask for help.

For a staggering second, I wondered where she'd learned to ask for help so unapologetically like that. Then I realized it wasn't that she'd learned to ask for help when she wanted it.

It was that she *hadn't* learned to be anything other than trusting.

And I guess I couldn't be mad at that.

Dominic was clearly touched by her ask, nodding and scooping her up by her armpits, holding her into his big chest. I blinked at her arms wrapped around his neck and her legs hanging around his waist; she hadn't looked this small in years.

"Are you coming down?"

I flashed a look up to Dominic who was waiting for me, but almost immediately skirted my gaze back down. It was still there, that unasked for *nasty* pity.

"In a bit."

Dominic stood in front of me a few seconds more, the burn of his stare a laser on my cheek. He left when my eyes stayed put on the sink, taking Charlotte with him downstairs.

I stayed upstairs probably longer than I would have if Dominic hadn't made it known with his concerned subtext and remorse-filled glances that he wanted me near him.

Just in case.

Just in case I wasn't eating. Just in case I started to cry. Just in case I went crazy in a bad kind of way.

He fell in love with my good crazy. He'd only had near-death brushes with my bad kind.

When I finally came downstairs dressed in black leggings and a black tank-top, Charlotte was perched on the kitchen counter next to Dominic where he flipped her pancakes on the stove. Her gaze jumped to me as I entered, but flitted back down to the pan Dominic was cooking with after a moment.

It stung, a fresh splash of acid on my already raw heart that she didn't give me her normal beaming smile or announce my entrance like usual. Maybe she was mad at me because I was the one who brought her the news about Mom.

Maybe, somehow, she already knew I was to blame for her death.

Maya and Dominic's mom sat at the kitchen table, the bay window behind them splattered gray with rain that continued to fall and splash rightful misery on the day. Meredith had decided to stay a bit longer now, Dominic told me.

Now that my mom was dead, and she felt bad for me.

Meredith's head rose from the magazine she was reading as I came into the kitchen, and I had to bite my tongue really fucking hard to keep from snapping at her to keep that pity gaze of hers in check.

"Oh dear, how'd you sleep?"

Peachy-fucking-keen.

"Swell," I went with which, admittedly, wasn't much less sarcastic than the answer in my head.

There was a pause before she spoke again, quick-acting guilt manifesting inside that pause as I wondered if I'd hurt her feelings.

"Do you want to sit or can I make you some coffee or tea or eggs maybe?" she went on.

Jesus Christ. She was worse than Dominic.

"I'm fine. Thank you," I replied, my gratitude stiff.

"You need to eat something."

That came from Dominic.

His bass voice vibrated down my spine, shaking my split nerves awake and setting them loose. My eyes slammed shut, a sigh pouring between my lips.

"I said I'm *fine.*"

A sigh streamed through his nose, much more concealed than mine, but I still heard it. He flicked the burner off, shoveled Charlotte's pancakes onto a plate, and sent her to the kitchen table. She thanked him and ran away, probably sensing my temper breaking beneath the shallow of my skin.

Dominic yanked open the stainless steel fridge door, stuck his arm in, and pulled something out that turned my sigh into an audible groan and turned my feet right back out of the kitchen.

He chased after me in pounding steps, a goddamn protein shake clutched in his hand.

Sturdy fingers grabbed my elbow in my race towards the front of the house, spinning me around before I made it to the giant front door. Bewilderment cut a clear line across Dominic's stare.

"Were you about to leave?"

My mind scrambled; I hadn't really thought about what I was doing or where I was going but now that I did—"*Yes.* Yeah, I need air."

"It's pouring."

"And I love the rain."

His dark brows curved in, saying that he found that sweet but also ridiculous.

"You know you can't go out there by yourself." *Now that Tommy is still out there.*

He didn't say it, but I heard it.

"Come back to the kitchen and eat something," he tried. "Please?"

My lungs squeezed out a bloated exhale, eyes shutting and pinching tight.

"Can you please, *please* stop trying to force feed me?" I jammed my eyes back open, glaring at him underneath angry brows. "I'm not a child. I'm not incapable. I'm just not hungry."

A wall of defense dropped over his expression. "I'm allowed to be worried about you."

"And I'm allowed to not be hungry," I snapped back, hand flying to my chest, fingers denting into my skin with manic energy. "Eating isn't exactly the first thing on my mind right now, *okay?*"

"I know it's not," he assured, pretending to understand. "Which is why I'm reminding you. You have to keep eating. Even if it's something small."

I heard his words, but I heard them how he *really* meant them.

I had to keep going, even in small steps. I had to keep moving and surviving, because he was worried after yesterday that I wouldn't.

And he wasn't wrong to be worried.

"I just need to breathe," I pushed, flattening my hands across my stomach. "I need to be able to breathe, and you're not letting me *breathe*, Dominic."

Hurt tried to pull a blanket over his expression, but he shook it off with a slow, defiant shake of his head. "I'm not going to stop checking on you or trying to help you."

My eyebrows sliced together like knives. "What if what helped me was you not checking on me and just giving me *space?*"

Reluctance pulled his head to the side and parted his mouth, careful thought going into his next words.

"I don't believe that's what you actually need."

"Then what is it that I *actually* need?" I dared, hands ducking behind my back to brace against the door, my lightning locked and loaded.

Silver-gray eyes swept between mine, a concentrated wrinkle chiseling between his brows. Hesitance held his tongue still as he thought and let me watch him think. He was letting me read him as he sifted through the alphabet in his mind to find the perfect set of letters to string together what he thought it was I needed.

He had to be mindful. One wrong word and lightning would shred my skin from beneath and strike whoever was nearest.

"You need someone to tell you that it's okay to be mad right now," he started, so *sure* of himself. My nostrils flared. "It's okay to feel something other than grief. I can be your punching bag for a while because I know you're in pain, and I know you don't mean it. But eventually, you're going to have to realize I'm not the one you're angry at."

"Oh yeah?" I pointed my chin up at him. "Then who am I angry at?"

A hard line carved in his forehead, spelling out her name.

"I'm mad at a dead woman, is it?" I barked a stiff laugh. "That would make me pretty fucked up."

My lightning, or maybe it was my heart, moved inside of me, slamming back hard as I heard myself. My voice was backed with less heat than I anticipated, this weird breathiness tying my words up on a weak little string.

Dominic heard it too, treating it like a magnet to bring him in closer. He shook his head slowly, eyes soft like the rain clouds outside.

"No. It would be understandable given everything you'd been through with her."

Given my fear that it would always end like this. Given her promises to be better and failing. Given her choosing her drug over her daughters for the last time in all our lives.

And the thing was… he was right.

I *was* mad at her. I was fucking livid that she'd left us just when things were starting to go up. I *hated* her for leaving Charlotte. I hated her for deciding we weren't good enough. We weren't worth living for. We weren't even worth surviving for.

I hated her more than I'd ever hated her in the entire course of our lives together. She *died,* and I hated her so fucking much for it.

I made myself sick with all the hate.

It soured my stomach, the acidic essence of it corroding my memories of her to burnt out ends of old film in my head. She was dying all over again in my memories, fading out to a black as bitter as the feelings she left me with.

My heartbeat *thunked* my rib cage like it was trying to break it. Dominic was holding my furious gaze or else I'd bet he'd be able to see the outline of my heart trying to rip through skin.

He knew. He fucking *knew* the hate burning in my veins for a woman who was dead that I was supposed to love and grieve.

And he wasn't judging me for it. He was telling me it was okay to be mad. He was telling me it was *so* okay to be mad, I could use him to take out all my wrath, and he'd still love me at the end of it. Wearing my bruises and bearing my scars, he swore to love me and be mine.

Beautifully mine.

Together, we were such a beautiful tragedy.

"You shouldn't let me be mean to you just because I have an excuse to be," I spoke thinly, my words getting chopped up by shallow breaths.

"But you can," he assured, so painfully sincere. "And I'll be okay."

Staring up at him, I wagered he'd let me slap him right across the face if I told him it would make me feel better.

Maybe he loved me *too* unconditionally.

Maybe loving me wasn't just his weakness. Maybe it was his greatest fault.

"I don't wanna yell at you. I don't want you to *let* me yell at you." The back of my heels came to stop against the door, and I realized I was shuffling back from him. "I don't want to be something in your life that makes you feel bad. Especially when you already told me you don't like—"

Tightness expanded inside my chest, searing it colder than ice in seconds flat. I grabbed over my lungs with eyes fluttering fast, trying to fight to keep breathing and keep talking.

"You said yelling makes you unbelievably sad, and I don't wanna be that for you. I don't wanna be—" *Heather*.

Quick thinking shined across Dominic's expression as he realized where I was going. "You can't compare the two, Kat. They're worlds apart. If you yell at me because you're in pain, I'll listen to every word so I can try to make you feel better."

A dry cry of sorts broke past my lips, my eyes darting all over for an out.

The walls of this monstrous house were closing in, Dominic feeling several feet taller and wider than usual in front of me.

"I don't—" My feet shifted, toes curling into the pristine flooring trying to lock into something stable. The points of my knuckles kneaded over my chest bone, trying to rub out the tightening feeling of dread. "I don't…"

What am I even saying?

Any train of thought I had dissipated into particles in my head, filling it with light and heady air. My skull was stuffed from front to back with so much compacted air, I was sure my head would either fracture from the pressure or float right off my shoulders.

In the middle of sucking down another hit of oxygen, body heat and the smell of crisp earth mingled along my front, taking a dip in my senses. Before I could catch up, arms were circling around me, folding me into a hard chest.

"Breathe."

And then he did, letting me feel the air lift his chest and come back down. The weight of Dominic's head rested on top of mine, his thunder rumbling.

"Just focus on me."

My eyes slammed shut to welcome in the darkness, the pitch black where only Dominic existed. My lungs were shaking, being beaten from behind by my heart, untamed and violent.

Dominic curled his big arms around me harder as if he was trying to squeeze the panic and pain right out of me.

His soft shirt got tangled in my fingers' grasp as I death-gripped his front, anchoring myself to him. He encouraged me in soft murmurs, telling me to keep breathing and keep holding onto him.

And I would. I'd glue myself to him and make him a shield to protect me from all the bad shit that kept coming for me.

Tommy, Layla, my mom.

Jesus fuck.

So much bad in such an infinitesimal amount of time, it didn't seem real. It had been, what, two weeks since Dominic figured out I'd been targeted? The second Tommy decided to slither into my life, I'd done nothing but lose.

And so much of the loss was my own fault.

"I hate this," I breathed harshly, nuzzling my nose into the placating smell of him saturated in the fibers of his shirt. "I hate so much of this. All of it. I hate all of it."

"I know." He nodded over me. "I know."

But he didn't know. Not really.

He didn't know that I included myself in all that hate. That I hated myself almost as much as I hated my mom for dying.

How couldn't I?

I deserved to hate myself for everything Charlotte was going through and the pieces of parents I was going to try my best to stitch together for her through me so she had *something* to rely on.

I hated myself for every moment I forgot to think about Layla and where she was because of me.

There was only so much headspace for all the chaos and misery, and at all times of the day, I felt like my skull was exploding. But it didn't mean I didn't feel like shit when I thought of Charlotte instead of her. Dominic instead of her. My mom instead of her.

My mom, who the last thing I ever said to her was: okay.

She told me she loved me, and I said *okay*. I'd always hate myself for that, and as it was with death, there was no changing it.

"You should let me go," I mumbled into him, eyes shut and the scent of him circling in my tired brain. "Heather's still home."

To that, he burrowed my head beneath his chin tighter. "I can hug you if I want to hug you. She can't take Maya away for hugging you."

"I'm not worth the risk."

A faint exhale of disappointment sprinkled down on me. "Don't say that."

Fine. I wouldn't say it. I'd just think it.

I'd taken down everything in my own life in a startling timeframe. Who was to say his wasn't next? I'd already taken a sledgehammer to his marriage, so it wasn't a far cry to think I might demolish everything else about him eventually.

I was bad for him before this, but I had been a willing infection.

Now?

I was a cancer, unstoppable and malignant, and a disease no sane man would willingly sign on for.

I shook my head against him, moving my lips against his shirt. "I could have been normal for you before this. Not, you know, *normal* but something like it. I was damaged before, but now I'm—"

"Perfect," he shushed me sweetly, lips moving against my hair. "You're perfect."

A huff of disbelieving air warmed my face as I exhaled it against Dominic's chest, shaking my head. How could he say that? How could he align me with a word strictly devoted to him?

He was perfection. I was a flaw with limbs to walk around and destroy everything I touched.

Pinching my eyes shut as hard as I could, I held onto him the exact same way. "I just want to fix everything and I don't know how," I confessed in mutters.

Affection traced up and down the ridges of my spine.

"We can start with breakfast and go from there."

His words were meant to be simple, an initiation to just take things moment to moment, but his infatuation with feeding me made me sigh against him.

Dominic pulled back just enough to fix me with his stare that begged I listen.

"Please?"

Staring up at him, my shoulders sunk low even as I tried to drill it into my brain that he was trying to take care of me. I'd passed out yesterday because I hadn't been eating enough, and Dominic, in his way of needing to be the hero, had to feel like he'd failed in some way because of it.

"Actually," He inhaled deeply, the rising air lifting his gaze into thoughtful territory before bringing it back to me. "Ms. Sanders, don't eat anything in the kitchen. Don't even look at it or think about eating it. That's a strict order."

Spirited eyes watched me closely as I caught onto what he was trying to do, and a damn curve caught the ends of my mouth. Dominic looked to the tilt of my mouth as if he was watching gold form, adoration—no, scratch that—*love* casting a spell over his handsome face.

"There it is," he heartened, reaching up and thumbing the corner of my mouth as if it really was made of gold.

My eyes rolled because I couldn't help it, and somehow the move dented both our grins deeper until they nearly cracked our faces.

How in the *fuck* was I smiling right now? It didn't make any sense to smile. It wasn't fair to anyone I'd lost to smile.

Dominic told me he was going to the kitchen to make me some coffee to start, and we'd work our way up to food from there. I stayed behind, still plastered against the front door as I watched him leave, gulping down a few calming breaths before I'd follow.

I'd have to apologize to Meredith for snapping when I got in there.

Which, *great*. I sucked at apologies.

I was less than halfway through my second breath when a sight lording at the top step of the stairs caught my eye, and my soothing inhale disintegrated to ash.

Stark blue eyes were honed in on me, blazing enough to burn the spot Dominic had just been standing. For a moment, I actually expected the white marbled floors to crack beneath my feet in retaliation to her fire-hot gaze.

Heather stood over me as the queen of her kingdom, me just some peasant who'd come in and seduced her domineering king. Murder brightened the slits of her stare to sapphires weaponized to kill at a glance.

I pushed myself off of the door, too past the point of caring if she wanted me dead.

"It was a hug," I called up to her, scoffing. "Calm your A cups."

And then I took off towards the smell of brewing coffee.

TWELVE

D ominic was watching me with approving eyes as I broke off my third bite of a banana when my phone sitting on the kitchen table started to dance.

The vibrations cut my gaze down, an unfamiliar number lighting up my phone screen.

I clicked it off with a heavy sigh and finished chewing the fruit rolling around in my mouth.

You know what had a really fucking weird texture when you weren't hungry? The kind of texture that made you wanna gag?

Yeah, that'd be bananas.

I was only halfway through and was seriously considering lobbing it at Dominic's face and making a run for it.

"Daddy?" Maya came up behind her father, her dark ringlet curls poofier today than usual. "Can you put on Netflix? Grandma can't do it."

"I just can't figure out your T.V. down here for the *life* of me," Meredith called over to Dominic, chuckling lightly at herself while giving the two remotes in both her hands a stare down. Charlotte was standing over her shoulder on the couch, pointing at buttons trying to help.

Dominic rose from his chair parallel to mine and went to go help with the T.V. With the food warden gone, I carefully folded the half uneaten banana back in its peel and set it down on the table in exchange for my phone.

I swiped up, the screen showing me the latest missed call from the unknown number. My lips pursed at it, the string of digits not looking one bit familiar.

I went to close out.

Then it lit up again, screen bright.

Same number.

A strange feeling rolled through my gut.

My thumb hovered over the screen, waiting and feeling each rhythmic vibration bleed into my palm. The sensations traveled up my arm into my chest, suspending my lungs in a freeze as I tapped my thumb on *'accept.'*

I pulled my phone to my ear, mouth parting—

"Don't say a single word, Catnip."

All breath *whooshed* out of me at once, and I couldn't have spoken even if I wanted to. The voice kidnapped all my words and the air I'd use to create them.

Just like the voice kidnapped my best friend.

The onetime familiar shadow's voice came through again, *ungodly slow,* chewing and savoring every vile word like spitting tobacco.

"Get up… don't make a scene… and go somewhere it can be just us two. You and I deserve some alone time together, don't you think?"

He then paused, forcing a knifing chuckle down my ear. "Or is Detective Reed the jealous type?"

Disgust scrunched my nose up tight, Dominic's name a thing of mockery in Tommy's mouth *shattering* my lightning's slumber. It felt like a fucking hot flash bursting beneath my skin as it came alive, filling my veins with fire as I shot up out of the kitchen chair.

This ended *now.*

The pathway to the back patio was a blood red blur as I tore through the house, phone clutched to my ear in my hand that was already beginning to sweat with the heat of my rage. I poured outside, the dew of rain-soaked air covering my hot face in a film as soon as I stepped onto the patio.

I swiped my hand over my forehead, breathing hard into the phone. "I'm outside you fucking *psychopath.*"

Tommy clicked his tongue on the other end, disappointment popping in the sound. "Your words hurt, Catnip. Words have power. *Your* words have power. Did you know that?"

"What kind of power?" I asked, teeth gritted.

"The power to save a life. Or three. Maybe four."

I whipped around, hunching into my phone. "Excuse me?"

"You remember our deal?"

"*Yes*, the trade. I was ready to do it days ago but you never called!"

Tommy chuckled, the noise locking up my spine. "Aw, were you hung up on me? Waiting by the phone to talk to me again?"

"I was waiting so I could get Layla back!"

"Careful, careful," he tutted. "You don't want your boyfriend to hear you and come outside and ruin our alone time, would you? Then I'd have to put a bullet between your pretty little friend's big eyes."

Horror bloated my lungs with a scream I struggled to swallow down. "Don't you *fucking* touch her."

"Oh, she's fine." He brushed me off, dangling my sanity by a thread. "A little banged up from the trip but still chirping like a songbird."

Oh *god.* I pressed the heel of my free hand to my eye, digging it in deep to keep out the flashes of her heart-shaped face flush with tears and decorated in bruises of my own doing.

"Let me hear her," I demanded through shaky breaths.

I needed to hear her voice, needed to hear that she was *okay* and tell her that I was coming to get her. Today. Now.

Noise on the other end crackled as Tommy shifted the phone away from his face to call out. "Sweetpea, make some noise."

Blood rushed between my ears.

"Kat!"

My heart *banged*, cracking in half at her piercing voice.

"Kat, oh my god. I'm—"

"See?" My hand jerked and flexed out like I could grab onto her voice and keep her there as Tommy's took her place, making my jaw fucking shake somewhere between a restrained sob and a shout. "The people down south kept her nice and breathing."

"Down *south?*" My eyes flared wide, fluttering fast. Memories prickled of Dominic saying they'd found one of the victims dead in Florida. "Where the fuck has she been all this time?"

"You're still asking the wrong questions."

Oh my *fucking* god.

Again with the right and wrong *questions*. Pain pinched my palm as my hand tightened to a shaking fist, holding against my forehead.

"It doesn't matter where she's been, but *why,*" Tommy pressed. "You still never figured out the why."

"The why to *what*? Why you're so fucking fixated on me?"

"Who wouldn't be?" His retort oozed with so much blood-curdling allure. For *me.* "You're a star, remember? All dressed in black with nowhere to go."

My hand slacked all tension.

My neck snapped up straight, eyes out on the rainy backyard.

I moved towards the edge of the patio in my black leggings and black tank top, feet numb and knees stiff. The pads of my fingers touched the stone-cold countertop sitting right up against the sheet of rain falling in front of my face.

The cords of my voice froze over. "Are you watching me?"

Every dark corner of the Reed's backyard morphed into hiding spots for the monster of my nightmares to be lurking. My heart stuck to my ribs, throbbing so hard I felt it pulse in my neck.

"Oh, you're always being watched, Gorgeous," Tommy preened—*delighted.* "All eyes are always on you."

Air kicked out of me, chest caving in with the assault.

He was here. He was fucking *here.*

My eyes jumped everywhere over the patio and around the huge backyard, narrowing in hard on every dewy blade of grass and forest green tree turned ominous black by the blanket of gray rain pouring over them.

Where is he, where is he, where is he?

Dominic should have been a thought in my mind to call out to, to scream that Tommy was here, he was *right fucking here* hiding in the bushes or some shit. But he wasn't, and I didn't.

Instead, I ran forward all on my own until my bare feet squished into wet ground and the rain that bled out of the sky covered me from head to toe. Each falling drop was a tiny bullet pelting my body that whipped in searching circles. The trees backed up to the fence were shaking in the tossing wind as bad as my lungs were as I sucked down shallow, rain-infused breaths.

I was a single bolt of lightning trying to take on the entire sky all on my own.

"Where are you? Where the *fuck* are you?!"

"God*damn*, that sweetfire temper is delicious." I pressed my phone to my ear harder to hear Tommy over the roaring rain. "I'd buy you myself if that was my kinda thing."

"Oh, do you draw your *outstanding* moral line at purchasing women?"

I kept turning in every direction in the backyard, searching out a thorn in the bushes as he spoke. "Believe it or not, I like my women willing, Catnip."

I swiped my hand over my eyes to clear out the dewdrops. "What a relief to hear chivalry hasn't completely kicked the bucket."

"Don't think I wouldn't take my shot with you if I didn't know I'd get in deep shit for it."

"How about you take your shot right now, huh?" I challenged, puffing my chest out like a bull ready to tear a hole right through a stadium. "Come out of the shadows and sweep me off my fucking feet, Tommy!"

He hummed something grotesque, his satisfaction churning the little food in my stomach. "Tempting offer, but today's not our day... and you've got places to be."

Taking a huge breath, I huffed, *"Where?"*

At this point, I wasn't even afraid to meet Tommy face to face. I *wanted* it. I wanted the look on his face when I went for his fucking throat.

"So eager," he mused deeply. Thunder crackled from above. "It's cute."

"Fuck you," I spat. "Dominic is going to rip you to *shreds* when he gets his hands on you, and I personally cannot fucking wait."

"Aw, I *hate* to be the one to tell you but your boyfriend ain't hot shit like he thinks he is. Trust me. He won't have anything more than suspicion to prove a thing."

He'll have me.

I was coming back from this 'trade' with Layla. There was no other option. I was coming back, I was bringing her home, and I would put this bullshit nightmare to bed for us all. What had started because of my mother would end with me, and it would end *my* way.

I'd create my very own paper mache happy ending from cutouts in the newspaper of Tommy's arrest and my victory over him.

"And…" He sighed into the phone, sounding really and truly hesitant. "You aren't planning on telling Reed about any of this, right? Because I'd hate to have to upset you by getting trigger-happy with your friend here."

"*No*, I'm not."

Lies.

I absolutely was planning on telling Dominic every single detail of this conversation when I got inside. Tommy couldn't hear me *inside*, could he?

"Because if you do tell him or anyone, I'll *know*," he said, almost like he was actually trying to warn me. "I know what you had for breakfast this morning. I know the episode you had by the front door with Reed. I even know what a button-cute face your little sister has."

Cold poured through my bones, and it had nothing to do with the rain.

"She looks real cute in that rainbow shirt you dressed her in this morning."

"Stop," I breathed, voice gone to the cold. The *dread*.

"Kids aren't the normal MO but—"

"Stop, stop!" I grabbed my phone with both hands, clutching at it and immediately begging, "Stop, I won't tell anyone! I'll come alone. I'll do whatever the *fuck* you want."

Oh my god. All my fighting tenacity was violently shoved beneath a raging swell of desperation.

Charlotte's sweet face, round pink cheeks holding up a toothy grin and innocent brown eyes, burned in my head. My stomach rolled, sicker than I'd ever felt before, pressing bile up my throat.

I gagged, choking on rain water and acid. Tears flooded my eyes and spilled over to mix with the rain falling down my face. My heart shattered, and I mean *really* shattered. It broke into thousands of shards so astoundingly fast, tiny cuts of its wreckage sliced all down my chest and left me openly weeping in seconds.

Not Bugs. Not her.

I would die a million deaths and then a million more before he ever got to her.

"Smart girl," Tommy's voice crackled into the phone, muffled by my heavy breathing. "Be at the back alley of the nail salon on Mills in an hour."

And then he was gone.

The line went dead, and all there was was rainfall. Splashing, plopping, battering. The earth, my skin, my clothes.

Drowning.

I was drowning, but I couldn't move out of the way. I couldn't move at all.

He'd seen Charlotte.

He'd seen *us*, our life. This morning and probably tons of others. He *threatened* her. I didn't even know him, and he'd threatened the first and truest love in my life because he *did* know me. He knew me enough to know it would work.

I wouldn't tell anyone about the trade.

I wouldn't even risk a whisper of it.

I would go to get Layla alone.

"Kat!"

Thunder boomed across the backyard, striking me through the blundering rush of rain like only he could. The power of his voice captured my anxious lungs and pulled me over my shoulder, finding Dominic standing at the edge of his patio, as imposing and consuming as the storm coming down between us.

He waited for me to run up to him out of the rain, and when I didn't move— when I *couldn't* move—he came to me. He grabbed a black umbrella from somewhere unseen and came to my rescue, jogging out into the middle of a torrential downpour just to get to me.

As he ran up, I thought about how often he'd saved me—small and big rescues alike.

The entirety of our knowing each other had been a storm like the one we were encased in now, built of passion, salvation, and inevitables.

Our meeting, our chemistry, our *loving* each other was inevitable.

We were the crossed stars tied up in the constellations, the twin flames unchecked and unbound, the mirrored pieces of a heart broken in half at birth. We'd been unwittingly set off on a path to find each other before we knew what we were searching for, but Dominic had figured it out quickly.

He'd always been five steps ahead of me so he could catch me when I jumped, let me crash into his arms when I tripped and fell over my own flaws and insecurities.

I never wanted the hero saving me. I wanted to be my *own* hero. I wanted to be Charlotte's hero, and now was my chance.

This was my chance to fix *everything*, save everyone I love.

Dominic arrived where I was standing, looking upset and strikingly so, jutting the umbrella over my head to shield me from the rain.

"I know you love the rain, but you'll get yourself sick like this."

His scolding was lathered with concern and love, as was his touch as he passed his rough hand over my face, pushing wet-strapped locks of hair from my forehead.

All my focus was on him, thoughts scrambling like ants being drowned for what to say to him. I couldn't say anything to him now because he'd know I was lying, but I would say *everything* to him when I got back. I swore it.

He'd be so mad.

Fuck, he was going to break his jaw in half clenching it with all the rage he'd have for me once I got back later with Layla. He'd yell at me, shake me, bruise my lips in a kiss that I used to think said he hated me but now knew meant he was scared to ever let me go.

I hated that I was about to hurt him, but he'd be proud of me when I got back. After, ya know, the anger.

He'd be proud, and Layla and Charlotte would be safe, and Tommy would be gone.

Dominic fixed all my hair back away from my face, thumb cleaning beneath my eye to gather what he mistook for a little fall of rain.

Inconspicuously, I slid my phone into the side pocket of my leggings so he wouldn't ask about it.

When I still didn't say anything, his umber eyebrows sunk together, and because Heather had left for work, he allowed his knuckle to draw down the curve of my cheek.

"What's going on in that head?"

So much. So fucking much.

But also somehow true: only him.

He was my so much, my *too* much, and he had been since the moment I met him.

There was this stupid freaking 'just in case' voice chirping in the back of my brain as I stood beneath him. A 'just in case' voice saying all the things I didn't want to think about on the off chance I failed.

On the off chance that the trade… happened.

A 'just in case' this was the last time I ever saw Dominic.

Which was *insane.*

It wasn't even conceivable or halfway acceptable that this was my last moment with Dominic. No, this was one of those bends in the river of our story. It was rocky and the current swept us up like a riptide, but it wouldn't take me away from him.

I'd be back by his side later today, and it was perfectly fine by me if he never let me go again.

Still, that 'just in case' voice wouldn't leave me alone. It got so loud, it was all I could hear *screaming* at me even in the roaring thunderstorm over us. Its screams burst into my fingers, latching them onto his shirt and wrinkling it up like always *just in case* I never got to ruin his perfection again.

The screams were in my muscles, rattling them with life to hold him close *just in case* I never got to hold him again.

The screams of the voice shook my born-again heart as I stared between those intense silver eyes—my *favorite* eyes—and memorized every dazzling shade of beauty they were made up of… just in case I never got to gaze up at my personal starry sky again.

Dominic thumbed the edge of my jawline, touching me as if he could read my thoughts being skin to skin. Maybe he could. He'd always been able to read me better than anyone; as if I was written in a language only he understood.

My smiles were poems, my frowns lyrics of a sad song. The looks I gave to him were paragraphs for him to unfold, our kisses entire novels written by loving lips.

Dominic *knew* me more than anyone had ever cared to know me before, and somehow, he fell in love with me because of it. And I loved him too, even though I couldn't say it.

But I could show him.

My hands turned to fists on his shirt, dragging him down while my toes pushed up to meet him halfway. Warmth pressed over my mouth, his lips softer than the water collecting on my eyelashes.

Sparks exploded in my chest, erupting electricity in shock waves beneath my damp skin.

The electrocution shot into my brain and glitched out all thoughts in my head, nothing telling me to stop, to slow down, to not consume Dominic as he always consumed me.

He was mine. Thunder and lightning *belonged* together, or else where would this rain have come from for us to kiss each other under like it was our last?

I kissed him hard, maybe harder than I ever had before. I poured *everything* I had for him in that kiss as if it really was our last. I kissed him like I was dying tomorrow and this kiss was my goodbye.

This kiss said everything I couldn't.

I'm sorry. I need you. I love you. Please don't hate me for what I'm about to do. Please don't stop loving me. Please don't ever let me go.

As if on cue, a streak of electricity broke in the sky, a rumble of thunder followed after to do what thunder did best and chase after its untamed lightning.

I wrapped my arms around his neck and held on *so* tight, moving my lips over his to spell out every unspoken word I wanted him to know.

A noise close to pain resonated from Dominic's lips to mine, and a second later, there was a clatter of metal beside us and nothing but rainfall above us.

His arm curled around my middle, dragging me into his hard-lined body and anchoring me in like I was a long-lost piece of him. My heart clamoured against my rib cage, trying to take flight as he lost to himself and let us both drown in the rain.

I was so small against him, so profoundly protected by all he was as he cupped the side of my face in his big hand and deepened our kiss until I tasted his soul.

Rain mixed between our greedy lips, slipping to our tongues and turning our hot kiss wet. Turning our passion to steam. I'd never been kissed in the rain before, but holy fuck, there was never any other way I wanted to be kissed again.

Dominic squeezed my waist, and I squeezed him back, pushing my fingers up his neck to split into his wet hair, holding onto him with all I had. Just like he was holding me.

This was love.

Love was running into the rain and getting drenched in it just to hold someone close. Love was kissing like no one or everyone was watching, and not caring which. Love was every tiny droplet falling from the sky; pointless as individuals, but an unstoppable downpour when brought together.

Dominic pulled back from the kiss way before I was ready to let him go, my whine of protest getting washed away in the rain.

Petals of water that were lucky enough to touch him slid down the rising peaks of his grin, getting lost in the grooves of his dimples.

"Just wanted to kiss me in the rain, Ms. Sanders?" he mused, deep and still clutching me tight.

A rock lodged in my throat, rising so fast, it shocked me how quickly my love for this man brought me to the brink of tears all over again.

"Well, it always looked so grand in the movies," I managed, my words hoarse.

He hummed, brushing his nose against mine. "And?"

Staring back and forth between his water-coated lashes and shining eyes, I breathed, "Better than movie magic."

His slow-rising smile was the stuff of dreams, making me go all starry-eyed beneath him and all that adoration beaming down at me.

He was happy. I made him *happy* just now.

Now if he could just hold on to that feeling until I got back later.

He passed a hand back through his hair painted black by the rainfall, water clinging to the stubborn dip in his chin. He blinked rain out of his eyes, focusing them on me.

"We need to get you into some dry clothes."

I nodded and let him guide me by the small of my back towards the patio. We ducked under cover and caught the not-so-sly arm of Meredith reaching through the patio door, dropping off two towels for us each.

Dominic breathed a laugh, and believe it or not, I did too. He dried me off first as if I wasn't gripping a towel of my own to my chest. He dabbed the fluffy fabric beneath my eyes, swiped it over my forehead and reached around the back of me to ring my hair out in the towel too.

I couldn't help but watch him as he dutifully took care of me, and that organ in my chest began to burn as his love set me on fire. He was *so* good. He was pure to his soul, and I swore down to *my* very soul that nothing as insignificant as Tommy fucking Lynch would come between us.

I pulled my towel over his head of dark hair, raking it back and forth to simultaneously dry it off and mess it up fantastically. When I dropped the towel down, his mass of hair stuck up in all directions and the lopsided grin he was sporting was nothing short of dashing.

He called me a brat, and I called him fabulous, and then his towel was pulling around my back. Dominic dragged me in close and kissed the smile on my lips softly. Then he did it again and again, each time growing less soft and more like he couldn't help himself.

Eventually he did, backing up just enough to put space between him and temptation.

"Would you send Charlotte out here?" I asked. "I just need to talk to her real quick."

He nodded. "Of course." Then, a stern finger aimed my way. "Then straight to a hot shower so you don't get sick."

My heart fluttered hard, all giddy and in love.

"Yes, sir."

A vexing warning flashed over his sharp features, and he angled his sharp chin low in a silent and playful admonishment. Then he was off, gone for less than thirty seconds before blonde curls and an upturned smile came in his place.

"Hey Bugs."

I squatted down to her level, big brown eyes taking me in.

Her mouth squished to the side. "Why are you all wet?"

"I ran out in the rain."

"Why?"

To save you. "I left something out there earlier and went out to get it."

She bobbed her little head, accepting the lie with ease. Her stare sunk to the ground, watching her toes curl inside her white socks that I needed to remember to throw in the wash when I got back.

It pained me, physically *pained* me, to see her like this—silent and her infectious neon energy muted so dark. She'd been through too much in only five years, and none of it was fair. Her life was *not* the life she deserved for as vibrant and sensational as she was, and I was going to fight with everything I had in me to change that.

Starting today.

"Can I tell you a secret?" I began.

Her big eyes popped up to me, intrigue undeniable. "Yeah…"

"It's a big one. Like a super-sister level secret, okay?"

Her head jumped up and down enthusiastically, promises that she wouldn't tell anyone falling from her mouth. She settled in and so did I.

"I'm gonna go get Layla."

Her gasp exploded. "You are?!"

"Mhm," I hummed with a smile finding my cheeks as I watched hers form for the first time today. "I know she's going to be so excited to see you, and she'll want lots of hugs. Like tackle her to the ground kind of hugs."

"I can do that!" She beamed, but then paused as her sweet face scrunched up. "Wait, why is it a secret?"

I inhaled deeply, finding the lie as I told it. "I just want it to be a surprise. You know, everyone's so sad today, and… I just wanna make it right." My fingertips touched her round cheek, thumb smoothing over her soft skin as I whispered, "I wanna make everyone happy again."

Thoughts buzzed all across her face, ones too serious and weighted for her age.

"Okay," she agreed slowly, nodding at the same pace. "You're getting her now?"

"I am."

She tilted her head at me. "How long will you be gone?"

Again, another stalling inhale as I tried to find an answer that wouldn't upset her or me.

"Hopefully not long at all."

I'd bring the mace, I'd bring a knife, I'd bring every fighting move Dominic taught me. It would be Tommy and maybe a goon or two, but Layla and I could take them now that we weren't caught off guard.

That stupid fucking 'just in case' voice began to murmur again…

The gravity of it caught in my throat, pain widening up the sides. I put a hand to my neck, trying to squeeze out the hurt while shaking my head.

No. Just fucking *no*.

Preparing to never see Dominic again was like preparing to never breathe again. Preparing to never see Charlotte though? That was like getting ready to rip my still-beating heart right out of my chest and pretend like I could survive without it.

My lips parted, a trembling breath tapering into my lungs.

"But if it is longer than I—"

A crack slipped past my defenses, snipping my voice in half.

I whipped my head back towards the rain over my shoulder, blinking out the rise of saltwater that welled at the ideas being whispered to me by the 'just in case' voice.

Rolling my lips together, I steeled my breath and turned back to Charlotte with a reassuring smile. "Mr. Dominic, his mom, Layla, her parents, Mrs. Sharon… they'll all take care of you until I come back, okay?"

My baby sister drew her chin down into her chest, regarding me with questions in her glistening eyes of why I would ever want to leave her.

Guilt shot from my gut straight into that pain wedged in my throat, exploding it and freeing the tears it was holding back.

Shit.

A groan tangled with my sob, trying to wrestle it away from Charlotte's ears. She shouldn't hear me cry. She shouldn't see me weak when she needed me to be a pillar of brawn for her to lean on.

I huffed like I was laughing, pretending to be her hero as I wiped away my cowardice.

Except only more weakness slipped through as a tiny hand touched my cheeks, helping clean my face. An ache of something halfway between a laugh and a sob poured out of me as my baby sister wiped my tears.

Dear lord, what the fuck was wrong with me?

I was coming *back*, but still I cried and she still cleaned my face like I wasn't.

With a smile so overwhelmed, I grabbed both of her hands and held them to my wet cheeks. Sorrow-blurred brown eyes watched me with downcast confusion, and I knew I was worrying her more than I needed to with these stupid tears.

So I kept smiling despite the moisture dripping into the facade, kept holding her hands to my face to leave her with a better memory of me today.

"If I'm gone longer than I want to be—that's a *big* if—there's something I need you to remember for me."

Her head cocked, innocence searching up at me.

"Never forget how much I love you and how much I will *always* love you. No matter what, I'm always proud of you, I'm always with you, and I will always love you more than anyone has loved anything else in the entire world."

One more tear crept between our locked hands, absorbing between our connection.

"To the moon and back, Bugs."

THIRTEEN

With the shower turned on in the upstairs guest bathroom to disguise my escape, I packed a small bag.

In it, I put a spare can of mace, my phone, and a kitchen knife I'd nabbed from downstairs while Dominic, Meredith, and the girls went onto the back patio to blow bubbles and decorate the cement with chalk.

I changed from my sopping black outfit to something with pockets to fit the mace Dominic made me carry around in my purse. Two cans of pepper spray between two pissed off women?

Tommy should look forward to a future with a sore nutsack and spicy eye sockets.

Before I left, I scribbled a note to Dominic to tell him what I was doing *just in case* I wasn't back in an hour or so like I planned on being. I *hated* the voice that was making me prepare in all ways for the worst case scenario, but it was too loud to ignore.

It was 'smart' to write down everything I could about Tommy's phone call and where I was going to get Layla. It was 'smart' to tell Dominic that we were all being watched. It was 'smart' to write down in words just how exceptionally I loved him so he'd always have evidence of it if he happened to have lonely nights in his future.

I placed the note on the foot of my bed in the spare room, touching the emerald of my necklace as I looked at it.

Steady breathing tried to conduct my heartbeat in normal rhythms, but it was pointless. What was going on in my chest was a rave of palpitations. I was stressed as fuck, but more than that, I was pissed. *Livid.* These were angry breaths.

There were justice-seeking flares of my nostrils with each fire-breathing inhale.

My touch over the necklace Dominic gave me turned fierce, to a fist of determination to fight for him, for us, for everyone I hadn't lost yet.

My fist holding the emerald he compared to my eyes shook. I'd use it to guide me like it *was* my eyes, the eyes of my soul steering me right out the front door to rewrite this mindfuck of a life using my own goddamn pen like a sword.

Making it downstairs without being seen, I backed out of the Reeds' driveway and tried not to think about it as my last time.

I'd be back. I'd be back with flying fucking colors of victory.

The drive to the nail salon was short, around fifteen minutes, and all fifteen were packed with overthinking exactly how this was going to go down.

Tommy would show up, I'd demand to see Layla for proof that she was okay, and then I'd pepper spray the shit out of him while making a grab for her.

I also went over every meticulous lesson of Dominic's self-defense training in the probability that I'd need to kick some criminal ass.

Honest to fucking god, I was sort of banking on it.

I *really* needed something to put my fist through today.

The nail salon on Mills had always been a sketchy piece of gossip in this town. It was rumored to be one of *those* salons, which would track with the sort of business Tommy was into. The back alley was barren of anything but a dumpster corroded in rust-red and a pile of sunken in cardboard boxes with the corners chewed out by whatever vermin frequented this shithole.

I felt like I could *see* the stench of this place radiating out in squiggly lines like in the cartoons as I pulled up and shifted my car into park. My heartbeat overpowered the not-so-gentle hum of my old engine, and I swallowed down the ball of nerves in my scratchy throat.

The keys stayed locked into the ignition in the likelihood Layla and I would need a quick getaway, and I couldn't wait to tell Dominic how smart I'd been to think about that. I also couldn't wait to see his perfect mouth peel up with pride when he realized I was *so* smart, I turned my Location Services on for this.

I was being so damn vigilant, Dominic was going to have to make me a medal when this was all over—shiny and obnoxiously large, engraved with my badassery and how I outsmarted the oh-so-infamous Tommy.

Stepping out of my car, I held my jacket closer around the collar. The zipper was busted, so it wouldn't keep out the chill of the colder-than-normal breeze, but it would keep my mace out of sight, tucked into the front pocket.

It had stopped raining right before I left the Reeds', but the evidence of the storm was all around us in pothole-filled puddles and in the crisp edge of the air.

I adjusted the strap of my bag over my shoulder as I closed my driver's side, the tip of the kitchen knife I'd nabbed poking my hipbone like it just couldn't wait for a taste of blood.

Me too, Knife. Me fucking too.

Minutes passed, a generator kicking on somewhere in the near distance and a car horn being smashed helping to fill the seconds. Impatience nipping at my nerves, I dug my phone out of the bag to check the time and for any missed calls or messages.

The screen was blank of everything but the digital clock reading that my date with Tommy started exactly two minutes ago.

He was late.

Groaning, I shoved my phone back in the bag and fixed my fingers around my bottom lip, pulling and tugging until I ripped skin.

"Fuck," I hissed beneath my breath, swiping my tongue over the raw flesh, touching and tasting blood. Rolling my eyes, I hid my bottom lip back between my teeth and away from my anxious habit.

My shaking fingers found the necklace over my vibrating heart instead, trying to fixate on a new nervous tick. The round of the silver heart was so smooth, gliding sweetly beneath my thumb as I rubbed it over and over, as if

I could feel Dominic's love touching me back.

Tires rotating on broken asphalt plucked me straight out of the necklace's solace, eyes snapping open and neck twisting towards a car.

A black van, to be more specific.

Just like the one they took Layla away in exactly one week ago.

It rolled towards me, rocks squishing beneath slow-moving tires. Polluted air saturated my lungs as I kicked back a huge inhale, my legs suddenly made of jelly as I stumbled back from the lurking van.

Breathe. Fucking breathe.

I tried to lock my knees together, willing my muscles to become steel as I stuffed my hand in my jacket pocket. All five fingers clenched around the cylinder of mace, thumb sliding the safety off.

My shoulders shoved back too, righting my posture stalwart and unshakable. I heard my breathing like I heard my heartbeat, both abnormally harsh and rattling between my ears like some alarm clock gone off rhythm.

The van stopped in front of me, crunching dirt beneath its heels.

My stare jumped between both doors facing me, trying to squint past the blackened tint of its windows. Was Layla really in there? Why wasn't she screaming for me?

Why wasn't *anything* happening?

Then, something did.

The back door to the van burst open, two men dressed in all black pouring out.

Fear struck my chest hard and fast, but so did my murderous adrenaline. With a violent screech, I wretched my hand out of my jacket pocket, finger poised on the switch as I aimed right at their dipshit faces.

My finger jammed down, spray flying out of the mace nozzle and hitting the first guy square in the face. He shouted and grabbed for his eyes, bowing over at his muscle-strapped waist to writhe in pain.

Fuck yeah.

The second guy dodged the onslaught, but I tried again, jerking around on my lightning-quick feet to hit him with the spray. Mist spurted into the air, the brutal features of the second guy contouring with an ugly sneer as he ducked the eye of the spray, waving off the outer bands as they coated his face.

Then, the breeze shifted my way.

I gasped and immediately coughed on the rancid kickback coating my lungs, squeezing my eyelids shut as bites of poison chewed at my burning eyes.

"Aw, *fuck*," I cried, digging my knuckles into my eyes like the pressure could make the stinging stop.

I couldn't see. I couldn't see a fucking thing even as I tried to blink back the tears, a thousand tiny knives lacerating my vision and bleeding my world out to a wash of black.

Hands, rough and built to bruise, clamped down on my upper arms, yanking them backwards. A cry split my lips as my shoulders wailed, the blades in my back dipping together to a point they weren't meant to.

"*Becks.*" The man behind me hissed out a name. "Get your shit together."

"She fucking pepper sprayed me! You have no idea how much this shit *burns.*"

'Becks', I assumed, wasn't wrong. This shit *did* burn, and I only got blasted with the kickback spray. Water leaked down the sides of my face, each drop infused with its own acidic burn, leaving simmering trails down my cheeks.

I huffed wildly and tried to blink out the sting tearing apart the ashen sky above me. All I could see were slivers of thick, swirling clouds. All I could feel was the unbearable stretch in my shoulder blades, muscles peeling and agony expanding.

"She got a bitter taste of her own medicine though, didn't she?"

My molars knocked together, grating his mockery down to dust beneath my teeth. Upper-lip twitching, I held my fucking breath with so much effort, the strings of muscle in my neck burned, but I couldn't let go.

I couldn't breathe, because if I breathed, I breathed *fire.*

And I had to restrain my fire until Layla was within sight.

The guy behind me was way too goddamn warm, sweat sticking his t-shirt to my back. Plus, he smelled like Old Spice. Like every teenage boy I went to high school with. The vivid stench was a nauseating fist in my gut, and I could have fallen over and kissed the dirty asphalt when he loosened his vice grip enough for me to drop forward.

The front door of the van remained closed, its driver a silhouetted secret.

"Tommy," I sighed, loud and still trying to right my vision. "Can we skip the dramatics and just get to it? This foreplay's getting tired."

The stinging in my eyes was beginning to dull enough to make out shapes and fixate on colors again—sleek black backlit by a sodden gray cityscape, muddy outlines of the van and circles of its giant wheels. Then, a crack in the outline. A widening of sorts.

A click against the road.

Two of them.

Porcelain white stepped out, so white in fact, it blinded like rays of the sun suddenly peeled out of the driver's seat. I squinted at the vision of white, blinking hard and fast to focus in on the face glowing at the center of it.

There was a dark halo of hair, a highlighted bridge of a pin straight nose and… fire blue eyes burning right at me.

Delight ticked up the corner of her pale pink mouth.

"Ms. Sanders."

Her greeting *sounded* like her, snobbish and her disdain tactless, but it couldn't be her.

I blinked several times, shaking my head and pinching my eyes shut. "I'm pretty sure the mace is still fucking up my vision."

The woman standing with her posture as strict as ever glitched in my sight as I tried to blink her presence away. After several tries and nothing changing but the fuzzy dots of white now snowing in around her, I stopped just to fucking stare at her like she was a hanging icicle in the dead heat of summer.

"Are you like my stalker now?" I blanched. "Did you *follow* me here?"

I swear to whoever or whatever was up there, if Heather Reed followed me here just to tattle on me for leaving the house to Dominic, and she *ruined* this meeting with Tommy, I was going to maim her. Slowly and painfully, I'd strip the perfume-stained flesh right off her brittle bones so she was nothing more than a delicate skeleton of stinking regret.

Keeping my eye, Heather flicked one of her boney fingers in a gesture towards Becks, who was still moaning about what a bitch I was for spraying him.

"Trunk," Heather clipped, her cadence an ooze of conceit.

Growling more friendly words about me under his breath, Becks moved his burly limbs in clunky motions toward the trunk of the van. My stare jumped from him to Heather, asking her with a severe slant of my eyebrows what the fuck was going on.

There was a pop from the trunk, the wide back door rising slowly.

Becks ducked out of view, reaching inside. There was a shift of something heavy, a chafing grunt from Becks, a curse to chase the noise.

The first thing I saw flop out of the back of that trunk were legs.

Limp, dangling, barefooted legs.

A ferocious pulse of dread stretched my neck forward for a closer look. Becks had his hands around the leg's small ankles, giving a sharp tug until hips and a waist came into view.

Purple.

A plum skirt crumpled up to the thighs of its owner, and also a mesh shirt on the same color spectrum. Tan skin pleated between the two garments, but there was at least one boot-shaped bruise on the skin trying to match the color of her outfit.

The rest of her came spilling out in a heap as Becks grabbed her arms and yanked her out of the trunk.

My heart stuttered.

My lips fell open.

My eyes dried in the toxin-polluted wind as they rounded large.

Her name tasted like ash in my mouth.

"Layla..."

She didn't move at the breathy sound of her name, her black hair smattered across her face and hiding her signs of life. In this back alley, she laid malleable to the divots in the asphalt, body like heavy rubber on the road.

My eyes tracked over every single unmoving inch of her with a wildness rushing my pulse. Every second she didn't move was a heavier pour of gasoline on the fire holding my lungs hostage. The seconds drenched, the seconds provoked, the seconds snapped, cracked, and fucking popped in a lacerating screech.

"Layla! *Layla*, I—"

My shoulders screamed in agony, my teeth grit towards the sky as the man behind me twisted my arms until he suffocated my shouts beneath waves of pain. Whimpers and shallow cuts of breath were all that made it past my lips as his too-hot hands enjoyed my torture, twisting harder the more I bowed back against the clouds and showed the heavens my pain.

Black tides lapped at the sides of my vision before he finally stopped, a cry of relief breaking through me as his assault gave way. I heaved, bent over at the waist as much as the imprisoning hands would let me.

In the middle of a dry heave, I locked sights on the bitch in heels who had a *lot* of explaining to do.

"What the *fuck* are you doing with her? Where's Tommy?!"

She crossed her thin arms, looking smug. "He's where I need him to be."

"*What*? How the f—" I stopped to think, but nothing I thought made any sense. "How do you *know* him?"

"He's been essential to business recently."

"Uh…" Did she hit her ego-thick head trying to fit it inside their van? "Realty? I'm pretty sure he's known for breaking into houses. Not *selling* them. Try again."

As Heather's tight expression marred with ire, my eyes kept drifting over to Layla on the ground. Why wasn't she getting up? She kind of needed to get up for the escape plan to work.

"Tommy was a happy accident that was deemed useful when you became an interminable *pest*."

My stare snapped back onto her, jaw slacking tension and eyes pinching at the sides.

"*What?*"

She was a well-dressed lunatic who wasn't making a damn bit of sense.

"I-This isn't about me. This was about, like, drug money that my mom owed Tommy, and then he just got fucking fixated on me."

"No, their history together just made him the perfect frontman."

"Frontman for *what*?"

An impeccably shaped eyebrow caught on a hook of ridicule. "I thought you said you liked surprises."

What the—

"I am so fucking confused," I breathed hard, shaking my head. I wanted to rip my hands free just to put them to my head, holding it to make my thoughts stop spinning.

The chaos in my mind was restless, escalating my breathing to panting as my focus frayed and heartbeat jumped. In the mindfuck of havoc, the immobile dark-haired girl on the ground gripped me hardest, terror slashing my voice out to a blasting scream.

"Why do you have Layla!?"

Why isn't she moving? Why isn't she getting up and running?

"Because they missed you that night," Heather replied simply, as if her answer made *any* bit of sense.

"*Tommy's* men missed me. Tommy called and—"

"You don't catch up fast, do you?"

Her insult smacked me in the face, but the truth she was weaving for me had a harder impact. It thwacked my brain, shaking it against my skull until a headache manifested behind my forehead.

"Are you trying to say that *you*," I pinned Heather with a glare as hard and pointed as my tone. "Planned *all* of this, the drive-by at my house, taking Layla, Tommy's threatening phone calls to meet up for this 'trade'?"

I waited, my eyes expectant on hers and my gullible meter reading at *'fuck off, I'm not that dumb.'*

When her only response was to ever so slightly poise her hip out, the needle of her heel scraping road, all I could do was laugh.

"No. Nope, you're a bitch, but you're not some secret mastermind criminal. You're a *realtor*," I drilled, leaning in.

Heather being behind all of this Tommy bullshit made about as much sense as the condom brand, Trojan.

Honestly, why name something that's supposed to provide protection and keep things *in* after possibly the most infamous example of failed protection in all of history?

Heather merely drew a closed-mouth simper, stalking closer in slow clicks until she was right there, until her waft of gardenias and her sapphire eyes, starved to the black pits of any humanity, were leveled right on me.

"I warned you, Ms. Sanders. I warned you to stay in your own *filthy* lane, and you didn't. So here we are. Your world, the pathetic thing that it is, is *mine...*" The harsh blue of her eyes glittered fantastically, *insanely*. "And I am going to love watching it burn."

"You're not gonna do shit," I sneered, upper lip twitching. "You're some bored housewife who's used to getting exactly what she wants, so you went *batshit crazy* when your husband decided he didn't want you anymore."

Murder slashed like a knife across her face, and in a snap, her hand latched to my jaw. Manicured nails that felt more like *real* nails bit into my skin. My cheeks ached beneath her forceful grip as she reared my head back beneath her height, the man behind me snickering as Heather displayed her dominance.

"It's getting involved in my marriage that got you here in the first place, Ms. Sanders. I'd watch it," she snarled, losing her hold on the porcelain mask she kept situated over her true self.

The *viper* beneath.

I think I even clocked her wearing snake-skin heels as she strolled over.

How fitting.

"Or what? You're gonna kidnap my best friend to scare me? Get some local drug dealer to play your part in the act so your hands stay clean until you reveal yourself like some criminal at the end of a Scooby-Doo episode?" My neck muscles tightened as I thrashed my head, ripping it from her cold grasp. "Even if this was all you, you're *trashed*, Heather. You played all your cards."

And Dominic was going to be heartbroken.

Blindsided and so, so heartbroken.

He may not still be in love with her, but he still had a *type* of love for her, and this would tarnish it. Any good he'd held onto of the woman he loved, the mother of his child, would be poisoned, the betrayal a scar too embedded in the years of life he spent with her to ever fully fade.

And I hated her for it. Fiery, bloody, writhing *hate*.

"This is so beyond jealousy if it's true, you know that? You hopped the fucking train from jealous and set up shop in institutionalized if you did all this just to scare me away from Dominic."

My eyes went back to Layla, relief blipping a momentary beat in my pulse to see her chest rise. "And what did you do to her?!"

"Oh, she'll be fine if she wakes up."

The stammer in my heart tore my stare back to her and her flippant fucking voice.

"… if?"

Lightning broke under my roiling blood as she had the nerve to whip out a prideful smirk. "Tommy assisted with getting her here and supplied her with a hefty dose of that stuff your mother *loves*… or loved, I suppose."

Her snake eyes slitted, pupils dilating. "My condolences, by the way."

Horror and rage clashed painfully inside my chest, the collision enough to knock me breathless. My focus jumped between her pursed mouth, wanting to wash it clean of her filthy sympathy, and back to Layla, almighty dread brewing now that I knew.

Now that I felt like I could see the death swirling in her veins.

"You…" Sound failed me, slipping between my rallying breaths as I went back and forth between cobalt eyes and ones I couldn't see. Back and forth. Blue to nothing. "You…"

Oh my god.

"Call an ambulance," I sighed weakly. Then I screamed violently. "Call a fucking ambulance! Now!"

The fire I'd been reigning back until I could get to Layla shred its bindings, peeling out of me in viscous snaps ready to whip and draw blood. "Layla, wake up! Get her some fucking help—!"

Salty sweat and muscle slapped over my mouth, muffling my shouts beneath a hand that outsized my entire face. Still, screams vibrated my vocal cords, the desperation supplying my air endless.

My head shook like a feral animal, jerking backwards in search of a nose to shatter. Dread spiked a cold wash over my skin when all I hit was a throat, the ball of an Adam's apple jabbing the back of my skull.

Husky amusement trickled out of the man behind me, and my gut pulled *hard.*

That wash of stinging cold dropped into my stomach, piling there like a meal undigested and ready to make a reappearance.

That move always worked before.

I gasped like I'd broken the surface of water as the hot hand slipped from my mouth but set beneath my throat instead.

Any voice inside of me shriveled up to dust.

Heather perched herself tall and superior in front of me, watching my struggle with full-hearted glee. "Maybe if you'd been better about shutting that arrogant mouth of yours, you could have avoided all of this."

My voice still cornered behind the threat of the massive hand, my conviction had to do the screaming for me.

"I'm still only processing all of this at like, 50% comprehension, but if you don't think I'm going to tell Dominic every single fucking thing you claim you did, you're even dumber than you think I am."

At that, she laughed.

She laughed, like, for the first time I'd ever heard her make the noise. It sounded like metal, clanking and hitting and making my shoulders touch my ears.

"You still don't get it," she delighted on a sigh. "You're not going back."

Her grin grew wicked, slashes instead of dimples cinching up on both cheeks.

"You're not *ever* going back, and you will never see my husband again. You're dead, Ms. Sanders," she stated simply, veering in close enough that her canines resembled fangs as she whispered darkly, "Just like all the women who came before you from this city."

She pulled herself back, venomous eyes collecting my falling expression as her words sunk in.

'Just like all the other women....'

Case files strewn across a desk back at their house flew across my mind, files with names of missing or dead women from this city and the outskirts. Cases that Dominic broke himself working over, women that Dominic grieved and punished himself over all in search for the sadistic fuck who hurt them.

The sadistic fuck who was standing right in front of me, disguised as pure white arm candy for a man in blue.

Holy fucking—

"Who *are* you?" I screeched, shocked horror a heavy brushstroke in my resonance.

Looking satisfied and disgustingly victorious, Heather stripped a pair of designer sunglasses from their dangling place in her blazer pocket, shelving them over her eyes.

"The wrong woman to piss off."

She cut back to me for a moment, sunglasses balanced on the bridge of her straight nose. Just before she hid those viper eyes behind the shades, she tossed me one purely *villainous* wink.

"Enjoy Hell, Ms. Sanders."

Heather showed me her slight back and trim waist as she stalked back to the car. I ripped open my mouth to scream after her when Becks rounded the van towards me…

A white cloth in hand.

Terror spun through my blood. Charlotte's face spun through my mind.

No.

"No-*No!*" I kicked out, both feet touching nothing but air as Becks got closer with the rag I just knew was soaked in my demise.

Not like this. Not happening. Not now.

The whispering 'just in case' voice was *not* right.

"Layla! Layla, *wake up!* It's Kat—" A fist around my throat closed off anymore cries for help. It squeezed, sticky hot breath creeping down my neck and telling me to stop squirming.

I wouldn't, and I didn't.

I thrashed even as he choked me, shooting my legs out blindly at Becks as he tried to get closer. My hands pawed at the one around my throat, fingers tearing at skin and gouging small chunks off beneath my nails.

The man behind me roared for Becks and crushed my windpipe harder, choking out wet, garbled noises as hoards of black dots split across my vision.

My heart was searing, crying, and trying to escape all at the same time. It wouldn't accept this. It wasn't happening.

This wasn't fucking happening.

I couldn't do this to Charlotte. I couldn't leave her. I *wouldn't* leave her.

Tears leaked lines down my cheeks as I fought for her and for Dominic, for the woman just barely groaning with life on the pavement five feet away. I had a life. I had purpose and passion and *love.*

I had so much love, I was willingly drowning in it, and it was the only kind of death I wanted.

To die of love was to be reborn as something better than yourself.

And that's what Dominic and Charlotte and Layla and Maya did for me. They made me *better.* They made me grateful and warm and totally blissed out on all their love. They were safety and comfort and the four new walls around me I'd resurrected to protect myself.

They were my *home...*

And I was being snatched right out of it.

Coarse fabric scratched along my lips and nose, and I jerked my head to the side away from it, rolling my lips together. Becks dominated over me, his hand crushing the rag over my mouth with rapture lighting up from the backs of his red-rimmed eyes.

The man behind me released his fist around my neck, enticing me to breathe again and suck down the poison on the rag, but I wouldn't. I'd hold my breath until my lungs burst sandwiched between these two giant men.

But then I did—*fuck.*

It was just a tiny gasp, a miniscule inhale in the effort of my fight. Once I breathed in a little though, my greedy lungs couldn't stop. They sucked back air, even if it wasn't sweet but like a hospital room instead, bleachy and tinted with death.

Beck's eyes gleamed with a sinister smile as I coughed and gagged, shaking my head to shake away the flicker in my brain as the chloroform mingled through. It might have been a minute, it might have been five, but a cloud covered my head and darkened all my senses and energy to a muted blur.

Before all lights went out, I forced my heavy lids up to the sky to take in the crisp color of the clouds and committed it to memory... *just in case* I never found myself beneath the most magnificent shade of gray again.

THE EYE OF THE STORM

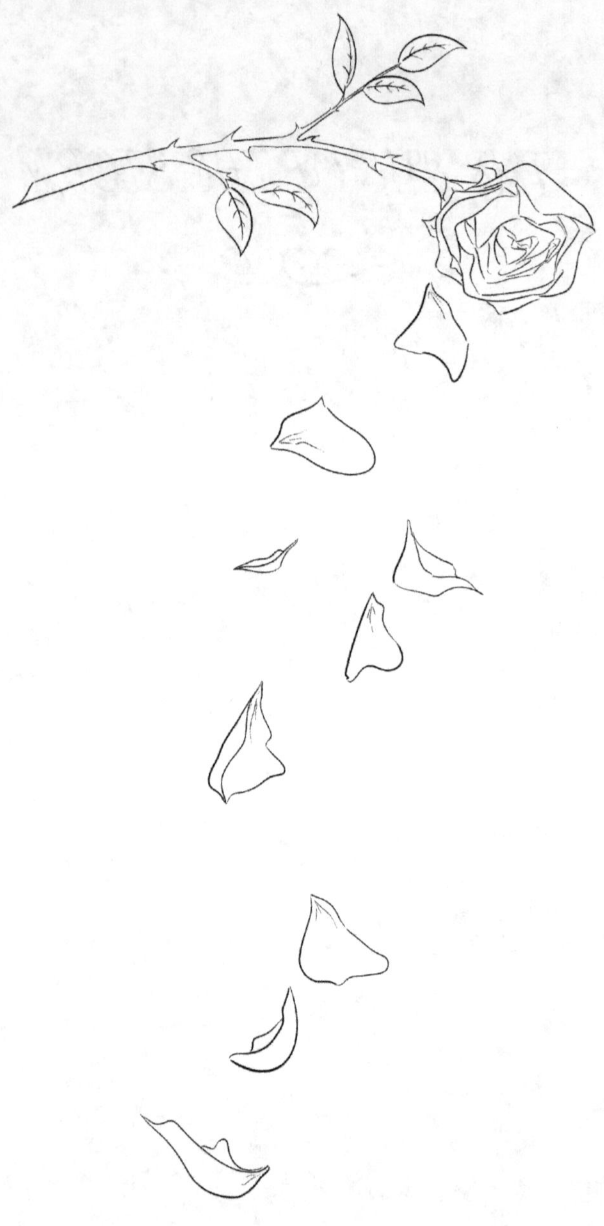

FOURTEEN

<u>DOM</u>

The shower had been running for thirty-six minutes.

I frowned at my watch, leaning a shoulder against the wall outside the upstairs guest bathroom. Kat never took long showers. I imagined it had to do with the scarcity of the dollar bill all her life. Shorter showers meant shorter water and gas bills.

Personally, the daydream of a long, scald-your-skin kind of shower when I got home was sometimes all that kept me upright when the days were hard.

Or, since meeting Ms. Sanders, a very *very* cold one.

Outside the bathroom door, I warred with myself over whether knocking to check in on her was too oppressive after the episode we had downstairs. She told me to back off, but I didn't want to and I didn't plan on it.

I wanted in her space and in that beautiful head of hers.

She was trapped up in that head of hers right now, wading through a swamp of heavy emotions she had no idea what to do with. She wore her feelings so vividly after yesterday, I felt as if I could see them like they were roots wrapped around her chest. Squeezing. Enlivening her fear. Making her want to rip free and run away from them and me.

I'd keep her quick feet on the ground though, right in front of me where she belonged.

My chest felt bruised ever since Ryan's call yesterday with the news about her mom. In fact, I caught myself rubbing my hand over the burrowed pain now while listening to the rush of the shower, hoping it would turn off soon.

I didn't like being away from her.

Not now. Not even before this. I worried about her more than I worried about my own daughter sometimes. Maya wouldn't mouth off to a stranger just because the breeze blew the wrong way or run away from me because the fear in her head told her to, but my spitfire would.

She'd survived hell before this, so I didn't even know what to call what was happening to her now. Whatever it was, she was suffocating in it, and all I wanted was to pull her out.

While Kat was speaking to her sister on the patio, I'd gone up to change out of my rain-drenched clothes. When I came out fresh and dry, the guest bathroom door was already closed, and after a few minutes, the spray of the shower kicked on.

Now, it was nearing over forty minutes since I'd last seen her, and I only allowed one more to tick by before rasping my knuckles on the door and calling out.

"Kat? Are you all right?"

A part of myself I'd pushed down—a *barbaric* part—that she'd seduced awake stirred at the idea that this was all a ploy of hers to get me to come in while she was in the shower, dripping wet and naked…

If it was, I'd have to make sure to lock the door *before* I let her completely overrun my mind again with those vixen lips and hypnotizing bottle-green eyes. This woman did lethal things to me.

She had from the day I met her.

The only response I got was the continued heavy rush of water, not the sweet siren voice I'd happily be dragged to the bottom of the ocean for. Wondering what she was up to, I twisted the knob on the door and cracked it open just enough to get a wash of steam over my face.

Head angled low to resist the urge to peek inside, I tried to coax her out with a dash of humor.

"Did you fall in there?"

Balance wasn't her strongest suit, but I loved catching her when she fell.

The corner of my mouth lowered at the absence of her voice. That wasn't like her. That mouth always had something to say. Usually something wildly inappropriate to make my lip twitch and cock stir.

Worry chewed at my gut as I pushed further into the bathroom, locking eyes on the glossy white shower curtain at the end of it. Steam billowed out of the top of the shower, swollen clouds of it breaking against the high ceiling.

"Kat?" I inched closer, quickly forgetting our house rules as I reached for the hanging curtain. "Are you—"

My words got sucked up in the mist, rising high to the ceiling and out of reach.

It was empty.

The shower was empty, the river-rock floor collecting water where a pair of feet should be standing. I jerked my head back over my shoulder towards the hallway.

Where is she?

I reached in and turned the shower off, the worry in my lower stomach biting down harder. She must have gotten out and forgotten to turn it off. She'd been out of it since yesterday, but that kiss she laid on me in the rain and how she smiled for me afterwards had given me hope.

Maybe that was getting ahead of myself, and as Kat would say, *'really fucking dumb'* to be hopeful.

That's who I was though. I was a hopeful man, who was hopelessly in love with a woman who would very much enjoy pointing out and making fun of that irony.

Charging out of the bathroom, I pivoted towards the room she'd been staying in where the door was already cracked open. Before I got there, a head of blonde curls rushed up the stairs wearing a grin so wide, it took over her entire face.

"Are you looking for Katty?"

My impassioned steps slowed, stopping in front of Charlotte and her giddy smile. My hands came to rest on my hips.

"I am. Do you know where she is?"

She nodded brightly, her tiny hands balling with energy. "But I can't tell you."

"Why's that?"

"Because it's a secret."

My chin tipped low. "Why is it a secret?"

"Because it's a surprise!" she announced with a jump, bursting from her toes to her fingertips with enthusiasm. A short breath of laughter parted my mouth, and I could feel the edges curving up.

A surprise? The concern in my gut smoothed itself down.

I already knew it before, but this just further confirmed that a life with this woman would be one lived on my toes, always wondering what would be around every glorious corner.

Crouching to her sister's level, I touched the bend of my knuckle to her rainbow bright shirt as I attempted to pull hints out of a five-year-old. "What kind of surprise is she planning?"

"I can't tell you because I promised!" *Damn.* Stubborn just like her sister. "You'll see when she gets back!"

The corners of my upturned mouth fell.

"Gets back?" My eyes tracked between hers, a tightness unfolding at my sternum. "She left the house?"

Big brown eyes turned even bigger with fear that she'd just outed her sister's secret. Suddenly, her socks seemed to interest her a lot more than me.

"Yeah… but she said that, um, she would be back soon hopefully."

That last word stuck out like a razor blade, sliding right through my chest.

"Charlotte," Both my hands wrapped around her shoulders, catching her worried eyes with mine. "Where did she go?"

"But it's a *secret*," she croaked out, loyalty contorting her expression.

The backs of my jaw set hard, biting back an exhale and trying to keep my voice free of any frustration even as it swamped me.

"Sweetheart, I know, but I need you to tell me where your sister went."

It was likely the store, the gas station, to pick up lunch maybe.

She wouldn't go anywhere else.

She was rebellious, and *fuck*, I loved and loathed it about her, but she was also whip smart. She was going somewhere to act out, to prove a point, to drive me up the fucking wall, but she wouldn't go anywhere dangerous.

She wouldn't do that.

Charlotte twisted her mouth to the side, peeking up at me beneath her flaxen brows.

"Am I gonna be in trouble if I tell you?"

"No," I reassured her, rubbing my thumbs along her sleeves to try and calm us both. My heart was pounding at this point. "Not at all. I promise. It's just really important that you tell me where she is." *Now.*

Hesitation stretched across her face as she thought it over, and I was practically vibrating with impatience. I needed her to put me out of my misery and tell me something simple. Kat was at the store. She was getting food. She'd taken my credit card and was at the mall downtown to therapy shop.

I wouldn't care. She could spend every cent I had so long as she was safe.

"She said she was getting Layla back," Charlotte said, her voice small.

My thoughts and air pulled to a freeze.

I searched between her eyes for more, but there was nothing there but worried guilt. My lip twitched. I blinked. My tongue touched the roof of my mouth to form words, but that froze too.

Pools of tears welled in soft brown eyes the longer I didn't say a word, her bottom lip quivering. I was scaring her with my silence.

I was scaring myself too.

My head broke the stiff freeze in my muscles to shake side to side.

"She wouldn't."

She would, my instincts whispered.

"She said she just—" A hiccup interrupted the wavering pattern of her tiny voice. "She just wanted to make everyone happy, and I think it's—" Another hiccup. "It's because of Mommy…"

My heart lurched as she wiped beneath her eyes with the back of her hand, big teardrops falling to her chin. "I think she's trying to make everyone happy because Mommy's gone," she whispered softly, giving me her full grieving eye contact.

'I just want to fix everything and don't know how.'

Kat's haunting words from earlier.

Trying to keep the panic out of my tone, I asked, "Did she say anything else? Where she was meeting Layla? When?"

Rolling her salty lips together, Charlotte shook her head. "She said you and Layla and Mrs. Meredith would take care of me until she got back."

The worry in my gut hardened to ice.

She was making long term plans.

I stood, my legs numb as I stared around the room at nothing, my thoughts wild.

What Charlotte was saying didn't make sense. Layla was with Tommy, and no one knew where that bastard was. Even if we did know, Kat would never go to meet him without me. She would tell me if something happened with him, I was *positive*.

Charlotte must have misunderstood. Kat wouldn't leave for something so dangerous without telling me, so it *had* to be a misunderstanding.

"Kat?" I called towards her bedroom, moving towards it in furious strides. "Kat!"

Where was her voice? I needed her voice. I needed to hear her and see her and hold her. Even the notion of a misunderstanding that she'd left me had my skin burning, the idea of her absence hurting every inch of me.

The bedroom door smacked the wall as I shoved it open, my wild heartbeat tearing my eyes across every single inch of her room in search of her wicked smile or spectacular scowl.

Instead of either, my gaze fell to the bed.

To the scrap of legal pad paper laying on the duvet, folded in half, my name scribbled across it in blue ink.

Ice shot through my veins. *Dread.*

My heart was already in my throat as I shot over to it and picked it up, opening it to read.

Dominic,

If you're reading this letter, you're already pissed so there's not much point asking you not to be angry. I'll just say that you can punish me when I get back later in any way you see fit.

(Handcuffs. Please use the handcuffs.)

Anyways, I'm only writing this out on the super super super off chance that what I have planned goes sideways. Tommy called earlier—finally, right?—and he had Layla. She cried and screamed for me. He said the trade between her and me was in less than an hour, and if I told you, he'd kill Layla and then come after Charlotte.

*He was watching me. He knew what both Charlotte and I were wearing this morning, and he threatened **her**.*

The indent of the blue pen drew violently into the paper over 'her', bolding her fury in the one word.

He knew I wouldn't say a word to you if Charlotte was at risk if I did, so I'm writing this letter instead—loophole!

The meeting is behind that sketchy nail salon on Mills, and I've turned on the Location Services on my phone in case anything happens and you need to find me.

I'm bringing all the mace and weapons, and I know Layla and I can take on Tommy. I'm getting her back, and then I'm coming home to you, and everything will be like it's supposed to be.

Everyone I love will be safe.

*And I love you, Dominic. I know I can't say the words out loud yet; I'm seriously dysfunctional, but I do mean them. More than I've ever meant anything. If-**If**—*

Her glorious temper chiseled deep into the paper again.

—Something goes wrong and I don't come back, I just needed you to have it in writing. Those three words. They've terrified me for years, those three words. But it's different with you. Everything is different with you.

Knowing you, loving you, and being loved by you has been the singular greatest experience of my entire life.

I'm gonna feel like a fucking idiot when I get back after having admitted all of this, but I just need you to know. Just in case.

You're my thunder and my greatest addiction. I'm your little lightning and your greatest weakness.

I'll be back, and I'll even promise it because I don't intend on breaking it.

I love you.

(Wow, writing it is so much easier than saying it.)

- Kitten ;)

I read each line twice, three times, a fourth even… and it didn't help. It was just letters all jumbled on a page that didn't *click*. I blinked at them over and over and over again.

A creak at the door pulled the muscles in my neck up.

It was Charlotte. Standing there. Watching me. Eyes wide. Tears shining on her cheeks.

In her big eyes, the message in the note finally cleared… and my free hand shoved into my pants pocket, snatching my phone out. Kat's name flashed across the screen in my contacts, and my heart punched hard behind my lungs as I skipped hers and went right for Ryan's.

He answered on the second ring.

"Hey, man—"

"Go to the salon in Mills street," I barked, folding Kat's note together and sliding it into my pocket. "Kat's doing the trade with Tommy. *Now*."

"*What?*"

I broke into a sprint past Charlotte, racing down the stairs and towards my car. "I'll meet you there, just go!"

Hold on, Kitten.

FIFTEEN

DOM

My Explorer skidded to a stop in front of the salon Kat wrote about in her letter.

The long stretch of road in front of the neon pink shop was deserted as I stepped out of my car, taking every bit of my self control to not slam the door behind me.

Ryan said the Chief ordered me to wait before breaching the property until backup got here, but he'd understand later why I broke the rules for the first time in my years on the force.

Gun drawn down at my side, I approached up the sidewalk in silent steps, ears honed in for any noise and eyes on the lookout for a sprinkle of wavy brown hair over this garbage wash part of town.

Nailz Salon had a front entrance and back, only two points of entry.

Tommy was the type of cockroach who did his dirty business in the dark of the shadows, so I started towards the back, down a narrow alley flanked by graffitied walls on either side.

From my vantage point, all I could see was the side of a beat up dumpster and deep puddles from the earlier shower. I crept down the channel, gravel crunching softly beneath my shoes. Nervous sweat slicked between my palms and the handle of my Glock, the wind as silent as it had ever been.

Glimpsing just around the corner, I caught the blue back end of a vehicle. The color of the car was weathered and sun-worn, each chip in the paint a familiar sight as I rounded the corner and poured into the mouth of the alley.

Her car sat so still, the driver's door open.

Empty.

I ran towards it before the pain of her abandoned car could hit or the notion that running into a crime scene blind wasn't only dangerous but also idiotic. I sprinted towards it, ducking inside and checking every space I could for a sign of her with frantic focus. Her coconut shampoo scent attacked from every angle in the car, swirling inside my chest like a newly formed memory.

A *memory*.

Kat wasn't a memory, though. She was my future and years of it. A lifetime.

In blind pursuit, I even popped the trunk to check for her, growing desperate with every place that turned up empty. The trunk door crashed as I slammed it shut and spun away from the car, running a hand through my hair as I looked out to the open alley for any signs.

A muffled groan arose behind me.

I whipped towards the sound, hope swelling in my chest.

For a moment, all I saw was the dumpster and I bolted towards it, grabbing onto the edges and readying to hoist myself in. Then, another tiny moan from the pile of cardboard boxes next to the dumpster.

I jerked towards the mound of sunken in boxes that, with one passing whiff, told me were soiled in urine. That wasn't the only disturbing find I garnered on my once over of the pile.

Legs.

Fattened boxes covered the rest of the body, but a pair of bare legs lay limp against the mess.

"*Kat*."

Her name rushed out of me, both a tangle of horror and relief on my breath. I was at her side in a second, calling her name again and pushing the damp and torn boxes from her face.

Except it wasn't her face.

"Layla," I sighed, shock and disappointment riding her name.

I wasn't proud of the disappointment, but it drenched my bloodstream in heavy measures and refused to leave. There was also fear. Dreadful, pin-prick cold fear circling my veins, but I refused to acknowledge it.

Just because I found Layla instead of Kat didn't mean I wouldn't find Kat any second now. And when I did find her, she'd kick my ass if she learned I didn't put all my energy into helping her best friend.

I picked up her slight wrist between my fingers and waited for the pump of a pulse.

It was weak, but it was there.

"Layla, can you hear me?"

Doing a scan of her from head to toe to check for injury, I waited for a reply. None came.

"Layla, I need you to squeeze my hand if you can hear me."

I looped mine through hers and counted the beats in my racing heart until the pressure of her response hugged around my hand. "Good. Good, keep squeezing my hand. Ryan and others are on the way."

Speaking of…

The scream of sirens and screeching of tires sounded not too far off, my neck twisting to see red and blue lights paint the streets. I turned my focus back to Layla, her eyes shut and no visible injury on her face.

"Don't forget to squeeze my hand," I encouraged, a graveled edge to my tone as I couldn't help but turn back toward Kat's blue Honda.

The keys were still in the ignition. She was planning a quick escape. Her letter also said she turned on Location Services on her phone, which was smart.

My girl was smart, even when she was doing something that was so goddamn *stupid*.

I'd punish her exactly like she wrote about in her letter when I got her back. *Tonight*. I'd find her by tonight, and the only thing keeping me breathing was picturing her and I back at my new place, buried under the sheets and buried inside each other.

I'd never let her go again after this. Not in a hundred years.

"*Kat…*"

My eyes snapped back to Layla, my pulse tripping over itself.

I hadn't imagined it. Kat's name came from those cracked and pale lips.

"What about her?" I pressed, quickly forgetting the outpouring of officers flooding the scene with us. Layla let out a moan, face contorting to look like she was about to be sick. I secured my fingers around hers tight, putting pressure behind my grip and voice.

"Layla, *focus*. What about Kat?"

I waited several moments for something, *anything*. Nothing came. Instead, her muscles encircled by my hand slacked.

"*Goddammit*," I cursed, dropping her hand to shift my arms beneath her body. I stood, her in my arms as men in blue funneled through the same alleyway I had, clearing a pathway for me as I stormed through.

"Medic!" I barked, spotting the flashing lights of an ambulance parked across the road and heading towards it. The paramedics saw me coming, ripping open the back of the emergency vehicle and pushing a white-strapped gurney out.

I laid her on it, and before I looked up, Ryan was there, panting and gasping over her limp body.

"What the fuck—"

"She was talking when I found her," I clipped, rigid and *barely* holding on.

"What'd she say?"

My head pulled to the side, muscles tensing, teeth skating together against her name. "Kat," I grunted low. "She said Kat."

The air tightened between us.

Two paramedics fussed over Layla, loading her in the back of the ambulance while Ryan and I stood silent. I could feel his eyes on me, burning with pity that I chomped at the bit with ferocity Kat would be proud of.

"Don't stare at me like that." Ryan's eyebrows jerked up on his forehead. "We'll find her. Layla will be able to tell us where she is."

"Officers, we're heading out—"

"I'm coming with," Ryan interrupted. He kept me in his strict line of focus for one second too many, his remorse glaring and premature before pulling himself up into the back of the ambulance. He saddled up next to Layla, scooping her hand up in his.

I watched his affection for her for only a second before the pain in my chest made me look away.

That pain was *also* premature. My palm rubbed over it, trying to knead it away as I headed back down the alleyway and towards Melendez, a man almost twice my age and a damn fine detective.

"What's the status on locating Kat Sanders' phone signal?"

He pivoted my way, hands hanging loose on his belt and brown eyes puzzled. "Says it's here, but we haven't found it."

That wasn't the news I wanted to hear, but I pushed past the feeling that my insides were melting in a quick fire and pulled my phone out of my pocket.

"Let me call it."

Within seconds, her ringtone filled the air and it came from the dumpster.

One of the new patrol officers trying to prove her salt jumped inside, weight vibrating against the metal as she hit the bottom. I was making my way towards her without realizing it until my nose was stuffed with the smell of rotting food and the patrol officer was holding out a black bag in front of my face.

The bag was ringing, and I grabbed it with numbing fingers.

It was one of my drawstring bags that I never used and had stuffed in the guest room closet. One touch said there wasn't much in it. All I pulled out was her phone and an unused can of mace.

Her phone, her mace, but no *her*.

Every inch of my skin started to burn again, the note she'd written hiding in my pocket starting the fire. My heart drummed between my ears, intensifying in decibel every second, drowning out the chatter and people around me.

I turned away from them all, the air thickening around me, making it feel like I was moving in slow motion while my thoughts were left flying. The hope inside me was a balloon and her phone in my hand was the needle trying to pop it.

It was pushing, poking, trying to deflate it and let my panic overrun.

I wouldn't let it, though. Not yet. Kat was a fighter, and a *vicious* one at that. Besides, there were still answers and clues to her whereabouts on their way to the hospital right now.

Knowing Melendez would take charge of documenting the scene, I ran back to my car and started it up, breaking every speed limit as I raced the streets to catch up to the ambulance.

* * *

The waiting room at the hospital wasn't all that full, but the tension in the air was.

Layla's parents and grandparents sat in one corner that Ryan tried to infiltrate while I sat on the opposite end with our Chief of Police, Richard Thomas.

He'd met us at the hospital and had a bullet load of questions to fire my way while we waited for an update on Layla.

The displeasure written into the heavy wrinkles next to Chief Thomas' eyes made me shift in these already uncomfortable hospital waiting room chairs. I'd always respected the guy and admired his dedication to the job. He'd always liked me too… until now potentially.

I went against direct orders today.

The dirty blond mustache hiding his upper lip furrowed. "Did you not receive the orders from Locklin to wait until backup arrived on scene?"

My hands were folded together over my lap. My right leg wouldn't stop tapping.

"I did."

"And you deliberately ignored the order?"

"The information I had was time sensitive, sir."

Chief leaned back, posing his hand that was beginning to liver spot over his chin. The hazel of his stare glinted with suspicion, and I knew with a roll of my gut what question was coming next.

"Detective Locklin said you knew the trade between Layla Montez and Karina—"

"*Katerina*," I corrected, almost immediately regretting my bitter flavor of tone. It was a slip, but a noticeable one. Especially for someone like me who never challenged an authority figure a day in my life. The chief watched me even closer as I swallowed back my frostbite disposition and spoke slowly.

"Katerina Sanders is her name, sir."

"She's your daughter's nanny, correct?"

Technically, no. "Yes."

"The one who almost gave Mueller a heart attack during her interview after the Montez girl was taken?" Amusement tinged his voice, and I curled my fists together.

I supposed it would be amusing to anyone who didn't give a damn about the panic attack Officer Mueller threw Kat into during that interview. I wasn't a violent man, but since meeting her, I'd wanted to lay fists into at least three men's faces.

Her pig of an ex-boyfriend, Detective Mueller, and her father.

I'd never even met her father, but I'd checked him out in the system and was a firm believer that he'd look even more the part of an absent, low-life father with two black eyes.

"That was her, yes."

As I answered, I held his gaze for any signs that he knew more than he was letting on. He'd find out once I handed him Kat's letter, but I had been careless with my proximity to Kat that day during her panic attack. I cleaned her tears and held her close, and I'd been on edge at work ever since, waiting for someone to ask me why.

No one had yet, and it didn't appear as if Chief Thomas was about to either.

"So, did she *tell* you she was about to go off on this trade with Tommy Lynch?"

The dubiety in his tone clenched my fingers together, my thumb reaching out to pet the spot my wedding ring used to be. Habit.

One I was trying to break.

"No, sir. She left me a note."

As I reached for the note in my pocket, I did a rundown in my head of how exactly I could phrase this information so I didn't come off like the opportunistic husband I knew I would. The catalyst for mine and Kat's relationship was one of cliche, and I knew that. Others would judge us, and I knew that too.

For weeks, I wrestled with how much I cared about other people's judgement before deciding I didn't care at all.

Not except for a select few individuals.

My parents, my daughter, and Chief Thomas.

I held the letter handwritten for me between my fingers, feeling her letters, her pen strokes, her brilliant anger through the pages. Hesitating before handing it over, I met the chief's waiting stare.

"Before you read this," I paused, loading up the words. "Heather and I are divorcing."

Shock stretched his eyes. He visibly blustered, and I set my jaw to the side and waited for him to finish reacting.

He liked Heather. From the moment they first met when she came to visit me at work that first week, he'd been keen to her and how she presented herself for him.

Classy, old-fashioned, and a dutiful cop's wife.

At home, she was none of the above and hadn't been in years.

"Well, I'm… I'm sorry to hear that. She's a lovely woman, and I thought you two always made a nice pair."

He dropped his gaze between us to the letter I held protectively in my grasp, his suspicion turning scandalous.

We shared a look where I dared to plead for him not to forget the kind of man I was. He personally hired me over a year ago now out of Atlanta PD, and we'd worked extremely well on both a professional and personal level. My relationship with Kat shouldn't change that.

He took the letter, sitting his back to the waiting room chair and folded it open.

With a tensing jaw, I watched his eyes scan the first few lines. Then, as I knew they would, his eyes blew open and ripped up to me.

"You're *sleeping* with this girl, Reed?"

With a sigh, I shifted forward in my chair and lowered my voice to match his.

"As I said, Heather and I are divorcing, and the papers have already been served. Things with Kat—"

"Your daughter's *nanny*," he interrupted to whisper and scold, his judgement poorly concealed if at all. "Does your wife know this is the reason you're divorcing?"

My jaw locked tight, smartly imprisoning the rise of rage his shallow assumption sparked. "Kat is not the reason Heather and I are divorcing. And no. Heather doesn't know, and I would consider it a personal favor if you kept this information between us. If mine and Kat's relationship were to come up in a court proceeding…"

Chief Thomas paused, idly handing the letter back to me without finishing it. Understanding clouded his muted green stare, and he nodded just once.

"I don't like it, but I also won't start up the rumor mill if that's what you're worrying on about."

I was worried about a lot of things these days, and losing Maya in a custody battle was one that kept me up at night.

"I just never took you for that kind of man, Reed." Chief Thomas shook his head, resting his elbows on his knees and gave me a look like he was seeing me through a new lens, one filthy and smattered in infidelity.

"Sir, it's not—"

"And you're lucky it's just messing around or else I'd have to take you off the case," he went on, wagging his finger and stopping my heart.

"Sir?" I questioned, voice and shoulders stiff.

He waved me off like he was relaying the weather outside. "If your relationship with Ms. Sanders went past physical and you had any type of feelings for her, I wouldn't be comfortable keeping you on the case."

My unblinking expression must have snagged his attention and curiosity, his head angling low and his question spoken as if he was afraid the answer might bite him.

"It is just physical between you two, right?"

My heart that was deeply and passionately in love shouted a profound *'No!'* that threatened to shake the walls of my impassive defense as my mouth said,

"Yes, sir. Strictly physical."

The lie tasted like dirt.

However, I'd done so much lying about my feelings and relationship with Kat that I'd gotten used to the flavor of lies the same way you get used to cleaning a toilet or doing your taxes. You hate doing it, and it makes you a little queasy, but you know you have to so you push through because the end result is worth it.

I pocketed Kat's letter, sending up a quick 'thank you' that the Chief didn't read past the beginning to where she'd penned her love for me down in words.

If the Chief *had* read the full letter, he'd have taken me off the case.

I couldn't risk that.

No one was going to find my girl but me.

Just like I knew it days after hiring her that she could ruin me for good, I knew I'd find her before anyone else.

I *felt* her in a way I never knew you could feel another person.

She was a constant whisper running over my skin, an awareness I couldn't block out. I tried for a while, but eventually, I welcomed it. I welcomed the heightened sense of her presence in any room, her overrunning fruity scent, her electric touch. I welcomed absolutely everything about the way that woman affected me because I knew it was special.

Ignoring that kind of awareness was like ignoring your sense of smell, taste, or sight.

Kat Sanders was my sixth sense. No one would find her before I did.

"Family for Layla Montez?"

Every head but two not with us turned in the direction of the feminine voice. A middle-aged doctor standing with a clipboard did a sweep over all of us, giving a stiff nod.

"She's awake."

SIXTEEN

KAT

Consciousness teetered in and out, swelling high enough to almost break the surface and then dipping back down into fathoms of darkness. It went on like this for who knows how long, my mind rolling in waves, tumbling and drowning, coming to just enough for the awareness to sting, but never enough to escape the density of sleep.

It took forever to find strength over the slumber, my mental footing slippery as I tried to latch onto the present so I didn't get dragged back down to where time didn't exist.

I started by shifting my shoulder, inching it every few seconds to keep myself awake until I was on my back.

Oh fuck, my *mouth*. I lapped my own tongue a few times, wondering when I downed a bucket of sawdust before passing out.

My arms reached above my head, joints popping and muscles stretching deliciously. I let my head fall to the side, a clatter of pain crashing in the back of my skull at the movement and pulling a weakened groan from my dry lips.

How much did I drink last night?

My brain tried to piece together memories of how I'd gotten in this miserable state, but thinking hurt. Like a lot. So I didn't bother and just rested the heel of my palms against my eyes.

"Okay..." My voice was such a pathetic croak. "I can do this."

Charlotte would be needing breakfast soon, and I would be needing water and painkillers.

Lots and lots of painkillers.

Sliding my hands down my face, I finally broke through the cinder blocks weighing down my eyelids, testing their openness with small flutters. My lashes flapped rapidly, glimpses of the guest bedroom coming in flashes.

Except...

My head cocked up at the ceiling, eyes squinting.

What the fuck happened to the ceiling fan? The place where it used to be was smooth and flat, no markings of a fan anywhere to be found.

Pain splintered straight through my forehead, reprimanding me for thinking so hard when it was still so early.

Moaning in exhaustion, I rolled over onto my stomach to check in with the sun's rays that bled in golden light each morning through the window. Depending on how vibrant the beams of ambered hue were would give me a general idea of the time. I was too lazy to get up and check my phone that was charging across the room.

I blinked sleep from my eyes, searching for the sun.

Except...

There was no sun.

Even on rainy days, there was still a muted glow that would stream through.

Okay, no ceiling fan and now no sun. Confusion tangled in the clutter of my head, and I wiggled my way to sitting up so I could make the Olympic stride over to my phone.

Except...

There was no phone. There was no familiar corner of the room with an outlet I used.

There was no familiar... anything.

Dread began to pump, thick beats of it crawling up my chest and clogging my throat. I didn't know these four walls. I didn't know the waist-high bookcase hiding in the corner or the lumpy bed under my ass.

I didn't know anything in this room at all.

Panic pushed my legs out from under the sheets they'd wrapped themselves in.

Sheets. Just sheets on the bed. No comforter like I had at my house or fancy duvet like at the Reeds'. Just scratchy fucking sheets the color of dried blood.

Blood—

—Fighting

Screaming—

—Layla

My manic train of thought slammed to a halt. Air inside my lungs pulled to a stop.

The only thing that moved was my jaw… and it fucking dropped.

"Holy fucking shit," I breathed.

Memories exploded across my brain, painted in a shade of fucked up I didn't even know existed.

Heather. Holy fucking shit, it was *Heather.* Her victorious face came to life behind my eyes, laughing, mocking, spelling out every dirty part she played in this game she pinned on Tommy.

I was a pawn who'd pissed off the queen, and this was her checkmate.

I put my hand to my throbbing head, needing to hold it up with all this heavy bullshit my brain was trying to wade through. My thoughts literally felt scrambled inside my head, trying to make an omelet out of eggshells.

Heather was the one who had targeted me. Heather hired Tommy to fuck with me and mislead the police. Heather's men had kidnapped Layla. Heather was the reason all those girls were taken that Dominic—

Dominic.

My reborn heart caved in on itself, squeezing out whimpers from blood vessels that pumped anew because of *him.*

Because he showed me what it was like to love and be in love, and now my love was in danger. He was married to the criminal cunt he'd been searching for for over a year, and he hadn't one goddamn clue.

My fingers made a grab for the necklace sitting against my collarbone, gripping it like it was Dominic himself and I could pull him through the necklace to right in front of me so I could warn him. My born-again heart screamed for him, ripping my head in every direction of the room, gauging which wall I could bash through so I could run out to him and warn *everyone*.

Fueled by the wild beat of my heart, I stumbled out of the bed, legs shaking as I wobbled on my own weight. My knees felt weak, like the muscles and bones in them had been replaced by soup. I looked down to them like I could x-ray through my leggings to see what was wrong with these stupid knees.

But it wasn't just my knees. My entire body felt… *wrong*.

Restless.

Every nerve-ending electrified and every muscle overrun with fire ants.

I had no other choice than to stretch my legs that were on fire to get the burn out, racing over to one of two doors I saw in the room and tearing it open.

Bathroom.

Simple and white. A shower, a toilet, a sink. With flames for blood, I ransacked through the cabinet below the sink, finding only a vanilla scented shampoo, a toothbrush, and a disposable pink razor.

With a snarl, I slammed the cabinet doors shut, elongating my arms as much as they could go to scratch that burn blazing beneath my skin. The feeling stretched into my hands too as I shook them out, almost expecting to see embers fluttering out of my fingertips.

This was either anxiety or adrenaline or some overloaded cocktail of them both, cooking my muscles from the inside out.

The fire ants had crawled up to my lungs, fucking biting over and over until my chest was aflame with the very same unbearable itch as the rest of my body. Every breath I heaved was an inhale of smoke and ash, but I couldn't stop the breathing.

In fact, I was hyperventilating at this point.

"Where the *fuck* am I?" I hissed, turning in circles in the bedroom of a stranger.

Then, the door on the far side of the room rattled.

I snapped towards it, my on-fire muscles twisting tight.

My best guess said whoever was about to come through that door was here to hurt me, and I had negative time to appropriately prepare. Maybe it was

Heather. Maybe she'd come to kill me. Maybe I could scratch her pretty blue eyes out before she did it.

I didn't know what I would do, but I had to figure it out fast as the knob clicked and turned, and someone came through.

That someone wasn't Heather.

It was a man.

He had his head down as he fiddled with a key ring sitting in his palm, showing me the crown of his dark head of hair. There was some curl to it at the longer ends, particularly over his ears, and it wasn't quite as dark as Dominic's.

Then, he looked up and showed me his eyes.

Which were much, much darker than Dominic's.

I dared to say black.

A reaction of surprise so subtle, it barely registered, rippled across the strong features of his face. Midnight-colored eyes gave me a once over, and I argued with my arms to stay right where they are at my sides and not sweep around my torso like they itched to.

I wasn't afraid of him.

I mean, I *was*, but I wouldn't show it.

"You're up."

His voice was much like his face, unobstructed by any substantial emotion but equipped with a hard edge. And deep. A monotone succession of two baritone words.

The man didn't wait for my reply before ignoring me to go back to the keys in his hand, pulling out a screwdriver from his back pocket. I watched him with his back to me as he messed with the knob on the door, casually changing out screws or bolts or whatever and discarding them in his dark-wash jeans pocket.

I remained near the back wall, the panicked sting in my veins and my overwrought brain colliding in confusion. Why wasn't he coming after me?

No, no—why wasn't he even paying *attention* to me?

I was here against my will, right? There was still a shitload to process, but I was *pretty sure* being chloroformed and waking up in a stranger's bedroom was like the definition of being kidnapped. Him showing me his back for the last half a minute either meant he was really arrogant or really stupid.

It took my lips a good moment to form the words, and even still, they came out stifled. "What're you doing?"

Carefully, his back rose, the fitted black t-shirt he wore stretching over muscles. On a constrained sigh, he answered. "Fixing your lock."

Still not sure, I asked, "Are you a locksmith?"

A beat passed between my question and his answer, a crackle heating the air.

"No."

His one word reply twisted my brows downwards, my confusion performing a quick change into hot-headed and senseless as my lip curled up.

"Then who the fuck are you?"

I needed *Heather*. Not some random asshole who did her busywork.

My lacerating projection hit the air… and his fingers around the door lock stopped.

I caught the pulse of his cheek tightening in his rigid profile. His shoulder blades outlined beneath his shirt had stopped moving too, telling me he wasn't breathing anymore either.

In that freeze of muscle in this total stranger, a wash of regret trickled down my rib cage.

Oh *shit*.

He squeezed the handle of the door, metal squeaking beneath his death grip as he spoke through clenched teeth. "I'm the fuck whose job it is to fix this lock and try to not break the fucking door while doing it."

Restraint vibrated a thin cord in his voice, my eyes blowing wide as the man who'd walked in here dispassionate and disinterested vanished as if he was only ever a shadow to distract.

His fingers were shaking around the bronze knob, and my stomach shifted as I realized how dangerously fast my sharp tongue had frayed the control he was holding onto.

My feet backed until my butt hit a wall, and I started eyeing any and everything in the room I could use to fight my way out in case the thread holding him together snapped.

Maybe mouthing off to complete strangers in this particular situation wasn't my brightest move.

To keep from plucking his cord anymore, I asked him a distracting question. "What's wrong with the lock?"

Another beat.

Another crackle of electricity between answers.

Then, the hollow of his voice carved deep. "It still locks from the inside."

My stomach muscles twisted, contorting in acts of pain-staking terror.

Fuck me.

In that moment, I was actually glad the man wasn't facing me. I didn't want him to see the reaction of a trembling bottom lip I wasn't quick enough to bite down.

I had to get out of here. Like right fucking now.

My arms swept around myself, hands grabbing beneath my elbows. "So is that the plan?" I started, inching closer to the bed set in the middle of the room. "Heather told you to lock me in here until I starve or beg for forgiveness?"

The question came with a force that leveled any quiver that tried to upend my voice. Apparently, it worked twofold: to quell the verbalization of any fear and to garner the attention of the man across the room for the second time.

This time, the surprise holding up his strict expression was more thinly veiled.

"You know Heather?"

He shifted on his feet, pointing the blunt tip of his black shoes my way. Having his full attention curled my toes into the bottom of my sneakers, but I tried to play it off with a normal scoff and deriding comment.

"Yeah, we're *real* close."

The man tightened his focus on me, opinions forming behind brown eyes burning black. My awareness on him was suddenly split between his feet as they came one step closer and his upper lip that quivered as he sneered, "You pissed her off, didn't you?"

My neck reared back, the *accusation* in his tone narrowing my eyes to slits.

"Excuse me?"

"You did something to piss her off and that's why you're here." His dark-eyed focus was so laser-locked on me as I watched him connect dots in his head, each one exciting his spurring contempt more. "It didn't make sense why you were brought *here*, but now I get it." He turned his voice to the floor, muttering sharply, "Now I fucking get it."

"Get *what*?"

Glare flickering up, he chewed his molten rage up and spat it at me through bared teeth. "Now I get why the next four weeks of my life are completely *fucked*."

His fire-breathing anger hit me square in the chest, boiling my own temper to the shallow of my skin.

I *felt* it stirring inside of me like a cheetah emerging from a nap, spine stretching, claws priming, teeth shining with promise in the overhanging sunlight. I could feel her climbing to all fours while a distant whisper got lost in the wind to lay the fuck back down.

"*Your* life is fucked? Are you shitting me? That's the most backwards thing I've ever heard right next to you saying it's *my* fault I'm here and not some psycho bitch's who throws a criminal-sized tantrum when she doesn't get what she wants."

Watch it, the voice of warning whispered.

More outrage pinched the man's mouth tight and wrinkled his nose, dispelling for good any perception I might have had of him as a man unencumbered by emotions. No, he was *ruled* by them as he jabbed a finger my way, fire-hot eyes burning a hole over my parted lips.

"I can bet it's that fucking mouth that got you here."

"And yours is *saintly*," I shot back, the mouth he was so hypocritical about still running defense.

The disoriented whisper tried to calm my temper again, warning that this wasn't smart, to back down, that I didn't know how sharp this lion's teeth were that I'd chosen to maul.

This was a stranger.

This was maybe a violent criminal.

This was a man whose eyes scorched *so* pitch black, they were like piercing screams in the dead of night.

He raked those howling eyes all over my face, his nostrils flaring like he loathed me in the couple minutes he'd known me.

"You've got fire," he said, gravel roughing up the words he let linger on his tongue. He continued to trace my face slowly, like he was savoring that too, taking in the warmth of the flames dancing beneath my skin. When he finally reached my stare, the mirage of warmth evaporated as he finished off his dissection with sobering hostility.

"It'll be gone by the end of the week."

A breath rattled in my lungs, shaking my determination awake and shoving it back into the driver's seat.

"I won't *be* here by the end of the week."

His stare hardened to coal, the corner of his mouth just barely trembling as he lowered his gaze to my chin. He stayed there like there was a fucking poem written on it, the stanzas agonizing and the rhythm offbeat. Eventually, he stalked back to work on the lock meant to keep me prisoner in this room.

I exhaled carefully, not realizing until he was gone how suffocating his darkness was. That man was a storm cloud, threatening doom and evaporating any light he hovered his shadow over. I needed to get away from him and everyone else in this hellhole. This house?

"What the hell even is this place?" I heard myself ask before thinking it through. "And *where?*"

I could be in freaking Mexico for all I knew.

A long pause lingered before he answered, making me wait and making me stew. Not taking his attention off of the lock, he muttered, "The girls will fill you in."

My pulse peaked, anticipation building it higher. "Girls? There are other girls here?"

Like the ones Heather ripped from their homes? Ones trapped like me? Ones I could save?

Pretty faces from the news and laying across Dominic's desk at home barreled through my head. Were they all here, locked in the walls around me waiting for someone to find them?

"Hey, I asked you a question." Annoyance shot an arrow across the room to the man still tinkering with the lock on my door, piercing him as he stiffened up the spine. He didn't answer me though. Just kept fucking with the screwdriver, tightening the bolts to keep me in here.

A scoff catching in my throat, I started towards him, all my good sense occupied somewhere else.

"Hey, I have a right to know—"

"No, you *don't*." A sharp gasp nearly choked me as he sliced around so fast, the air around him chilled. "You don't have any rights anymore, you got that? You fucked up, got yourself put here, and now we *both* have to deal with it."

The shock of his lashing words kept me locked on him, collecting every threatening flicker of animosity that fueled his fire. His heated hatred poked at mine, challenging it as the biggest and baddest in the room.

Except his hatred didn't make sense. Mine? Yup, fully fucking justified, but *his?*

"Why do you make it sound like I'm such a goddamn burden to you?"

"Because you *are*," he bulleted back, not taking a single second to think about it.

Not taking a single second to think *at all* as he trudged at least two paces away from the still open door. My eyes bounced to it for less than half a second, only a glimpse of freedom over his shoulder, but a glimpse was all I needed.

"Then let me *go!*"

I made the move, stupid or brave, limbs flashing in a storm towards the open door.

Did I think I'd make it? Not really. But as the door slammed a resounding *bang* right in front of my face, the whip of the wind it created still stung.

It shattered my very next breath, jolting me back from the white wood blocking my way. A large hand splayed across the wood, long fingers spread wide, the tips a pressurized red, veins bulging beneath sun-tanned skin.

The man hadn't moved aside from his arm, but I had run forward, so I'd brought myself right up to the mouth of the inferno. My blind determination had led me here, close enough to the fire that the hairs on my arms raised against the heat of his scorching gaze.

"Running, fighting, screaming…" He dragged his hard-bitten gaze between mine, the flesh beneath his nose twitching like he was disgusted by what he saw. "It's all useless here."

Give up, he was saying.

Give in, he was saying.

We own you, he was saying.

But I wasn't listening to his threats or his fear mongering. I was too busy picturing exactly how I'd tear this asshole to the ground and take this place with me. This man had clearly kidnapped and threatened plenty of women into a state of submission or tears, but he'd never met a woman like me.

I would never stop running. I would never stop fighting. I would never stop screaming. I'd scream until my voice shattered the walls of this place and the hands that built it were crushed under the wreckage.

I was a tenacious motherfucker, and the only man I submitted to was made of thunder and silver eyes.

This man of fire and raven eyes in front of me was beginning to see just that. In the thinning of his lips and twitch of his cheek, he realized Heather maybe hadn't filled him in on the handful I'd be during my stay at the Hellhole Inn.

Which, fingers fucking crossed, wouldn't be the four weeks he mentioned.

Dropping his big hand to the knob, he fisted the damn thing and jerked it open, not sparing me his final glare.

"Stay in your lane, keep your head down, and stay the fuck out of my way."

Then he left, slamming the door shut on his way out…

The lock shifting into place from the outside.

SEVENTEEN

<u>DOM</u>

"Nothing?"

"Nothing," Ryan confirmed.

"A week with the suspects and she remembers *nothing*?"

Ryan pinched his mouth tight, warning rising to high-tide in his blue eyes to watch my words. I took his glare in with a sigh, turning away from him with a hand roughing up my hair that was already falling out of sorts just like I was.

I'd been waiting outside Layla's hospital room for over half an hour between the emotional and noisy reunion with her parents and Ryan going in next as 'family', not as police. He promised before he went in that he'd come out with answers, but instead he'd come out and handed me nothing.

"She was blindfolded whenever they moved her and was kept in one room the entire time."

"Were there windows?"

"She said no."

"What about people she interacted with? She was fed while she was there, so *someone* fed her."

"*Barely.*" Another warning flashed over his face. "She said some days, she didn't eat and some days, she'd find some fruit waiting on a bookcase inside the room when she woke up. She slept for most of the day."

Sleep.

How in the hell anyone slept through their trauma, I'd never know. I knew a lot of people did it just to get through the days, but I couldn't get my brain to shut off long enough to even come close to sleep when something large was disrupting my world.

I had to work and push and *fix* whatever was wrong. I couldn't go to sleep and hope it would all be better when I woke up.

"What about the phone call with Tommy?" I pressed, hanging my hands on my waist standing in the middle of the hallway. "Kat says in her letter that she heard Layla screaming for her during the call."

Ryan released an exhale, shaking his head and looking anywhere but at me. "Man, you *know* there's no way she remembers him with all the shit they pumped into her. They had to flush her system just to get her conscious."

The disregard with which he plucked at the lasting feathers of my hope readied what I could only describe as a growl in the pit of my throat. Yes, I felt *animalistic* at every growing second without Kat or any answers to where she might be.

My heart was racing, sweat building on the back of my neck, my skin itching like there was something crawling beneath that wanted out.

Pivoting away from Ryan, I pinched my thumbs over the bridge of my nose and tried to level my breathing.

The same people who, by doctor's terms, said 'Ms. Montez had been injected with enough heroin to take down a man twice her size' now had their hands on Kat. They could be injecting her bloodstream with enough of her mother's drug to take her away from me and her sister at literally any second.

This second.

Or this second.

Or this one.

Layla's survival was a miracle, her doctor said, and only because we'd found her so fast. Other than the attempted overdose, all she'd come away with was some mild bruising.

It was still too much. A bruise on her meant a bruise on Kat, and I was only one more warning look from Ryan away from putting my fist through a wall. I had to move. I had to get my hands around something they could squeeze until it popped.

"We have enough with Kat's letter to bring Tommy in to question him at least." Reaching for my walkie strapped to my belt, I ripped it free and up to my mouth. "All officers advise, we're issuing an APB for the suspect Tommy Lynch. Again, that is Tommy Lynch. Report when you have a confirmed hold on the suspect."

Stuffing the walkie back in place on my belt, I moved back around to Ryan to find him watching me. Concern was set firm beneath his rigid brows, and I allowed us a moment of eye-contact that didn't require words.

The look gave more meaning than any words could.

Sniffing sharply and dropping my stare to the floor, I swallowed the thickness that had grown in my throat over the last few seconds. There wasn't time for that or time for standing around in a hospital with a victim who couldn't help me or Kat.

There was only one man who could get me the answers I needed now, and I'd squeeze them out of his goddamn throat if I had to.

* * *

In less than an hour, Tommy was in our custody.

Which was alarmingly fast.

He'd always been slippery to pick up, but the officers who'd found him said he was waiting for them in one of his known locations down by the docks. They said he offered to come in willingly.

Tommy was now sitting only fifteen feet away behind a quarter inch of glass. He'd been in the interrogation room by himself for over thirty minutes, and not once had he let that smug smirk on his mouth falter.

I wanted to take my fist and fucking wipe it off for him.

"You sure you wanna talk to him? I can get Melendez—"

"I'm sure," I cut Ryan off, flexing my fingers at my side. Tommy hadn't taken his shark eyes off the two-way glass since he'd been put in the room. He knew I was out here.

He also knew where Kat was.

I'd tangoed with the bastard in these walls exactly six times over prior incidents, and not once had I been able to pin him down. Technicalities or a lack of evidence had let him wriggle free before, but not this time. We had Kat's letter, heroin in Layla's system—a drug he'd been linked to but not proven to deal—and a couple patrol officers were checking on the alibi he'd given when he was being driven down to the station.

That alibi would fall apart, and he'd fall right into my lap.

Determination boiled the undercurrent of my blood, Kat's mischievous eyes streaking a line of green rage across my mind.

My heart squeezed, and then my fists. "Let's go."

Ryan clapped me on the back. "Let's finish this fucker off fast so I can get back to the hospital."

The way my teeth pinched and jaw stressed made me glad I was walking away from him. He was happy to have Layla back, I got it. We all were. But we only had her back at the expense of Kat, and that was a loss I expected him to take seriously.

If it took the rest of the day and into the night for Tommy to break, then we were staying in this 8x10 box until stars poked holes in the sky tonight.

I wasn't walking out of that room with anything less than the exact coordinates of where I would find her.

My little lightning, as she so appropriately named herself.

The door leading into interrogation room C squeaked as it always did whenever it opened. The noise, however, had never seemed more fitting than with the biggest vermin in South Carolina sitting snug in the middle of it.

Tommy Lynch twisted his thick neck my way, a smile that *never* reached his eyes stretching from cheek to cheek.

"Detective Reed."

I hated a lot of things about Tommy Lynch. So much in fact, my hate-loving girlfriend would be proud. His smarmy face that was misleadingly average-looking, the soul that was missing from his eyes, the fact that he was always wearing some worn out 80's rock band t-shirt.

What I hated most though was how he said my name.

Like he knew a secret of mine and was hiding it between the letters.

The sound of it today set my jaw to the side as I charged up to the metal table, hating him the closer I got. Tommy arched one of his salty gray eyebrows. He was only thirty-nine, but he'd been silver-haired since I met him.

"Uh oh. You don't look too happy." He jumped his focus behind me to Ryan. "Kid, what's wrong with pretty boy?"

Ryan brushed by me, grabbing and yanking out his chair on our side of the table. "All right, why am I *Kid*, and he's Detective Reed?"

My hand tightened around the back of my own chair as I pulled it out, mentally sighing at Ryan. Tommy's grin deepened, leaning with his arms across over the table.

"Because he's my favorite."

I lowered myself into the seat as Tommy reclined back in his, arms still folded and soulless gleam targeted on Ryan. His forehead drew fleeting grooves as he jumped his browline up and added, "Plus, you lean more towards man-child than actual man."

The second thing I hated most about Tommy was when he was right.

Ryan was a good partner and better friend, but his downfall was maturity. It couldn't have felt good on Ryan's pride that even the lowest of the low knew it.

"If I'm such a child then—"

"That's enough," I broke in, handing Ryan a warning look. He rolled his mouth together, and I watched his ego battle it out over his face before he sank back in his chair and conceded to behaving for this interview.

Less than a minute into it, and my patience was already zapped.

Sighing deeply, I shifted to pull my phone, keys, and walkie from my pockets and belt, setting them with a controlled clink on the metal tabletop.

The two others in the room were silent while they waited for me to say something, and the silence only reminded me of Kat.

She hated silence so passionately. She was willing to let that wild mouth of hers say anything to avoid it, and in my days of denial about us, I was truly and honestly afraid of what would come from between her lips next. As the weeks went on, not only did I come to crave the weaponized words she'd wield to destroy me and the silence, but filling the silence with her became the best part of my days.

Laying both my palms flat against the chill of the table, I massacred that loathsome silence just for her.

"Where's Katerina Sanders?"

Her name shook the room like she shook my world. A twinge dug inside my sternum, and in that moment, I missed her like she really was gone. Like I wouldn't be seeing her tonight or even tomorrow.

"*Wow.*" Tommy kicked back, resting his ankle over his knee. "Now that's gotta be a pretty woman to have such a pretty name. *Katerina,*" he tested her name out, like he was taking it for a fucking joyride.

My fingers twitched to smash his face into the table so the teeth he needed to properly say her name were knocked right out.

Perfection like hers didn't belong in the trash.

"Is she as alluring as her name, Reed?"

"You know *exactly* what Ms. Sanders looks like."

My hand shot to the folder Ryan brought in with us, flipping it open and grabbing the photo sitting on top. I shoved it towards Tommy on the table, showing him what he looked like photographed in black and white entering the grounds of East Lions High School.

"Why were you trying to pull Katerina Sanders' school records two weeks ago?"

He touched his fingers to the corner of his glossy photo, spinning it his way and pretending to act surprised. "Oh, yeah. Forgot about that 'cause they wouldn't give 'em to me."

"What did you want with her school records?" I paused, the words left unspoken darkening the pitch of my voice. "We both already know you know where she lived."

Those dead-inside eyes met mine across the table, flashing to say he heard what I didn't say. Then he fucking shrugged.

"I was just following orders."

"From who?"

He inhaled through his nose that was still so straight, it didn't make sense how no one had broken it for him yet. Sitting all the way back in his chair, he thumbed the bottom of his chin, a glint to his vacant eyes as he stared me dead in the face.

"Now that I think about it… Sanders was a looker. I got to see her Junior yearbook photo." He winked at me, and I heard the symphony of his nose cracking in my head. "She was a beauty even then. Long raven hair, pretty little face. Just my type."

The itch was back beneath my skin. That feeling, animalistic and feral, scratching at my composure. The feeling wanted out. It wanted me to reach across the table and put my hands around Tommy's neck until his lips cracked blue.

Kat said he knew about our relationship in his first phone call. I couldn't figure out how he knew until she wrote in her letter that he'd been watching her.

He'd been watching us.

Wondering exactly *what* he saw was the current madness roiling in my blood. How much did those shark eyes see of moments that were privately ours, stolen from the real world where we weren't allowed to hold or kiss or love each other.

Not yet, anyways.

Not knowing how many of Kat's sunshine smiles he'd thieved for himself or heavy teardrops of hers he'd watched me clean away enhanced that scratch under my skin to a violent *burn*. Tommy hadn't taken his eyes off me, watching the invasion of him in my world cook me alive from the inside out.

He slid his stare from me over to Ryan.

"Your boy seems like he's getting a little red in the face. Something happen to the young Ms. Sanders?"

"Answer his question," Ryan snapped back and shut him down. "Who gave you the 'orders' to pull Kat Sanders' school records?"

"That'd just be bad business to tell. Sorry, Kid."

A heat wave of anger burst out of Ryan next to me, torching the savage burn eating away at me hotter. I tried to breathe through it like I did back at the hospital, ignoring the smoke rising and clouding my head of what was right with everything I wanted to do to Tommy for coming anywhere near Kat.

"You called her," I stated, voice flat and dry.

He swerved his head to the side. "Did I?"

"You know you did. One week ago. I was standing right in front of her when you called."

He sat forward, his whole body invested and mocking. "How'd you know it was me?"

My hands on the table retracted, one fitting over my mouth and the other hiding beneath the table on my thigh. It started as a fist but ended in a vice grip over my knee, squeezing it until my bones whined because I just needed to grab *something*.

Tommy may be vermin, but he wasn't dumb. He knew I didn't have anything other than Kat's word to back up the claim that it was him who called her. If I did, I would have thrown him face first into a jail cell by now hoping his nose finally caught that crack it deserved.

Another tactic unfurled in my head as I held a stare so cold, my lashes could catch frostbite.

"You said I'm your favorite?" I drawled, the words muffled by my fingers resting against my lips.

He shifted in his chair, getting comfortable. "You flattered, Reed?"

The corner of my eyes twitched, a chuff pushing through my nose. A minuscule reaction to fuel his inflated ego. Breathing deep, I moved my hand over my mouth to rest my knuckles beneath my chin.

"Is that why you targeted Ms. Sanders? Because I'm your favorite and you wanted my attention?"

A ribbing grin peeled up his face. "What does the little lady have to do with you?"

"She worked for me, but you already knew that."

My reply was cool and fast, and now Tommy and I were finally playing the same game.

"Now what's a married man doing hiring a girl that looks like that to work for him?"

"Did you target her because she's attractive or because it would make my life difficult if you went after my employee?"

"Employee?" He scoffed the word like he didn't understand it. Then, he dropped his focus to my left hand supporting my chin. It took every bit of restraint I had not to curl my fingers into the palm, knowing exactly what he was looking for. "I don't know, Reed. I wouldn't take my wedding ring off for just an employee."

Burning clawed up my scalp, sweat building on the back of my neck.

Beneath the table, my kneecap screamed from the pressure my hand was crippling it with.

"That's enough of the meandering bull, Tommy." Ryan's interjection couldn't have come soon enough. "We *know* it was you. You had connections to her mom, you called her, you tried to abduct her once but got *my* girlfriend instead, and today you finished what you started by taking the girl you wanted in the first place. We've got you. We've fucking *got* you."

The wiser part of me pictured me putting a hand on Ryan's shoulder and telling him to rein it back. Except the part of me that was purely primal was being smoked out by the fire in my chest that rampaged for *her*.

Kat was a wildfire, and I was the forest she'd set ablaze that would burn for an eternity for her.

Feigning innocence at Ryan's outburst, Tommy touched his palm back to his chest. "I have no idea what you're talking about, Kid. I was at the Seafood Shack all day until your boys picked me up."

"*Bullshit.*"

Cold black pupils cut over to me as I spit the first flame out, a genuine recoil of shock over his face.

"*Woah*, Detective Reed." A goddamn smile touched his mouth that my knuckles begged to smear away. "I always knew there was a streak'a passion in you. Just took the right kinda woman to bring it out."

"*Where* is she?" I pressed, needing this to end now—needing *Kat* now.

"Your wife know about her?" He blew right past my question, pointing a knobby finger at me, and let his arrogance trickle out in spine-curling chuckles. "Oh, I bet Christmas will be a blast at the Reeds' this year with the wife *and* the tail you're keepin' on the side."

I lowered my hand from beneath my chin to a hard-knuckled fist on the table. "You sure running your mouth right before patrol gets back and blows a hole right through your alibi is the smartest idea?"

Empty eyes glinted. "Oh, that ain't gonna happen."

"Oh, I'm very sure it will."

A stubborn line tethered between our locked stares, severe confidence gripping my voice and heart. Tommy's head began to shake, loosening his neck up with a long inhale.

"Man, I feel sorry for you, Reed. I really do."

"Your pity is noted."

He sniffed loudly, slouching back in his chair. "What's that thing all cops say about missing girls?" He shoved his tongue across his front teeth. "Something about the first forty-eight hours or they're dead, right?"

My airways narrowed as his glare did the same.

Was that a threat?

The way my chest tightened and breaths started coming and going faster and harder said a definitive *yes*. He'd just threatened Kat. To my face. My heavy breathing grew louder, shoulders rising as I held the stare of the man arrogant enough to do such a stupid thing.

The man arrogant enough to hide my girl from me and think I wouldn't tear a hole through the universe to find her. The man who wasn't a man at all, but a *monster*. A monster who'd likely *touched* her, *hurt* her, *scared* her.

The beast slanted his head. "You okay there, Reed?"

"I'm *fine*," I snapped, teeth clenched hard.

Kat's wildfire flame burned my chest hotter, burned my self control *brittle* thin.

Tommy came forward in his seat, excitement sparking his eyes brighter than New Years Eve fireworks.

"How long's it been since your girl disappeared?"

My fist slammed against the table, metal vibrating the air and sending out a warning signal.

"*Quiet.*"

Tommy heard the warning like an encouragement though, leaning even closer to the detonation he was stoking, gasoline pouring between his yellow-stained teeth.

"Must have eaten up at least a quarter of that precious time already."

"*Dominic...*" Ryan's voice was a cautionary tale dulled beneath the crackling flames between my ears. It got noisier and noisier, my nerves breaking and snapping one by one, the temperature in my head reaching nuclear levels.

With a spark in his eyes, Tommy ignited the explosion.

"You gonna go back to the misses if this one turns up dead?"

Heat erupted across my chest, a fucking growl tearing from the hellfire in my soul.

Ryan shouted as I shot up from my chair, arm rearing back with a battering fist at the end of it. He locked himself around my shoulders, jerking me away.

"Dude, don't!"

"*Where is she?*" I slammed both fists to the table, roaring as Ryan yanked at my body with his whole weight to keep me from breaking through the table and shaking Tommy's throat until Kat's whereabouts fell out of it.

Laughter echoed around the room, coming at me from all angles like a haunting as I fought towards the beet-red face of the thing supplying the ghostly laugh.

"He's not worth it, man," Ryan grit out with force. "He's not worth it!"

Tommy clapped along and chimed in, goading Ryan to let me go.

"Come on! I wanna see what Reed has in him!"

Ryan shoved me back and I let him, catching myself in a few steps. He held up his hands in front of me, breathing hard.

"Dude, *stop*. He's pissing you off on purpose."

"I know," I breathed harshly.

"And you're letting him."

Roughing both hands back through my hair, I snapped, "I *know*."

Suddenly, the door behind us burst open and two pairs of eyes fell on the scene. Ryan, huffing and holding his arms up to barricade me back; me, looking like a bull ready to take down a china shop; and Tommy, tickled pink at the whole thing.

"Detectives…" The newer officer who'd jumped into the dumpster earlier to retrieve Kat's bag stepped forward, expression cautious on us both. "Everything okay?"

"It's fine." Ryan answered for me, daggering me a glare.

The second officer jumped in, bushy-eyed and misreading the energy in the room.

"Good news! We just got back from checking Mr. Lynch's alibi, and it checks out."

I only saw a flash of Ryan's expression breaking in shock before I whipped around to the female officer.

"*What?*"

She staggered back even though I was sure she didn't mean to. Fear spliced into the umber of her stare. Any other time I might have felt a slap of guilt over intimidating not only a new officer but a female officer at that, but I wasn't thinking about powering down my dominance at the moment.

I was just thinking that the words that had just come out of her partner's mouth had to be wrong.

She blustered and fumbled over her breath, cutting a '*save me*' gaze back to her copper-haired friend who was leaving her out to dry.

"Sir, uh, we talked to four people working at the Seafood Shack, and they all confirmed Mr. Lynch was there since open."

I sliced a sharp look back to her partner to confirm. They had to be wrong.

The man shrunk smaller than a pebble in the ocean, speaking even tinier.

"It wasn't him."

Denial pumped between my ears, mouth drying out. "That's not possible."

On heavy feet, I turned back to Tommy, finding him with his arms spread wide and the grin peeling from ear to ear even wider.

"It wasn't me."

EIGHTEEN

KAT

There wasn't a clock or window to gauge the time of day or how long I'd been in this room, but the ache of hunger gnawing in my stomach felt like it had been a year.

A full fucking year without a scrap of food. In reality, it had probably been around a day, but my stomach didn't want to hear that bullshit. It only wanted to hear the moans of its own pain and desperation for something to chew on.

I'd gone hungry before like when my mom forgot to pack me a lunch or there wasn't money for a lunch *to* pack.

Even those times, I'd steal a bag of chips from the kid next to me or give the lunch lady my best argument for why I deserved a snack pack that day. Mrs. Sherry would always cave and swipe me a chocolate cup except on the days where she handed me a stupid fruit cup instead and told me, "You'll thank me when you're still skinny in ten years."

Well, Mrs. Sherry. I'm *still* skinny, and I'd *still* like my damn chocolate snack pack.

A groan rolled me over into a ball on the bed, clutching at my empty stomach and wondering for about the billionth time if I had the strength to make it to the bathroom to lap water out of the sink faucet like an actual cat.

Kittens who got too curious and got themselves locked up in a cage really

231

didn't get preference between Aquafina water or sewage water.

It was stupid of me to expend so much of my energy banging on that locked door for hours before giving up. I shouted to anyone who would listen, kicked at the door with both feet, and one time even sang the entirety of *'Memory'* from Cats the Musical.

Mom loved the show and would play the record on repeat before Dad smashed our record player one night. We used to sing it together in dramatic fashion, and I hoped my mom was looking down on me as I sang our song as loud as I could, hoping someone's ears in this place would bleed enough to come in and stop me.

No dice.

Another violent cramp chewed through my gut, the acid boiling around at the bottom of my stomach folding the feeling of pain into the feeling of, "Oh fuck, I'm gonna be sick."

Huffing, I turned my face into the only pillow on the bed, breathing my own day-old breath back into my lungs and trying to swallow back my gag reflex.

I needed a toothbrush.

Scratch that. I needed an entire bottle of Listerine to gulp down. That way I'd be minty fresh *and* I'd probably pass the fuck out.

As I was contemplating death by mouth wash and dreaming of the fresh peppermint taste on my tongue, the door across the room jammed.

The slow-pumping organ in my chest jammed next.

Seconds later, the lock unclicked and a man strode through. *Another* man.

Not Heather. Not the asshole from earlier. Another person entirely.

"How many freaking jackasses work for this lady?" I wheezed, sitting upright in bed.

A throbbing detonated behind my forehead, my brain beating like it had a heartbeat. My eyes squeezed shut, squinting through the pain that spiraled up the cords in the back of my neck.

Hunger headaches were such a *bitch*.

The man across the room was big. So big, the bed I was on vibrated with every step he stomped over to me. My headache rattled with his heavy steps, head falling into one hand to stabilize the pulsing pain while I used the other hand to scurry back from the man coming my way.

His face screamed murder, and my heart screamed for him to get the fuck away from me.

"You know you're a noisy bitch, right?"

An honest to god shiver shuddered up my spine at the serrated sound of his voice, the husk of it gravel at best, knives in a blender at worst.

"I've been called worse if you're trying to hurt my feelings."

The man scoffed a broken curse not in English right before he swung one of his huge hands towards my ankle.

My heartbeat skyrocketed a scream right up my throat.

"Get off!" I yanked my leg away, tumbling off the bed ungracefully. I snapped up, pain breaking like an egg and spreading down the back of my skull with the sudden movement. My legs holding me up were fragile twigs trying to steady a waning tree, but I managed to retreat back to the furthest wall.

I stood with my feet apart, breathing in ready for an attack and mentally going over what Dominic told me about breaking someone's nose if they came at me from the front.

Heel. Nose. Heel. Break the fucker's nose.

"Fucking come *on*," the guy whined, sliding his giant hand down his face that was almost too angular to be human. "Boss wants to see you, so either I take you walking or I take you kicking and screaming over my shoulder. Those are your choices, girlie."

My fight or flight adrenaline sloshed to a rest, shoulders dropping.

I blinked. "Boss?"

Heather's still here?

"Yeah, so lets go." He jabbed a thumb back towards the stretched open door, freedom and vengeance calling to me sweetly. The cloying pair rolled over my shoulders, burrowing their sweet encouragement between my ears and whispered how *perfect* an opportunity this was.

Getting a second face to face with Heather would be like getting a second chance to get the upper hand and *win* this time. I didn't know exactly how I'd win just yet, but coming up with half-assed plans on the fly was sort of my gift.

Lets fucking go.

* * *

So, I was in a house.

No, I was in a *mansion*.

Rooms stacked on top of rooms lined the first hallway I was led down.

'Led' was also a loose term where *dragged* would have fit much better. My shoulder whined as this new guy lugged me down the hallway by my upper arms, his hands uncomfortably hot and inhumanly large.

I clocked at least four closed doors—presumably more bedrooms—as I was yanked to the corner end of the beige carpeted hallway. We curved around it, spilling out into the mouth of a zigzagging staircase. My feet wobbled, eyes sucking into the back of my head as I realized we were up at least one story from the ground floor of this hell house.

Light split across the ceiling in rainbow shards, drawing my neck up to the very point of it to drink in the sight of a chandelier so big, I couldn't be sure it didn't have its own gravitational force.

It was either that or the common sense in my feet had dulled as they took each step down the staircase willingly.

This place was *massive*.

Gaudy as all get out with decorations so pretentious they could rival a few in the Reeds' house, but massive nonetheless. I always knew Heather had deep pockets, but this was *ocean* deep territory.

My entire home could fit in the foyer we descended on the first floor.

Maybe even twice.

"*Hey,*" I hissed, bowing back into the pain twining up my spine as the monster of a man twisted my right arm back. "That fucking *hurts.*"

He grunted and pulled the same move with my left arm, securing both behind my back in a way that cracked a wince across my face. My sneakers fell over one another as he shoved us forward, growling at me to walk straight.

"Kind of hard to walk straight when you're fucking shoving me," I pitched over my shoulder, putting one foot blindly in front of the other.

Another curse in another language got muffled beneath his breath as we walked. I ignored trying to figure out what language it was to focus on everything I passed as we toured the house.

Two gargantuan front doors were nestled side by side at the front of the foyer, their wood darker than the souls of everyone who worked here. Right past them on their left was another door, but these were French in design.

We sunk deeper into the maze, pushing a turn towards the back. My eyelashes blinked in fast shock as a kitchen fit for a fancy hotel and not some house jarred into frame.

Then… sweet *sweet* sugar.

The aroma of it stuffed up my nostrils, tying a candied high around my brain that made my mouth salivate in seconds. My parched lips split, a cry for food sitting in the back of my hungry throat.

Then, something more important than all the sugar and food in the world slid into view.

Jet black hair peered around the edge of the kitchen, a limp rag in hand.

A *woman's* hand.

Oh my god—

"Hey!" I shouted, jerking all my limbs in her direction. "Hey, help! Hey, call the—"

A terrible screech shredded through my cries for help, my head flying back to scream at the ceiling as the hands around my arms crushed like they were trying to burst my bones back to dust.

"You don't talk to Theresa unless you're spoken to *first*," the voice of knives snarled in my ear.

He didn't even give me a chance to recover. He just shoved us forward until the kitchen and the woman named Theresa passed us by in exchange for another length of hallway.

We had to have been getting close to Heather now, and my brain had just been taken for a dizzying spin. I was all out of sorts, not thinking fast enough to log what I was seeing as he dragged me along, not coming up with that half-assed plan my freedom was banking on.

I was dumbstruck and malfunctioning as we reached the end of the hallway and stood before a tall door. There wasn't even a chance to open my mouth and protest before the man tapped his knuckles against it, the sound unnerving the emptiness in my stomach.

"Come in," a voice rang out. A *female* voice.

Cold swept the spot on my arm he'd been strangling as he lifted it towards the door, turning the knob in his mammoth hand.

It swung open, pieces of a darkly decorated office sweeping into view.

The air in the room crept its claws out, scraping the smell of sweetly sick cigar smoke and mahogany against my nostrils.

Somewhere in my subconscious I noted the missing smell of gardenias.

My sneaker rose off the floor, hesitating for a *fraction* of a second before the oaf behind me let a curse roll off his foreign tongue and thrust both hands against my back.

With a sharp gasp, I went tumbling into the room, feet working to catch my fall so the first time I saw Heather again after all of this wasn't with a mouth full of floor.

"Mother*fucker*," I seethed, snapping my neck around to the closing door to give a homicidal glare to the asshole shutting it. The click of the door ricocheted around the office, such a tiny noise to signal such a monumental confrontation.

Again, I was sans *any* type of plan for what to say or what to do to the 'boss', but I'd always heard you didn't need anything more than balls to trap a venomous snake.

And I had ovaries of goddamn steel.

Lip sheathing my sharpened teeth, I flicked my shield of hair over my shoulder, lightning burning a scraping fire up my throat.

Both my curling lip and ready-to-strike lightning died immediately as I laid eyes across the room.

Confusion rose beneath the ashes of my dead reactions. Two pairs of eyes observed me across the space, one from behind a semi-circle desk providing the smell of rich mahogany that perfumed the room, and the other perched on the edge of the desk.

"Who are you?" I breathed, stare switching between their strict expressions.

The one behind the desk was a man probably in his sixties, ghost gray hair retreating from his five-finger forehead, and eyes of brown that'd been smothered of most of their vibrancy. They were deadened as they tracked down my length, taking stock of every inch of me with a pinched scrutiny.

He had that expression of someone solving a really long math problem in their head, and I wondered with ice in my gut exactly what numbers he was working with and what they had to do with my body.

The woman leaning her blush pink, pressed skirt against the corner of the desk crossed her ankles, stealing my attention towards her feet.

Holy shit, was she wearing *pantyhose*? I thought we as a society decided those rip-prone contraptions were awful? My appraisal went up to her face that was tacked with too much makeup to hide the fact of her age, rouge that was too dark marring her high cheekbones and lipstick a peachy pink painted on her thinned lips.

The skin around her mouth was wrinkled and tight in a contradiction I'd wager money on was the result of too many needles in her face. It was just like the crows feet next to her glacial eyes…

Familiarity lurked in the shadows of my brain, whispering behind faded memories.

My head cocked, stare narrowing on the blue-eyed woman.

"Why do I know you?"

Conceit leveled her chin higher, withering sapphires reducing my worth to pennies beneath the pointed tip of her nose. Dulled memories began to sharpen, struggling to rip forward and be recognized.

The two strangers just kept *staring* at me, the silence in the room loading up like pop rocks behind my anxious teeth until I spit them out in a not-so-sweet explosion.

"Are either of you going to say anything or are we all just gonna stand around with our dicks in our hands?"

Impatience jutted my head forward, waiting for one of them to respond.

Heavy-coated black lashes rolled in a fit, a click of the woman's tongue echoing off all four walls. She drew her gaze back to the man behind the desk, a secret passing between them as her thinly plucked brow arched and his mouth gave a tilt.

"You were right."

The woman preened. "I know."

My neck stretched even more, sticking out like a goddamn giraffe trying to get closer to the point of this meeting.

"Does anyone wanna fill me in or can I just go?" I kicked a thumb back towards the door, hooking up a brow with enough attitude beneath it to crush this place back to rubble and insects.

"No, Ms. Sanders." The man behind the desk sighed my name, intolerance elongating each syllable. "You cannot *just go*. A lot of resources and effort were put into getting you here."

"For me?" My hand aimed back towards the door changed to touch the fingertips to my shoulder, really leaning to the mocking flattery. "Sounds like a lot of effort for a little payout."

"Oh, it won't be little, Ms. Sanders." Muddy brown eyes flickered with savage promise. "I can assure you of that."

Bits of information from my phone calls with Tommy resurfaced, crawling out of the top of my brain. Words like *buy* and *sell* twined together, braiding their meanings in my head to create an overarching picture of horrors.

"Right." I nodded, tapping my toe. "Because Heather's gonna 'sell' me, whatever that means."

"No, I'm going to sell you, Ms. Sanders," he corrected with pointed nonchalance, shuffling papers into neat order on his desk. "I'm only allowing you to stay here as a favor to Heather."

Choosing to forego the millions of questions I had about what he exactly meant by, 'sell me', I settled for another burning question.

"Why would you do her any favors?"

The woman still perched on the edge of the desk pushed her weight off of it, standing to her full height plus the two inch chunky heels she had on.

"Do you remember me yet?"

My focus snapped to her, that thorn of familiarity poking again.

"So, I *do* know you?"

Her hands folded around the bottom of her blouse, tugging it straight. "You quite literally ran into me."

The smooth ride of her voice over the soft consonants of her genteel accent confused the harsh line of her words.

I'd run into her before? I knew I was clumsy, but you'd think I'd remember the freezer burn of bouncing off of someone whose exterior was pure ice. The chill coming off of her even now was arctic, her glare narrowing in a challenge that *dared* me to forget who she was.

My brain was trying, pumping and tearing overgrown vines apart in my mind that protected the memory. Clarity was right there, the thorn pushing itself out, gasping for freedom, fighting to be plucked and—

"At Maya's birthday party..." The remembered words fell out of me in a trickle of disbelief. Holding the discovered thorn in my hands, I felt it pierce my heart, bleeding out memories of this vile woman standing in Dominic's home. I bumped into her while I was mid-run and mid-panic attack, trying to escape from Dominic after his mom found us in the shed.

She was in the house I'd been living in. In the same house with Charlotte.

Shaking my head, I started to asked, "Why were you at—"

Her cobalt eyes flashed, locking up my tongue.

It was actually *another* thorned memory that stabbed my tongue dead in its tracks... the callus shade of blue her eyes were made up of looking far too familiar.

Holy—

"You're her mom." My stare switched over to the man behind the desk. "And you're her dad."

The shock in my breath dried out my gaping lips, the words sounding impossible even as I said them.

"You're Heather's parents."

Her *parents*.

The people who birthed and raised the woman hellbent on tearing my life apart, and my *god* did they both look so proud. Proud of what they'd raised. Proud of what she'd become. Proud of every single part of her down to her black and ruthless heart.

And I thought *my* parents were fucked.

"We are." Heather's *dad* produced a ball tip pen between his fingers, his attention fractured between the girl he kidnapped and some note he was jotting down. How desensitized he was to all of this might have been the scariest part of all. "My wife runs the brothels. I run the trading and sales side of our business."

"Brothels?" The word spit from my mouth quick, accusation ringing in my tone. "Aren't those like, illegal prostitution rings?"

"Yes, Ms. Sanders." The ballpoint pen paused on paper, sobering black pits lifting to me. "And you're standing in one."

Realization dropped my stomach to my feet, all the pressure in my body fixating there.

The unspeakable things that went on in this house grabbed onto my legs like ghosts reaching up through the floor, their touch clawing up my body, covering me from head to toe in a chill of disgust.

'The girls will fill you in' that man with the black eyes had said. Girls brought here like me, I thought. Girls that were being used as prostitutes in this very house.

And if they had no trouble forcing women into illegal prostitution…

"When you said you handle the selling and trading, you meant…?"

Crossing a T and dotting an I, Heather's father replied in casual.

"Girls, Ms. Sanders."

Trafficking.

The word flashed in my head, unbelievable and turning over the nothing in my stomach. That's what that was, right? I didn't know a lot about it, but you'd hear horror stories in passing about human trafficking in other countries.

Stories of women who get into a cab in a foreign land and never come back. Stories of women there one second and gone the next. Stories that didn't fit with the narrative of life in America.

Or so I thought.

Heather's mom chuffed. "Pick your jaw up off the floor, Ms. Sanders. It's not nearly as taboo as you may think."

My neck pushed forward again, eyes bugging out in their sockets.

In what world was that *not* taboo? Taboo was actually a mislabel to nicely disguise what it really was: barbaric. Inhumane. *Insane.*

My thoughts were zig-zagging all over the place, trying to keep up with the lunacy of what she'd just said. Normal people didn't say that. *Normal* people didn't act like selling a human was the same as selling a candy bar.

Normal was not a word I would use to describe this hellspawn of a family at all.

My hands came up the side of my face, fingertips holding at my temples as chaos squinted my eyes at them both.

"What the *fuck* did Dominic marry into?"

How had such a good man attracted such bad people into his life? I knew there was something about him and his goodness, a gravitational pull to people broken like me, but this was beyond that.

Dominic's pure and perfect orbit had attracted something *beyond* imperfection. Something beyond evil.

Her daddy dearest made a noise in the back of his throat, placing his pen down gently. "We were never in favor of her relationship with him, but my little girl always gets what she wants, and for whatever reason, she decided from a young age that she wanted him."

The chaos in my head expanded my disbelief to something outrageous.

What kind of mental gymnastics did he have to do to see what Heather had done to Dominic as admirable *persistence*?

She *tricked* him into falling in love with her. Wanting someone because you love them is different than manipulating them into falling in love with a version of yourself you have to put on display because the real you is a fucking psychopath.

"She convinced us from a business standpoint how valuable it would be to have such close access to an officer, and she was unsurprisingly correct. She's been an unbelievable asset in turning those pigs on their head and sending them sniffing in all the wrong directions."

Her father leaned back in his chair, crossing his arms over his stomach and chuckling at his daughter's deceitful prowess.

My fingers twitched, a fist *dying* to be born at my side.

"So, she kidnaps innocent girls for you two and then comes here and… *laughs* about how miserable her husband is looking for them?" I pressed, my lightning unfurling beneath my tingling hot skin.

Her father rocked in his chair, so *painfully* casual. "I have no idea how their relationship works. I don't care for the man."

He tipped a degrading look up at me, his unkempt brows set in heavy knowing. "But you certainly do, don't you, Ms. Sanders?"

My empty stomach shifted around nothing. I didn't like him talking about Dominic. I liked that evil glint in his eyes when he talked about him even less. The violent pitter-patter of my heart begged to get the spotlight back on me.

"So Heather wanted me out of the way, and you two just swooped in and offered to destroy my life?"

"Actually, acquiring you was mutually beneficial."

My stare was sent back to her mother and her brutal coldsnap of a glare.

I felt—physically *felt*—the fire warring in my blood snuff out to cowardice smoke, one look from her stealing all heat from my body. Goosebumps rose to try and hold in whatever warmth they could, but there was something downright chilling about this woman.

"After Maya's birthday, I was the one who sent a car for you the next day, but it was reported back that you weren't *alone*. It's unusual to target someone so specifically as we've targeted you, but after your display at the party, you were a piece we had to have."

"It's true," her husband chimed, slanting an admiring look up at his wife. "She came home and wouldn't stop talking about the little bitch with the big green eyes."

His admiration withered away as he drew his gaze to me, gut-churning approval crawling from the dirt in his mud brown eyes.

"And she was right. You're a goldmine, Ms. Sanders."

Well, that's a compliment I never thought I'd hate to hear.

"Heather wasn't even involved at first," she continued. "I assumed you were part of the catering staff, not my granddaughter's new nanny. Had I known, I wouldn't have made a grab for you considering the last incident."

Ice trickled down my back, shivering each vertebra of my spine.

"Last incident?"

"Maya's nanny that you replaced. She stumbled on some information she shouldn't have." Reflection bobbed her head from side to side, refocusing her blue flames on me. "Things got messy on our end."

More memories I never would have given a second thought to ripped front and center. Particularly Maya's shining eyes as she grieved the loss of her previous nanny who just stopped showing up to work one day.

"Shelly…?" I breathed, her name a ghost's chill on my lips.

Her mother dismissed me with a glance. "I don't care to know their names."

Defense for a woman I'd never met broke out in quick flames beneath my flesh, flaying the ice inspired by this woman to shards.

"Well, you should. Her name is *Shelly*—"

"Was, Ms. Sanders." The man behind the desk sliced me off with a cut of his *brutal* stare. "It was."

The ice was back just like that.

It'd frozen my eyes wide open and my lungs mid-breath. This time, it felt like a permanent paralyzation as I stayed locked in a stare-off with a man whose eyes weren't just deadened like I thought.

They were lifeless.

The soul inside of them was just… gone. I thought the color of his stare had been dulled by time, but time hadn't a thing to do with it.

He'd killed someone. Possibly many someones.

I was standing one desk length away from a man who had taken life from a person's lungs, and the incisive look he'd pinned me with told me he'd do it again as easily as he'd blink.

For the first time since arriving here… fear trickled rightfully into my bones.

Heels clacked across hardwood floors, fading out as Heather's mom stepped onto a rug separating us.

"Heather wasn't happy when I told her who I'd sent the boys after that day, but she was even less happy when she heard her husband was at your house. My mistake of going after you turned into the perfect opportunity for us to both get what we want."

Like she was leading me to the question, I asked with hesitance, "And you wanted me because I ran into you at a party?"

She *almost* smiled.

"I wanted you because the type of clients we service will pay an offensive amount of money to beat the attitude out of a pretty girl like you."

Though she didn't smile, she still beamed like she'd swallowed the sun.

This woman fed off of my terror like she was a succubus to it, and the resemblance between mother and daughter had never been so distinguished.

"The nearest auction is in four weeks and no sooner, unfortunately. You'll be in attendance." Even though her husband was talking, her focus was still trained on me, the both of us locked in a stare down I was honest to fuck too scared to lose. "Until then, you'll be under Claudia's ruling here at the brothel and interact with the customers as she sees fit. We don't operate on Sundays, but you'll start up tomorrow."

His wife watched with wicked glee as my eyebrows curved into question marks.

"I expect you to service our clients to the fullest as any other girl we have staying here," she answered to clarify, the words sounding like butter on her gentle accent.

Their meaning, however… sounded like gunfire closing in.

Dread flushed the length of my body, my head shaking back and forth. "I'm not *working* here for you. That's insane."

"That's not insane, Ms. Sanders." She even cheapened my words with air quotes and a peachy grin. "That's karma."

My breathing might have been choppy but my conviction was *fierce*.

"You're out of your fucking mind, you know that?"

A warning noise came from the background.

"Ms. Sanders, *enough*."

My heart jumped, the snap of the voice behind the desk a laceration across my chest. Heather's mom pivoted to the side and put me right in the bullseye of the daggered glare of her other half.

"You've already made it *quite* clear that when it pertains to manners, you have none. I can appreciate that to the degree of just how much it will increase your sale value, but that's as far as my appreciation goes."

Shivers replaced the marrow of my bones, a visible tremble conducting my body no matter how hard I tried to hide it from the callous stare I was under.

"My business is widely successful and respected across continents. Your brain couldn't even fathom the amount of money I bring in each year for something as simple as women. They are a disposable gender with only rare gems…" He gripped a lengthy pause, giving his pupils time to transform into glass shards. "You've already lessened the shine of one of my gems, and I'll be damned if you cause any trouble for my other."

He palmed a letter opener from his desk, sticking the sharp end beneath an envelope's flap and slicing it open. I gulped, my throat scratchy and dry as the threat of his gesture bounced off the blade and settled in my gut.

"There are girls who would kill you to be where you'll be for the next month," he went on even as my brain *screamed* that couldn't be true. "To gain employment here is a rigorous process, and being chosen as one of Claudia's girls is an honor. You're only here as a favor to my daughter, but I will not hesitate to exterminate you if you become a problem. Am I understood?"

From across the desk, he fixed his focus on me, the letter opener winking a promise at me in his right hand. Eyes on the silver blade, my mind tried to find some sort of footing to help *any* of this make sense, but it kept flailing and failing because none of it did.

This was all insane.

Clearly, I'd grossly underestimated my circumstances and who I was dealing with. This wasn't just a housewife out for revenge.

This was a family out to *ruin*.

Retreating on feet I could hardly feel at this point, I warned, "I'm not having sex with anyone…"

Claudia took back the reins. "You most certainly will be."

"No, I'm fucking *not*," I shot back, quick-rising horror masquerading as anger.

Staring at a woman who was readying to take a sledgehammer to my free will, I forced myself to remember who and what I was.

I was stone. I was goddamn *stone.* I had cracks, sure, but where I was broken was infused by lightning.

"I'll kick and I'll scream and I'll tell anyone who comes in here exactly what you guys do and why I'm here and you'll be out of business." I blinked rapidly, my thoughts coming in just as manic a frenzy. "You'll be in *jail* actually. You try to force me to have sex with anyone, and you're risking your whole operation. Plus! You don't even know if I'm clean. I could have fucking herpes for all you know."

Maybe I should lie and say I do.

"Your blood was taken while you were out and sent off yesterday." I gaped at her father, mouth falling apart. "It came back clean, but your blood sugar was low. Have Sergio grab you food on the way back to your room so you don't pass out during tomorrow's Line Up."

"You took my blood?" I breathed, beyond shocked, beyond terrified, beyond anything I'd ever felt before.

"And we'll take so much more than that from you, Ms. Sanders." Claudia turned to face me, showing me the pride chiseled into her botoxed face as I lost grip on the mask hiding my fear.

It was splashed all over my face, clinging to my expression like splattered war paint.

She started towards me, and even only a few inches taller, Claudia managed to look five times more intimidating during her prowling gait up to me.

"Four weeks, and then you'll be off to the auction. In the meantime, you will fuck who you're told to fuck, go where you're told to go, and if you *do* try to fight or run, don't think that the men who frequent this house will have any issues bedding a woman who is unconscious. In fact, some of them get off on it."

The easy way she spoke almost made it sound like she meant her words as sage advice rather than the disgusting threat they were. They reached inside my throat and snatched my voice clean out, the extraction scathing my insides raw.

I put my hand to my throat as if I could feel my muteness, as if I could grab my pulse thumping inside of it. Claudia completed the distance to me so I could see every imperfection chipped into her face up close.

"You act like a whore, Ms. Sanders, and you get treated like one."

Venom pumped in her glare, stinging each spot on my face she passed over in her inspection of me. Her eyelids lowered with an unimpressed glower.

"Everything about to happen to you, you *deserve*. I just wanted you to know that."

From behind her, her husband let out a quiet chuckle, and the sound from him and look from her were both enough to sour my stomach past the point of hunger.

I wasn't hungry anymore. I was too full of dread to have room for anything else.

With victory holding up her thin smirk, Claudia went back to her place by the desk, circling around to stand next to her husband.

Both parents of Heather stared at me, satisfied in the voice they'd stolen from the girl who'd stolen their baby girl's husband.

"By your expression, I can only assume you understand the severity of your cooperation." He reached next to him, finding his wife's hand on his shoulder and giving it a pat. "That will be all, Ms. Sanders."

He raised his guttural voice a mere octave. "Sergio."

The oaf apparently named Sergio busted through the door at his boss's slightest command. I didn't even get another look at either of Heather's parents before he dragged me out by the same arms he'd twisted out of place on the way down.

I left the office with a splitting cry, forgetting to tell him I was supposed to be fed as he threw me back in the bedroom upstairs.

I forgot everything aside from the horror story I'd just been told, worse than any scary ghost story I'd been fed when I was little. I kept thinking about it and how it couldn't be real.

I kept thinking that I'd really like to wake up from this nightmare right about now.

NINETEEN

KAT

I hated scary stories.

I had since I was little. There was this friend I had growing up, Lawrence, who was known for his ghost stories at sleepovers and on the school playground. It was my own dumb fault for listening to them. Morbid curiosity was my downfall even as a child, and I'd listen to every creepy word Lawrence weaved together until there were knots in my stomach and tears in my eyes.

I couldn't help it. I wanted to know what happened because, even as a kid, there was a part of me that was fascinated with tragedy. There was something in me addicted to horror and the things that went bump in the night.

In all my years of addiction to the fictional tales of ghosts, goblins, and masked killers, nothing was more terrifying than the nonfiction reality I was living now.

I passed in and out of sleep for the next however many hours until the morning.

Or what I assumed was morning by the bustle of movement happening on the other side of my locked door.

I hadn't wanted to sleep—I couldn't be caught off guard in a place like this. Unfortunately, not having eaten in probably two days now didn't make staying awake easy.

The pain of hunger had dulled its excruciating bite in exchange for obliterating all of my energy. At one point, I'd crawled up onto the bathroom counter to palm cups of water to drink and ended up falling asleep with my cheek pressed to the mirror.

By now, I'd made it back to the bed, huddled up with the crumpled crimson sheet and my almost three-day-old leggings and t-shirt. I'd taken my bra off at some point when the underwire started digging into the emptiness beneath my ribs. My sneakers were in the corner too by the shelf of books I'd tried and failed to sustain the energy to read.

Which sucked. This all sucked.

I needed to be *prepared* the next time I saw anyone in this house, not a pathetic lump who couldn't even hold her head up.

Yesterday's talk with Heather's parents made it *harrowingly* clear that their goal was to dehumanize and demoralize me. They wanted to reach between my legs and rip my dignity clean out and save it to serve at Thanksgiving as an amuse-bouche.

But they wouldn't get it.

No, her parents might have scared me, but they also inspired me with their nightmare tales. They took a woman whose tenacity was already a level above sane and sensible and cranked it up to off-the-rails.

I would *bleed* before I submitted how they wanted me to.

For Charlotte, for Dominic, hell, for *myself*, I would fight until I found the weak spot of this Jenga house of horrors, snatch it out, and watch it all fall.

I just had to get some motherfucking food in me first.

In the middle of wallowing about food and wondering what Dominic and Charlotte were doing right now, there was a sudden jiggle on the doorknob.

My heart punched a weakened beat behind my ribs. *Shit.*

My muscles and nerves all scrambled to get me to sit up and be on defense for whoever was about to come through that door. I couldn't show them I was weak. I couldn't be anything less than the lightning I was born to be, fired up and deadly to whoever was brainless enough to touch me.

Pushing my palms to the mattress, I went to lift myself up with a shaking breath. That breath tasted like desperation as I tried and tried and tried in the two or three seconds I had to sit up…

And failed.

I didn't just fail though.

I failed *fantastically*, slumping back down to the mattress more exhausted than I'd been before to the point that my only defense left was to pretend to be asleep.

Fuck this *fucking* exhaustion.

My cheek had just settled into the pillow when the door clicked open. My heartbeat was bouncing off the walls, overworked at the bare-minimum exertion and crashing against my rib cage.

Footsteps creaked the floorboards, drawing closer. My eyelids were heavy but my ears were perked high like a canine's, tracking and listening to the weight shift beneath the—

"Get up."

"Hey!" I gasped, eyes flying open as my head fell a few inches to smack the bare mattress. My neck snapped up to attention, finding my pillow in the strong fist of the man with black eyes.

A noise of warning rumbled in the back of my throat.

Fuck this guy.

"You know there are other ways to wake me up that don't include stealing the pillow right out from under my head." I hit the guy with a feeble glower, straining to get up on the back of my elbows.

Find the strength. For the love of fucking god, find the strength.

The man set something folded in a white napkin on the stand next to the bed. "Right. I'll get the choir of morning birds to sing you awake next time."

My sore neck jerked back at his slap of sarcasm. "Who the fuck pissed in your cheerios this morning?"

He ignored me with a dramatic roll of his dark eyes, moving to the foot of the bed where he unshelved a load of clothes he had draped over one arm. I cocked my head at the drop of neon and sequins falling on the bed's end before the man pointed a long finger towards the folded napkin on the nightstand.

"Eat."

My neck cranked towards the idea of food so fast, a twinge splintered up the back of my skull.

My jaw dropped with a tight hiss, hand flying to blanket my eyes as pain burrowed behind them. Hot air swirled in my head, dizziness poking black dots behind my eyes, all of them whirling in anarchy devoted to making me feel like I was falling while already laying down.

I needed that food, whatever it was, badly.

Except my untrusting tongue was determined to make it difficult for the both of us.

"I don't need you to feed me."

"Seems like you do."

"I'm *fine*."

That lie wasn't an easy sell with my hand still stabilizing the tornado of pain in my head.

"Clearly," he mused, his mumble deep. More sarcasm.

The floorboards cried again as the man came closer, curiosity squinting my eyes open to watch his moves. He stopped in front of the napkin, flipping the folded top off.

"It's a donut. Eat the donut."

My stomach straight up *lurched* like it could rip out of my flesh and consume the sweet dessert all on its own accord. I loved donuts.

"Who's to say you didn't poison it?" I shot back.

Oh god. My stupid freaking stubborn mouth.

I was going to tear it off myself if the man in front of me didn't do it first. He tried to internalize a heated sigh, steam practically billowing from his ears.

"It's store bought."

"People in stores can be bought off to poison the pastries."

"Oh my f—" The man turned to show me his profile, trapping a big hand over his mouth. He aimed his stare up at the ceiling, likely counting the seconds and counting ways in which he could hurt me. That hand over his mouth swept back down to his side, a fist rearranging in and out of shape as he turned back to me.

"As much as I would love for our time to be cut short, that would defeat the point of you being here, so eat the fucking donut. Or don't. I don't care."

He said he didn't care, but he huffed and puffed like he did, crossing to the wall closest to me and putting his back to it. He crossed his arms and ankles, watching me beneath thick and angry brows, waiting for me.

We stared across the space at each other, neither of us backing down. I wasn't sure he was even blinking. His black eyes were on full assault, brutalizing what was left of the air in my lungs, setting it all on fire until my chest burned.

There was something about this guy. Something about him and his *eyes*.

I didn't believe in seeing auras and shit, but if I did? This guy's aura would be a cloud of black, radiating out of him in pulses that sucked the air right out of you if you got too close.

Yeah, that's *exactly* what it was. There was something downright suffocating about him and his dirty emotions that were swiped so vividly across his skin.

His anger was a strike of crimson red, his passion a splatter of burnt orange. The midnight sky when it deepened to purple was the color of his hatred, and the golden rise of sun that pushed the night away was the color of his resentment.

He had too many emotions thriving on the surface of his skin that they all smattered into the darkness he walked around wearing.

This guy was raw. A flesh wound thriving in a constant pour of peroxide.

I didn't like him. Not one goddamn bit.

But I *did* like donuts. And I liked surviving.

With stubborn fingers, I reached out and picked up the donut in the napkin while holding his stare. He wouldn't look away and neither would I as I parted my lips for the first bite of food in over forty-eight hours.

Plain cake passed over my tongue that somehow found the fluid to salivate, but I didn't even take the time to taste it before wolfing it down to settle the ache in my stomach. There was hardly any flavor at all considering it was a *plain* donut.

Who the fuck got plain donuts when powdered and chocolate were options?

Stormy eyes were eventually the first to skate away, sitting heavy in the corner of the room with a curse hanging off his lips.

"Christ, you're stubborn."

I lobbed off another piece, talking around the food in my mouth. "And you have boring taste in donuts."

He wore another black t-shirt today, and it stretched over his chest as he held back whatever insult was likely sitting in his next exhale. The backs of his cheeks pulsated as his anger tried to take flight, but he clenched it back and pushed himself off the wall and started towards the bed.

"These are the clothes Claudia approved for Line Up. Get dressed and be ready in an hour."

Shaking my head and clearing my throat of crumbs, I asked, "What the hell even is that? Everyone keeps saying it."

He grabbed a fist full of the clothes on the bed, slowly thumbing through them with a 3rd degree burn in his glare.

"The women line up. The men come in and choose."

Another swallow of dry cake tumbled down my throat as I considered his words. Choose? Confusion narrowed my focus on the man's face until what he meant *clicked*, and the confusion drained down my face in a cold wash of dread.

"You mean the men come in and choose which woman they want to *rape*."

"It's not—" He paused, slamming his eyes shut and dropping the clothes as if they'd scorched him. Long legs spun him around and headed for the door, throwing a final command over his shoulder. "Just pick out something to wear."

"*No*."

My denial was an electric shock through his legs and back, freezing up both and stopping his stride.

"I'm not picking out shit from this pile of—" I sat up, aided by the strength of the sugary fat donut sitting happy in my belly, and reached for the garment closest. Stringing it up by bewildered fingers, my eyes roved the animal print dress that couldn't have been finished.

"What the fuck even is this?" Using my other hand, I poked a hole through one of the sides that just *didn't* exist. This was like a hooker meets Jane of the Jungle kind of getup, tears in the cheap fabric included.

The man swiveled around, dropping an unenthused glance down the dress I was holding before meeting my eye.

"It's what the customers like."

"Yeah, well *fuck* what the customers like." I tossed the dress back on the pile, sitting with my arms crossed in defiance over my chest. "I'm not wearing this, and I'm not going down there as a willing participant."

That donut was already beginning to work, the spunk in my veins creeping back. The man across the room hung his hands on his hips, dragging his hard-bitten stare to the floor.

He stayed silent for a moment, the tip of his nose twitching as he wrestled back his vibrant streak of red rage.

"You don't get it."

The weight of whatever it was I didn't get lowered his voice to the point I almost leaned forward to hear him better. Good thing I didn't, because the heat wave he sent my way next with his furious scowl could have singed my eyebrows right off.

"You don't *have* to be willing."

Abhorrence rounded my eyes as they tracked back and forth between his, searching for something that was clearly missing.

"Do you have a *soul?* Do you even care how fucked up what you just said is?!"

"My soul is irrelevant," he clipped, a dark acceptance to his tone. Moving back towards the bed in furious steps, he picked up a fist full of fabric. "Pick something to wear, don't look any of the men in the eye, don't cause a fucking scene, and maybe you and I can both get through this without breaking someone's neck. *Yes?*"

"*No.*"

His knuckles drained of color, and I swore I heard the clothes trapped in his grip gasping for air.

"Fuck!" A rainbow of cheap colors flew back to the bed as he threw them, nailing me with a hard glare. "You don't have a *choice.*"

"Yes, I do! I know what kind of girl you're probably used to getting in here, but I'm not her."

I imagined he was used to women who played by the rules here so they didn't get hurt. Except life had already taught me that playing nice is oftentimes what brought the pain.

Giving into what people wanted from you didn't make them *nice* to you.

It made them take advantage of you.

The man's stare drifted down, unfocused on anything in particular.

"You're right," he stated, his baritone voice quiet. Thoughtful. Then those unfocused eyes found me at the center of their attention again, honing razor sharp. "You're *worse*."

And goddamn proud of it.

Seconds lingered in silence, the hate stretched between us something I *swore* you could reach out and stick your fingers in.

It was a tangible creation. Sticky and messy and *dark*.

The man was the first to sever our tar-like tension, stomping over and swiping the empty napkin off the stand and crumpling it in his white-knuckled fist.

"It won't be me coming up to get you for Line Up. It'll be Sergio, so *be ready*. And—" He stopped mid-sentence next to me, nose wrinkling. All my muscles jerked back to plaster against the headboard of the bed as he leaned in closer, sniffing in my general direction. Thick eyebrows crammed together and he retreated back, waving his hand in front of his face.

"And take a fucking shower. You smell like horse shit."

Oh, was the big bad criminal repulsed by the 'I haven't showered in three days' fragrance I was rocking? Shame.

"Nah, I'm good. I'm sure the kind of clients you service here will love a girl who smells like the embodiment of what they are."

His eyes sliced over to meet mine. "You're a real comic," he spoke dryly.

Before I could send a quip back, he was moving into the bathroom and disappeared inside. Yellow light flickered with life at the same time an overhead fan kicked on, whirling a white noise tune through the bedroom. A moment later, a twisting squeak and a sputtering rush of water followed.

The man appeared, leaning around the door frame of the bathroom and cocking his head inside. "Get in."

My shoulders perked up and back, poising a pensive pointer finger to my lips. "How about *you* go first, drown yourself in the bathtub, and then I'll take my turn?"

The sugar rushing my blood aided an extra *oomph* to my fraud enthusiasm, and the man groaned at it, pinching his fingers over the bridge of his nose.

"I don't have the energy to deal with you this morning. Just get in the damn shower."

"Um, how about *bite me?*"

I thought he might break his own nose he was squeezing it so hard, a swell of violent energy leaching out of him.

"You can't show up smelling like *shit*."

"I'm not showing up anywhere," I argued back, leaning forward and shoving the pile of laughable wardrobe to the floor. With flames licking across my bones and uncapping my temper, I snapped. "I'm not *doing* this rapey fashion show, I'm not *wearing* these trash clothes, and I am not getting in the fucking shower!"

Each of my last words nailed into existence, malice coming off my body in charging waves that could throw any normal person back and *demolish* them.

Except my waves didn't demolish this guy as they reached him. Instead, they powered him up like an extra life, filling in the whites of his eyes just as malevolent black as the rest of him.

His jaw moved to the side, a momentary flash of Dominic passing behind my eyes before he asked, "Really?"

"Really really," I challenge right back.

He nodded subtly, wrinkling his nose up yet again. "Okay."

A lump moved beneath his upper lip as he passed his tongue along his teeth, his black eyes a flurry of unhinged thoughts speeding through. He nodded again as he squished his mouth together and stepped forward.

"Have it your way."

"What the fuck—"

My world went upside down with a scream as the man swooped both arms around my waist and threw me over his shoulder like a sack of flour.

"Get off of me!"

"If you're gonna act like a child, then I'm gonna treat you like one."

He pivoted towards the rushing water in the bathroom, carrying me with him even as I thrashed and kicked my legs out. His hands were *on* me, touching my waist and the backs of my legs, places they didn't belong.

The feel of someone else's touch spurred my mind into a frenzy, fists lashing across his back and screams pouring out of my mouth like fire.

"Put me down! Put me down right fucking now!"

The sound of the running shower was right behind me now, the screech of the curtain being yanked back digging into my ears. His grip on me shifted, my shirt bunching up at the waist as he lugged my body forward over his shoulder.

"As you wish," he grunted.

The series of events that happened next lined up seamlessly with the parade of misfortunes that made up my life.

An animalistic screech shredded through my throat as excruciating pin pricks of ice cold water pelted down on my skin, drenching me in seconds. My t-shirt soaked up every drop of frozen water, reforming to a brick of ice around my torso under the roaring stream of the shower.

I'd only been in the assault of the shower for mere moments, and already, I was jumping out of my skin, sinking my claws into his back, desperate to escape the torture as he tried to pull away.

"Let go," he gritted through clenched teeth, trying to force my weight off of his back. He was getting hit with the spray too, but not nearly as much as me. Still gasping out tiny shrieks, I made a grab for his shoulders at the same time he made a grab for my waist, trying to pry me off of him.

Then, also at the same time, I lost my footing in the puddles at my feet as he gave one final, powerful shove.

A gasp sliced the air, getting suspended in time as I fell backwards.

My stomach plummeted, my heart choking on its next beat, knowing the hard ground waiting for me at the end of this fall. I could see it now, my name spelled out in my own blood on this tile floor as some unlikely gravestone.

A masculine curse squeezed its way into the drama of the moment.

And then—the world stopped.

My fall was suspended just like time was, holding still to allow me to catch up to it. Darkness consumed my frozen world, eyes shut in preparation for my deadly meeting with the ground. So I couldn't see anything.

But I could feel it.

Warmth. A lot of it.

Wrapped around my waist and melting the ice on the tip of my nose. The warmth was scented with… smoke? Its smell was faint, but unmistakable in the sweet and bitter notes that crawled up my nose.

The steady sound of the shower was still prevalent, but the downpour of ice on my skin was lost. Cautiously, I tested my eyes open with a few gentle flutters.

However, what was right in front of them shocked them *wide* open.

Black flames waited for me, burning from just above.

The warmth was *him.* On my stomach, clutching my back, fanning over my face. His flame was all over me, holding me so I didn't fall to the death he pushed me towards.

He caught me.

He threw me, and then he caught me. His body was shielding over mine, taking the brunt of the cold spray with me hidden beneath him and rescued from a grisly fate at the bottom of the shower. With one arm hooked around my waist, his other was holding us both up, sturdy and strong on the wall behind us.

I was frozen. Inside and out—*frozen.*

He was close. *Too* close, but I couldn't melt my brain fast enough to do anything about it. In my head, I was still falling and waiting to crash, bracing for the pain of smacking the ground.

I couldn't fathom that I wasn't on the floor right now, a crack in my skull bleeding out a puddle of red, diluting in the mix of water. Instead, I was *here,* being held by a flame that had no intention of burning me.

At least not at the moment.

The man with black eyes was holding me in a dip, and I was holding him too. My hands had gripped the globes of his shoulders mid-fall in a flash of instincts, but now all those quick-thinking instincts were lost in the ride of water droplets sliding down his smooth face. It was sort of mesmerizing, watching them roll over the rise of his cheekbones before jutting out to follow the defined cut of his clean shaven jawline to the dip of his chin.

I didn't *mean* to watch him, but in my defense, he'd started it.

His eyes were a flickering of intensity over me, unchecked in their exploration of my face from up close. From my chin to my hairline. From cheek to cheek. He was shameless and unyielding in his examination of me, as if he was making notes about every inch and what he despised most about it.

The fire of his eyes roared as they fixed on mine, trying to melt my emeralds back down to minerals. Part of my brain that was racing to get back on track wondered why he didn't let me fall, and then wondering became asking in a voice quieted by the spell of the shower.

"Why didn't you just let me fall?"

Strange puzzlement gave a pass over his stare, lines in his forehead knitting just enough to collect a water image of curiosity between his dark eyebrows. My eyes rose to the collection of droplets clinging to his browline, a shadow of a memory tingling in the pad of my thumb that knew I'd wipe the water away if he were Dominic.

He wasn't—*obviously*—but he saved me like Dominic would. My brain trapped in this slow-motion confusion couldn't make sense of it. Why push me just to catch me?

Through lips so stiff, he gave me the answer.

"I didn't want to clean up the mess."

The cruelty he spoke with sprinkled down from his lips to my face, each touch of his smoke-tinted breath a dip of poison melting through to my brain, *shattering* whatever freeze had taken over me.

I nodded, filtering thinkable air back into my lungs. "Makes sense."

A selfish reason to save someone's life from a selfish criminal like him *did* make sense.

My feet found their footing again, socks squishing wet against the tile floor as I swatted his arm from around me. He righted himself back with a string of unfriendly curses, ducking out of the shower space and retreating into the bathroom.

He was soaked, doused from head to shoe like he'd been hit with a firehose. I watched him with a scowl screwing up my mouth as he shook his head, splattering water from his now black mop of hair as he dug his thumbs into his eyes.

With a jerk, I cut the water stream off and stepped out myself. The bathroom without the soundtrack of the shower was a dead echo of slow drips and shivering teeth. If I thought I was cold before, that was jackshit compared to now, standing in clothes drenched in below freezing water and *braless*.

Yeah, my nipples were having a field day right about now.

"You're such a *jackass*," I breathed, the waver of my voice chopped and chattering.

Raking both hands back through his hair, his glare stuck to the floor.

"Your 'thank you' needs a bit of work."

"Yeah, thanks *so* much for pushing me to my almost death."

Puddles were growing beneath my feet as I wrapped my arms around myself, trying whatever I could to preserve the memory of heat in my bones. The man tried to wring out his shirt in the sink, abandoning it with an exacerbated sigh.

"You're so dramatic."

"Yeah, *I'm* dramatic when you're the one who manhandled me into the shower."

He shrugged, voice detached. "You smell like shit."

"*God*, I hope you weren't this much of a prick to Layla if this is where she was," I scoffed.

Saying her name out loud inspired a chill to circle my stomach, sweeping up what little food I'd eaten in a frostbite wind. My arms cinched around my waist as every bite of donut solidified to ice, sitting heavier in my gut as I thought about my best friend. Whether she was okay.

I didn't know.

She was hovering over the doorstep of death when I last saw her, and I *didn't know.*

"Are you talking about the girl here before you?"

The almost abrasive intrigue flavoring his voice guided my head up as if a finger beneath my chin.

So she was here. He knew her. He knew Layla.

"She's my best friend," I told the man whose eyes had gone severe.

My reply made him tilt his head at me, the subtle but new angle delivering his intensity like a match lit right between my ribs. I wanted to shift beneath its uncomfortable heat, but wouldn't dare.

"And now you're here instead of her?"

"She was never supposed to be here, but they grabbed her instead of me. Now it's fixed." Loyalty vibrated a thick cord in my voice, and the blaze holding together his expression went supernova.

"You're here on *purpose?*"

"Uh, I wouldn't call it purposeful given the whole chloroform thing, but if you mean I traded places with her, then yeah. It was my fault she was here in the first place."

The backs of his wet cheeks pulsated, animating his fury. A trickle of water made the trip from his forehead down to gather on his surprisingly long lashes. Even from here, I could see them glistening with every hard blink he gave me.

His hanging jaw clamped together hard, the tip of his nose twitching again. "That was stupid," he ground out through gnashed teeth. "Really *fucking* stupid."

Offense slapped the words right outta my shivering mouth. "Oh, fuck you."

"*Watch it.*"

The scorch of his glare was a warning that I promptly ignored.

"No, I'm not gonna 'watch it.' If you tell me I'm stupid for caring about someone other than myself, I'm gonna tell you to fuck off. *Especially* now that I see the kind of creeps she was stuck with! I'm glad I got her out of here. I'm glad she isn't trapped with you, having who the fuck knows what done to her—"

"Nothing," he cut me off, his cadence made of rocks. His eyes were pure coal. "She stayed in this room the entire time she was here."

Shock inverted my brows from vengeful to relieved.

It flooded in fast and put out the fire in my chest. Sure I could wonder if he was lying, but the sensation of breathing all the way down to my belly button felt too good to consider it wasn't the truth.

On an exhale that felt like I'd been holding my breath all day, I sighed, "Good."

Good.

Tension left my shoulders, dwindling in the damp air hovering in the bathroom too. I had to drop the man's gaze to fully immerse myself in the relief, instead finding focus on his shirt instead. I breathed in as he did, observing the material of his shirt, now heavy with water, and how it clung to ridges of muscles beneath.

Huh. I guess even dipshits can workout.

Walking past him, I wrapped my hands around my soggy hair and began to wring out over the sink. Drops of water strangled from the locks, and I watched them peel down the rim of the sink and swipe over the ring of rust around the drain before disappearing from sight.

I wished my escape could be that simple.

"You still need to finish showering," came from behind me.

Pulling back an inhale of frustration, I decided it was the only way to get him to leave me the hell alone. "You would need to leave in order for me to do that."

"I will. Just—"

He cut himself off. I glanced up in the mirror over the sink to see why. He was directly behind me, so all I could see was the top half of his face reflected in the mirror. Lowered eyelids and a fan of long lashes over his cheeks.

He'd lost whatever he was about to say in his head, thickly-shaped eyebrows pointed inwards to frame the disappearance. Impatience rolling my eyes back, I whipped around my brows halfway up my forehead.

"Just *what?*"

The slap of my voice didn't move him an inch. His breathing was an even and deep push and pull, his stare swimming in the puddles at our feet. There was something off about him all of a sudden, as if someone had taken that glowering black energy cloud around him and turned it to simmer.

Confusion started to move the muscles in my face when the backs of his jaw suddenly pulsed out, and his eyes snapped to mine.

Not until now did I realize how close he still was, only a foot or two away. It was way too close, and as he searched back and forth between my eyes from above, the suffocating effect of him began to take hold.

It was just a scratch of a feeling at the back of my throat, but it was the exact same kind you got when you inhaled smoke. The way he was *staring* at me was a mirrored sensation of the time I tried pot at a house party in high school, and the bitter burn didn't leave my lungs all night long.

Black flames traced my face, but there was something different about them from the times before. Something *more*. A flicking of a color I hadn't seen yet dancing in his eyes.

Another brushstroke of emotion to add to his palate.

This one a melancholy blue.

Just as the string on my curiosity was singed by the arrival of this new color, the man flared his nostrils in defiance of it and muttered, "Wear the red dress."

Then he spun around and left.

TWENTY

KAT

I specifically did not wear the red dress.

How dare that bastard use my best color against me. Unfortunately, the red dress was one of the few in the pile that wasn't laughable or animal print or both, but I'd sooner gag myself with the disposable razor in the bathroom than wear anything he told me to.

I actually *did* finish showering up just enough that I couldn't smell myself anymore, but not with any intention of going downstairs for this so-called 'line up.'

I would sit my happy ass in this bedroom and draw blood from anyone who tried to pull me from it.

At the hour mark, someone did show up just like the man with black eyes told me would happen. Sergio practically crashed through the door, a groan leading his way when he saw me perched on the bed, barefoot, arms crossed, and a "get the fuck out of here" locked and loaded.

I'd put on a layered, short black skirt that had been provided because my leggings were soaked, but left my t-shirt on and tied it up on one end so the wet material didn't chafe my stomach.

Sergio scoffed at my attire and bitched at my welcoming comment. We went back and forth only a few times before I told him I would die before going downstairs to be a part of this visual diatribe of sexism.

It was after that declaration that he showed me the handle of his gun sticking out of the waistband of his pants.

He was walking me out of my room less than a minute and a minor heart attack later.

I didn't know what else to do.

If I died, then I couldn't get back to Charlotte or warn Dominic it was Heather behind all of his personal *and* professional heartache.

I had to survive to tell them, but how in the fuck would I survive something like this?

We arrived downstairs, and I think my legs had gone numb by the time we reached the final step. It felt like I was walking on air, but not in the blissful kind of way people usually meant. The kind of way that felt like, at any moment, the next step I took would have the floor disappearing from beneath me, and I'd plummet straight through a false sky to an almost certain death.

What was most *definitely* dead was the air when I arrived on scene. So corpse-stiff, it was like walking into an invisible wall.

The gigantic foyer I'd been led through just yesterday morning was no longer empty.

There were a dozen pairs of eyes staring back at me, every single one of them narrowed in some degree of disapproval.

Ten of them I'd never seen before. Two pairs were familiar. One, a searing black and the other a blue so frigid, a chill tracked up my spine as she stomped my way.

Her heels clacked in a straight line past all ten girls standing in a row facing the front doors. They were all done up in outfits like the kinds that had been dropped off in my room, leather and lace and *lots* of skin all glaring back at me.

A quick scan of their faces showed me two things.

One, they wore way too much makeup, and some of them had spray tans that could rival an orange's complexion. It was all Vegas showgirl glam and zero style.

Two? They all hated me.

There wasn't a single friendly nor petrified face in the crowd like I expected I might find. I thought these girls would be like me. Scared, dying to get out of here, unwilling participants in this fantasy from hell, but not a damn thing about them screamed 'unwilling'.

The only thing about them that screamed was their appearance, and it screamed Julia Roberts from Pretty Woman pre-makeover.

A cold front washed over my body, an imposing shadow of royal blue falling over me. Every single bone in my body froze to icicles, straightening my posture on an involuntary shiver.

Claudia's outfit was blue from head to pointed toe today, making her cobalt eyes outshine even her daughter's most heated glares.

"Ms. Sanders, you are *late* and you are *barefoot*."

I parted my lips, and they went dry before I spoke. "I don't have a clock in my room."

Her pink lip twitched. "That's your excuse?"

I paused, inhaling a hit of her perfumed condensation.

"No, my excuse is that I don't want to *be* here."

There it was. The comforting spark of lightning. The fight breaking through the ice congealing in my veins.

The flash of the gun had blown my fire out, but like a trick candle, it had found its way back to life, burning a determination in the pit of my chest. Warming, boiling, charging up every nerve ending beneath the casing of my skin so even the hair on my arms rose against conduction of brewing electricity.

The man with black eyes stood to Claudia's side, and in the reincarnation of my spark, his very own *blazed*.

It roared with life, screaming at me to shut the fuck up like how glass explodes sitting in the middle of a fire.

He was pissed. At my attitude, my outfit, my existence, the whole lot of it.

And I didn't give one flying fuck. All the fucks I had to give were reserved for proving to this shitstain of a woman that I would not just roll over and give in.

An echo of heels clicked against the hardwood floor. "But you *are* here, Ms. Sanders, and you'll participate, and you'll be good…" Her cadence was so assured, so apathetic in that gentle accent and easy smile that twirled across her cheeks. "Do you know how I know this?"

The way her eyes glittered like a thousand thumb tacks with their pointy ends up made the breath to answer her with catch in my throat.

"How?"

"Because even if you don't care about your own life enough to follow my rules, I suspect you care enough about your younger sister's, hm?"

That spark between my ribs went out, coldness sweeping in to fill my chest. Plumes of it seeped out all the way to my fingers hanging at my sides.

My hands grew heavy the colder they got, weighing down on either side.

I couldn't move them.

I couldn't move anything.

Glee struck at the core of Claudia's stare, taking advantage to revel in my paralyzation. "Heather is always one call away from something just *terrible* happening to her," she drawled out, a miserable act for concern playing with the tone of her voice. "She tells me how close the two of you are."

Just behind her in my peripherals, smoking eyes shifted from me and transferred to his boss. He was staring at her now the same as I was. I couldn't stop staring though, because I couldn't move, because I couldn't do fucking *anything*.

Claudia fluttered her mascara smattered lashes at me, composed cruelty tightening her smile lines.

"Declawing you was rather easy and… disappointing, Ms. Sanders."

She angled her head at me, taking an appraising last look at the crumbling masterpiece she'd created before walking back to where she was, giving a flick of her wrist.

"Open the doors."

The man lingered back a moment as his boss strode away, the sizzle of his gaze on my face for a few seconds before he left to go meet Sergio at the front doors.

My stare went to his back, glued there as if I had no other choice than to watch him. As if all I could do was stare as they each grabbed a hold of the brass handles on each massive door. A metal fastening unlocked in unison, the sound *banging* inside my chest.

Terror held my eyes wide as both men pushed down on their respective handles, and the doors to hell swung open.

Both men stepped out, and nothing happened for a few moments.

Nothing except the implosion of my world in my head, tiny bombs going off in each area of my brain. My thoughts were screaming in panic, chaos running around my mind as everything I relied on caught fire.

It was calamity up there, nightmare images melting down in my head to crayola horrors where every mouth looked like it was screaming and every pair of eyes were a long drip of tears.

I didn't know what to do. Any second now, men were going to come through that door with enough money in their wallets to buy their dick's way into me, and I didn't know what to do.

If I fought them off, Charlotte got hurt. If I didn't fight them off, I got raped. *Raped.*

Oh holy fuck, nausea swarmed in my gut, that donut churning fast and saliva pouring into the sides of my mouth faster. I was gonna puke. I was gonna puke all over myself. Which, maybe wasn't the worst thing in the world if it repulsed any of these men away from me.

As I willed the donut from before to make a reappearance, the first of the men walked through.

A doctor.

My jaw literally dropped. A fucking doctor still wearing his scrubs sauntered in, looking somewhere in his mid-forties and not even unattractive.

My tongue touched my teeth in a silent 'what the fuck?' as I watched him greet Claudia like they were old pals and give a wink to one girl at the end of the line. The wink was even *charming* for fucks sake, and the girl burst into a fit of giggles and called out, "I love it when you come in your scrubs."

Fishing out his wallet from his pants, his mouth drew a smirk for her. "I know you do, sweetheart."

"Coming in early today, Richard. No appointment?" Claudia interjected, moving towards that setting of French doors I'd noted yesterday off to the side in the foyer.

"I've got a double today at the hospital. Couldn't make it to the usual time to see my girl."

"Ah, well. Let's get you squared away, and then Lori is all yours."

The doctor followed in Claudia's designer steps, stopping as she laid both hands on the knobs of the sealed doors. Each side whirled open in a grand gesture, an office of sleek black waiting just behind.

Claudia and the not-so-good doctor disappeared inside, my hanging jaw gawking after them as they went.

Before I could think too much, another man funneled through the front doors, and then another behind him. One could have been anything from a lawyer to a congressman with the sharp gray suit dawned on his broad physique.

This guy *also* wasn't a noticeable creep from first appearances.

Just your average Joe who just so happened to stroll dick first into a crime house.

The other? Yeah, the oil layering his hairline and belly hanging over his belt aligned with the picture of someone I expected to pay for sex. There was a seediness to his roaming stare, and a fucking pit of dread in my stomach as it passed by me.

My eyes dropped to the floor, lids slamming shut as I tried to make myself invisible. This would be a great time for any one of those Disney fairytales to come true. I'd take anything: a magic carpet to whisk me away, fairy dust to help me fly far far from here. Hell, even a fairy godmother to poof me into a pumpkin for the next hour would suffice.

Anything close to magic had always terrified me with its ability to disappoint so fantastically—prayer, love—but right now, I'd take anything. I needed magic and miracles and fairytale rescues at the very last second when it seemed all was lost.

I needed Prince Charming to be the very next man to step through those doors.

Squinting an eye open, all hope disintegrated to wreckage in the bottom of my stomach as the *literal opposite* walked in.

A biker. Hulking muscles, ink swirling all the way up his thick neck, boots so heavy they could kick a hole straight through my chest. He even had a handlebar mustache hanging over his mouth, a cigarette stuck between.

I wasn't an expert, but I was pretty sure Prince Charming didn't come with a sagging caterpillar on his face.

The two other men from before were gone, and so were three of the women from the line. I was shit at math, but three men—the doc, the lawyer guy, the greasy creep—had all come in and now three women were gone.

Which meant I'd kept myself small enough on the radar to avoid *three* encounters.

I just had to keep it up, and I did.

The biker came and went, choosing a tiny blonde next to me that was half his size and triple the energy. I had no idea the energizer bunny was real, let alone a platinum blonde prostitute with tits the size of Texas.

That made four, and another two men came in after that, both sporting wedding rings and semi-hard ons for women who were not their wives. One was for the Asian woman on my left whose name was apparently Ginger, and the other for a woman of color standing tall at the center of the line who looked like she could and totally wanted to squash me beneath her six-inch sparkle heels.

So far, six women had been taken off to where the fuck ever, and there were four left, plus me. My heart was racing on a track of anxiety, but the odds were stacking in my favor as only one more man came in before they shut the front doors behind him.

That had to mean he was the last one, right?

This dude had such a close-shaven buzzcut, he almost looked bald as he sauntered in, taking a slow peruse of the women left for him. He stuffed his hands in his front jean pockets, watching us all like a kid in a candy store whose parents had given him their whole paycheck to play with.

"Hey, Sugar. You're a fresh face in here."

"What're you lookin' for today, baby?"

"Gawd, you're so fuckin' cute."

"Look at those *arms*. Somebody works out!"

All four women left made their play for the payday, stroking this guy's dick through his ego. The two were synonymous in a man if you really thought about it, and these girls were clearly pros. They were *clearly* the obvious choices, all dolled up and begging for his cock while I kept my trap shut and eyes on my bare feet.

A slow chuckle rolled out of him, slim slicking up its delivery. "You're all beautiful ladies. I wish I could take all of you with me."

"There is a package for that," one of them quipped.

The buzzcut man hummed an approval deep in his throat. "A business gal. I like it."

Swell. Take her and leave me the fuck alone.

"I think I'll start with two of you today. Work my way up to that *package*."

My heart seized up, a fist of terror reaching through and squeezing it.

Two?

My odds sliced in half just like the air flowing into my lungs.

Breathless. I was suddenly breathless, even as pressure started to push against the backs of my eyes, screaming for me to *breathe;* It wouldn't happen.

Shoes tapped in slow clicks across the floor, *heel toe, heel toe, heel toe.*

It was like the fucking Jaws theme music. Such a minimalistic sound, but every daunting beat was a fresh pump of fear straight to my heart. It was getting closer, too. The shark was coming my way, swimming up on a whiff of panic in my blood.

"I'll definitely take the business gal," he commented aloud. "I like the silver skirt, and I think I'd like it even more around your ankles."

The woman who spoke up about the package chuffed a laugh riff with polite enthusiasm, a laugh all women had to perfect for the sake of a man's ego.

"I think we can arrange that, honey."

Worn brown leather shoes stopped in my visual, pointed right at my bare feet.

"And then what about you?" *Fuck.* "You're awfully quiet down here."

My toes recoiled from the proximity of his, curling under and trying to stabilize against the hardwood floor.

Leave me alone. Leave me alone. Leave me alone.

"She's new, baby. You don't want her. *Trust* me." Whichever girl from down the line that comment had come from, I could have jumped out of my skin and kissed her.

"Is that why you didn't dress up for me, baby?"

Out of the corner of my eye, I saw his hand lift. A flash of skin coming my way, fingers outstretched towards my arm or shirt or hair. I didn't know what the fuck he was about to grab, but my heart screamed as if he was coming at me with a switchblade.

"*No touching,*" a voice knifed from somewhere in front.

A voice splashed with livid red that belonged to a pair of black eyes.

The hard-edged voice nailed the reaching hand in mid-air, upturning it into a position of surrender like the tone of his voice.

"All right, all right. Can I see your face at least?"

Oh god. Standing still, my body was trying to do everything *but.* My flesh was crawling, fresh fire ants birthing from my pores and stinging my skin with the need to peel it right off. The furious feeling ate down my legs and into my feet, energy just *dying* to unleash right out the front doors.

But I couldn't. I couldn't run. I couldn't fight. I couldn't do anything but squirm and try like fucking hell to disappear into myself.

Maybe if I didn't talk, he'd leave. Maybe if I didn't look at him, he'd leave. Maybe if I pretended to be deaf, dumb, and mute, he'd walk away and *leave.*

Oh my god, please just leave.

I stood there, knees loose and wobbling, muscles pulled as tight as a fucking piano string, waiting for this stranger to pluck me and make my screams crescendo.

Buzzcut leaned in, heat from his body washing a humid film over my itching skin. Warmth prodded at the back of my neck, my stomach folding into itself, bile sloshing up my throat in the collapse.

Oh god, here it was. The puke. Any second now I was going to be sick all over this fucker and Heather's mom would come out of her office and lose it.

On me. On my baby sister.

The boiling in my stomach bubbled up to between my ears as the weathered tip of his shoes pivoted with a shift of his weight.

"Hello?" Fingers snapped in front of my face, each hit of flesh on flesh another tremble in my back. "Are you even *allowed* to ignore me?"

"Come *on.*" Irritation heightened the volume of one of the other girls. "Let's be honest, you don't want some inexperienced chick for a threesome."

Buzzcut held a considering beat, the roiling in my ears almost deafening. Then, "What if I wanna break her in?"

Oh god.

My hand flew to my stomach, sitting over the cramping vomit getting ready to spew.

"Hey, my man." Over the gag in my throat and the rush of sickness, the guy with black eyes spoke up. "Come here."

Not daring to look up, and not daring to breathe, I held myself still as the heated presence of the buyer disappeared in front of me. The click of his steps faded further off and when that sound stopped, a rumble of whispered voices took its place.

My heart was in my throat, throbbing a rhythm of panic beneath my skin. The voices were too hushed to make out anything being said; all I could hear was the monotone vibrations of *his* familiar voice.

The man with black eyes could be saying anything, giving Buzzcut tips on how to hurt me, how to humiliate me. Maybe he was bargaining a deal for Buzzcut to film the exact moment my pride was ripped out of me so he could point and laugh and say I told you so.

Fuck, I had to know.

Risking a single glance up, I saw both men standing rather close, the man with black eyes nodding his head in my direction with a wrinkled nose.

In my impossible-to-help peek, our eyes caught, and his mouth slowed the formation of whatever he was saying, his words tangling between our connection.

For just a flash of a second, the ever-present intensity burning his stare wasn't aimed *at* me.

It was *for* me.

A secret passed beneath heavy-set eyebrows right to me. Then it was gone and his attention was back on Buzzcut, who was shaking his head in a show of disappointment. He clapped the man with black eyes on the back, squeezed his shoulder and threw him a, "thanks for the heads up."

He traveled across the floor past me, holding a finger up towards another one of the girls with a hungry smirk on his mouth.

"Looks like you're the winner, Blondie."

The girl he'd chosen burst into laughter and overly enthusiastic cheers, and Buzzcut pivoted towards Claudia's office, he and his oversized ego disappearing inside.

I blinked after him, mouth hanging open, thoughts in my head stuck in a rudder.

"All right Jackie, Kira, go get breakfast or whatever until your afternoon appointments. You know I don't care." My rounded eyes soared over to the man who'd spoken—the one who was currently walking my way.

His paces up to me were long and dictated, simmering pupils rooted on me the same way I was rooted on him. Well, not in the *exact* same way.

Not when he looked like a looming hurricane and I was more like a house one storm away from a total collapse.

He reached where I'd been petrified in place, stopping only a foot away. The smell of smoke lingered in my nose as his heavy-lidded stare lingered down my face.

A beat of tension crackled between us.

"Are you hungry?"

His stiff question fanned over my cheeks, warming the blood in them that had frozen over. Everything about me was still frozen, layered in ice forged from terror and now shock. My voice, my thoughts, my focus on *him* were all stuck in disbelief.

Mindless and numb, I shook my head.

There was a slight flare in his nostrils, a tick in his jaw. He was the one to break our stare, casting his over my head while keeping his head angled low. He was such a *severe* man, everything from how he glared behind me to the weight of whatever was running through his head right now was a concentrated intensity.

If he were to put the tip of his pinky to my chest right now, I think it'd have enough electricity in it to restart my frosted heart.

"Come on," he muttered, still not looking at me. He hooked a hand around my upper arm right beneath my sleeve and urged my feet to turn. They did, walking in blind steps wherever he pulled me.

Which ended up being the kitchen.

I followed on numb feet as he walked us up to a spread of food across a countertop, breakfast meats, pastries, and fruit set up like a buffet. The man palmed an orange from the basket full of them, and then we were leaving on a wordless trail back upstairs, back up to the room I was actually happy to be back in.

He set me in front of the door and then set the orange in my hands. The heat of him pushed against my back as he fished out his keyring and unlocked the door, a press of five fingertips to my lower back guiding me inside.

My feet went, still riding on that wave of shock that had turned them senseless. I was floating above my own axis, not quite off of it but not quite on either. It was loose, wobbling in a daze as I rotated around to face the cloud of black hovering in the doorway.

His stare was on the floor but his arm was reaching for the doorknob, fingers readying to slam it shut and be done with me for the day. My hand not holding the orange shot out, splaying across the wood to stop him before I could think *why* I wanted to stop him.

My lightning just did it. Shot through my veins and put my hand on that door, suddenly awake and wanting answers.

"What did you say to that guy?"

A steamed breath poured through his nostrils as they broadened, his gaze still fixed on the ground. I could practically hear his teeth grinding to dust.

"Doesn't matter."

"It does," I pressed, desperation to *know* upending my breath. "Because whatever it was got him to leave me alone."

Whatever he said *saved* me.

I knew it, and he knew it too, and maybe that's why he looked so uncomfortable as he stuffed both hands in his front pockets, shifting to lean a shoulder up against the doorframe.

"Just gave him some insight."

"Like what?"

His teeth nabbed the corner of his bottom lip, and he spoke through the bite. "*Fuck*, you're nosy."

"I know. Now tell me something I *don't* know, like what you said to stop him."

"I didn't *stop* him." Bladed eyes sliced up from the floor to pierce my next breath. "I told him you were a shit lay."

His aggressive delivery of such a batshit comment jerked my neck back. "*What?*"

Contempt speckled like embered ash in his flaming eyes. "I told him not to waste his money on you. Said every guy who works security here gets a pass at the new girls, and you were a lazy and unimaginative fuck."

My lips recoiled over my teeth. "Gross."

He shrugged, pretending to be casual. "It worked."

I blinked up at him, the gravity of what his little white lie saved me from weighing down my voice. "It did..."

First the shower. Now this.

That was twice now that this man who was supposedly monster through and through showed signs of something more. Something almost human.

It moved behind his eyes, lurking in the shadows his darkness created, but *it* itself wasn't dark. It was a speckle of light, a single snowflake falling in the dead of night. He tried to hide it, tried to melt it away with his quick-trigger flame, but it persisted as if made from diamonds and shined just the same.

My curiosity narrowed on it, trying to catch a closer glimpse to better understand it. Every snowflake had its own design, and I bet if I got close enough to see his, I could make out the shaping and read between every intricate line.

He wouldn't let me though, demonstrating a slow and heavy blink as if to flurry the snowflake back into the darkness so I'd never find it again.

"All right." He tipped his chin up to tell me to back up. "I gotta go—"

"*Wait.*" My hand snapped out to hold the door again as he tried to leave.

"What's your name?"

The way the blacks of his eyes blazed, you'd have thought I'd asked him to roll over and die. I needed to know though. I didn't know *why* I needed it, but it felt as crucial as breathing to know him in that moment.

He swallowed—*hard*—his Adam's apple bobbing, his eyes smoking. It was a simple question. Just his name. The tension that ebbed out of him as he considered answering it though was heady, a hum of energy moving over my skin.

He searched across my face, trailing the burn of his stare over my cheeks, nose, forehead, mouth, *everything*, until the simmer made its way back up, settling on me.

"Blake."

Blake.

My mind wrestled the letters of his name down, coiling around each one to get used to the feel of it.

"Blake," I tested his name out, the single syllable feeling heavy on my tongue. "It suits you."

A beat rested between us, subtle vibration humming in the air making sure we didn't sit in silence. His focus lingered on my mouth that had spoken his name and slowly came back up.

"And you are?"

I blinked up at him. "Kat."

He nodded, not once taking his eyes off of mine. "Okay."

A few more seconds passed before my hand fell from the door and I let him leave.

The door shut and the lock clicked in place from the other side, but I didn't move away from it. That small interaction hung in the air like the smoke he was scented with, slowing my thoughts and compacting my head.

What happened was strange. It was… unexpected.

It was my fucking fairytale miracle.

TWENTY-ONE

DOM

Three days.

Seventy-two hours.

Too many minutes to waste time counting.

That's how long Kat had been missing. That's how long it'd been since I'd seen those big and beautiful bottle-green eyes or heard her siren-song voice.

That's how long it'd been since someone put a hole in my chest and walked away.

I sat at my desk, clicking through Kat's phone I'd hooked up to my computer to search for evidence. *Evidence*, because she was gone. Taken. Someone had taken her from me, and my world hadn't stopped spinning since.

I'd known her less than half a year, but I already didn't know how to live without her. Before meeting her, I thought my life was set. An unhappy marriage but a daughter who made the days brighter and a career I'd worked hard for.

All in all, I considered myself a relatively lucky man.

Then Kat blew into my life, foul-mouthed and foul-tempered, and set it on fire.

She set *me* on fire.

Before Kat, I hadn't realized how numb I'd become to so much of life,

279

moving where I was supposed to, following orders at work and at home, going to sleep at night in a bed that was cold despite the warm body sleeping next to me.

I'd accepted complacency as a form of happiness because I wasn't aware there was anything past it.

Then there was her.

Being with Kat was like waking up one day and finding out you'd been living in a grayscale world where a rainbow of colors had always been waiting to sprout. You accepted the ordinary because you didn't know there was anything extra beyond it.

Kat was my extra. She'd splashed color into my life and embedded her fire inside my heart, and by the time I realized I was burning alive in her colorstorm, I hadn't the faintest interest in reversing it.

Her burn was intoxicating, and it wasn't dramatic to say it was also addicting. My girl was as close to taking a drug as I'd ever come.

And I missed her like hell.

Sighing, I clicked out of Kat's text threads on my screen having found nothing and went over to her storage of photos and videos. There wasn't going to be anything on this phone, and I already knew that.

My index finger rolled down the ball of the computer mouse, scrolling through photos of mostly Charlotte, some of Kat and Layla where the best friends were clearly less than sober, and even one of Dickhead Daren from months ago.

An exhale steamed from my nose while I fought not to scowl at a computer screen.

Moving past it, I was nearing the end of her camera roll when my hand over the mouse froze, the cursor hovering over a video file.

It was timestamped six days ago.

My finger tapped play before I could reason myself out of watching what I knew it was in such a public place.

The video opened up and spread from corner to corner of my computer screen, a perfect shot of my backside in only a pair of black briefs taking center focus. I slipped a quick hand over my mouth to muffle my breath of reaction as I angled the screen away from anyone who walked by.

This was the only time since I started working here that I was grateful to be given a corner desk.

The picture of the video started to move, and I raised the volume only high enough so I could hear.

"That, ladies and gents, is an ass worth dying over. I mean, look at it."

A smile peeled up behind my hand at the sound of her voice. She was such a shameless pervert.

I loved it about her.

She'd taken the video at my new townhome when we came downstairs for a water break after our third round that night. After wanting her so maddeningly for so long, it didn't register how exhausting it was going at it for hours until we'd finished up in the shower, and I was sweatier than when we got in.

I hadn't gone at it like that in over a decade and *never* quite like it was with her. I couldn't help myself from touching her, tasting her, and taking her in every way I'd felt guilty for wanting to for months.

She was my compulsion, and I'd never been so okay having such little control over anything before.

In the video, I was standing bare-chested in front of an open fridge door, the painfully white light from inside brightening the picture of me as I turned to face her, a water bottle still tilted back against my mouth.

"God, even the way you drink water is sexy. How do you get anything done?"

"I could ask the very same thing of you, Ms. Sanders."

"No, you were in the bathroom while I got my refreshments. I downed that water like a fucking lion at a watering hole. There was nothing cute about it."

I laughed both on and off screen, an ache pouring between the bones in my chest as I kept watching us. In the video, I recapped my water bottle and set it somewhere off-screen, knocking the fridge door shut with a tap of my elbow.

"If you were so thirsty, does that mean I finally exhausted you?"

"You wish, old man."

"If you get to call me old man, then I get to call you young lady."

"You'd like that wouldn't you?"

"Honestly, it's like Pandora's box discovering what I like with you."

She laughed aloud, and it was such a goddamn beautiful sound. I wished I could see her face, but the camera was aimed at me as I closed the distance between us in the video. I remembered she was sitting on the island at the center of the kitchen, draped in only the shirt I'd worn to work that day.

The rest of her was bare, and she'd done a flimsy job buttoning the shirt up, missing almost every button but two. The visual I had of her in my head from that precise moment could have been sold as art if I could transfer it onto canvas.

She was this sin-wrapped temptress from the moment I hired her, and in that memory of her, I'd unwrapped her down to everything but sweat and my loose shirt.

That wasn't what I remembered the most, though.

It was her glow. That full-face smile.

Her happiness that night was breathtaking.

I had such a perfect picture of her in my head, it was almost startling when it manifested on my computer screen. There she was, wicked grin and all, as she quickly adjusted her arms to loop around my neck as I closed our distance and went out of frame. She fixed the camera at her face and the back of my head, the stars in her eyes as she looked at me making mine mist.

"Next thing you know, I'll find a crop whip and a schoolgirl's uniform laid out on my bed."

"Are you trying to give me ideas, Ms. Sanders?"

"Of course not, Mr. Reed. Why, is it working?"

"A little."

"What do I have to do to make that 'little' a lot?"

"How about a kiss?"

Her beautiful eyes rolled back in her head, a grin still very present on her perfect mouth. *"Such a sap."*

She leaned in and closed the space between us, and that's where the video ended.

Her lips on mine, and my heart beating outside my chest.

I couldn't look away from the screen, a sweat building at the back of my neck against my shirt's collar as I stared at her. At *us*.

Even as a boy, I couldn't wait to be in love and married. Next to being on the force, becoming a husband and a father were all I wanted. I wanted a family like the one I grew up with. I wanted the dream, and I wanted it badly.

The idea of being in love had always been so romantic to me, and perhaps that's why I married Heather as young as I did. We fit well as teenagers, and at the time, she was the most wonderful thing in the world to me. I didn't see that ever changing.

After the first year of marriage, the wonder began to wear off even though I tried like hell to bring it back. The truth that I denied for the better part of our relationship was that it wasn't love with Heather.

Not true love.

It was a first love, and it had faded as time intended.

However, the love I had with the woman on my computer screen was a lightning strike kind of love.

Rare and explosive, just like her. *My little lightning.*

Our kiss on my computer screen was so goddamn bittersweet to look at. Sweet for the recorded memory I was without prior, bitter for the sting it put behind my eyes.

Over the top of my computer, a pair of designer sunglasses I recognized well carried over and stole focus. They sat over a face that made my stomach drop and arm shoot out to click off the incriminating image on my screen.

The picture of Kat and I went black just in time for her to reach my desk.

I shifted in my chair, buzzing with uncomfortable energy.

"Heather, what are you doing here?"

She propped her ridiculously expensive glasses back on her head, batting me a lighthearted smile.

"What, a wife can't come check on her husband at work?"

Her choice of words straightened up my spine, tightening my shoulders. She'd been throwing those words in my face as often as she got the chance ever since I asked for the divorce. She used them—and Maya—as weapons to guilt me with.

It worked every damn time.

Diving my focus back into the files at my desk, I asked, "Do you need something?"

She came around my desk, perching herself on the lip. "I thought I'd stop by for lunch. Take you to that French cafe on 5th."

I hated that place.

"I'm working, Heather."

"Yes, but all you've done these last three days is *work*. Take a break. Come enjoy some quiche."

Her mindless suggestion of tarts and eggs reduced my nerves to dust in seconds.

I knew what she was doing. *She* knew what she was doing. Years of marriage had given me a decoder to each of Heather's tones and what they really meant behind the surface sounds. This particular tone was one of want.

And what she *wanted* was for me to stop searching for Kat.

"Ms. Sanders' disappearance might mean nothing to you, but it means everything to her sister who is waiting by the door every second she doesn't come home." Folding open a file with Kat's name on it, my voice rolled out low and unforgiving. "If that doesn't break your heart, it should."

She made a noise with her mouth, disregarding and infuriating.

"Her sister is none of our concern, Dom. Is it tragic, *of course.* Is it our problem though?" A silence set, and I knew she was waiting for my attention before answering. When I didn't give it to her, her heel tapped the floor and a sharp sigh heated the air. "The answer is no. As soon as we can ship her off somewhere else to stay, it is not our problem."

Now *that* got my attention.

"Ship her off?" I rebuked, looking up at her finally.

She waved me off. "Oh, you know what I meant."

"I do. You meant you can't wait to get a grieving little girl out of your house while her only family left is missing."

Heather dared to hold eye contact as she showed me with those blue eyes I used to love to death how right I was. She wasn't sorry or sympathetic. She looked how she always did: pissed at me and bored with the conversation.

She got comfortable against my desk, resting her palms behind her against the edge and her right hand an inch from mine. "So sue me, Dominic. She's not our child and therefore not our responsibility. I've allowed them *both* to live in my house, and I'd say that earns me some credit."

"It might've had you not complained about it the whole time."

"Did you expect me to be as *thrilled* about their stay as you were?" She narrowed her stare down at me, her subtext fire-breathing and not at all subtle.

"We're not doing this right now." Sighing heavily, I cleared my hand away from hers and found busy work rifling through papers. "I've got work to do, and I'm sure you have a busy day too."

"On the contrary. I cleared my schedule so I could take you out to lunch." She slid herself across the edge of my desk, inching closer to where I sat.

Internalizing a groan, I rolled my chair back to a distance that wasn't so perfumed with her flowery scent. "You should go see Maya with all this free time you have now. I'm sure she'd like that."

Heather's eye roll was practically audible, and no matter how often she dismissed our daughter, it never stopped hurting.

"I came here to see *you*, Dom."

"You shouldn't have," I mumbled, tired of her too-little-too-late attempts. "You know that."

"*Dominic*." She scoffed my name, and the pages in my hands crinkled as my grip on them tightened. "When are you going to stop this? You're being ridiculous and you know it."

My eyes slammed shut, a weighted inhale filling my chest.

"Heather, I don't have time for this," I motioned between the two of us, "today. You and I haven't gone out to a meal just the two of us since we moved here."

A brush of delicate, cool fingers moved over mine.

"So why don't we change that?"

I jerked my hand away from hers so fast, you'd have thought her touch was acidic. In a way, it was. The feel of her skin on mine was all wrong now. Where I used to crave it, now a touch from her made my gut boil like I'd swallowed a mouthful of poison.

Rejection splashed every pretty corner of her face, and a look like that from her a few years ago would have gutted me.

Heather wasn't a woman used to being denied what she wanted.

There was a part of me that still cared for Heather as the mother of my child, and that part squeezed, hurt palpitating in my sternum as I watched her grasp for straws. She'd been doing that a lot since I asked for the divorce, and I'd have to be inhuman not to feel sad watching a woman who'd always taken without asking grasp for anything.

"I think it's time for you to go," I spoke carefully.

Her tiny nose ruffled with indignation, her mouth pursing. "You're still my husband, Dominic. Without a court date set, your wagon is still hitched to mine. For better or worse, remember?"

I did. I remembered my vows and how confident I was when I made them. In front of friends, family, and God himself. I'd vowed to love this woman to my dying breath, for better or for worse.

"I don't think anyone is ever prepared for how much worse worse can get," I replied, my tone leveled by years of fights and resentment.

For so long, all I wanted to do was make my wife happy.

I worked every day at it, finding ways, big and small, to put a smile on her face and ease the worry in my gut that something was wrong between us. Nothing I did was ever enough, though.

That kind of failure as a man and husband were nearly debilitating.

"Dominic, I think you forget how *good* we were before we moved here." Heather's glare was like frostbite on the top of my head as I refused to look at her. "You didn't have these asinine whims back in Georgia. Everything was *fine* before we moved down here."

Taking her millionth jab at the move we made for my job in stride, I slid my hand up my nose, pinching the bridge between my dry eyes.

"No, it wasn't. We hadn't been fine in a long time, Heather."

"Oh, so I'm just making up all the good times we had?" she pressed. "Like our Honeymoon in Mexico or our dates to the drive-in or the midnight trips we'd take to that bakery on the corner when we were teenagers? You'd always get the chocolate chunk cheesecake and I'd always get…"

She trailed off, memories of a past with her cluttering my head as I pictured her nose scrunched up like it got when she thought too hard, a sigh of nostalgia slipping out.

"Key lime pie," I answered quietly.

I loved that bakery. I loved the memories we'd made there. I used to love my marriage just the same.

I tilted a pitying look up to her, the corner of her mouth rising in victory.

"So you do remember."

And she did too. She just wanted to make sure I also remembered.

"Yes, I remember, but every memory you just mentioned was made over a decade ago. We were kids, Heather. We're not kids anymore."

Denial flooded in from all sides of her stare, her upper lip catching on a sneer.

"You're just confused."

And now we were back to this. Her go-to argument. That I was 'confused' and I would get over my 'whim' of wanting a divorce any day now. She blamed my confusion on everything from stress at work to Kat coming into our lives but never stopped to accept what I'd been telling her the whole time.

Our marriage had been a dead thing dragging us down for years, and I'd just found the strength to cut it loose.

We'd had this same argument a hundred times by now, and I couldn't handle having it again at the moment. I moved forward in my seat, resting my elbows on the desk.

"I really think it's time you go."

"So you can get back to working on the nanny's case?"

The accusation in her tone was so booming, it could have vibrated the walls of the police station. Lifting my gaze to hers, I kept my control in check and my bravado implicit.

"Yes. That's my job."

Thoughts moved behind her eyes, fast and calculating, as if every argument we had was a game of chess she intended on winning.

"You and I both know the likelihood of finding Ms. Sanders at this point."

She dangled those words in front of me, focusing the shards of her pupils razor sharp to quickly stab out any slip up I gave her. This was how any mention of Kat went between us. From even before anything happened with her, Heather would jab accusations my way about my lurid intentions with Kat.

It used to piss me off in the beginning.

After having been nothing but loyal to her in the near thirteen years we'd known each other, I had a right to be offended. I never so much as looked at another woman while I was with her, and in our first fights about Kat, I admit I was overly defensive of myself.

Later on, I realized my being so defensive even before I'd kissed Ms. Sanders was because I knew I wanted to. Even then.

Thoughts of her strawberry lips had slipped into my mind within the first week of her employment. By the second week, I couldn't get her out of my head. She was there when I woke up and there when I went to sleep at night.

When Heather's accusations turned into the truth, I was mindful enough to change my stance to impassive whenever we spoke about Kat. No more oversensitive blow ups to hide my guilt inside.

I had to be smart. I had to be tactful.

Except now, with Kat gone and Heather relishing in it, I just couldn't stop my jaw from ticking.

And Heather caught it.

She jumped on the reaction, contempt teeming in her slitted glare. "And try not to care too visibly or you'll blow your cover."

Leaning back in my work chair, I breathed out a mundane sigh of deniability. "I don't have a cover, Heather. I just have a heart."

One that belonged to the woman she was so fastly casting into a grave.

"Have you gotten anywhere on her case?"

"Heather—"

"What?" Her blue eyes flashed. "I'm showing interest in Ms. Sanders. *Compassion.* Isn't that what you want?"

Internalizing a steamed sigh, I said, "What I want is to get back to work."

She promptly ignored me, gliding her manicured nails along a stack of files to take a snooping gander. My hand slapped down the papers she was sneaking a look at, handing her a warning glare. She raised her hands in mock surrender, and I snatched every file Kat's name was printed on and moved it to the other side of my desk aside from one.

I singled out the folder with every detail Layla gave at the hospital.

"I'm waiting on her best friend to come in for another interview," I mumbled, all my patience frayed. "See if she remembers anything else."

Heather tutted next to me, her voice drifting off with a calculated awe. "It's still a phenomenon she survived her ordeal."

I grunted in agreement.

"When is she coming in?"

"Should be here any minute."

Beside me, Heather went quiet. The steady push and pull of her breathing I knew as well as I knew my own stilled. I tipped a look up at her, catching her dainty features doused with a little more chill than usual.

Her gaze skirted mine as she righted herself to stand, clutching one of her several designer purses under her arm.

"In that case, I should go."

Before I could verbalize my agreement, Heather had strutted past me in a blur of perfume and fast clicks of her heels, sunlight bleeding in as she took the emergency backdoor outside rather than the way she came in.

She swept out of here fast, two other faces towing around the corner on her tailwinds.

There was no time to recompose after the collision with Heather before both Ryan and a nervous Layla reached me. Her nose was to the floor, her steps slowed as if each one was a potential encounter with a mine. Her posture was tight, too.

Scared.

"Hey, man." Ryan clapped me on the shoulder, keeping his other hand firmly locked around Layla's.

I swallowed, a thickness greasing up my throat as I nodded at him but didn't look away from Layla. I hadn't seen her since I found her halfway to dead in a pile of trash. She looked small then. She was even smaller now.

And she wouldn't look at me.

"You getting anywhere trying to find her dad?" Ryan spoke up when no one else did.

My head started in a slow shake before I found a voice to speak with. One deeper and rougher than normal.

"No. The guy's a ghost. No records of where he moved to after he left town three years ago. No bank statements, no address. All I found was an old phone number."

"You call it?"

"No answer. Left a voicemail."

"You really think her *dad* could be a suspect?"

"It's worth a shot." We had nothing to go off of since Tommy's alibi checked out. Even Kat's ex, Daren, had been brought in with an alibi too. "At the very least, we can rule him out and I can stop wasting time on him as a potential."

Ryan packed his chest with a digestive inhale and nodded, a curious smirk whirling up the side of his mouth.

"Boy, I hope you're not expecting to get her father's blessing this way."

I slanted him an unamused glower. The only blessing I'd need if I found him would be that I didn't punch his face through the back of his skull.

"What's that smell?" Layla suddenly spoke up.

Both Ryan and I dropped our focus to her.

She wasn't staring at the floor anymore, big, dark rings hanging beneath both eyes as she sniffed the air. Ryan glanced to me in confusion, giving his own whiff of the room to smell what I knew they were both getting at without having to nose the air.

"White gardenias." Ryan's browline bunched in confusion at me. "Heather was just here. That's her perfume."

His mouth formed into the perfect shape of an O and Layla simply nodded, a bit of dark hair falling in her face. She didn't seem to notice, and Ryan swept it away before she could.

Ryan had been unevenly splitting his time between work and being with her, and it was getting harder not to take it personally. When I needed him here to comb through case files and bounce theories off of, he was by her side instead.

In the year I'd known him, he'd never taken any woman he'd been with seriously, and I was more than glad he finally manned up with Layla. I wasn't mad that he was taking care of her when she needed someone.

I was mad he was blowing off helping me find Kat to do it.

Getting him to agree to bring her in for this interview alone had been like pulling teeth.

"Babe, you wanna sit?" Ryan gently guided Layla into a nearby chair, rolling her over closer to my desk. She still wouldn't look at me, and if I wasn't mistaken by the lighting, there was already a sheen of wetness gathered in her eyes. She blinked rapidly, inhaling a lungful of the flowered air again.

Ryan stood over her, both hands on her caved in shoulders, rubbing support into her every so often. She wore a loose t-shirt, but at the angle she was hunched into herself at, I could see bones in her shoulders poking out. I wondered if she'd been eating since being back.

I wondered if Kat had eaten since being taken.

My chest pinched tight with the thought, a lonely ache blooming from the pain. I tried to breathe past it, picturing her cheek-to-cheek smile on my computer screen. It and she were radiant and lively, and I would have my little lightning back, brightening up my world as soon as her best friend pointed me in the direction to go.

"How have you been?" I asked, easing into things.

Or so I thought.

She stiffened up, flashing me a weakened look. "How have *you* been?"

Point taken.

I nodded solemnly, though she didn't see it. Her focus was already back on her hands that she tangled in Ryan's. The palm of my hand tingled with the memory of Kat's in it, and I squeezed it to a fist to make it stop.

"Ryan already tells me you don't remember anything from when you were away, but I'd like to talk about when I found you."

She was shaking her head before I even finished my sentence.

"I don't remember," she murmured, her volume cracked in half.

Frustration tickled at the back of my throat, but I brought my fist in front of my mouth to clear it out.

The woman sitting in front of me was fragile. Nothing like the one I'd met at Kat's side that day in the park or spent time with at the hotel by the beach.

That woman was wild and carefree. One look at her back then profiled her as someone who'd had an easy life and sailed right through it. She was naïve to heartache and strife, likely living her life up to that point in a safe and warm bubble.

That bubble had been popped since. Brutally.

Whoever had traumatized Layla's rose-colored view of the world now had Kat. I didn't even want to think about how much they'd try to smudge her already corrupted view.

She saw things through an over-corrected lens that painted everyone as monsters, and after this, I wasn't sure how I was supposed to convince her of anything different.

I pressed on. "Do you remember saying Kat's name to me?"

Again, she shook her head before I finished the question, and I repeated the process of clearing my throat when irritation itched the back of it. My nerves had been shot long before Layla got here, but her dismissing the questions before she even fully heard them was making my skin burn.

I was just so fucking tired of *no* direction and *no* answers.

Layla's lids were lowered, her attention on her hands still as she fiddled with her fingers between Ryan's. Her nostrils flared, another smell of the air rattling down her chest.

"Layla, will you look at me?"

She rolled her lips between her teeth, biting until the skin turned white from blood loss. More hair fell into her face as she shook her head.

Confusion angled my head at her. "Why not?"

In her seat, she rocked back and forth, still shaking her head.

"I can't," she whispered, torment mangling her voice. She was coming apart at the seams bit by bit, breathing harder, a desperate well of tears pooling fast in the cusp of her eyes. "I look at you and I see *her*."

Her honesty hit me like a goddamn brick wave, smacking the air right out of my lungs. I blinked at her tears, forgetting how to breathe, forgetting how to think. All I did was feel her words and grapple with the poor stitching coming undone over my heart.

I didn't talk about how much I missed Kat out loud.

I didn't talk about the last three nights I'd spent alone in the dark, wishing for her, praying for her, doing everything I could to keep my thoughts off of what was happening to her. I didn't talk about the crack in my chest that felt deep enough to swallow me up in my grief.

I didn't say these things out loud because then it made them real.

Saying she was gone made a reality where she might not be coming back real, and that wasn't a reality I had any interest in entertaining.

Not now. Not ever.

My Kat *wasn't* gone. She wasn't lost. She was somewhere inside Layla's head right now, and I needed to rip her out.

I leaned forward in my seat, the mark of grief branded into my chest searing hotter, the agony impossible to ignore. Wet brown eyes jumped to me, and I smartly deepened my voice to muffle the stitch of vulnerability digging into it.

"I want her back, Layla. I need her back. You can help me."

"I can't," she croaked out.

"You *can*. You were there and I wasn't. You can help her more than I can right now. You just have to think." I ran the tip of my tongue over my upper lip, watching her carefully as blood pinked her cheeks from beneath and a splash of tears washed over them. "She was there in that back alley, wasn't she?"

"I don't know."

My chin kicked to the side, jaw sawing hard. I didn't give up.

"You saw her that day, and that's why you said her name to me, right? She went there to get you, and you *saw* her. You saw Kat in that back alley."

More rapid blinking. More frantic dashing eye contact. She touched her fingertips to her mouth, mumbling out, "Maybe…"

Maybe. Maybe wasn't 'I don't remember.' Maybe I could work with.

"Who else did you see Layla?" I urged, leaning forward in my chair. "Voices, smells, *anything* distinctive you can tell me."

She put a hand to her chest, and I noted the tips of her fingers shaking against her shirt's fabric.

"I don't feel good," she whispered, more to herself and Ryan than me.

Ryan knelt next to her, squeezing her hands in his. "We can stop if you want."

"No," I denied, offense surging in my bloodstream as I locked my attention on Ryan. "We're just getting somewhere."

"Dude, she's crying."

Layla let out a succession of quick breaths, her hollowed chest pumping faster than seconds ago. In more innate confusion than anything else, her watery gaze fixed on me, a silent plea for help screaming from the pits of her eyes. My mouth parted as I watched her, her slipping tears, her gasping breaths, the helpless sheen casing over her wide eyes.

Familiarity kicked me in the gut, the diagnosis rushing out.

"She's having a panic attack."

A severe one from the looks of it.

"What—" Ryan blustered next to a hyperventilating Layla, rivers running down her puffy cheeks. "Babe, it's okay. It's okay." He snapped a red-faced look back at me over his shoulder. "I told you this was a bad idea."

Layla began shaking her head back and forth, panicked eyes switching back and forth between me and him. "I-I don't know wh-why it's happening. I don't—"

A violent sob ripped through whatever she was going to say next, folding her over at the waist. Ryan helped her up out of the chair and practically carried her out the same back exit Heather had taken.

I watched them go but didn't stand, the sunlight waning through the closing backdoor until it slammed shut. Silence took over in their absence, crushing down on my chest with a profoundness I'd never experienced before.

I was beginning to understand why Kat hated it so much.

TWENTY-TWO

KAT

The next Line Up went the same as the first.

And the one after that, too.

I'd made it through three morning Line Ups so far without being chosen for slaughter, and the reason had a name I'd been thinking a lot lately.

Blake.

Him and his inexplicable mercy had absorbed many of the unending hours I spent trapped in my room. I thought about him a lot and why he did what he did. Every time a customer would turn their small dick energy my way, *Blake* would come out of the shadows and mutter something to them. The men would go from horny to disappointed and set their appetite on another fresh pick from the line.

I hadn't asked him to do it, and I didn't know why he did it either. I tried to ask him after the second Line Up, and he slammed a door in my face. On the third day, I hid under the bed when he came up to get me for that morning's torture fest, positive my luck in his criminal kindness had run dry.

Not only did he repeat exactly what he'd been doing so far, but he also didn't kick my ass for hiding from him. Just dragged me out by my ankles, both of us cursing and yelling, and reminded me what was at stake if I wasn't downstairs on time.

Claudia's threat was always ringing in my ears, Charlotte's sweet face beaming behind my eyes.

And that's exactly how her face would stay no matter fucking what.

Today was a Thursday, my fifth morning here, and it began with another failed escape attempt.

It wasn't all that clever—I didn't have a lot to work with here—but I'd seen the whole 'hide behind the door' trick work in enough movies to at least give it a try. I had to give *everything* a try to get out of here. I wasn't ignorant enough to think I could keep up this streak or that Blake wouldn't decide he was done saving my ass any day now.

I had to get out of here. Back to Charlotte. Back to Dominic.

Today, un-fucking-fortunately, wasn't that day.

The lock on the bedroom door unfastened, swinging wide open with me standing in waiting behind it. My heart beat for one, two, three seconds before a dark head of hair peeked around the edge of the door, unsurprised eyes falling to me.

My shoulders dropped as my bottom lip reeled back between my teeth. *"Fuck."*

His heavy-set browline was curved up on one end, arrogant intrigue holding it up.

"You really think that would work?"

"Wasn't sure how stupid you were," I said with an obvious shrug.

He nodded just once, unamused. "Flattering."

Blake herded me downstairs for the Line Up, and to my sanity and vagina's relief, did what he had done the last three days. He steered the two men—one trucker, one army guy—away with whatever lies he came up with, and before I knew it, I'd survived my fourth Line up.

Blake walked over at the end of it, only me and that platinum blonde energizer bunny left standing. Well, I was standing. She was pouting and stomping her way back towards the kitchen, the clack of her plastic heels cheapening her backwards walk of shame.

"What'd you tell them this time?" I asked when he reached me.

He averted his gaze over the top of my head like he always did when I tried to talk about what he did.

"Same stuff."

My nose pulled to a wrinkle. "That's boring. Next time, give me a fungus or something."

Neck craned back to stare directly at him, I was there to witness the exact moment pigs took flight, hell froze over, and any other idiom phenomenon as the corner of the grumpiest mouth in the world twitched up.

You couldn't even categorize that as a technical smile, but coming from him?

It was like the sun itself just burst through the front doors.

He took me by the arm and led me back towards the kitchen, currents of melt-in-your-mouth bacon and processed, sugary syrup guiding the way. The breakfast buffet, as Blake explained, was for the staff before operating hours and for the morning patrons after the day had begun.

Since I was neither, Blake usually let me do a drive-by snatch of everything I could fit in my hands before locking me back in my room for the day. Since I couldn't exactly *carry* bacon or eggs, my diet had been mostly palmable fruits, muffins, and donuts.

Not exactly my *worst* breakfast.

Today, I didn't feel like a moderate sugar high just to sit in that boredom chamber. Today, I wanted to fill up on fat and grease and have a conversation with someone other than myself before I passed out in that blank, four-walled prison where sanity goes to die.

The only other person in the kitchen when we got there was the blonde who didn't get hand-picked to be rammed by a stranger all morning. She sat at the long stretch of countertop in the middle of the expansive kitchen, picking sections of fluffy scrambled egg out of the silver buffet bin in front of her between her long, hot pink nails.

No eggs for me today. Thanks.

The warmth of Blake's hand loosened around my upper arm as we stopped in front of the pastries section, blueberry muffins, chocolate donuts, and biscuits all sweetening a smile up at me.

I didn't fall into temptation with any of them, turning to face Blake instead.

"Will you eat with me?"

He pulled that face again. That one he made when you asked him something simple and he reacted like you'd asked him if you could spit in his food instead. Swarthy brows curved in, a wrinkle of confusion forming between the two.

His eyes, well, they were doing what they *always* did.

Burning a little too hot to not sweat beneath.

"I already ate."

I shrugged. "So watch me eat."

There was just the slightest part to his mouth that disappeared as his pink lips thinned under the pressure he clenched his jaw with. His gaze skimmed over my head yet again, a storm billowing within dark sky eyes.

"No. Grab what you want—"

I dodged the grab he made for me, slipping an arm's length away from him and stood my ground. "Just ten minutes!"

Just because I'd put distance between us didn't mean I couldn't feel his temper pulse out, heat prickling tiny jabs of warning across my bare skin. Those eyes of smoke blackened, Danger a cloud quickly manifesting around his frame as he started towards me.

"I said no—"

"Please?" I cut in, not swaying an inch even as his temper brought him so close, I could taste him on the tip of my tongue. A fusion of cigarettes and potent electricity, like a sip of the headiest, smokiest wine.

My heart throbbed the same way it would if I took a long pull of any alcohol, over-pumping and over-stimulated. Maybe breathing too much when he was this close wasn't smart. Maybe *being* this close to him wasn't smart, but I couldn't move now. I needed him to know I meant it. The 'please.'

The *begging*.

The word had done a loop through his stare and come back to his pupils, crackling the black like embered coal. 'Please' wasn't a common word in my dictionary, but I'd beg for this if only to see if it worked.

If only to see just how deep his mercy went.

The power in his stare pressed up against mine, challenging it, *scrutinizing* it. I'd always heard a woman's pleading gaze could end wars, but I'd never tapped into that power until now.

Never wanted to need to.

Blake rolled his eyes up and away from mine, the whites of his eyes showing a white flag.

"Eat fast."

A breath of disbelief swept from my lungs, victory attempting to dent my cheeks. I rolled my lips together to keep it from showing, turning my focus from him to the stretch of hot food laid out for what felt like miles.

Never before had a victory looked so fucking delicious.

I started with bacon, shoving two slices into the hole in my face without even chewing. There was enough saliva drowning my mouth that I didn't need to. It all just slid down my throat and made room for the next thing my greasy fingers picked up, which was a sausage link.

I wolfed that down too, and sometime in between that and making a grab for a stack of golden pancakes, a plate materialized in front of me, a large hand shoving it into my free palm.

My neck cranked around to find Blake at my side, watching me beneath brows of heavy-judgement.

"At least try to pretend you're civilized."

I held up a finger in between us, waiting for the savory breakfast meat rolling around in my mouth to go down the pipe. Swallowing thickly, I said, "I'm only accepting this, not because I give a fuck about being civilized, but because I need it to drown my pancakes in syrup and biscuits in gravy."

One of those thick, judgy eyebrows hooked up, and I couldn't exactly tell if it was derision or intrigue doing the lifting.

I didn't stick around long enough to care or find out, moving down the line and only skipping the bin full of sun-yellow scrambled eggs still being hoarded by the woman with hair the same color. She gave me and my overloaded plate a hazel-eyed glance before diving back into the world of her phone.

Which is why it shocked me when she spoke.

"So what's your deal?"

The high-twangy pitch of her voice jerked my head in her direction, but I found white-light from her phone screen still washing her face. She was simultaneously nosing into my business while keeping her nose buried in her own.

The ceramic of the plate clattered carefully on the marble as I set it down, wrapping my fingers around the handle of syrup.

"It's hard to answer such a specific question."

Sarcasm dripped along my words like the sweet pour of thickened sugar over my stack of pancakes, the golden fluff turning darker and candied and so fucking mouth-watering.

I set the syrup back where it belonged, handing blondie a furtive glance.

"Why are you here?" She shifted her brazen stare to Blake. "Why is she here?"

"Clearly for the *bitchin'* buffet," I replied before Blake could.

A heated sigh fanned down my neck, exposed by the sequin tank top I'd lugged on for today's Line Up. I craned my head back to Blake, a look of innocence sitting heavy on my face.

Black eyes disappeared behind heavy lids as they rolled, and an itch to call him on it tickled at the back of my throat. Mainly because of that damn sunbeam twitch wrestling up the corner of his mouth again that was a traitor to his eye roll.

"Seriously, come on." Blondie garnered my attention, twisting on the stool she sat on to face me. "All the girls are curious about you."

With a click of my tongue, I perched myself on one of the stools at the end of the counter. "Good to know I'm a water cooler topic of conversation around here."

"Well, *duh*. Ray's never brought in anyone like this before. It doesn't make good business sense."

Across the expanse of marbled countertop, a flash of silver forks sitting on a flourish of napkin cloths caught my eye. I leaned over my plate, stretching my fingers as far as they could go for one. "And who's Ray?"

"Our boss?" The dubity of her tone curved my slanted focus to her, still straining across the counter. "The guy who runs this whole shindig?"

Oh. *Him.* "Heather's dad."

My reach for the throng of forks was cut short by a sun-kissed hand getting in the way, plucking one from the batch and folding it between long fingers, handing it out for me to take. My stare tracked up to the face the hand belonged to, lingering for a warring second before snatching the offering.

"Wait, you know Heather? I've been here for three years and I've barely had two conversations with her."

Lucky.

"We share a few of the same interests." Or really just one.

The double meaning flew right over her head of bleached hair like a volleyball soaring over the sand at the beach. She nodded slowly, bringing her greasy pointer finger to her lipsticked mouth and sticking it in, sucking off the egg residue.

With the fork Blake got for me—that I could have gotten for myself with just a *little* more reaching—I dove prongs first into a cut of pancakes, sectioning out a bite too big for my mouth.

But fuck it, I was hungry, and this was happening.

Jaw widened, syrup-soaked cake sliding across my tongue, I almost jammed the triple stack bite all the way in my mouth when some rando came around the corner from the hallway and broke my focus.

"Aw, *shit*," I mumbled beneath my breath, sticky globs of syrup falling across my chin.

The new guy on scene jabbed his pointed chin in Blake's direction. "Claudia needs you. Brett was a no-show at Reeves."

Next to me, Blake sighed a curse and I cut a look back to him as I thumbed a drop of syrup off my chin. He clocked the gesture, lingering the weight of his black stare on my chin before moving it up and over my head.

"Hey, Sergio," he called through the house in the direction of the foyer. A few seconds later, the beast of a man known as Sergio came into the kitchen, scary-looking as ever. Blake rounded the countertop in his direction.

"I gotta go to Reeves. Can you bring Kat back up when she's done eating?"

"Who the fuck is Kat?"

"Oh—" Blake fumbled, realizing his mistake. He shook his head as if shaking my name from his brain and nodded back in my direction. "Her. Take her back when she's done."

And then he left. Just like that. Here one second and gone the next, leaving me under the charge of a man who honest to fuck looked like the bones in his face were too big for his skin to hold in. A shiver tickled down my spine as he passed a molten glare my way.

"Is that your name?"

My attention jumped back to Blondie. "What?"

"Kat. Blake just said it."

"Oh, yeah."

"Cute. I'm Zoey."

"Cool." I nodded, barely registering her name with a burning question melting my focus on anything else other than, "What's Reeves?"

She smacked her bright pink lips. "Our second location."

My fork nearly fell out of my hand.

"You mean another *brothel*?"

"Don't act so shocked." She crossed one leg over another, a whole lot of ass cheek making an appearance. "What, are you a *prude*, Little Miss Newbie?"

"I'm not a prude, I'm just not a…" My voice cut away as my brain floundered, searching for the spelling of the correct label in the mossy green of her eyes. "Prostitute?" I tried, a preemptive wince heightening my pitch.

"Oh my god." Her laughter bubbled up, light and unoffended. "You can say the word. It's not gonna bite you."

My chest deflated with a breath of worry, a pit I hadn't realized formed in my stomach unclenching around all the food I'd hoofed down. Tension untethered in my posture, sinking back down to normal as I stuck my fork into another bite of pancake.

"I wasn't sure. I've never met a prostitute before." Raising my fork to my mouth, I added, "I've never done *any* of this before."

"I can tell." She gave me a once over. "It's not your stuffy nine-to-five job, but before you say anything," She held all five manicured fingers up to me. "I love what I do."

Skepticism lowered the tilt of my head. "Sleeping with strangers?"

"Having sex for money," she corrected. "*A lot* of money. Plus, working here is a step up and a half from being on the streets or with a pimp. Food, a warm bed, free control over your schedule—"

"Being forced to fuck a brand new dick every day," I added in for her, stuffing the bite between my teeth.

Heat flared up the back of my neck as I heard myself say it, and I wanted to grab the words and swallow them down with my pancake.

Damn. Maybe I *was* a prude.

Thankfully, all Zoey did was flash me a side-eye that made the wad of cake going down my throat stick just a bit.

"We have a *lot* of repeat customers, mind you. All of them have to be approved by security before even getting the address to the place anyway. There's no real creeps or anything, so don't worry about that. The Line Up is a way we test new customers out, and from there we get to make our own schedules, decide how many appointments we want a day, who we're seeing, yada yada. And nothing's forced. We all wanna be here. We're all *lucky* to be here. You can ask any of the girls. This place got a lot of them out of bad situations."

A grunt vibrated in my throat as I wandered my fork around my plate. "Yeah, well this place is my personal fucking nightmare."

"Then why are you here?" The veracity in her high-pitched voice strung my attention over to her. "Like, seriously. All Claudia told us about you was that you were gonna be out in a month and to ignore you, but like… why?"

"Why *what* exactly?"

"Why are you here when you obviously don't want to be? None of us get it."

The corner of my mouth inched up, the rest of the muscles in my face doing their damndest to wrestle down my amusement at the sake of her stupidity. "I think that's the whole schtick of being kidnapped. Being somewhere I *don't* want to be."

She scoffed a laugh, one not as lighthearted as her last. "Claudia and Ray do not need to kidnap anyone."

I blanched, setting my fork down. "How the fuck do you think I got here?"

Hazel green narrowed on me, a ring of neon disbelief circling around the edges. Her mouth parted, thinly plucked eyebrows peaking up and back down. It was like I could physically see her trying to make the hurdle to understand what I was saying, and she kept missing the jump, falling flat on her face instead.

"They did not kidnap you," she denied, telling me as if she was leading the blind—*me*—to the cliff point of comprehension.

"Yes they fucking did," I almost laughed at the absurdity of what I was defending. "Chloroform and all."

When all she did was blink at me, a new layer of doubt coating her stare each time, I pivoted in my stool to face her with a fizz of lightning circulating my bones. "I don't know why you seem so shocked. You said it yourself. I *clearly* don't want to be here. I'm not jumping up and down for all the guys they parade in here."

"Well, you're new so…" She uncrossed and crossed her legs again, shifting in her chair. "Everyone's nervous when they first start."

"I'm not *nervous*, I…"

A strange sensation bubbled between my ribs as I stopped to stare at her. At the loose strands of understanding yet to be connected in her curved-in eyes.

I'd met some first-rate liars in my life, ones who could convince a sheep they were a lion, but those people always had something off in their eyes when they spoke. Something a little too shifty to nail down and trust.

I wasn't stupid enough to trust Zoey, but all she had in her eyes was genuine confusion.

She *wasn't* lying, and she *wasn't* acting.

Holy shit.

She was in the dark about all of it. The sex-trafficking, the kidnapping, the countless young women her employers had ruined without a goddamn care in their high-and-mighty world.

The hunger in my stomach vanished, swept away by shock and something comparable to that godforsaken hope. Both emotions swelled in my heart and dragged me off my stool to get closer to her, excitement trapped beneath my humming skin.

"You don't know about the sex-trafficking?"

Pretty green eyes bulged. "The *what?*"

Time to act fast.

"Zoey, I'm not supposed to be here. I'm supposed to be home with my baby sister and best friend and this guy, this *great* fucking guy that kind of sort of is the reason that I'm here," I rushed, words spilling out of me faster and faster by the second. "You could call him. You could call and—"

"I don't think I should be talking to you." She cut me and my excitement right off, hiding her stare in her lap as she began to move off the stool, readying to leave. Desperation shot me forward, *almost* reaching out to grab her arm.

"No, *no*. Wait—"

But she didn't wait. She bolted instead, leaving dust in her high-heeled steps, going off to her room or wherever she wanted. Because she *could*. She could go wherever she wanted in this house, in this city or town or wherever we were.

She wasn't a prisoner here like I was.

I watched her until she disappeared, my heart deflating back down to its normal, crippled size.

My stupid heart was all confused ever since Dominic loved it back to normal health.

It wished for more than it knew better to wish for with people.

People were the fucking worst, but Dominic was *so* good, he outweighed so much of the bad in others that I almost forgot it was there.

Until they reminded me.

Until I could tell someone point-blank to their face I was trapped here against my will and they could walk away. Not just someone either. A *woman*. A fellow uterus before duderus. Before Dominic, the only people I'd been able to depend on had all been women. Mrs. Sharon, Layla, Charlotte.

Now, between Zoey, Heather, Claudia…

Maybe I had it wrong all these years hating men.

I shouldn't have discriminated.

I should have been hating *everyone* until proven otherwise.

Out of the corner of my eye, a dark-haired woman in a light gray dress with pleated white around the collar and sleeves came out of a door at the back of the kitchen.

Theresa, I remembered Sergio called her. Right as he was twisting my arm nearly out of its socket and threatening me to not talk to her unless she talked to me first.

"Hi," I tried.

Theresa scurried around the countertop, eyes laser-locked on the floor as she whipped a white rag out of her dress pocket. She ran it across where Zoey had been sitting and then lifted my plate still half full of food and walked away with it, disappearing behind the door she'd come through.

I cocked my head at the swinging white door, a click of my tongue echoing in the emptiness. "Or not."

Seriously, fuck *everyone* in this house.

"Guess I'm done eating," I mumbled, lifting my foot towards the entrance of the kitchen where Sergio was.

Or…

Where he was supposed to be.

My eyes scanned, breathing pulling to a stop as I searched for signs of the man left to watch over me. A peek of his burly arms hanging too long at his sides. A rumble of his gravelly voice down the foyer or hallways.

I waited several, several seconds.

For nothing.

Not a single peep.

Holy shit, did he forget about me?

Inching closer to the entrance of the kitchen, I dared a glance down the hallway. The parallel walls were lined with doors, all of them closed shut.

No Sergio either.

I canted back, astonishment righting my shoulders as I thought one and only one thought.

I was alone. Forgotten.

Whatever feeling went along with *holyfuckingshitholyfuckingshit* parted my lips, but I clamped my palm over my mouth before any smile could spring. Even though my pores were buzzing like I'd hit a million dollar stroke of luck, I would *not* get ahead of myself.

Not yet.

My heart lodged in my throat. I tiptoed out into the open, eyes wide and wary on every corner of the house that was still so awake. Voices, some muffled and some moaning, came from all directions. Clatter from back wherever Theresa had gone trickled out in staccato chimes.

So much noise. So much liveliness bustling behind each and every wall…

Except for the foyer.

Where *I* was.

It was dead, the dark wood floors spotless and the air still as a static breath. My neck elongated around the corner, sweeping a surveying glance around the barren space, my pulse tripping over too many beats as my gaze passed the front doors.

The doors to my escape. The doors I could leave through *now,* tear them open and scream to the first person I saw to call 911 and have the crazy bitch living with my boyfriend arrested and her family thrown in the loony bin with her.

Boyfriend.

For all that was going on, I almost stopped myself as I thought the word. My disjointed brain realized it was the first time I'd called Dominic my boyfriend even in my own head, and it made my heart fucking ache in that good love kind of way.

That way that told me I missed him more than I might miss breathing if that were taken from me too. I missed him and his hands and his voice and his laugh. I missed his goodness, his *perfect* heart.

My body ignited with painful longing for him and all he was, all his staunch-heroic, cheesy-romantic, straight-laced facets; I loved all of them. I loved all of *him.*

He'd turned me into this sap sack, and I needed to get back to him ASAP.

Turning the corner into the foyer, I thought about how much danger he, my sister, and even Maya were in being around Heather. Taking my first few silent steps across the mahogany-colored flooring, I thought about how badly I wanted to wrap my hands around her thin little neck and squeeze. Inching out into the open, I thought about the look on Heather's face when I showed up on her doorstep, a prized grin holding up my cheeks as I brought her facade of a life to a fiery end.

I was exactly four steps in the direction of freedom when I glanced aside and nearly choked on the oxygen in my lungs.

Claudia.

Fuck, Claudia was still in her office. The one that sat *right* next to the front doors, her mouth pursed and her head down towards her desk as she fussed over stacks of cash sitting in a neat row in front of her.

My heart reined me back, pulling to the back of my chest and stumbling me behind the corner. My heels barely caught my frantic fumble, every muscle in my body coiling to petrified stone as my plan for escape shattered in a miraculous few seconds and left me stranded.

I was an aimless doe, wide-eyed and out in the open, staggering blindly and a perfect target to prowling predators.

My head whipped in every which direction, up and down the hallway, eyes zeroing in the very first door plastered along the far wall. I didn't think, which was probably a given at this point. I just darted towards it, hoping and praying all in some last-ditch desperation that it wasn't locked or occupied.

Tears could have sprung when, for once in my fucking life, the magic of prayer and hope paid off and I felt no resistance against the door handle as I turned it.

Again, no thinking was going on at this point. Just a lot of sweaty panicking and throwing myself in dark rooms, which is exactly what I did.

The door shut behind me, a click breaking apart the quiet air and making the muscles in my neck tense against the sound. My breathing wasn't any better, choppy and hot, filling the tight dark space like a humid summer night.

I swallowed to coat my drying throat, jerking my neck around. Light from outside spilled in beneath the bottom of the door, illuminating a spotlight on my feet and the boxes that surrounded them.

Boxes?

Squinting, I leaned closer to them, the wording printed on the cardboard edges flitting in and out of focus as I rapid blinked to force my eyes to adjust. Black words sharpened, printing labels unblurring their inscriptions against the cardboard.

My sight strained in the darkness as I read the lettering on the first box.

Trojan: Ribbed and Bareskin.

Surprise jostled my head back, a cautious curve painting my lips. The box was for… condoms? I looked to the one next to it.

Dental Dams.

And alongside those were stacked boxes for tampons, lube, flavored lube, and batteries.

As I read the labels and admired the towers of boxes piled high all around me, I realized with a huffing chuckle exactly what I'd stumbled into for shelter.

I was in a closet. A sex storage closet.

Spinning in a tight circle, a balloon of relief deflated inside of me as I realized my luck. My *stupid* luck. This could have been a bedroom, this could have been a bathroom, this could have been someone's office, but it wasn't.

Thank fuck.

Spotting a nook at the back of the closet, I inched carefully towards it and made a home for myself, sitting my ass on the cold, hard floor. I exhaled another bout of relief and got as comfortable as I could as I came up with a new plan.

One not-so-impulsive and ludicrous.

I'd wait in here until the house fell asleep and everyone in it too.

That's when I'd make my move. That's when I'd escape into the night and run home to Dominic.

Come nighttime, I was getting the fuck out of my own personal hell.

TWENTY-THREE

KAT

I wasn't sure how long I waited there.

Long enough to regret not jumping into a bathroom instead of a kinky sex closet. My bladder was sore by this point, crying for relief that I denied it over the hours until it eventually gave up and let me sleep off its torture.

That's how I spent most of my time in there—sleeping, listening to the conversations that passed by the door, or daydreaming about going home.

By the time the crack of light bleeding in beneath the door dimmed and left me in total and utter darkness, I'd daydreamed about what it would be like when I got home so much, the thoughts of it followed me into my subconscious.

Sleeping or awake, I thought about calling Dominic and hearing his voice, clinging to its bass deep solace over the phone and daring to let a few tears leak as I told him I loved him for the first time in real words.

I'd yell at him for making me fall so sick in love with him, and he would soothe me over the phone and tell me he was just as sick and that he was on his way to me.

I imagined seeing Bugs again and how I'd scoop her up and cry out so many apologies for leaving her longer than I meant to. Her springy pigtails would tickle my cheeks as she clung to me as hard as I clung to her, and I'd promise to never leave her again, and she would make me pinky swear it.

I'd saw off the whole finger before I ever broke a promise to her again.

Eventually, the bustle of footsteps and voices on the outside of the door grew fewer and the silence grew more frequent. I waited what was probably another hour in nothing but silence, hating every second of it but knowing this silence was the only good kind there had ever been.

This brand of silence meant freedom.

I needed to ride this silence all the way to the front doors, and that started with turning the knob on the closet slow enough that the pulse of my heartbeat was louder than any momentum of rotating metal.

It was a quick-rhythmed gong banging between my ears as I guided the closet open, touching my toe to the outside as if testing the temperature of a pool before jumping in feet first.

Coming out into the open, all of my senses were on high alert.

Any shadow could be my doom. Or Charlotte's.

I hadn't been thinking about anything other than escaping when I threw myself into hiding earlier, but all that time alone forced the worst kind of ideas in my head.

Like what happened if I got caught. Would I die? Would they go after Charlotte like Claudia had threatened to teach me a lesson? If they didn't kill me, would they still hurt me? Make me beg for them to stop?

I didn't want to think those things, but that fucking *what if* voice wouldn't shut up. It had been right before, and it touted that it could be right again.

Moving out of the closet, I pressed my back flush to the hallway wall, trying to control my breathing. Inching one step down it, a terrible scrape from my sequin top scratched a deafening noise along the walls. I jolted off of it with a spike in my heart rate and froze.

Panic set fire to my chest, all my oxygen burning alive in it as I waited…

And waited…

For nothing.

Just more silence.

My hand came up to my neck, clutching around it as air filtered a slow breeze back down my throat, eyes falling shut. My pulse thwacked against my palm as I steadied my breathing, beginning the slow descent down the hallway again.

I made it all the way to the edge, teetering around the corner that poured into the foyer.

God, I was close. So fucking close to making it. Risking a peek around the corner, my gaze fell over the wide-birthed entrance to the house, checking against every corner for any shadows in the shape of lurking men.

But there was nothing. Just darkness and stillness.

There was barely a speck of light in the foyer, but somehow the handles rooted to the front doors glowed with a shine.

They were glowing for me.

The people who embodied this house were more than evil, but the house itself wasn't. It wanted me to succeed. It was holding itself still for me, not even allowing the bones of it to creak and moan, cheering me on in its gift of silence.

A lump of too many emotions moved up to settle in my throat.

My exhilaration. My relief. My impossible to demolish hope.

The house wanted me to run for it and so did the electric energy in my feet. Run for Charlotte. Run for Dominic. Run for the happily-ever-after I'd had at the tips of my fingers before everything went so fucking wrong.

And so I did.

Lump lodged in my throat, I pushed off the wall, stepping my electric feet out into the pool of black—

Only to make it two paces before getting shocked by a flash of tan that shot into the darkness, a hand clamping over my mouth.

The ball trapped in my throat morphed into a scream as I was pulled back, terror skyrocketing up the back of my skull, tingles so fire hot spidering all over the top of my head as I was shoved back first against a wall.

Devastation poured through my veins in buckets as a hard body sealed over top of mine, a cry firing up my throat.

Before I could get it out, the sight of a finger pressed against a set of pursed lips caught the noise in place. In wild confusion, my eyes tracked up from the finger, taking in a nose with the tiniest bump blemishing its bridge before finding a pair of black flames burning down at me.

A cocktail of relief and blood-boiling rage intoxicated my brain in milliseconds.

Blake lorded over me, his finger warning me to be quiet and his palm still glued over my mouth making sure of it. I bucked my shoulders against his chest, jerking my head against his silencing grip.

His fingers holding down both sides of my cheeks tightened, the flames of his eyes glowing hotter.

"Are you really this fucking stupid?" he spat in hushed tones.

His insult slapped my eyelids back, widening my temper up my warming face as I shook his hand from over my mouth.

"Trying to save my life is *stupid*?" I whispered back, my lightning peeling up my throat.

"When all you'll do is set off the house alarms as soon as you step outside that front door and get us *both* killed? Yeah, I'd call that stupid."

Like its plug had been abruptly pulled, my lightning powered down, jaw hanging open.

All that was left was muted shock and disappointment. Droves of it.

Alarms.

Why didn't I think of that?

All that time to strategize and ponder in that closet, and something as basic as alarms never crossed my mind. I lowered my stare to his chest, feeling my stupidity weigh down my heart, sinking my shoulders to cave in around it and protect from any more blows tonight.

Stupid. Fucking. Hope.

Blake sighed above me, drowning our shared space in the tint of cigarette smoke and frustration. "Jesus *Christ*, why do you have to make everything so difficult?"

"I wasn't trying to be difficult. I was trying to—"

"I know what you were trying to do," he sliced me off with a serrated voice, smoky bites of breath chewing across my lips. The blacks of his eyes had consumed them completely, and somehow even out here where there was a near total absence of light, his eyes were still the darkest thing in the room.

His anger clouded around him, around *us*, thickening the air until that quiet trill of electricity began to hum.

"Are you gonna tell them?" I asked softly.

If he told Heather's parents, I would be punished for certain. Or dead.

He let a breath cut through his nose, backing a step away from me and rested his hands on his hips. A heavy and humming beat of tension passed before, "No. I'm not."

That answer both did and did not surprise me.

Blake helping me when it was in his job description to do the exact opposite was sort of becoming his thing.

The thought to be thankful and say the words ruminated in my brain, but he was still a bastard criminal and I was still a stubborn brat, and that sentiment would stay locked behind gnashed teeth until the day I died.

I shifted against the wall, wondering how far I could push my luck. "You don't maybe wanna turn off the alarms so I can sneak out, huh?"

Unamused dark slats flattened over his heavy eye contact.

"There's a night guard and cameras on the outside perimeter."

Well, shit.

"So then, back up to my room and forget the whole thing happened?" My timbre was a light and wishful suggestion, but it was met with a shake of Blake's dark head of hair.

"I can't do that either."

"Why not?"

He sighed, digging his fingers into his eye sockets. "Because there's a camera watching your room too. Morning crew wouldn't notice that you weren't brought back to your room this morning, but they'd notice me sneaking you back up now. They'd know you tried to leave and that it was my fault."

"Well, Sergio's fault."

My eyes were beginning to adjust fully in the darkness, seeing his thick brows jump up in bemused agreement. We both stood there for a bit, him deciding what to do with me and me, chewing over my bottom lip as I waited. Helpless.

I hated being helpless.

"*Fuck.*" His curse streamed out, exhausted and fed up as he hung his head low. "You're gonna have to stay in my room tonight."

"*What?*"

The exclamation was out of my mouth and piercing the night in one thoughtless second, and Blake's hand was back covering my lips in the very next. He towered over me, his unique delicacy of smoke and electricity tingling the tip of my nose as he breathed deep, eyes blazing.

"We'll both be dead if you don't learn to keep that mouth *shut.*"

The barbaric growl of his voice crawled through my ears, shaking my ferocity off its chain. "*Okay.*" I wretched my face from beneath his heavy and large hand, snapping my sharp teeth up at him. "But I'm not staying in your room."

"You pretty much made sure you had no other choice with this stupid stunt."

"I—"

"It's the only way this works." He shut me up with an all-too-serious gruff, holding his position over me. "You stay in my room tonight, get ready in there in the morning, then we resume things as normal."

I searched back and forth between his eyes, looking for the joke, digging for the catch to upend this entire *ridiculous* idea.

I couldn't stay the night with him. He was a criminal. I was a captive. He was a criminal keeping me captive.

This was so dangerous. This was so *backwards.*

But Blake didn't look like he was joking, and he also looked about as happy about it as I felt.

Holy shit.

He was serious.

And I was seriously fucked.

TWENTY-FOUR

KAT

Blake's bedroom was nothing like I'd expect a hardened criminal's bedroom to look like.

His room was towards the back of the house on the first floor, tucked away where most people would never find it. Good for him.

Bad for me in case I needed to do any screaming for help tonight, because *no one* was hearing me back here.

Not like anyone in this house would help me anyway, but still.

Walking through the threshold into his room, three things about Blake jumped immediately into focus. Things I never would have known about him any other way.

I knew he was a smoker given the flavor of fire always wafting from between his lips, but now I knew he smoked Marlboro Red cigarettes. And thanks to Daddy Dearest, I knew that Marlboro Reds were some of the worst cigarettes you could pack your lungs with.

If you smoked Marlboro Reds, you didn't care about your health and you didn't care about living long. You just cared about the addiction and the comfort that came from giving into it.

The second thing that jumped out were his walls.

They were covered, and I mean *covered,* in posters, pictures, and artwork from movie classics. Casablanca, Rebel without a Cause, Gone with the Wind, A Streetcar Named Desire, and a shit ton more I hadn't even heard of owned real estate all over his room.

Blake created his own wallpaper out of James Dean, Marlon Brando, and that guy with a ridiculous mustache who didn't give a damn.

And the third thing I noticed in his room threw me off the most.

Where there weren't grainy movie posters, framed cinema artwork, or packs of cigarettes, there were books.

Poetry actually.

Stacks and stacks of it.

Walking over to his bookcase, I fingered my way past softly worn copies of Emily Dickinson, John Keats, Robert Burns, Lord Byron, and on and on and on. Each spine was cracked with faded white creases, the covers on almost all of them curling at its corners from too many page turns.

His bookcase stretched to nearly touch the ceiling, and every crevice was jammed with words on pages too eloquent and beautiful for the boorish man across the room.

I turned in place to find him standing with his back against the farthest wall, feet and arms crossed, black eyes waiting for mine.

"You like poetry."

His lip twitched. "I like a lot of things."

"A lot of *old* things."

There went his eyes again, rolling into the back of his head as he pushed himself off the wall. "I'll sleep on the floor tonight. You take the bed."

Apprehension flooded my next inhale as I looked to the bed, sheets all nice and primped straight, two inky black pillows fluffed and sitting side by side.

He slept there. *Blake* slept there, his body heat infused in the linen fibers, the shape of him grooved into the mattress, his burnt scent lingering where my face would lie on the pillows.

A shiver trickled down each vertebra in my spine as I thought about sleeping where he slept, trying to find a comfortable position in the bed of my enemy.

"Oh, no that's okay." I shook my head and waved him off. "I'm fine on the floor."

"Look," He yanked open a closet door and took out a blanket. "I don't know if you're being polite or stubborn, but just take the damn bed."

"I *am* being polite, which is kind of a rarity for me, so soak it in. It's your room. It's your bed. I don't wanna sleep in it."

More eye rolling. "Whatever."

He chucked the blanket my way, and I caught it against my chest with both arms. It was surprisingly soft as I rolled it between my fingers, woven of maroon and black yarn in a striped pattern.

"Did someone make this for you?"

He went over to the nightstand next to his bed where all his cigarettes were, not looking up at me. "One of the girls who used to work here."

"An old flame?"

Ew, did I just say flame?

That got his attention, dark eyes peeling up to land on me. "No. She just liked to knit."

I nodded slowly, the information bopping around in my head. "A prostitute who likes to knit? Sounds like the making of a 90s trash sitcom."

His burning focus still aimed at me, Blake plucked a fresh cigarette from its pack.

"The girls here are more than just their job. Just like I'm sure you're more than just a pain in my ass."

Shadows darkened the rise of his cheekbones as he lowered his eyelids to the stick of white he placed between his pink lips. Long fingers picked up a metal lighter off of his nightstand, one of those old school Zippos.

"You're right," I said at the same moment he flipped the lighter's top back, raising it to the hanging cigarette. His movements paused, midnight eyes finding me across the room.

"I also happen to be an excellent karaoke singer."

Several seconds passed with us both staring at each other long and hard, neither of us blinking. If there were an Olympic sport for pressing other's buttons, I'd bring home the bronze, silver, *and* the gold.

It was a skill, really. It got me through *a lot* of uncomfortable situations I didn't know how to handle. Like this. Like being trapped in a room for an entire night with someone I was supposed to hate.

Blake was the first to drop our staring contest with *another* rotation of his eyes that danced the length of his lashes in shadows over his face before his focus fixed on the cancer stick. Orange flared up from his lighter as his thumb kicked down the back of it, the end of his cigarette glowing with golden embers before blackening to ash.

His cheeks hollowed as he pulled back a drag, threads of white pirouetting up in the room as he parted his lips in a slow release.

The smoke drifted from his mouth like a visitor who didn't want to leave, lingering and dancing in curvy, high-rising twirls, Blake controlling its exit as if he didn't want to let it go either.

As soon as the first inhale and exhale were finished, he did it again.

"What if I don't like smoke?" I asked, more to break the tension than anything.

His jaw ticked almost like he forgot I was there. He blew out his second puff much faster, keeping his stare down. "Don't care."

"Well, that's rude."

"Never said I was nice."

"Oh believe me, *nice* is not an adjective I would associate with you."

"Do you ever stop talking?" His dark voice sliced my vocal cords right in half, leaving my jaw stunted open. My thoughts dangled in suspension with my voice as I stared at him, hunting out that diamond speck I *swore* I saw contrasting in his jet-black eyes days ago.

Right now, all I saw was a night sky of nothing.

No blinking stars. No halo of moonlight. Just an unending stretch of ominous black threatening from above me.

"Not when I'm spending the night trapped in a room with a guy I barely know. My mouth kinda runs the show."

Blake angled his head, curiosity rippling across his stare.

"Because you're nervous?"

"I'm not *nervous*," I defended brashly, the implication catching my short-wire temper. "I think it's pretty fucking understandable to be on edge around someone like you."

"What's someone like me?"

The way he asked it, the severe concentration on my mouth as he waited for an answer made it seem like he genuinely wanted to know. He wanted to know what someone like me thought of someone like him.

"Well," I jutted my chin up, catching his gaze with mine. "Last I checked, you still worked in the sex-crime business, yeah?"

Just as I had raised my chin, Blake lowered his.

"You think I'm gonna try something with you tonight?"

The idea went right from his mouth into the atmosphere, thickening the air between us until it pressed around my throat, narrowing my airway as if it had hands.

As if he was already choking me. Touching me. Violating me.

"I'd kick your ass if you did."

My threat was a breathy mess, unease hacking my conviction to pieces for Blake to play with. Just like he could do to me if he really wanted.

Whether or not I wanted to, I remembered the muscles I'd seen carved into his body when his shirt clung to his waist from the shower. I'd felt the strength in his grip whenever he escorted me to and from the Line Up the last few days.

He could overpower me if it was something he wanted to do.

"Really?" He erased a single step between us. My body stiffened. The flames of his eyes fanned. "You think you could fight me?"

Raising my chin, my confidence was unwavering. "I think I could make you bleed."

Blake stood there unmoving, taking over the bedroom with all his suffocating severity. Especially now when we were on his turf in such an enclosed space, the cloud of black that followed him around felt even more stifling, pressing down on my heart and making it race.

The tip of his nose gave an angry twitch. "Your arrogance is going to get you killed before anything else in here."

"It's not *arrogance*. It's survival instincts."

"It's stupid," he spat.

"*Fuck* you."

I hadn't considered that I might have done that thing where I push too many buttons too many times until Blake was charging towards me in quick strides, giving me nowhere to go but backwards.

With a wide gasp, I stumbled over fumbling feet into the wall behind me, plastering myself to it as he came so near, the taste of him went far past the point of smoke.

It was goddamn fire.

It singed the tip of my tongue as I breathed him in on an unintentional inhale as he towered over me, both hands slapping the wall on either side of my head. He didn't even leave enough space between us to get my arms through so I could shove him back.

He was just *there*, everywhere around and over me, heating the surface of my skin like he was the sun and I was every drop of water on Earth he intended to evaporate.

My heartbeat ricocheted around my head as Blake took his fire-breathing eyes between mine, watching me like he planned to destroy me, like he was a hair-trigger away from finishing me off himself before this place could do it for him.

Except…

From this close, where I could count every single one of his dark long lashes or see a tiny, faded scar next to his left eye for the first time, I also saw *light*.

That diamond snowflake flurrying around lonely winter night eyes.

That tiny dot of light poked at the swell of my chest where I'd trapped all my anxious oxygen, letting it out slowly so something else could filter in its place.

A simmering, tapping, *needling* curiosity.

For as black-hearted and bitter as he was, that dot was a clue to something else buried under his layers of smoke and ash. A diamond in the rough of all his dirty, foul-tempered, stormy emotions.

I wanted to touch whatever it was and dig it out.

I wanted whatever it was up front and center, unfurling the mystery of this man right before my eyes so I could know him better. My downfall curiosity had been plucked days ago when he saved me for the first time. It started with wanting to know his name, and now I needed another fix.

My addict-prone genes were drawn to this guy, itching beneath my skin to get under his.

A barely controlled exhale warmed my cheeks, my nose, my lips with fresh smoke, the words that followed just as poorly tethered.

"You still don't seem to get where you are or that it's *dangerous*."

I could tell he meant the clenched teeth comment as a threat, but I heard its disguise of caution now. Of *warning*.

"I do," I breathed out, watching that fleck of luminance float in his depths. "I just don't think it's as dangerous as you want me to think it is."

Hot gaze locked on me, Blake inhaled my double meaning, his shoulders lifting and chest brushing a graze over mine for the length of his breath. His nostrils flared, every muscle in his angular jawline moving and tensing.

"It is. More than you know."

My head rested back against the wall as we watched each other from up close.

"I'm not so convinced."

"*Trust me.*"

"I don't."

Blake waited a beat, still hovering over me. He nodded just once. "Good."

"Do you trust me?" I asked in return.

"No."

I waited my own poignant beat, a hum beginning to sing in the silence. "Good."

Neither of us moved.

That serenade of energy began to build in the tight air. A little louder. Then a little more. The sensation of it scratched delicate lines up my arms and down my legs, covering me in its live-wire presence until I was buzzing beneath him.

It was in my ears next, shaking my brain so the world felt like it was shaking beneath my feet too.

It was a gentle rumble, but somewhere in my head, I knew it had earthquake potential.

Whatever was happening, whatever connectivity was going on between the disciplined hold of black eyes on green, was catastrophic.

And not like the aftermath of a thunderstorm or lightning strike. This was *more*.

This was deadly.

Blake backed away first, retreating to his bed. "Bathroom's to the right if you need it."

With his distance, the humming scratched to a halt like a needle zipping off a record. The buzzing second skin it wove around my body fell away too, leaving my pores feeling clogged and my head too.

What I really wanted was a shower, but I settled for running off to the bathroom he'd pointed out to pee like a fucking race horse like I'd been dying to do for hours.

When I finished and came out, Blake was lying on top of his covers, an onyx notebook opened in front of his face and a pencil in hand.

"What's that?"

He snapped the notebook shut and shoved it underneath a pile of different sized books on his nightstand. "None of your business."

I puffed an absurd noise between my lips. "Well, now I have to know."

"No, you don't."

"You said it yourself how nosy I am."

He reached his arms back behind his head, laying down on his pillow to point his stare up at the ceiling. "Doesn't mean I have to entertain it."

In his repositioning on the bed, I realized he'd changed since I went to the bathroom. Where a shirt of standard black used to stretch around the muscle of his biceps was now bare.

It was all tan, all smooth, all exposed muscle aside from the white undershirt he left on to sleep in.

The flash of toned muscle was a fresh reminder of what he could do to me tonight if he wanted. It should have been enough to zip my mouth shut and lose the key somewhere between responsible and sensible.

Unfortunately for me, my mouth was always driving along the edge of devil-may-care, usually sending me right off one of those proverbial cliffs.

"Do you write? Is that what you were doing?"

His eyes closed shut, a sigh dispelling through his nose.

That's a yes.

"Can I read some of it?"

He turned his head on the pillow to lock eyes with me as he dead-panned, "Abso-fucking-lutely not."

I will neither confirm nor deny if a pout found my bottom lip.

"Why not?"

He rolled his stare back up to the ceiling, staring at nothing but the shapes in the drywall. "Because I barely know you and you barely know me."

"Okaaay." I popped a squat on my spot on the floor and leaned back, resting on my hands. "So we've got time to kill. What's there to know about you?"

"Nothing."

"*Liar.*"

"Go to sleep."

My head dropped back with a scoff, rife with frustration. "Come *on*. I need to know more about the dude I'm spending the night with other than he's a criminal with a fetish for poetry."

"I don't—" He stopped himself, sighing out an audible gust before twisting those ashen eyes back to me. "I don't have a fetish for poetry. I just enjoy it."

Now we're getting somewhere.

"Is that what you were writing when I came in?"

Annoyance flitted his gaze back to the ceiling, showing me his near perfect profile.

"I think we've talked enough for one night."

"We've *barely* talked."

"Not everyone likes to yap as much as you."

"Well *excuse me* if this is the first semi-normal conversation I've had since I've been here and I'd like to keep it going."

"Well, I don't." He rolled to his side, reaching for the table lamp flooding amber to every corner of the room.

"*Wait.*"

His hand froze mid-reach, his skin glowing golden under the cone of lamp lighting. The other thing in the room that glowed were his eyes, smoldering as he waited like I asked, lowering his reach for the switch.

"Are you scared of the dark?" he rumbled.

My head jerked back in offense, nose wrinkling. "No. I'm just not tired."

Blake wasn't impressed, going back to the lamp. "I am, so lights out—"

"Why don't you wanna talk to me?" I cut him off again, desperation propelling me forward on a backwind. I was sitting up on my knees when his gaze found me again. "I get that you're probably not supposed to talk to me, but you're also probably not supposed to have me in your room either. Or feed me or help me, so why can't you just *talk* to me?"

My minor outburst sat heavy in the air, and yes, I 100% realized that I sounded like a whiny child throwing a tantrum over not getting what I wanted, but I *wanted* to talk to him. If I was going to be stuck in here all night, I wanted more than just the occasional grunt or brusque comment.

I wanted answers. I wanted to *know* him even though I definitely shouldn't.

Blake's burning focus was hotter in the amber light.

"Why do you want to talk to me so badly?"

"Because you don't make sense. Why you're here, why you help me, why you're so *mad* all the time. None of it…" I paused, licking my lips and finding the tail end to my thought. "None of it fits. *You* don't fit here."

This place was like a library of horror novels that all looked the same. Their covers were dingy, dark, and bone-chilling, but what you found on the inside were nightmare inspired.

On the outside, sure, Blake looked the part. He matched the tone, the menacing *feel* of this library. It wasn't until you cracked him open that you'd realized he was misplaced, sitting on the shelves of a genre he didn't belong to.

Or so I was willing to bet all the money I didn't have.

"You really believe that," Blake stated—not asked—dragging his charred eyes up and down my face in a slow peruse. "Maybe you're not stupid then. Just naïve."

I grit my teeth against the insult, buckling down hard.

"I'm not naïve *or* stupid, just like *you're* not as bad as you pretend to be."

Challenge lowered the tilt of his head, the new angle glinting his eyes as gorgeous and intimidating as fuck onyx.

"I'm plenty bad."

"Then why do you save me *every time* I need it?" I threw back in his face, my hands coming to the edge of his bed to give my argument some up close leverage. "You don't have to but you *do*, and someone as evil as you're trying to convince me you are wouldn't lift a finger to help someone they barely know."

Through pinched teeth and severe focus, he ground out, "Would you like me to stop?"

I tried and failed to hold back a scoff. Or the eye roll that followed.

"Obviously not. I just want to know *why*."

Where I came up to sitting on my knees in front of his bed put our faces all but level. I remembered how I'd told myself just this morning I should never get within dangerous distance to Blake again.

Dangerous being where I could inhale his exhales and feel his potent energy tingling all the way down to my belly button.

And yet here I was again, filling my lungs with his smoke and watching that diamond snowflake fight for a spotlight in his midnight eyes. I was too close to be safe, but the addiction in my veins chewed up all my ability to care.

It just wanted *more*.

More of him, more answers, more of everything that didn't make sense.

Blake dragged the simmer of his stare over mine, picking up my heartbeat with every patch of skin he skimmed.

"You want to know why I'm here? Why I help you? Why I'm always so *fucking* mad?"

The languid succession of his words felt like the slow drip of wax falling from a candle, both taunting and so completely satisfying.

I nodded fast, holding my breath for his answers.

He held those answers behind closed lips and watched me wait for them. He observed me for so long without saying a damn thing. The idea to reach up to the seam of his mouth and part his lips to spill out the answers myself stirred in my head.

Thankfully, I didn't have to wait much longer.

"I'm mad *because* I'm here." The point of his glare refocused razor sharp, and my chest pinched in anticipation. "I'm mad because you're here too."

So many fucking questions.

"You don't wanna work here?" I rushed to ask.

He handed me a sharp look that said all he needed, and my question load tripled.

"I *knew* you weren't a complete piece of shit!" Victory sprawled up my cheeks. I was getting pretty good at this whole reading people gig. "If you don't wanna be here, then why haven't you left?"

"Does this seem like a job you can hand in a two weeks' notice for?"

It only took about three seconds of him staring at me under those heavy brows before my stomach folded over in realization and my smile slipped…

Oh.

I supposed it didn't.

The weight of Blake's stare was too heavy not to sink under. My shoulders went first, my bottom lip next. Blake tracked the deflation in my body, watching me absorb his fate with sullen understanding.

"Once you're in…" His curtain of black lashes lifted, a show of obsidian sorrow beneath. "You don't get out."

I sat back on my heels, blinking up at him. "How did you… get in in the first place?"

His lips pursed together, the upper define of his pecs rising as he breathed deep, eyeing me closely.

"You won't drop this, will you?"

I shook my head. "Uh-uh. I'll keep you up all night until you talk."

His shadow of dark lashes fluttered fast as he rolled his eyes, flopping his head back down on his pillow. "You're such a goddamn pain in my ass."

"And you're a motherfucking thorn in my side," I countered with ease. "That makes us even."

Blake stared up at the ceiling for a long while. So long, in fact, I wondered if he'd fallen asleep with his eyes open. A snarky, alarm-clock of a comment was working its way up behind my teeth when his throaty voice slipped into the air.

"I started here when I was sixteen—"

"Holy *shit*, that's young."

His mouth froze halfway open, stare stuck to the ceiling. Slowly, his head rotated on his pillow until he faced me, the bite to his glare making me stiffen.

"Got anymore interruptions?"

My lips parted to an 'o', muscles in my neck tensing as I cringed in regret. *Whoops.*

In a flare of dramatics, I circled my pinched fingers around my mouth, zipping them across the front and mimed throwing the key over my shoulder.

I even went so far as to fold my hands in my lap, sitting up straight like a good little listener. Blake's lids lowered halfway down his granite eyes, and I could tell with a smirk jumping at the corner of my mouth that he was trying *really* hard not to roll them.

He turned his profile to me again, filling his chest wide with a quiet sigh.

"My home life was shitty, and I fell into the wrong crowd to sum up a sob story. The people I ran with did some pretty heavy shit, so I did it too. Got addicted. Got arrested the week after my sixteenth birthday. Few months later, I was high at a friend's house, some guy showed up looking for money, and everyone else bailed. I was too fucked up to make it out."

The anticipated twinge of grief for my mom did not disappoint.

"That guy turned out to work for Ray back when operations were smaller. Instead of beating the shit out of me, Ray and Claudia said they saw potential. Gave me a job, got me clean, put a roof over my head."

"You make them sound like saints," I inserted before I could remind myself not to.

He spared me a cursory glance. "That's how it felt at the time. I was a fuck up of a teenager who already had a rap, no home to go back to, no money."

"No family?" I cut in—*again*.

"None that gave a shit."

A knot tied itself together at my sternum for the quick way he wrote himself off.

I knew how that felt. Family was supposed to be unconditional. It was a special kind of hurt that never went away when it turned out they weren't.

Blake anchored an arm behind his head, all his intensity focused on the story he was writing across the ceiling in vivid words. "Claudia and Ray made it feel like I had a purpose. Some semblance of a family. They only gave me minor jobs to start out. Money or product drops, surveillance, easy stuff."

"What's your job now exactly?"

"Head of security for the brothels. I run backgrounds on all our buyers, keep the properties secure and the girls safe." He paused, sustaining a poignant beat, dropping his pitch. "Usually."

There was a culpability in that one word. One that stained the air with knowing tension. It grabbed my voice, wrestling it soft, smothering it with burdens.

"And then there's me."

Blake looked to me, shadows playing in his eyes. "And then there's you."

Me. Who he wasn't supposed to keep safe. Me. Who he went out of his way to keep safe anyway.

"Is that why you were so pissed when I first got here?" *And every day since.*

Proof of his brilliant anger smoked in his gaze, his fire ever-present and ever-captivating.

"You're not part of the job."

My head shook, disbelief bringing me forward and tugging at my brows.

"There's never been anyone here before like me?"

At that, everything about him hardened to stone. His jaw, his browline, his serrated pupils.

"I didn't say that."

Curiosity *chomped* down on my gut.

"So there *have* been?" His mouth remained hard-locked, so I pressed harder. "Lots?"

As if I held the brush in my question, that same melancholy blue I first saw during our shower incident smeared across his eyes, painting them the loneliest shade of indigo.

"Just one."

The way he said it, a chill lifted all the hairs on my arms.

The room that was already so still, so overcharged and amplified on a swell of tension as if each particle in the air was a nerve-ending of its own.

Every breath we breathed pressed against it, every word we spoke threatened to shatter it.

"Who was she?" I asked gently, *carefully*.

As if he felt the same sensitive danger compounding our shared space, he spoke her name just as delicately.

"Abigail." From his tongue, her name sounded like something angelic. "They brought her here when I was seventeen."

"In this same house?"

Blake shook his head, looking back up to the ceiling. "No, back at our first location, Reeves. We've only been operating out of here about four years. Ray and Claudia have a few different facilities all around, and I knew they did back then, but I'd only ever worked at Reeves when Abby got brought in."

More out of certainty that I was wrong, I asked, "Did she piss off Heather too?"

"No. Some *fucker* requested a virgin," he spat up at the sky, hatred scorching his words and stabbing our finely-tethered friction. "That's Heather's part in the business, by the way. She executes requests clients give for a specific type of girl, finds a match, and delivers."

For that slice of information, he twisted a look back at me.

Just to watch the disgust ripple across my face and shock part my lips, a sickness unsettling my stomach.

What the actual fuck is wrong with her?

Satisfied, Blake moved his attention back up high. "Abigail was before Heather picked up that job though. I don't know who found Abby. I didn't even know there was such a thing as 'requested product'. All I knew was the drug-trafficking and brothel side of the business back then. Abby's buyer fell through, and that's how she got to stay with us while Ray looked for a replacement."

"How long was she there?"

"Eighteen days." A lull tangled into the conversation, a heavy tide shifting the air. Blake's voice shifted with it, sounding like the softest wave emerging from the deepest cavern in the ocean. "I found a way to see her for every one of them…"

In all I knew about Blake, I knew he wore his emotions on the outside of his skin because there were just too fucking many to keep locked beneath. Even so, how he looked and sounded *now*?

This was an expression of something else entirely.

A new level of wearing your heart on your sleeve.

His was bleeding all over, vibrant agony stained on his flesh.

"She was so fucking scared and so fucking sweet," he rasped, throwing a glance my way. "Pretty much the exact opposite of you."

And she was special to him.

He didn't have to say it outright. The way he reminisced about her was loud enough, which is why there was a fucking fist of nails clawing at my chest as I wondered aloud about this story's ending.

"What happened to her?"

Seconds ticked on, and my heart was beating all the way down to my stomach as I waited for him, each thump against my chest a violent plea for a happy ending.

It wasn't likely, and I *knew* it wasn't likely, but I still let my reborn heart pump with that stupid optimism Dominic had infused it with when he decided to love it.

It slapped harder and angrier, impatient and desperate for the answer it wanted to hear. It needed it to be something good. It needed the selfish proof that this place and every wicked person in it was survivable.

Blake fixed his black flames on me, burning me, my heart, and all of my useless optimism right up.

"She was sold. Probably raped. Definitely killed." He stopped, jaw pulsing. "I couldn't stop it."

My body didn't know what to feel first between the terror, disgust, and pity that all attacked at once.

I couldn't even hide the overload of emotions consuming my face from him because he was watching for them. He collected the part of my lips, the swaying hitch in my breath, and could probably even taste the dryness in my mouth as I left it hanging open.

Probably raped.

Definitely killed.

My stomach rolled into itself, folding into a tight ball of dread. Blake knew the girl who'd originally been cast in my role and died while playing it. Not only did he know her, but he *cared* for her, grieved for her even still.

I was Abby's reprise, walking in the same damned shoes she did, and Blake had to watch it happen all over again. No wonder he hated me so much.

I'd hate me too.

A lot of quiet seconds passed before I found the ghost of my scared-to-death voice.

"Did you love her?"

If three months was enough time for someone like me to fall in love with Dominic, then I imagined eighteen days was enough time for someone like Blake to fall in love.

"I was only seventeen so I didn't have a good concept of love, but I like to think I did."

As someone who knew jackshit about romantic love until recently, even I could tell he had loved her. Didn't matter the age, didn't matter the circumstances, he fell heart first in love with this girl, and he'd basically watched her die right in front of him.

And he couldn't stop it.

It was right then, *right there*, as he spoke about his lost love and didn't hide a single drop of his radiant grief, that his dark skies finally cleared and I *saw* him for the very first time.

The first *real* time.

I saw a boy who'd been dragged into a world he didn't have a choice in and couldn't escape. I saw a boy that fell in love for the first time only to have that love ripped away and burnt up into hell. I saw a man who loathed himself for letting his love go, who beat himself up every day he still worked for the people that took his love away, and who still was too scared to say no to them.

I was right before. Blake *didn't* belong here in this library of horrors.

Nightmares were not his genre.

Tragedies were.

"That's why you help me," I said, soft and quiet.

Because he couldn't help her.

Blake dismissed the relation with a signature eye roll, jabbing me a pointed glare. "It's why I stress how careful you need to be in here, even though you haven't listened to a fucking bit of it."

"I have!" I defended, posture righting.

He shot me a look. My shoulders deflated.

"I'll start tomorrow," I mumbled.

"Good." With a labored sigh, he sank back into his pillow but kept his eyes on the ceiling. "This place will fuck you up. Trust me."

"I don't."

A dent formed in his cheek that faced me, a slow blink following.

He slid a glance my way, reaching an arm up to finally switch off the lamp. In that glance, and in that last ray of amber glow, that diamond speck shined a bit brighter in his black eyes.

"Good."

TWENTY-FIVE

<u>DOM</u>

Six days.

It had been six miserable days since Kat's abduction. Six days of crushed leads, sleepless nights, and an unending barrage of morbid thoughts popping up through my brain like poisonous weeds, strangling any optimism I had until all that was left were mangled heaps of unavailing hopes littered like carcasses through my mind.

With each day that passed without her, I could feel myself sinking into an obsessive decline. My focus had been splintered into fragments for those around me while the majority of it was dedicated to finding Kat.

I hadn't touched any of my other cases all week, my mom was picking up the slack I was leaving around the house, and I'd committed a criminal lack of goodnight kisses as a father over the week.

Today I had off, but that didn't mean I wasn't working.

Currently, Maya was sprawled across the living room floor with her nose buried in one of those beginner's books for reading. I was sprawled out in my red chair, my nose buried in reports I'd combed over a hundred times already.

"Daddy, I'm bored." Maya rolled over with a dramatic sigh. "Can we go get Charlotte?"

"No, sweetheart. She's spending the day with her neighbors. Mrs. Sharon used to watch Charlotte like Ms. Kat watches you."

A few seconds went by, my eyes scanning the same lines over and over.

"Is she gonna stay there?"

When I glanced up from the paper, Maya was in front of me, a curious twist to her mouth. Exchanging my files for my daughter, I grabbed her waist and lifted, setting her on my knee and brushing a curl from her cheek.

"She's just there for today. You and Grandma will pick her up in the morning."

Her stare dropped to her fingers, a pout that had the power to bring me to my knees pushing out along with a quiet voice.

"Is Ms. Kat coming back?"

On instinct, my jaw set against the throb of longing that built in my throat. I tried to rid it by breathing past it or swallowing it down, but it was set like stone and refused to budge. The ache of longing was a part of me now just like the woman it was born for.

I missed her.

Goddammit, I missed her.

Maya tilted her chin up to me, a similar longing highlighting the blue of her eyes.

Grabbing the tip of her chin between my fingers, I told her, "I'm doing everything I can to make sure she does."

"Because you love her?"

My hold on her chin loosened.

Nervous energy bounded through my tightening chest as I searched between my daughter's eyes. "What would make you say that?"

She gave a bashful shrug.

"I don't know. Charlotte thinks so too."

My eyebrows almost hit my hairline. "She does?"

She nodded, screwing up her mouth like she did when too much was going on in that little head of hers. If I needed any further proof that I was a poor man's actor, this was it. I hadn't even been able to hide my affection for Kat from two five-year-old girls.

Shame began a slow trickle through my ribs…

Then Maya said this:

"We want you and Ms. Kat to get married so we can be sisters. Then I get to marry you next."

The shame loading up my chest got overshadowed by the sudden infusion of warmth. Warmth the first time I held my baby girl in my arms or when she held onto me extra tight when she didn't want to go to bed and begged me to read her another story.

That warmth climbed within my chest, the heat rising to the corners of my mouth.

"You want to marry me?"

She nodded brightly, grabbing my thumb in her little palm. "We'll have a wedding just like Ariel and Prince Eric."

"I don't think we have room in the backyard for the entire ocean to attend, Munchkin."

"We'll make it work," she assured me. "But you and Ms. Kat have to get married first so they can live with us forever. I wish her and Charlotte were here now."

The warmth didn't stand a chance against the cold that swept in its place and iced everything off after a comment like that.

My chest still burned, but this time with frostbite.

I rested my chin atop Maya's soft head of curls, wishing alongside her for my own many things.

I wished that my daughter didn't have to experience the downfall of her parents' marriage at such a young age. I wished my wife hadn't devolved into a person that was only beautiful on the outside. I wished my partner and best friend would come into work once in a while and help me find who'd stolen the girl of my dreams.

I wished no one had *taken* the girl of my dreams when I'd just found her.

If I had any faith in the truth of shooting stars, I would stand outside all night, searching out a falling ray of fire to wish upon so I could have her back.

I wasn't juvenile enough to put all of my hopes, or any for that matter, into wishes. Wishes were for children and for birthday candles. The only hope I had for them was that the smoke from the candles would travel through the wind to wherever she was and caress her face like I couldn't, and she would be reminded of just how much I loved her.

"Can I at least go wake up Grandma?" Maya broke me from my smoky thoughts, peeking a pleading pout up at me.

"No, let's let Grandma sleep in, okay? She's earned it." *And then some.* I lifted my arm, flicking my wrist to check the time on my watch and the temperature outside. "It's a little too chilly to play outside yet, so how about we put on a movie that'll lead into lunch? Then naptime for both of us."

"You're already planning on taking a nap?" Her sweet face scrunched together. "Is it 'cause you're old?"

A breath of laughter pushed through my nose, the build of tightness easing in my chest.

I hadn't come close to laughing in over six days.

"You know another name for a father *is* 'old man,'" I told her, tapping her on her button nose.

She digested the new information, bouncing the new name around in her brain. Then she shook her head of curls.

"I like calling you daddy."

Before I could stop it, an anticipated flash of vixen green eyes blurred past my mind.

You're not the only one.

Towards the front of the house, a clank of heavy doors being opened and closed sounded off. The precise click of pointed shoes came next, nearing in echoes that reintroduced the twisting tightness to my sternum.

"Is Mommy home?"

Drawing in a gulp of air not yet permeated with the scent of citrus flowers, I nodded just once. "Sounds like it."

On cue, Heather came around the corner dressed in a gray pencil skirt that went all the way to mid-calf and an unnerving smirk that went all the way to her sharp eyes.

I wasn't expecting her home so soon, and she was likely counting on it.

Trapping me where I couldn't leave and where I couldn't yell was a new tactic of hers to argue about the divorce. It was getting tired, and so was I.

Not even 9am, and I was ready for that nap.

"I thought you had a showing this morning?" I asked her, keeping my irritation leveled for Maya's sake. Heather gave a flick of her delicate fingers my way, unshelving her purse from her shoulder.

"I packed it in early. Only one couple showed up."

"That's too bad."

"I'm not bothered. It meant I got to come home early and spend the day with my family." The lie didn't sell well given that she hadn't so much as looked at the other family member in the room. Her calculation was solely stuck on me, sparkling with purpose and boiling my skin. "Nothing's more important than family, right?"

Maya perked up on my lap, twisting to face Heather.

"Daddy wants to watch a movie."

Heather dropped her first glance towards our daughter, flicking a strand of lengthening hair over her shoulder. A beam brightened her face as she smiled, stalking towards us both.

"How about we all three watch a movie? Does that sound nice?"

The excited gasp that pierced the living room went straight through my heart too.

"Yes!"

Heather came up right next to my chair, lingering her hand on the back of it and right next to my head. The presence of *it* and *her* were suppressing, sharpening my exhausted nerves to a fine-tip breaking point.

Over my shoulder, enveloping the oxygen beneath my nose with her signature scent, she drawled out, "You love spending time with both Mommy and Daddy, don't you?"

My back and shoulders stiffened. Fists too.

I needed something to grab, to squeeze, to hit.

Maybe I'd find the time to workout today after all.

Maya was clearly confused by Heather's fishing question, nodding out a slow, "Mhm."

The empty space next to my head was suddenly blocked by another, my awareness of unwanted body heat prickling like the wildfire stoking between my ribs.

Kat's inspired wildfire.

I could only imagine the colorful choice of words my girl would string together right now if she walked in and saw what Heather was doing. My chest would burn with pride as my browline peaked in shock at whatever brilliant fire shot out of her mouth to incinerate Heather with for crossing lines and using our daughter to do it.

I couldn't and wouldn't say or do anything to put a stop to it with Maya watching. Heather was vindictive enough to know it, too.

She went on. "Are you happier when we're all together like this?"

The purr of her goading burned in my ear, my brittle nerves snapping.

"Heather—"

"Well… yes," Maya started, stopping me as she laid her hand over my forearm, scratching her tiny fingers in light distractions over the hair there. "But when we're together is when you fight a lot."

A dismissive tuff of laughter went off over my shoulder.

"Maya, all married couples fight."

She looked up to me instead of Heather, her small voice so honest, it broke my heart.

"Every day?"

Water pooled at the brim of her eyes, drowning all my breathable air in their emergence. I wiped my thumb beneath both her eyes, cleaning her sadness away and wanting someone with an iron fist to sock me in the stomach for being the cause of it.

I never wanted this.

Fathers were meant to wipe their children's tears away, not cause them.

"We never meant for you to hear any of those conversations, sweetheart." I passed my fingers across her forehead, twisting a dark curl of hers gently around my finger. "Mommies and Daddies just get angry sometimes."

Maya sniffled, her cheeks flushing cherry red. "You never get angry with Ms. Kat."

A cold front swept the side of my face as Heather stood to her full height, enhanced by the heels she was wearing that I bought her last Christmas.

"Ms. Kat isn't your mommy," she said. "She doesn't count."

"I know she isn't," Maya conceded, craning her head back to show her innocent confusion to Heather. "But Daddy loves her and he doesn't fight with *her*."

Heather tutted above us and gave a chuckle. "He doesn't love her, Maya."

"Yes, he does! I saw them kissing in the backyard after Daddy fell!"

Out of nowhere outside, a crash of lightning blasted from up above and deafened the silence.

Thunder rattled the house next in all its anger, the walls around our quiet family shaking.

Moments later, the pitter-patter of unexpected rainfall drummed over our heads.

It wasn't expected to storm today.

Nothing that just happened was expected to happen today.

That day in the backyard, I knew it wasn't smart to kiss her. We were out in the open in the backyard of the home I shared with my wife and my daughter had just run inside. Or so I thought. Kat was so miserably worried about the meeting with her mother, and I just wanted to make her frown disappear for a moment. The length of a kiss.

The rational part of me knew better, but rationale didn't stand a chance when a woman like Ms. Sanders was pressed against you. Her sweet smelling hair draped over her shoulders, wavy tangles falling into my eyes, her beautiful face silhouetted by the burn of sun just behind her head.

I was weak for her, but I was weakest of all for her sadness. Her temperamental vulnerability.

Kat Sanders was an addiction, but her vulnerability was an obsession of mine. She gave into it so sparingly that whenever her firewalls collapsed, I couldn't get enough. I wanted to help her, heal her, protect her from demons she'd collected over the years and slay every last one of them.

I was so thoroughly wrapped up in my obsession that day that I didn't see anything but her. Kat was the blinding sun above me, the warm breeze around me, the solid earth beneath me.

And now she was gone.

And I was about to pay the price for being so careless.

I shut my eyes in the silence, listening as my world crumbled around me.

"Daddy?"

The tiny voice of my daughter whispered for me, and I opened my eyes for her. Seeing her. Smiling at her. Memorizing her. I touched my thumb to the roundest part of her cheek, brushing it.

"Can you go wait upstairs for a bit, Munchkin?"

Panic widened her stare, blinking up at me like she'd done something wrong and was already so sorry for it. She wasn't the one who'd done anything wrong though.

I brought her head forward, pressing my lips to her forehead, whispering softly, "It'll be okay."

I pulled back, looking down at the most perfect face. Even splattered with plops of tears and with blotchy red cheeks, she was far and beyond the best thing I'd ever done with my life.

My slice of perfection stole away upstairs like she'd been asked, sparing me one last sad look over her shoulder before disappearing. With her gone, there was no stopping the grenade she'd pulled the key from before running off.

It was behind me, ticking down the seconds before it would shred me to pieces.

Three...

Two..

One.

"You fucking *liar.*"

I pushed myself up from my chair. "Heather—"

"Again and again, I asked you and you *denied* it. Were you trying to make me feel crazy or just plain stupid?"

"Neither."

Her expensive heels took her into the kitchen, hands fit into the dips of her waist as she paced back and forth. All I could do was watch her. There was an urge I didn't think would ever die to comfort her like I had in the past, but I didn't know how to do that anymore.

She used to fit so well into the crook of my chest when she shed her tears, but she'd outgrown me since then. Or maybe I'd outgrown her.

I also hadn't seen her cry since she was eighteen and we hit a Blue Jay driving to the movies. Birds were her favorite animal, and none more than Blue Jays. When I asked her why, she said it was because they were her mom's favorite for their symbol of confidence.

They were assertive birds for the sake of survival, and she couldn't hold back her tears that we'd killed something so strong so easily. She wept on the side of the road over that bird while I held her, and it was the moment I knew I was going to ask her to marry me.

I saw that Blue Jay in her today, wings bent and light going out though she fought like hell to keep flying.

"I *knew* it." A slap of flesh against granite exploded through the air as Heather slammed her palms to the kitchen counter. "From the moment she stepped into my home, I knew she would be a *disease* to everyone in it."

Her comment took my jaw to the side and my stare to the floor.

I was used to how she spoke about Kat. Didn't mean I didn't want to put my fist through a wall each time she did it.

"Is that why you're so desperate to find her? So you can have your fuck buddy back?"

My teeth set so hard, there was a tiny crack up the back of my jaw.

She was goading me. And she was allowed to.

"*No.*" Exasperation took my gaze up. "I'm not treating her case any differently than the other missing girls."

Her lips parted slightly, the harsh cobalt of her eyes sparking like the hit of metal on metal.

"Lying to me about her is about as easy as breathing is to you now, isn't it?"

Guilt speared my chest like she'd thrown a javelin across the room and hit me square on. All that nasty guilt spilled out of the hole it created in my chest, filling my body so heavy I couldn't even hold Heather's gaze.

Because she was right.

I wasn't a man who lied easily, but I had become one.

Not just when I met Kat, either. I'd started lying years back when I told myself that my marriage was stable or that Heather and I were still in love. Or that she was a good wife.

Or that I was a good husband.

I was at one point, but that good husband died under years of winless battles and inadequacy in all departments that mattered to my wife.

Money. Status. Presentation.

I had been lying to Heather long before Kat came along, but she wouldn't care about those lies. She'd only care about the lies I told over the last few months because they interrupted her world.

"Was the first time you fucked her in our home before or after that chunk of video tape went missing on the nanny cams?"

A sigh lowered my head parallel to the floor, the guilt unimaginable.

I suppose I should have seen that one coming.

I'd been on edge ever since that night I lost control with Kat in the very same red chair I was standing in front of now. Heather checked those tapes religiously, and her eye was keen enough to notice the missing hour of tape I'd edited out to hide my crime.

I had a lie all prepared for when she asked about it, but she never did.

Now I knew she wanted to keep the information locked and loaded for when she had enough proof to tear me down with it.

Hanging my hands on my hips, I shook my head.

"Let's not get into details, Heather."

She blew out a raspberry with her lips, something I'd never heard her unmannered enough to do. "So, that's a yes."

"*No*, it's not," I quickly corrected. "But I don't think talking about when it started will do either of us any good."

"Because you just couldn't wait to cheat on your *wife*."

She didn't even flinch before throwing those words in my face. Deepening the pitch of my voice, I dared to use the thin defense I had.

"We were separated before anything happened." Aside from the first time I kissed her. "I know that doesn't excuse what I've done. It was never my intention to be unfaithful."

"Oh, how noble of you, Dom." She clapped her hands together, huffing out a faux laugh and smiling just the same. "You didn't *intend* to cheat on me with the help." Hands still clasped, she fixed the pale blue of her eyes on me, her acute focus unsettling. "But you did. You *were* unfaithful. You broke your marriage vows, and all for some poor slut."

Tension screwed up every inch of my body, eyes slamming shut.

That *word*.

I couldn't take it when she used that word for Kat. Aside from the fact that it was degrading and purely invented, it was also far too easy for that woman of mine to convince herself it was true. She took blame and insult so easily, wearing them like her favorite sweater she felt the most comfortable in.

Peeling my eyelids up, I nailed an unwavering scowl her way.

"She is not a slut."

Heather set herself forward on her countertop, not backing down. "She opened her legs for my husband when she was supposed to be watching our child. She is, by definition, a *slut*."

Both my fists curled at my sides, knuckles stretching against skin. My teeth knocked together, jaw tightening up as I held her boiling stare.

"I don't want to have to defend her to you, so please don't make me."

Her head shot back in a sharp, single exclamation. "Oh, wouldn't that just be the icing on the cake? You fuck her in our home and then defend yourself for it."

"I'm not defending my actions. They have no defense, but I won't listen to you slander her right in front of me."

"*Oh my god.*"

Heather dropped her head down for one splitting moment, her nails a glazed shade of beige clawing at the countertop. The bones in her lithe hands protruded with the force she buried behind her fingertips as she tried to take a fistful out of the counter. Then, her head shot back up, and the hurt crawling all over her face was like a swift slap across mine.

"Stop protecting her! She's *gone*, Dom. She's gone, and you know as well as I do that she's not coming back so you can drop this whole fucking act. Drop the lying, drop the divorce, drop everything to do with her so we can just get back to our lives *before* her."

A thousand bricks crushed down on my chest as the woman I vowed to love until my dying breath showed me the cracks in her stone-faced composure. All this time, she'd been nothing but mad or cruel or dismissive about the divorce and how I felt.

When I finally worked up the courage to ask for a divorce, a part of me thought she might be relieved to end it. We'd been miserable for so long, and if she wasn't fighting with me, she barely acknowledged me.

In my hopeful mind, I'd pictured myself asking her for the divorce and her shoulders sagging as she said something along the lines of, 'I was wondering which one of us was going to pull the trigger first.' Then, we'd embrace, and for the first time in over a decade, finally be at peace with each other.

I never anticipated her pain.

I never imagined it would inspire her to dig her heels in deeper.

When I asked her why she wanted to stay with me, her answer was because I was her husband.

Not because she loved me. Not because she wanted to grow old with me.

I was a trophy she kept on display, and she didn't want an empty spot on her mantel.

All she wanted was to go back to before.

Perhaps before I met Kat, we could have.

"You never should have had to find out like this," I started low, taking a soft step towards her. "I'll never be able to apologize enough for it. You deserved better, and I'll talk to Maya about what she saw."

Agony loaded up my throat as I prepared to say it, trying to cage the words where they couldn't break free and inflict anymore scars on this woman. It felt like I was gearing up to ask for a divorce all over again, bracing myself for the potential volatile trajectory of the conversation from here forward.

I breathed deep, rooting myself in place.

"But Heather, there is no *before* Kat for me."

She blinked a few times, wrinkles bunching up her forehead. "What do you mean?"

The pressure lodged in my throat tripled. Swallowing past it was useless. The block in her head keeping her from understanding proved just how convinced she was that this was all just some bump in the road, and how necessary it was to clarify to her it wasn't.

I closed the distance to stand against the outside of the kitchen countertop, the length of it separating us. It was only a few feet, but it felt like miles and had for years.

"You and I are not getting back together." I switched my eyes back and forth between hers, a finality settling in the surrounding air. "No matter what."

As I said the words, I anticipated anger.

Maybe even a glimpse of those long-lost tears she used to shed.

Instead, all she did was roll her eyes with a flick of her wrist. "You'll change your mind once the sex fog clears from your head."

Frustrations plagued my muscles, every one of them coiling tight.

I would definitely need that workout after this.

"Heather," I knew I might regret correcting her, but I didn't see a choice at this point. "It's not just sex."

"What, do you *love her* like Maya said?" she mocked, air quotes and all.

However, both her hands and the mockery on her face dropped when I stayed silent.

I hadn't wanted it to happen this way.

I thought about how I'd tell her about my relationship with Kat a hundred times, and not once did it involve hitting her over the head with the infidelity and pouring salt in the wound.

I would have waited the appropriate length of time before telling her. We would already be divorced and living separate lives, and it wouldn't have been an easy conversation, but it wouldn't have been anything close to as painful as this.

Heather's disbelief was practically palpable, her mouth stuck open.

"You don't," she denied, as if stating a fact. Something she was dead sure of.

I remained quiet, letting my absence of words speak for me. The angular cut of Heather's chin jutted forward, her eyes narrowing their disbelief into slits.

"Dominic, tell me you don't *love* her."

Again, she sounded so sure of herself. As if I were telling her an awful joke and she was waiting for the punchline so she could pretend to laugh and move on to something sane.

Not knowing what else I could say, I shook my head with guilt thickening my voice.

"I'm sorry."

Her eyes bulged, white stretching into view around her sky blue shock. In a flash, she was rounding the kitchen counter towards me.

"Don't say sorry, say you don't love her!"

A wave of citrus and scalding wrath hit me fast as Heather came right up to me, so close she had to tilt her head back. I didn't move. I couldn't. My guilt had turned to a lead brick and held me cemented to the spot so I *had* to watch the devastating collapse of such a controlled woman that was all my fault.

Slaps lashed across my chest when I stayed quiet. "Say it! I need the fucking words, Dom. Say it!"

Fingers twisted into the fabric of my shirt, greedy and desperate. I let her shake me using her balled up fists, demanding with her blazing eyes one last time.

"Tell me you do not *love* her."

Staring down at her, I couldn't remember a single time in our entire relationship where I'd known her to beg for anything. I hated myself for reducing her to something so out of character. I hated how this was all happening now instead of later.

Mostly, I hated knowing it was only going to get worse as I told my wife the truth for the first time in months.

"I am unavoidably and permanently in love with her," I spoke quietly, the confession pulling out slow.

It sat heavy between us, her hands still latched onto my shirt as I searched her stare for a reaction. She'd frozen. Unblinking, unmoving, unspeaking.

There wasn't a right way to react to being told your husband had fallen in love with another woman, but *some* reaction was expected.

And then I saw it.

The reaction.

Glistening from the backs of her eyes.

My heart clobbered itself to see even the mist of tears from my wife, but before I could give into that rooted urge to comfort her pain, another reaction of hers emerged.

"*Liar.*" Rage built beneath that one word hiss, boiling over and spilling out in a scream. "Liar!"

Fists swatted at my chest, pounding over and over until pounding became pushing and pushing became scratching. I absorbed every strike of her fury until it became clear she wasn't going to stop until I made her.

I dodged her next hit and captured both her wrists between my fingers, trying to calm her rage. "Heather, *stop.*"

With staggering strength, she ripped herself from my hold and retreated backwards. Chest heaving, eyes a wash of fury and pain, hands balled tight.

"She is *never* coming back," she seethed, leaving a trail of venom behind her as she stomped over to her purse, fisted the thing in her grasp, and left out the front door without another word.

I stood there shocked, watching where she'd just left.

A very, *very* bad feeling unfolded in the pit of my stomach.

TWENTY-SIX

KAT

The night passed by strangely fast.

I didn't think I'd sleep much being trapped in a confined space with Blake all night, but as I found out last night, a lot of what I thought turned out to be wrong.

I did sleep. Not a whole lot, but enough that a sleepless bubble of nausea didn't swallow me up as I moved around the next morning. When I finally decided to stir, Blake was still passed out on his bed, one arm thrown over his face and the sheets kicked down to his feet.

I thought about trying the bedroom door to see if it was locked, but the threat of alarms and guards kept me where I was on his bedroom floor.

Eventually, he woke and used the bathroom, coming out and telling me to go in and get my business over with. I did, taking a bit longer to ransack his bathroom for anything I could use as a future weapon or clue to tell me my location.

All I found to use was mouthwash.

Not a *total* loss, I suppose.

Pulling the whole, mouth slurping at the faucet bit, I washed the taste of minty alcohol into the basin of the sink, using the back of my arm to swipe off the residue. When I came out of the bathroom, Blake was already dressed and holding a strappy pair of heels and—

"Is that the red dress you told me to wear?" I cocked my head at the draping of wine red fabric in his hands.

"Yup."

My curiosity flattened under my plummeting brows. "Really? One word? That's all I get after last night?"

Black eyes rolled up to me beneath heavy lids, a flash of irritation like all the times before, but something *wasn't* like all those other times. The black that met me head on wasn't the same ominous shade I'd gotten used to.

The recoloration was subtle, as if streets of city lights had been switched on from somewhere beneath, doing what they could to lighten up the night sky that was so far out of their reach.

"Still obsessed with talking to me, hm?"

"I'm not *obsessed.* Don't flatter yourself."

He tossed the dress my way with a throaty mumble. "Wouldn't dream of it."

My hand latched around the fabric in a swift catch, intrigue running the pads of my fingers over its material, my focus still on him.

"Talking about obsessions, why do you keep trying to put me in this dress?"

I knew why *I* liked it better than all those other trash bags he'd brought me to wear, but why was this the second time he tried to get me to wear it?

"It's not just a strip of fabric like the rest," he answered, palming his open pack of Marlboro Reds and plucking one free.

"Ah, trying to cover me up."

Sliding his chosen cancer stick between his lips, he muttered around it, "That's the idea."

My toes curled into the floor as I watched him kick back the wheel on his Zippo lighter, bright orange sparking to life and starting the slow burn to a surefire death.

Ivory smoke billowed from between his lips, rising a romantic line of curves and swirls in front of his dark eyes as they found mine through the vapor.

"Plus, it's a good color for you."

His baritone words played between my ears, blurring everything like the smoke from his cigarette was inside my head now too. Was that a compliment to me or the dress?

My eyes switched over his, wondering aloud.

"*Good* like someone will choose me, good?"

It might have been with the help of the smoke toiling through the room, or it might have just been him, but the intensity of his stare crackled the immediate air around my skin. Every hair on my bare arms lifted in surrender to it.

His hard-edge voice was just as severe.

"You know that won't happen."

* * *

The red dress wasn't half bad.

It looked even better with the gold heels Blake had snagged from who-the-fuck-knows-where.

It cupped just under my ass, hugged the curves of my waist, and finished with a cute sweetheart neckline that made my tits look perky as fuck but didn't dip so low that my nipples were falling out.

On any other occasion, I'd feel like a bombshell all dolled up in this kind of dress, strutting through a mansion-like house. If only it wasn't *this* house, and I was only wearing this kind of dress in the hopes that Dominic would be shredding it off of me later.

Still, I'd say of all my mornings here so far, this one came with the least amount of stomach cramping.

I wasn't worried. I wasn't nervous. I wasn't starved or about to puke all over the expensive mahogany floors.

I was... *okay.*

And all because of the man leading me by the wrist to today's Line Up.

Last night took my kaleidoscope view of Blake and spun it all around, colors and shapes shifting, views distorting, white light splintering a crack through this world of darkness.

I knew he couldn't be all bad, but last night showed me that he wasn't even *mostly* bad. He was this swirl of light and dark, a painter's palette where contrasting shades bled together and created a chaos of moral gray confusion.

Blake was not bad. Blake was not good.

What's more was that the wicked that ran in his veins wasn't there by choice. *He* wasn't here by choice.

In a less literal way, he was a prisoner here just like I was. He was trapped under the thumb of Ray and Claudia because of choices he'd made when he was young and stupid, and there wasn't a way out that didn't involve a body bag.

He was dying here and *would* die here. Blake was working in his own grave, and now I knew why he smoked those god awful Marlboro Reds.

To speed up the process.

We arrived about five minutes earlier to Line Up than we normally would have to miss a run-in with Claudia. Only she would have cared that we didn't come from my room upstairs like normal, and last night would have been all for nothing.

The foyer was sans one old rich bitch, and a few of the other girls were still trickling in, some finishing off makeup, some finishing off breakfast. A pang hit my stomach as I locked my sight on the last of a blueberry muffin being shoved between two red-painted lips.

My palm rested over the hollow ache.

I couldn't wait 'til this was over so I could bury myself in carbs and grease.

Blake escorted me to the end of the line closest to the stairs, his steady grip around my arm loosening as he planted me in place. Thanks to last night, I wasn't worried about today's Line Up… or any in the future for that matter.

Because of Abigail, Blake wouldn't let anything happen to me if he could help it.

I was his chance for redemption.

I was his chance to get right what he got so wrong with her.

The press of Blake's presence was still at my back as I turned to face the front doors. It was comforting, actually, to feel him there.

To know my secret wall of defense was nearby.

"You snore, by the way," I whispered back to him, tugging at the hem of the red dress.

Burnt warmth breezed over my ear, my attention prickling.

"I'm not the only one."

I stifled a gasp but not the gape of my jaw, whipping my head in his direction. "I do not *snore*."

A glimpse of white teeth shined beneath his rising lips in the widest half-grin I'd seen him give yet. "Soft and trill like a fucking kitten."

My head jerked back with a funny scoff.

"Well, that actually sounds pretty fucking adorable then."

A noise cracked out of him that sounded a hell of a lot like a laugh.

It was short lived, but holy fuck was it robust and exquisite and surprising at the joy it filled me with just hearing it.

I liked making him laugh, I decided right then and there. I wanted to do it again.

The short noise died out fast, but left his voice riding the high of levity as he scanned over my head.

"It wasn't the worst."

A ghost of humor still speckled his grumpy mouth, and I swear to fucking god, it was so spectacular. Like an eclipse or meteor shower, or some other natural phenomenon that captivated completely without even trying.

My whole focus, my whole body was entirely enamoured by that gentle curve on his lips, and that's why it was so personally devastating as I watched it slip and fall out of existence.

A frown took its place. A deep one.

Dangerous smoke rolled in from both sides of his stare, darkening it back to a sheet of brutal black.

Grief erupted and chewed its sharp teeth at my chest at the loss of his light and smile. I wanted them back. I wanted them back *now*, but his severe glare was locked in on something over my head.

I turned to see what it was that had soiled his rare joy.

I froze.

So did everyone else in the foyer.

I hadn't even heard the doors open yet to let her in.

She was staring at me and I was staring at her, and no one was moving. No one was breathing, either.

At least, I didn't hear any. I didn't hear anything over the rush of blood in my ears.

Roiling. Crashing. *Screaming.*

The energy in the room stiffened to a freeze with everyone else as they watched us, as if they knew the secrets we shared, the connection we possessed, the destruction we'd laid on the other's life.

I couldn't move. All that time I'd had to sit up in that room and stew and think and plan what I'd do whenever I saw her again went right out the wide open front door.

All I could do was *stare.*

At her scowling face. At her fire-blue eyes. At the glinting diamond ring sitting on her finger where it most certainly did not fucking belong.

The weight of her presence held my body down, slowed my thoughts as if they were swimming through trenches of muddied water, polluted by hatred and a scathing rage. My emotions were just as ensnared as the rest of me until…

Until she spoke.

"You homewrecking *slut*," she spat.

And that was it.

Heather's vile voice electrocuted my body out of its trance, and I took in a gasp so *audible* with hate, everyone in the room simultaneously flinched when the sound of it hit them.

"You fucking bitch!"

A whisper of a touch grazed my shoulders as I screamed and Blake attempted to grab me and stop me, but it was too late. I wanted her fucking blood dripping through my fingers, her head hanging on a rope made of her own hair; and I would do about damn near anything to get it.

I ran at her with memories of Dominic and Charlotte and my mother pressing through my furious feet. My lungs rose with the hurt she'd inflicted upon me and fell with determination to deliver the same degree of pain to her.

Blood boiled in my head. Screams pierced in my ears. A feral cry tore apart my lips as I closed in on her. Heather looked neither afraid nor shocked as I charged, flawless arrogance perched on her features.

Just a second later, I discovered why.

Sergio came out of nowhere, wrapped a big fat arm around my waist, and then I was airborne.

Another gasp punched my lungs as I soared backwards, knowing what was coming.

I hit the floor *hard*, pain knocking against my spine as I skidded across the unforgiving floors until I came to an abrupt stop against a pair of legs. Groaning through gritted teeth, familiar hands appeared beneath my upper arms and hoisted me up.

Blake's fingers pinched my dress at the small of my back, tugging me back against him.

"*Don't,*" he hissed in my ear, a warning and threat in one.

I wobbled against him, head spinning and trying to find focus on anything other than the splinter of pain throbbing up my neck.

Laughter cut through the stiff air, mocking and circling my dizzy head as my vision tried to right itself on the woman across the foyer where the laughter was coming from. It took a few seconds, but eventually, instead of three or four vindictive bitches, there was just one.

And she was grinning so wide, showing me all her fangs.

"I can't say that wasn't fun to watch."

Blake's grip on the back of my dress tightened as Heather delighted in my pain, holding me back from a take two.

She was here. She was fucking *here*.

"What the *fuck* are you doing here?" I spat, heart pounding up my throat. *Where's Dominic? Where's Charlotte?*

"I gave my mother the morning off." She beveled in her heels. "I'll be running the Line Up today."

"*Why?*"

She breezed right past my question, slanting her pretty little head at me. "You look right at home here, don't you? Finally right where you belong."

"I *belong* back home with my sister, you fucking psychopath!"

The front doors still wide open, Heather took a thoughtful step away from them. "You know, maybe without you around, she won't grow up into a life of slutting it up with any man she can find…" She paused, thin pink lip twitching up. "Married or otherwise."

With the emphasis she put on those last words, I felt the curiosities of every single person in the room spike, including Blake's.

"You don't know what the fuck you're talking about," I denied, and would continue to deny until I was out of here and could break the good news to her when she was behind bars and Dominic was by my side.

Her vengeance went ocean deep and morphed her eyes ocean dark.

"I know exactly what I'm talking about, Ms. Sanders. Do not *insult* my intelligence."

"Why not? You always insult mine."

Her mouth parted, icicle sharp gaze refocusing. "And I'm beginning to see I was wrong about that. I pegged you as a stupid high-school dropout. But you're not stupid… are you, Ms. Sanders?"

"Is that rhetorical or do you want me to insult myself or say I'm a fucking genius? I don't get what you want here, Heather. I don't get *why* you're here."

"I'm here because I underestimated the *impact* you've had on my life." She angled her sharp chin up high and mighty, but not high enough that I didn't see the fan of anguish that rippled across her slender face. "And just how much you *ruined* it."

The look of torment in her razored sapphires plus those words pulsed a wave of dread through me, my heart tripping and falling over what it meant.

Oh shit.

Maybe she does know.

"In that case, you've done a pretty *bang up* job ruining mine right back."

"Oh…" A sick enjoyment tilted her head, the sanity in her eyes entirely unhinged. "I can assure you I've only just begun."

Apprehension churned in my gut as echoes of her heels brought her closer to the opened front door. Facing me, she raised her arm out to the side, fingers poised as if to welcome someone in.

I felt the wave of her fingers move in my stomach, my heartbeat climbing into my ears. A man came through the doors not too long after, his shoulders set so wide, he almost didn't fit.

Behind me, Blake stiffened.

The uncomfortable shuffling of a few other girls down the line caught my attention, too.

Blake's hold on the back of my dress vanished. "He's not allowed to be here."

"Why not?"

Zoey, the bleach blonde girl from breakfast, was standing right next to me and added in a whisper. "He almost broke my arm the last time he was here. I thought he'd been blackballed."

"He has," Blake answered, his voice darker than his burning eyes.

My rounded stare went down the line of every girl in the room, all of them regarding Mr. Six-Foot-Something with fear fogging their expressions. This guy was huge. He was practically bald. He had a particular glint to his eyes that shined like the blade of a machete, deadly and truly fucking evil.

Heather touched her hand to the man's arm, her dainty fingers not even spanning half his bicep. "Mr. Smith here is a special client," she told me. "He's an expert in dealing with *problem girls.*"

Her elegant hand lifted from his arm, gliding up through the air until she landed a pointed finger my way.

"And that's my problem."

A saunter brought 'Mr. Smith' forward with a raking chuckle, his wickedness zeroed in on me as he cracked each of his knuckles. "You picked me out a real pretty flower, didn't you?"

All of Heather's explosive crazy was fixed on me. "With petals just *dying* to be plucked."

Horror parted my lips and upended my stomach.

Oh my god.

She…

"You—" But words failed.

All my life, I'd pretended to be strong and brave and fearless. Lying about being brave came easier to me than being honest about being weak. *Weakness* didn't pay the bills, keep the house running, or food in our stomachs.

I hated feeling weak or scared so I lied and said I was the opposite.

But I couldn't lie right now.

I couldn't pretend to be brave with a man twice my size coming my way. I couldn't pretend I wasn't scared—more scared than I'd ever been in my entire life—as starving eyes took a long taste down my body and came back up hungry for more.

I couldn't pretend to be anything other than weak as the man Heather hand-picked to violate me got within grabbing distance.

Denial swept a freeze through my bloodstream, telling me this wasn't happening, this couldn't be happening, that no one was this fucking *sick* in the head to make this happen.

My bones locked, joints stiffening. I'd survived this long. Blake had done so *good* at helping me survive.

This isn't happening, isn't happening, isn't happening.

A big fat hand swiped at me, and all denial shattered on a piercing breath.

Moving fast, I ducked out of his reach and bolted for the stairs. *Go, go, go.*

My legs pumped with my hammering heart as I pushed up one, two, almost three steps before—

Hands wrapped around and tugged at my ankles, a yelp stabbing the air as he yanked my legs out from beneath me. Jarring pain clattered through my head as my chin bounced off a step, my brain knocking around my skull.

Black and spots of white clustered my vision, stars suddenly inside during the daytime even though the sky was so dark. Then I realized it wasn't the sky and those weren't the stars. My eyes were pinched shut, and those tiny bright dots were signs that I wasn't going to make it.

They were spelling it out for me in my head, telling me that this was it. I'd made it as long as I could avoiding what I'd been promised since day one.

Agony was singing a painful tune through my jaw as I tried to wrestle myself up from the stairs, but those snatching hands got to me first. They flipped me over, the man with no soul in his eyes hovering his monstrous silhouette above me.

"Oh, Darling," he tutted playfully, shaking his big head from side to side.

"Am I gonna have some fun with you."

Saliva pooled from the sides of my mouth at his lecherous tone and sickening smile, hot bile sloshing up around my stomach. I needed none of this to be happening. I needed to wake back up in Blake's room on his floor. I needed this *not* to be reality staring me in the face with savage intentions rolling behind his eyes.

"No-no!" Before I could even properly scream, I was hoisted up and over his shoulder, gravity working its magic and sinking my heart up into my throat.

I pushed my palms against his back, hitting and swatting and yelling. I caught a glimpse of glittering sapphires watching the show with glee in all my thrashing, and I yelled out to her next.

"What the fuck is wrong with you?! Tell him to stop! Stop!"

One shaking breath later. "Stop," Heather called out.

He did.

'Mr. Smith' kept his arm anchored around my legs so I couldn't kick out, but he stalled in place just like Heather had said. Shock blasted a film over my body, encasing my skin in buzzing, manic energy just *sitting* on the surface.

She actually told him to stop.

Relief was waiting like a weight to drop in my stomach as Heather came closer, halting only about a foot away. She was right there, my entire fucking fate in her hands and she knew it. She *knew* she had everything over me just how she wanted, and maybe that was all she wanted.

Maybe she just wanted this. My fear. My surrender. My begging.

Switching her snake eyes between mine, she dropped her voice to just between the two of us like the dirtiest little secret.

"This is what you get for fucking my husband."

My relief dropped like a bomb, exploding the secret assailant of despair hiding inside. It ripped its shrapnel through me, scouring down my stomach and bleeding out a curdling scream.

"You bitch!" I made a useless swipe for her, the man holding me already making his way past the stairs down to wherever he wanted. "No! No!"

Desperation snapped my head up, wild panting working my lungs until I found him.

Blake, who was watching me being taken away from him with heartbreak cracked into his crestfallen features. He was devastated. He was fucking livid.

But he wasn't moving.

"Blake!" I cried his name, watching it slap him in the face and tear those thick brows of his down his forehead. He still didn't move, though. He just fucking stood there as the exact same thing that had happened to his Abby was about to happen to me.

He might get in trouble if he helped me now, but no matter how selfish it was, I didn't care. I didn't fucking care. All I cared about was him saving me one more time as a final scream seared up my throat and ripped through the air directly at him.

"BLAKE!"

And then he was gone.

Everyone was gone as Mr. Smith turned a corner and opened a bedroom door. I continued to thrash as he dipped us inside the room, throwing my arms out to grab onto the door frame with every ounce of strength I had.

The attempt was futile as he jerked my body forward, each finger slipping free from the frame one by one and hammering my fate into existence with every hold lost.

The door slammed with a resounding echo as he kicked it shut.

Seconds later, I was falling upside down in a heap, bouncing unceremoniously on a bed. Flopping around on it, I scrambled up to my hands and knees and shot up to my feet, teetering on the unstable mattress.

The man had his sinister gaze on me, standing at the foot of the bed with his arms crossed. My back hit the wall as I stumbled as far away from him as I could towards the headboard, chest heaving and insults flying.

"Don't you fucking touch me!"

He let out a slow chuckle, hanging his thumbs through his belt loop.

"You know I used to love coming here before some bitches got too whiny. So I was mighty pleased to get a personal ring from Mrs. Heather this morning about some chick that needed handling. For her to be calling *me*, I thought for sure she'd be a wild child, but honey, I ain't never expect nothin' as lovely as you."

He stepped towards the bed.

"You ever been punished before, Darlin'?" His filthy stare elevated to mine. "And I don't mean that pussy-bullshit, spanking or choking or rough fucking. I mean *really* punished by a man who gets off on your pretty tears and screams."

I could hear them, those scraping screams and cries peeling down the walls in my ears as his hands dropped to his gaudy brass belt buckle. Slowly, he began to undo it.

"If you ain't, I'll start you out nice and easy. How about I let you use that pretty little cock loving mouth of yours to suck my dick?"

I sucked in a sharp breath of disgust. "How about *fuck off*?"

His cruel laughter was muffled by the thump of my heartbeat getting louder and louder inside my head.

"Mrs. Heather warned me about that mouth of yours. I told her not to worry. That I'd stuff it full of good ol' southern boy cock for her."

"You're a sick motherfucker, you know that?"

"Honey, I've been called all the names in the goddamn book." Languidly, he slid the length of his belt from around his jeans, my pulse crescendoing as I watched. "Nothing you're gonna say is gonna stop you from choking on my cock and loving every second of it."

"I find it hard to imagine that anyone has *ever* loved sucking anything of yours. Let alone your pathetic little dick."

"Oh, there ain't nothing little about me, darlin'." A crack sliced the air as he snapped his belt using both hands, his unsavory gaze trapped on me. "I'll fuckin' break you."

"Not if I break you first," I growled out, fight overriding flight in my lightning bloodstream.

If I could just get to the bedroom door, I could run free. *All* I needed was to get to the other side of this room, and I'd be free. There was only one pigheaded roadblock in the way.

I could do this. I could fight him. I could win. I could run.

I could be my own hero.

I *had* to be my own hero. No one was coming for me this time. No last minute rescues, no fairytale miracles. Just me, myself, and my motherfucking lightning.

Mr. Smith stalked in deliberate steps around to the edge of the bed, drool practically hanging from the corner of his mouth as he eyed my legs.

"Now, are you gonna play nice, or are you gonna be a little bitch?" He flashed me a deviant look. "Either way ends with me painting your cheeks with tears and your ass black and blue."

"I think I'll pass on both," I seethed, countering his steps on the floor with my own on the mattress to keep us a good distance apart.

"Aw, sweetheart, you don't have a choice."

"Yeah, that's kind of the fucking definition of *rape*, isn't it?"

He pushed his thighs up flush to the side of the bed, and I nearly stumbled off of it. "What I'm about to do to you won't be rape when you're beggin' for more, trust me."

"I *don't*."

A flash of black eyes blurred past my mind, and my chest fucking ached for Blake to be here. But he wasn't. He was too scared, and I didn't have time to waste thinking about him.

"This game of cat and mouse is gettin' old, green eyes. How about we get started?"

I was so stunned when he actually made a reach for me, I nearly forgot to move.

His hands shot out across the bed, fat fingers making a grab for my legs. With a startled yelp, I half jumped, half tumbled off the bed to get away. The walls of the room dragged by in a blur as I fell to the floor, my hands blindly trying to stop the fall while my shoulder did most of the actual catching.

I rolled onto my back, heaving as if I'd been fighting for hours instead of seconds. My heart was just racing so fucking fast, it'd exhausted me before the battle really even began.

Swallowing down a dry gulp of air, I burst to my feet, snapping around in the direction I last saw him in, ready to let my lightning shred my skin and strike him down.

Just as I turned, he got me before I could get him.

A cry broke the atmosphere as his heavy palm smacked the side of my face. The force of it was so hard, my neck even cracked as it jerked. Pain exploded up my cheek, lights in my brain went haywire, strobing bright and black and every shade in between.

My footing staggered as I tried to stay standing, cupping my cheek as it throbbed all the way up to my temple. Moans of agony infused my next few breaths as I held my face, trying to focus on standing and breathing and where the fuck this guy was in the room with me.

A snaking hand around my hips gave me the answer to the last one.

He gave a violent jerk of my waist, and my arms flew in front of me to try and catch myself as he bent me over on the bed.

Except, I failed with that too as he snatched both my arms behind my back, shoving me face first into the mattress.

My nose and mouth got smothered into the bedding, and the scorch of self-loathing I felt at failing *so* fast to be my own hero was almost worse than the panic chomping at my stomach.

"Get off of me!" I struggled beneath his hold, dread rising a heatwave through my body as my breathing grew stronger, faster, and began to sound more like cries than anything else. "Get off!"

"Nah, why would I do that?" The brush of jeans grazed my ass, the feel of his hard excitement pushing against me and turning my gut inside out. "We're just starting to have fun now."

"Stop-stop!" I screamed, squirming beneath him and bucking my shoulders, kicking my legs out, all in blind pursuit to get him the hell off of me. Pain made bracelets around my wrists as the man tightened his grip around them until the fucking bones beneath whined for him to stop.

"Stop *moving.*" Impatience poured through his clenched teeth, but I kept on. Kept thrashing and kicking and jerking myself between him and the bed. "I said stop fucking moving, bitch!"

"Ah!"

A cry tossed my head back, sending my agony into the air as my elbows were bent in directions they shouldn't be. *Fuck, fuck, fuck,* I could feel the bones bowing to the pressure of his twisting hold, marrow chipping, the sting of tears stabbing the backs of my eyes.

I gave in so fast, I'd never be able to look myself in the mirror again if I survived this.

"Okay! Okay! Please! I'll stop, I'll stop!"

Plumes of black were fading in from the sides of my vision as I begged and cried out in so much goddamn pain, I almost couldn't wait for the darkness to consume me so I could escape it.

Then, it was gone.

The pressure released, and I slumped back down onto the mattress, panting and expelling every ounce of pride I had through every haggard breath.

A violating palm swept over my ass, circling the flesh just beneath the fabric of the red dress.

"Think you might wanna play nice now, don't ya?"

Everything inside of me screamed, *no*.

But my scrambling brain didn't know what to do. It was overwrought with panic, the feel of this pervert's erection touching me glitching out my lightning so it zapped tiny tremors throughout all of me but not at *him* behind me. It didn't know how to reach him, how to get to him and make him wail like he'd made me.

In all of the chaos, in all of the terror, in all of the nasty *weakness* overloading my system, a voice of thunder rumbled through my head.

And the memory of it made me want to break down into a puddle of tears and never come back up for air.

Dominic's deep velvet voice burrowed in my ears, sweet and perfect and everything I needed it to be. I pictured him just like he was—pressed in behind me, trying not to touch me more than he had to so he didn't fall for me more than he already had—when he told me the piece of advice echoing in my head:

'How I have you now, your easiest way to hurt me would be to step on my foot as hard as you can, especially if you have heels on.'

And heels I had.

I only wanted one thing more than to stay in this memory solitude with Dominic's thunder rolling through my head, and that was to get this fucker off of me. Plus, Dominic would be so goddamn proud of the hole I was about to put through this guy's foot.

Leaving my thunder behind, I lifted my right foot with a battle cry rising just the same in my throat.

Simultaneously, I released them both.

My pointed heel came down on Mr. Smith's awaiting foot just as my screech shredded the barriers of sound.

At the exact same time, a loud bark of pain shot off behind me *and* the sweaty palms locked around my wrists vanished. Cold swept in where they'd been, and never had an empty chill across my skin been so relieving.

There wasn't time to celebrate though.

Freedom had a closing window, and I wouldn't waste a second of it.

Bringing my knees up to the bed while Mr. Smith wallowed behind me, I scampered across the entire bed until I made it to the other side, feet scrambling to touch floor. I didn't even stop to smile as my toes touched solid ground, making a desperate break for the bedroom door.

I wouldn't celebrate or smile or anything close to it until I was on the other side of it, and I was so fucking close. My heartbeat was in a mad dash with my legs as I ran towards it, closer and closer and—

A large hand shot into my hair, fingers tangling tight as my jaw dropped to let out a scream straight from my heart.

That scream struck like my lightning meant to, tearing through the room as knuckles dug into my skull as they dragged me back by my hair. The arch of my neck was as far back as it could go as he yanked my hair hard, snapping my head back to gape at the ceiling.

That ceiling had two blood-curdling eyes that *roared* for my pain and submission.

"That wasn't so *nice*, was it?" Another cry split my lips apart as he tightened his fist, his knuckles like spikes pushing into my skull. "Little bitches like you need to learn to be nice to men like me. You know why, green eyes?"

"I don't *fucking* care," I ground out through my teeth, struggling beneath his grip.

"Oh, but you will." In a quick move, he hoisted me upright, trading his hold on my hair for one around my shoulders. It brought us almost face to face, a terrible glint winking in his sordid eyes that promised suffering. "I guarantee you will."

Then, he shoved. *Hard*.

My skull connected with the wall behind me, pain exploding through the back of my head as I cried out. It was like he'd stabbed me from behind, the knife driving into the back of my head and coming out the front. The starry spots from before sprouted in my eyes again as the agony radiated, swirling and dancing and confusing my sight.

Oh god, I just wanted to fall. I wanted to sink to the ground and fall asleep, but I couldn't. Not now. Not yet.

Not with this blur of a man still in my way, nothing but burning eyes and a sinful smirk.

"How'd that feel, darlin'?"

"Fucking peachy," I huffed, trying to blink the bright dots away so I could see him. So I could fight him. So I could *win*.

I made a pathetic shove at his chest that got my arms thrust back against the wall and his humid breath right in my face. "Mmm, I haven't had a real fighter in a while. I am just gonna *love* rippin' into you. Tearing out that goddamn attitude and shoving some manners into you."

Vomit tightened in my stomach, and I jerked my head to the side so his mouth wasn't so close to where it didn't belong. He was too close to headbutt, too close to knee in the balls.

He was just overall too fucking close.

"Why you turnin' your head baby? You don't wanna kiss me?"

"I'd rather *choke*."

A hum vibrated his wide chest. "Oh, we'll get to that. But first..."

His hands dropped from my wrists and bunched at the sweetheart neckline of my dress so fast, I didn't even have a chance to gasp before it happened.

The wine red dress split in two right down the middle, the sound of shredding material ripping through the room and my pounding heart. Horror expanded my lungs as I watched the blanket of defense flourish to the ground, my bare tits spilling out.

I hadn't been able to wear a bra with this dress, but I didn't think it would matter.

I didn't think *this* would be happening today.

My manic focus snapped back up as a perverted groan rattled in his throat, Mr. Smith leaning back to give his greedy eyes a good look.

"Now those are fucking perfect."

I swatted at his incoming hands, slapping and yelling louder, "No, no, *no!*"

A yelp ripped up my throat, eyes slamming shut to block out the violent touch pinching my nipples.

The violating feel of him where he didn't belong chewed across my flesh until I felt like I was all raw, all exposed, bleeding acid down every single inch of me. My reborn again heart spasmed, bellowing out that where he was touching was only for Dominic, begging me to make him stop.

This wasn't happening. This wasn't fucking happening.

He palmed both my breasts like I wasn't doing everything I could to pry him off, tearing with all my might at his forearms, dragging my nails over his arms 'til red hot lines bloomed from his skin.

He only grabbed harder, *twisted* my body tighter.

I screamed, tears flooding in to sit on the brim of my eyeline ready to fall, ready to give up and give in. Except, my lightning *wasn't* done. It wasn't ready to give in, because it knew if it did, and this man put himself inside of me, it would be the death of my lightning for good.

He would rip it clean out of me like he said, and I'd be left a girl hollow and cold.

My lightning needed one more fighting chance, and it took it as soon as Mr. Smith leaned back just enough to give it room to strike.

"Gah!" The heel of my hand smashed under his nose as I thrust it up just like Dominic taught me.

A god awful cracking sound bounced through the room, and Mr. Smith shouted.

Stumbling back, he grabbed his nose with both hands, crimson blood already pooling through the cracks of his fingers. Victory went off in fireworks through my chest, ignited by the lightning and how *proud* it was to see blood.

"What the fuck is wrong with you?!"

I didn't stick around long enough to give him the lengthy list of answers. My feet pivoted towards the door only a few strides away, lifting off the floor to make a break for it.

A sticky hand fisted around my neck, smashing my head back against the wall.

This time, instead of white polka-dotting my vision, black appeared instead, swimming all around and much bigger than the tiny bright stars were. These black dots were everywhere, bleeding in and out of size, consuming my dizzy head until the darkness swallowed me all up.

It was all dark and all pain.

And no air. Not even a gasp of it.

My eyes bulged in my head against the pressure the man was squeezing my neck with, pushing out farther than they were ever meant to go. Gargled cuts of wet air tried to suck down life, but nothing was coming and nothing was going either.

The black shadows cast over my vision only showed me flashes of red rage eyes and streaks of blood the same angry color.

"You know when I got here, I wasn't so sure I was gonna break something of yours." At this point, he was just a grating voice in the void of pain. "Now I'm gonna break *everything* you got. Fingers, wrists, your fucking *nose* to pay you back."

His fingers crushed my windpipe, the desperation to breathe scratching between the friction of my esophagus folding against itself. My head was filling too tight, too compacted with all the oxygen I couldn't breathe as I clawed at his hand.

Blood-stained teeth spotlighted in the filter of fading black, growling at me like a grizzly. "By the time I'm done with you, you're gonna bleed from places you didn't even know were possible."

And it was right then, with his threat lurking in my ears and my consciousness fading in and out, that I felt it begin to happen.

A mist of cold crept in, slinking beneath my skin and melting into my electric veins.

My lightning… it couldn't take this. It couldn't fight this. It had already tried, stomping on his foot and breaking his nose, and nothing worked.

This man was stronger. He was bigger. He would rape me.

And my too-proud lightning wanted to die out before it happened.

The fire my blood ran hot with was smothered to a smoking simmer, a chill rising from its ashes to possess my body from the inside out.

The chill was safe. The chill was numbing.

The lasting lights flickered in my head, readying to dissolve.

A sudden crash jolted my sinking subconscious.

Next thing, the hands, the body, the stinging fate of a violent desecration were gone.

My lungs gasped for air like I'd breached a surface of water, choking down sweet, sweet oxygen too fast and ended up coughing it all up.

The force of it bent me over at the waist, hacking and scratching that itch for air as another crash went off somewhere in the bedroom.

My sore neck jerked to the side just in time to see two bodies hit the ground, a slew of grunts and curses rising from the collision. One body was Mr. Smith's, and he was facedown on the ground, his already broken nose taking another beating.

The second body jumped up to his feet and spun around to face me.

Black eyes that were anything but met mine, and I swore if everyone in the entire world had been quiet at that very second, we all would have been able to hear the audible *click* of our connection.

He was here. He was *here,* and all of his brightly colored emotions were smeared in a disarray across his stare as he drank me in. My torn dress. My wild panting. My battered cheek.

He didn't speak, and he didn't need to either. I heard him. I heard him without words by the roaring hum we created in the air around us. I heard his relief that I was still standing. I heard his regret that he ever let me go. I heard his magnificent rage that this man had laid a finger on me.

I heard him so powerfully, I was breathless all over again with no one even touching me.

Movement behind Blake caught my gaze, and I tore it from his to gasp. "No!"

The word pierced the air with panic as Mr. Smith rose behind Blake with murder in his beady eyes. Blake snapped around in a whirl I couldn't keep up with, his arm rearing back.

He didn't even make a sound as he slammed his fist into Mr. Smith's face, knocking him back to the ground... where he didn't get back up.

My shocked-wide eyes watched the man's back for movement, for any signs he was about to stand and take his own swing. All there was though was the easy rise and fall of his breathing.

Holy shit.

Blake stood over his prize, back rising and falling as he looked over the man twice his size that he'd knocked out with a single punch.

He eventually stepped over him, grabbing a blanket from the bed I'd almost been raped on and walked over to me. He wasn't staring at me though. All his hard-bitten focus was on the floor while I could do nothing *but* stare at him.

Blake reached where I was huddled against the wall, nothing but my underwear and hands to shield me. Other men might have looked when a woman was so bare and helpless, but Blake didn't.

He just widened the wool blanket in front of me, holding it open for me to walk into.

At this point, I was something *past* dazed and barely holding on. All the strength I had left was going into not collapsing where I was. As I lifted one foot to step into the blanket, that last vertebrae of strength gave out.

I fell into Blake, and he caught me.

Strong arms locked around my back and supported most of my weight as he held me against him. Soft fabric brushed around my shoulders as Blake wrapped me up in it, burrowing me into the blanket and into his chest.

He wrapped me in his arms, his warmth, all of his fierce protection, and I let him.

Right now, I wasn't stone. I wasn't anything stable or invincible. I was a dam overflowing and breaking down, losing all my power and all my strength in this destructive place.

Every touch, every slap, every vile word from the man now laid out on the floor had stolen another brick from my wall.

I was collapsing in, one by one, going down fast and rivers ready to run down my cheeks.

There was only one thing keeping me from crumbling completely, and it was him.

Blake.

He was strength, and I was weakness. He was comfort, and I needed it.

Fuck, did I need it.

My exhausted muscles let go of the tension in my neck so it could fall back and stare up at the thing I needed, unapologetic in showing him just how veritable that need was.

"I didn't think you were coming," I whispered, tracking my eyes over his face.

He breathed in, slow and deep, something so comforting about the feel of life lifting his chest over mine. "Sorry it took me so long."

"I fought." I tried.

A softness feathered his dark eyes as he took that in, barely parting his lips. "I saw his face."

"Will you get in trouble?"

He swallowed thickly, his Adam's apple riding under his skin. "Probably."

I inhaled his answer, stretching my fingers up to the collar of his signature black shirt, rolling the material in my grasp until my knuckles met his skin beneath. I didn't think about why I wanted to touch him. I just did it, brushing my thumb over the rise of his collarbone, our eyes still locked.

"I'm sorry."

I didn't want him to get in trouble because of me, but staring down at me like he was, he didn't look like he'd care if he did. In fact, something profound passed across his gaze like a shooting star streaking across the night sky.

"It was worth it."

My eyes dropped shut as I breathed in his words. Petals of water filled in behind my lids at the degree of certainty in his rough voice. He thought I was worth it—and I wasn't worth anything.

How fantastically I failed just now proved it.

Exhaustion brought my head up to rest my forehead to his chest just in case any rogue tears went for an escape. I stayed there, counting the beats in his confident heart and trying to match my erratic pulse to his rhythm.

Seconds later, a weight settled on top of my head, Blake nestling his chin into my hair.

We stayed just like that for a bit, holding onto one another and pretending time had stopped.

"Can you walk?" His voice vibrated through the top of my head, shuddering through my body.

I shook my head against him.

Pathetic as it was, I had nothing left in me to stand with let alone walk. Blake seemed to understand. The weight of his head disappeared from mine, and I swear to fucking god, I almost whimpered at the loss of heat and pressure and *him*.

Thankfully, he wasn't gone for long. He bent at the knees and scooped me up, keeping the blanket secure around my nakedness. With my feet off the floor, he cradled me into his hard chest, and I buried my face in the crook of his neck, trying to pretend like I didn't know how pitiful it made me.

How pathetic and needy I was as I breathed a hit of his burnt scent off his skin just to feel the familiarity of it fold into my mind.

Whether I liked it or not, in this place, Blake was my calm.

He was my sanity and safe haven wrapped up in smoke.

As he walked me out of that room, out of the den of would-be horrors and moved down the hallway, I melted into his embrace and became the weakness this place made me into. There was someone to hold me, to carry me, to protect me, and at that very moment, I gave into it despite how unlike me it was.

Right now, I didn't care to be me. I didn't have enough energy for it.

Blake brought me up the stairs, and I spared a look over his shoulder at the crowd behind us. Several pairs of curious eyes watched us ascend, but I only searched out one pair.

She was in the corner of the room with Claudia, who from the looks of it was scolding her daughter. Claudia's back was to us but Heather was dead on, and I waited and waited and waited for her to look up at me.

When she finally did, you can bet your sweet fucking ass I did not let her go.

I held her.

An ugly, thick mass of tension threaded between our staring, every second writing out another letter of the silent message passing between us. A message that dripped with violence and vengeance.

A message that read whatever this thing was between us had just taken a deadly turn.

However this ended…

One of us was walking away with blood-stained hands.

And one wasn't walking away at all.

TWENTY-SEVEN

KAT

By the time Blake and I made it upstairs to my room, I wasn't feeling so vulnerable.

More so nauseous.

Blake carried me into the bathroom and set me on the sink countertop, probably feeling it in my muscles that they wouldn't work if he tried to make me stand.

We were in there for less than sixty seconds before I threw up.

It happened so suddenly, I barely made it to my knees in front of the toilet before it all came up. Not food, since I hadn't eaten that morning yet.

The memories.

Mr. Smith's touch. Mr. Smith's voice. Mr. Smith's threats.

They all came up, expelling from my body like the poison they were. Blake grabbed my hair, moving it from around my face as I puked up every horror from the last however many minutes of my life.

He waited patiently until I was done, then grabbed me a towel to clean myself up with. While I wiped the puke from my chin, he reached around me to turn on the shower.

We weren't talking.

The rush of water was all there was. Oh, and the humming. The *energy*.

It was still there even now. Even as the thing that made my fire and song alive had died out. It wasn't gone completely. Just hiding well enough that all I felt in its place was numb.

Totally fucking numb.

Blake squatted down to where I sat on the bathroom floor, balancing on the balls of his feet. Still, not a single word moved that strict line across his closed lips. He was waiting for me.

To speak if I wanted to. To stay silent if I didn't.

The shower still running in the background, my voice broke in a mumble over it. "Can you go?"

He was watching me when I glanced up at him after a beat of nothing.

"So I can shower."

His shoulders rose with a deep breath, dark eyes tracking between mine.

"I'll be back in ten minutes."

Standing up from the floor, he headed out of the bathroom, carefully closing the door behind him. I watched where he'd left from for a while, zoning out on the door until I came back to, remembering I only had ten minutes to bathe, and I'd probably just wasted three of them.

Letting go of the blanket around my body was surprisingly difficult.

Well, I suppose not surprisingly.

All I had to take off after freeing the wool blanket to the floor were the same pair of underwear I'd been turning inside out for almost a week now. They were fucking disgusting, but I didn't have anything else to wear.

The spray of water when I tiptoed inside the shower hit my skin with a wash of heat.

Not enough, though.

My fingers found the knob of the shower, twisting it until it wouldn't twist anymore and the temperature turned molten.

It was the only way I could feel it though. Anything less than fire couldn't burn off the handprints left on my body without permission. Only something equally as scalding could strip my flesh of the blistering stain the feel of his erection pressed all over me had left.

I needed to melt my skin off so I could watch the memory of him swirl down the shower drain and be gone for good.

I didn't want what he'd done to me. I didn't need *more* baggage.

My back was already so fucking broken as it was.

I wanted to pretend like it'd never happened. Furiously scrubbing my arms, my legs, my stomach of his criminal fingerprints, I washed them off so I could move on without the memory of his touch. My fingers scratched and scratched in my hair until a burn chewed along my scalp when my skin got too raw for the chemicals in the vanilla shampoo.

But he'd touched my hair. Made my scalp burn and probably bleed.

Scrubbing each strand of hair and inch of my skull was all I could do without shaving it all off.

"Kat?"

My body froze beneath the spray, fingers strapped in ready over the pink disposable razor.

"Blake?" I tested.

"Yeah, it's me."

My hand relaxed its reach. Still, being naked in the same room as him felt more exposing than I liked. Uncomfortable, like the shower curtain was invisible and so was my skin, and Blake could see down to the most exposed parts of me.

A squeak signaled the end of my shower as I turned the knob. The spray cut off, and there was teeth-chattering silence.

"Can you hand me a towel?"

I stuck my hand out of the curtain, coarse fabric meeting my fingertips seconds later. Pulling the towel in with me, I brought it to my face and swiped it down until a wince of pain jerked my hands away. My cheek throbbed where I'd run the towel over, and my heart shuddered as I remembered where I'd been hit.

The numbness replacing my lightning burrowed deeper.

Wrapping the towel around myself, I slid the shower curtain back and stepped out. Blake was there, standing against the far wall, eyes on me. I kept mine on the small puddles building at my bare feet.

"You're shivering," he observed, voice monotone and thick.

I probably was. I didn't notice. That was thanks to the numbness, icing out all feeling in my body and in my mind so I couldn't feel the beginnings of bruises forming over either.

The gentle touch of fingertips appeared under my chin, guiding my head up from the floor. Severe eyes were waiting for me to scour my freshly washed face, lingering over my sore cheek.

The rough patch of his thumb grazed in inspection along my jawline, softly turning my head to the side. I let him.

"You'll need to put some ice on that."

Knowing that was true and just not caring, I moved my face from his hold. "I'm fine."

Except I wasn't, and we both knew it.

"I brought you some clothes." He gathered up a fistful of clothes he'd laid out on the counter, handing them to me.

A black t-shirt and dark blue boxers.

"Yours?" I asked quietly.

"Yeah. Those leggings and shirt you've been wearing since you got here—"

"Smell like shit, I know."

It was true. I wouldn't say it out loud, but I was glad for the new clothes. I was glad they were *his* clothes. I folded the black t-shirt through my fingers, feeling Blake with every touch of soft fabric.

"I'll wait on the other side so you can get dressed."

He left me again, and I yanked on his t-shirt and tugged on his blue boxers. Both were loose around my body in the best way. They weren't confining. They weren't flashy. They didn't reek with seven days worth of sweat.

They were just comfortable. And they were his.

I pulled open the bathroom door and found Blake exactly where he said he'd be. Waiting for me.

A wet spot seeped against the back of this shirt from where my sopping hair lay. I found myself wishing for a hair tie.

For whatever reason, my eyes went over to the nightstand next to my bed. Dominic's necklace was hidden there so nothing bad happened to it. I decided that more than a hair tie, I wished I could run over to where it was stashed, grab it, hold it close, and pretend it was Dominic.

I was cold. So fucking cold.

My thunder knew how to warm me right up.

"Are you hungry?"

On a blink, my stare went back to Blake. Something inside my chest moved around as we found each other across the distance. I'd been shit at reading people all my life, but Blake read differently than anyone else I'd ever met.

Reading him wasn't like reading at all. It was like feeling. Like feeling emotions that weren't my own but, somehow, I knew them.

Blake was a movie playing out in bright colors—*every color*—and his visuals made so much sense to me. Like his regret right now. His rage. His understanding.

I saw it all—I *felt* it all—as easily as I breathed.

Slowly, I shook my head. "No. I'm not."

Solemnly, he nodded and didn't push it. I was thankful I didn't have to fight him on this. I didn't have any fight left in me.

I didn't have *anything* left in me but the cold.

Blake shifted where he stood, focused on me. "Do you want me to go?"

A lot of responses went through my brain, but I asked something to deflect from them all.

"Don't you have to work?"

A heavy pause. "Line Up was cancelled."

Mimicked shock jumped my eyebrows up about half an inch. The effort was too much though, and they fell back down in place a second after. Whatever.

"Claudia must be pissed."

All those clients. All that money. All the cover-up she would have to do to convince all the girls who worked here that what they saw was a show or planned. Or pay them out to pretend they saw nothing.

They'd probably pretend for free. Not one of them tried to help me. Not even a peep.

This was the place where humanity went to die, I guess.

And freewill.

Blake muttered in agreement, not denying the fury of his boss. Then, something unexpected happened.

"Speaking of..."

Blake reached into his jeans back pocket and pulled something out. Something rectangular.

Something game-changing.

Underneath my skin, there was a surge. Trying to break ice, trying to unearth itself, trying to heat up.

A phone.

He had a fucking phone.

Why that fuck hadn't I seen it before now?

My mind began to spin, ideas and plans coming into shape in milliseconds as my eyes glued themselves to the freedom vibrating light from his palm.

Blake rounded towards the bedroom door. "I have to go che—"

"Wait!"

Blake cut back to me, and I had to think fast. With his stare on mine, the words fell from my lips as fluidly as the idea formed.

"Can I stay in your room again tonight?"

Surprise flashed like heat lightning over his dark sky eyes. Thickly-shaped eyebrows moved wrinkles into his forehead.

"Why?"

Why? A pause fogged over my brain as I thought up a lie.

"I don't really feel like being alone tonight." I tagged on a shrug for effect, dragging my stare to the carpet. The lie stuck to the inside of my cheek, and I nabbed the inside of it with my teeth, chewing it over and wondering why it didn't taste much like a lie at all.

Enough quiet friction passed to where my curiosity couldn't take it anymore and peeked a glance up at him. Or, what was meant to be a glance.

Blake didn't let go though. He held me there with all his smokey fire, and I wondered if he was even trying to sustain me like he was.

Inside of me, that buried *surge* of sensation gave it another go. Another pulse.

I shifted around the feeling, the pores of my flesh itching. Frazzled.

Say yes, say yes, say yes.

Blake rolled his eyes back, and my stomach rolled with them.

"Shit. Okay." *Yes!* "But *only* tonight." He raised and pointed a serious finger my way. "This is not a regular thing, okay?"

I nodded fast in agreement, trying to hide behind my ghosting smile the fact that there wouldn't be a tomorrow night here for me once I got my hands on his phone. I'd call the cops. I'd call Dominic. He'd come for me and rescue me like the goddamn damsel in distress I'd been made out to be.

Blake moved towards the bedroom door, readying to leave. "I'll pick you up around midnight when there's a security switch out." He nailed me one final, chest-clenching look. "Be ready."

"I will."

Ready as I'd ever be for anything.

Because tonight was the night.

Tonight was what I'd been *waiting* for.

Tonight, I was getting the fuck out of here.

TWENTY-EIGHT

❦

<u>KAT</u>

Blake arrived just as he said he would, whisking me off to his room in the dead of night.

The blanket I used from last night was neatly folded on the floor where I'd left it in a crumpled ball this morning.

This morning.

It felt so far away now, like another year rather than just a rotation of the Earth. This morning was full of Blake's half-smile and his once-in-a-lifetime laugh. I was being carried around on this foolhardy easiness after a night of learning all about him, meeting his demons and knowing they would keep me safe.

There was nothing safe in this house though.

Not a goddamn thing.

And tonight, I was getting out.

Blake shut his bedroom door behind us with a discrete click, making a smooth cut across his room to his bed. "Zoey gave me some clothes to give to you if you wanted them while you're here."

I almost—*almost*—laughed loud enough to blow our whole cover.

Sauntering over to his bed where a small pile of clothes sat, I fingered through them with cruel speck curving my lips. "Are a few tank tops and pity thongs supposed to be her way of making up for doing *jackshit* earlier?"

"None of them were allowed to do anything." The fistful of garments I'd grabbed fell back to the bed as Blake put his toes against mine, defense burning a path across his face. "Claudia whipped up NDA's for them all to sign before anyone could move onto any of their afternoon appointments."

A click of my tongue bounced off the walls. "Swell."

"They're not bad people."

"They're not good," I shot back.

Severity like I'd become accustomed to smoldered his eyes. "None of us are *good*."

My first instinct was to agree, but something stopped me. Something diamond-like flickering in the heat of black flames.

So instead, I asked, "How's your hand?"

The backs of his jaw set *really* hard.

By his side, he flexed his red-knuckled hand and grumbled. "It's fine."

Keeping his gaze, I made my subtext extra pointed. "*Good*."

He needed to know someone thought it even if he wouldn't believe it. There was good in him. There was *potential* in him other than the kind Claudia and Ray saw.

When I left tonight or tomorrow, depending on how fast Dominic or any help could get wherever *here* was, I already knew that I was going to miss Blake. For a moment, I considered telling him about my plan so he could get in on it.

But logic and reality both stomped all over that pipedream. Not only would Blake not go for it, but I didn't know what would happen to him on the outside if he did.

He'd probably be arrested for a long list of felonies I didn't even know the half of.

No, Blake would have to stay and I would have to leave, and that was just the way our stories were meant to go.

Leaving Blake with the pile of Zoey's clothes, I went to use the bathroom and throw back a swish of mouthwash. By the time I came out, he'd changed into one of those white undershirts again and was lying on his bed, book in hand, a lit cigarette between his lips.

And I had only one mission.

Find the phone.

"Whatcha reading?" My oh-so-casual question lingered in the room as my eyes gave a scan of his bookcase. No dice.

"Poetry," he replied dryly.

"Okay, but what *kind* of poetry?"

I kept pushing him to talk so he wouldn't notice my purposeful wandering around his room. The bookcase was empty of the phone I saw earlier, and a sweep of the other side of his room delivered disappointment too.

"It's a collection of John Keats best work."

"I've never read anything of his."

What the hell was I saying? I'd never read *any* poetry. Not willingly. I was emotionally inept enough as it was; I didn't need rhythmic stanzas and messages hidden between flowery verses to make me feel any dumber.

"He's one of the most famous Romantics. Only became well known for his work after he died."

"How'd he die?"

"Tuberculosis."

I flashed him a side-glance. "Well, that's the pits."

Cigarette hanging between his lips, he mumbled his sarcasm around it.

"Poetic."

I gave a shrug and moved my search closer to his bed, idling around his nightstand and trying not to be too obvious.

"Could you, uh, read me something of his?"

From beside me, I could feel the sizzle of his gaze on the side of my face. Nerves in the pit of my stomach broiled from the heat of his focus. When I couldn't take it anymore, I turned my neck to find him scrutinizing right up at me from where he sat against the headboard.

With long fingers, he plucked the cigarette from his mouth. "Why're you acting weird?"

"I'm not weird."

"You're definitely weird." *Rude.* "Your behavior from earlier to now is totally different."

"What, do you want me to throw up again?"

Disapproval lowered the strike of his chin. "No, but you're off."

"You don't know me well enough to know when I'm *off*." The bitter edge of my tone sliced an opening through Blake's stare, an inclination to disagree with me running over. But he didn't let it sit long, lowering his fan of lashes back to his book, the weight of a quiet sigh pushing down his chest.

My own inflated with the sting of guilt, poking and festering like a colony of bees took root between my ribs.

I was leaving him as soon as tonight. I didn't want it to be on a sour note.

Especially after today.

Gaze sinking to the floor, I twisted my mouth to the side, curling my toes into the carpet. "I'm not being *weird*. I just feel better in here."

It wasn't a lie either.

All morning after Blake left me in my room, I'd been tossing and frazzled and just overall *heavy*. I couldn't stop moving or feeling like I needed to, but on top of all that anxious energy, there was something big loaded up on my chest.

Every fall and rise of my lungs was harder than the last.

Being next to Blake didn't cure the burden.

But I liked knowing I wasn't struggling for breath alone.

After too much uninterrupted stillness that put an ache in my jaw, I hooked a glance his way. All that stinging, pestilent guilt berating my chest caught on fire as I met his eye.

My whole chest went up in flames because of him and the honest-to-fuck look he was offering me.

Not bad flames. Not good flames. *Blake's* flames.

They didn't hurt. They didn't soothe. They just *felt*.

My truth had unveiled his as he told me without words that he shouldn't enjoy that I felt safer here, but he unreservedly did.

His all-consuming gaze fell back to his poetry, and a breath of release rattled my lungs. He went back to his thing and I went back to mine, roaming to the end of his bed with my eyes scouring in secret over every inch of the mattress.

Nothing.

Then…

"I almost wish we were butterflies and lived but three summer days - three such days with you I could fill with more delight than fifty common years could ever contain."

The words floated up from behind me, riding every roughed up syllable from his lips over my shoulder, taking a hold of my chin and pivoting me back around to him.

He was, of course, already watching me.

I didn't like or understand poetry, but I liked whatever he'd just said.

I liked the pretty words on his gruff voice. I liked how they burrowed into the space below my collarbone and tingled like fireflies dancing under my skin.

I was also a little terrified at the way simple words made my mind go dizzy.

"That's intense," I said.

"That's John Keats."

My eyes tracked down to the poetry unfolded on his lap, propped up on his thigh, wondering what other sorts of dizzying words were in there. "Still, 50 years for three days? Seems like a lousy deal."

Blake cracked a soft smile. "He was a hopeless romantic."

His smile, however imperceptible it was, made my lips pull up to match. "Does that mean you're a hopeless romantic too?"

That sought-after uptick to his mouth vanished. Mine went next. The lamp of golden light sitting right next to him couldn't help brighten how pitch black his eyes grew.

"No. I'm just hopeless."

How absolutely certain he sounded made me want to scream. Ball my fists up, kick back a gulp of fire-hot air and blast it right at him until he got the message.

He wasn't any of the things he thought he was. Not bad, not hopeless, not damned for eternity.

"You're only hopeless if you actually believe that bullshit," I argued.

A loud slap bounced off the walls as Blake snapped his book shut. "Whatever you do, don't become a motivational speaker."

A scoff rode up my vocal cords, but before I could respond, Blake put an end to the night.

"Lights out."

I stopped with my debate-ready mouth open when he reached down to the floor, blindly searching until—

My heartbeat tripled. Cold sweat dampened the back of my neck.

Caught in his fingers was a charging cord. He stuffed his other hand into the side pocket of his black sweats and pulled out what I'd been looking for all night.

My gaze was strapped tight on his phone as he shoved the butt of the cord in it, then wedged his hand underneath his pillow to tuck the phone away. He reached out to a lamp on his nightstand, and without so much as a goodnight, clicked it off with me still standing.

Lost in the darkness, I walked back through his room in careful steps and felt my way around until my toes brushed the blanket I used last night.

My throbbing heart lowered me to the floor, beating a song of impatience inside of me. It was screaming to get up, get the phone, and get the fuck out of here.

Thank fuck my brain wasn't so trigger-happy. It laid me down on his bedroom floor, forcing my eyes shut and to wait for the right moment.

I'd spent almost a week in this nightmare. I could survive one more hour if it meant I got to walk out of it tonight.

Back to Layla to see if she was okay. Back to Charlotte to hug her and never let her go.

Back to Dominic to… *everything*.

I wanted to do *everything* to that man once I saw him again. Hug him, kiss him, love him, fuck him, scream at him, whisper sweet nothings to him, tangle myself in him in an impossible knot so nothing could separate us.

Dominic had turned me into a sappy motherfucker, but I didn't care. I *needed* to see him. Not a want, but a desperate need. I didn't *just* miss him. No, this was something beyond longing, beyond pining and melancholy dreaming.

This was all our heroin love going into relapse.

I was dumb for falling into the kind of love that I had with Dominic, because it wasn't an easy or simple love. It burned in my veins just like it burned through everything in its way when it was forging. It was entangled in the core of my makeup, and without it, the tremors were setting in. The shakes, the aching, the unquenchable thirst to have what I lost back.

If I went too long without a hit of our love, the withdrawal would be lethal all on its own.

I waited until Blake's breathing slowed into a perfectly timed rhythm, and then I waited some more for good measure. I waited until my heart felt like it was going to beat right out of my chest, jump up, and get the phone itself before I rose to my knees on the floor.

My eyes had adjusted as much as they would by then, making out shapes and shadows and that would have to be enough.

My hands were anything but steady as I crawled over and reached out in search of the bed, brushing over what felt distinctly like the lip of the mattress. I trailed my fingertips ever so slightly up and up until the fluff of a pillow touched back.

All my breathing pulled to a stop as I flattened my hand to the bed right next to the pillow Blake's head rested on. His breathing was so soft. So even.

Slow, slow, slow, I slid that hand along the cool-to-the-touch sheets until the tips of my fingers breached the pillow.

It felt like a fucking lifetime before they bumped the hard, rounded edge of a phone beneath his heavy head. My heart, *god* it was tearing up inside of me, feeling like it was running a marathon and taking a hit of cocaine at the time.

It wouldn't shut up. It wouldn't calm down. It wouldn't stop spinning out of control—

Until I gave a swift and smooth pull and was staring down at Blake's phone in my palm.

Holy fuck.

A blank and black screen stared up at me, somehow finding a shine in the dark room for me. It shined *just* for me.

Holy shit. I did it. And Blake hadn't moved an inch.

Victory shot me up to my feet, forgetting my stealth mode for half a second to celebrate. Cheeks aching and adrenaline coursing, I found my footing across the room until I made it to the bathroom. Without pause, I slid inside and quietly shut the door behind me.

I left the lights off. *Just in case.*

The only light I had was from the phone as I swiped my thumb across the screen and it lit up right in front of me.

The time read 12:28am.

I memorized it, logging the time away as the exact moment I found a way to checkmate Heather in her own fucking game.

I was coming home.

And she would fucking *rot*.

Making another swipe on the phone, I moved the screen over to Emergency Dial.

My thumb tapped the numbers I needed, all three of them. I pressed the green call button, and with adrenaline shaking in my blood, lifted the phone to my ear.

Ringing.

It was ringing.

It kept ringing. I listened to three sets of it.

"911, what's your emergency?"

A shrill voice came through the other end, and the shock of hearing it clogged my throat.

Oh my god.

Oh my fucking god.

"Um..." My mouth watered, disbelief coursing through my brain. Holy shit, *talk.* "My name is Katerina Sanders," I rushed out on a breath, heart slapping. "I need-I need someone to come get me. *Now.*"

"What's your current address?"

I pressed the heel of my palm to my forehead in the darkness, shaking it. I couldn't believe I was talking to someone outside of this house. "I don't know. I don't know where I am. Listen, you have to get Dominic Reed for me. He's—"

Sharp lighting erupted to life above me, stabbing painfully against my vision as I hissed out. Panic shot out into every inch of me as, in that blinding second of shock, the shape of the phone in my hand was snatched out.

The hollow clutch of my palm sliced a gasp straight through my heart, and I whipped around to see who'd done it.

Just in time to watch his thumb hover over the red button to end the call.

Desperation pulled into my lungs, and I screamed.

"Blake, *no!*"

He did it anyway, smashing his thumb down on the call that was the only chance to save my life. Then I watched on in horror as he tossed it into the toilet bowl and ruined it for good.

Another scream of denial ripped out of me, and I threw myself to the ground and plunged my hands beneath the water. The phone slipped between my fingers as I fumbled, as I shook, as I fucking lost it.

"Kat, it's trashed. *Leave it.*"

I didn't listen, his words as inconsequential as my life he just threw down the toilet.

Hands fastened around my upper arms, too hot and too inescapable, lugging me off the ground and away from the submerged phone. I fell back, my feet quick to catch me and my temper quick to light.

"What the *fuck* is wrong with you?!"

It was a goddamn slap across the face to lock eyes with him and see his temper just as red-hot. "Lower your voice."

"Are you fucking *serious*? Do you know what you just did?"

A step disappeared between us as he prowled closer, eyes cracked coal black. "I said lower your goddamn *voice.*"

"*No.*"

"*Kat,*" he warned.

"Why did you do that? *Why?* That was my chance! My *only* chance and you just fucked it up!"

Lightning strike fast, he was flush against me, his big hand clamped over my mouth and his flaming eyes burning over me. "You can be as mad at me as you want so long as you do it *quietly.*"

The flesh sealed over my mouth, the body pressed to mine, the brutal fire in his eyes—a flash of this morning swamped my skin in frostbite terror.

Shards of dread exploded through me, bleeding out a strangled scream. "Get off! Get off!"

My hands slapped, body jerked, and before I knew it, I'd bolted from the bathroom and ran to the other side of his room. As far away as possible.

I stood towards him, finding his face through the dust I'd kicked up in my escape. Chest heaving, heart racing, skin crawling. That festering, gnawing, overwhelming feeling that had been brewing all day spread like wildfire in my veins, conforming me into a chasm of living, breathing *fear*.

It was all over me, stained on my face like splattered mud, dirty and disgusting just the same.

Blake stepped out of the bathroom, fading out of the fluorescent light and into shadow. His eyes moved over me, drinking in my terror-stricken reaction as if he was seeing me in new skin.

Veiled and one tear away from falling to pieces.

Swallowing down the emotion peeling up my throat, I spoke low and accusing. "You just killed me. That call could have saved my life and now if I *die*, that's just more blood on your hands."

That magnificent streak of rage I'd seen in him in the bathroom was gone now, a somber tone smoothing out his face.

"That's not fair."

"None of this is *fair*." My voice, my breath, my hands; all of me shook with intoxicated betrayal. "*Being* here isn't fair. This *morning* wasn't fair. You *ruining* the one chance I actually had to save myself isn't fucking *fair*."

Unable to hold that goddamn penetrating gaze of his one second longer, I spun around to face the wall, locking my arms around my body. Trembling. I was doing it so, so badly. I couldn't stop even my teeth from chattering in the fight to stay still.

A breaking point was swelling, extending into every fingertip, stretching my skin, fighting to get out.

Blake didn't help, his deep voice traveling through the silence. "Do you really think they don't monitor our call logs or search histories? I'm Head of Security. I've gotten people beaten and fired for less than what you just did."

The trembling stilled for a moment so realization could set in.

Shame rolled my eyes shut next, mouth parting on a heavy breath. *Oh my god.*

I didn't think about that. I didn't *think* at all. I just saw an opening and took it, logic and lives be damned.

"Half of the police in this town are in Ray's pocket to add to it. If any one of them had gotten that call or been able to trace it here, whoever's phone the call came from would be dead in hours."

A sharp breath shocked my lungs, sinking my head past the peaks of my shoulders into my awaiting hands. Palms pressed into my eyes, I squeezed and dug pain into my scalp with my nails as Blake said what I just realized was true.

"You and I would both be dead if I hadn't stopped that call."

Guilt swam up my throat, throbbing there and trying to break out. Trying to explode just like my heart as he kept going, painting such a goddamn tragic picture for us both.

"If there was a way to save you, I would have done it by now. I've thought about it, gone over it in my head a hundred times since you got here, and there's nothing that doesn't end with bullets in both our heads."

"I'm not *dying* here."

Denial flourished in me, my hands moving away from my eyes so they could stare at the bleak shadows of this bedroom. "I have a *sister*, I—"

I couldn't die here. I *couldn't*. Charlotte was waiting for me back home. She *needed* me to come home. She didn't have anyone else like she had me. No one who knew her like I knew her or loved her like I loved her or had been there her *whole* life as a promise she could hold onto.

I was her *promise...* and I left her. I left her to save her, but still. It wouldn't matter why I left her if I never came back to her. She'd grow up alone, those big brown eyes I loved so goddamn much stripped of their light because every person in her family had left her in some willing way.

I left her.

"I have a sister..." I whispered, grief blocking my voice.

Picturing Charlotte's sweet face, with her smile that took over the whole thing, that grief moved up my throat to press behind my eyes. *Stinging*.

I sucked back air against it, holding my breath so the sobs wouldn't come. I hadn't cried since being here. I refused to let this place do what it intended and break me. I was stronger than that. I was stronger than *all* of this.

The persistent burn of weakness in my eyes tried to prove me wrong.

It flooded in with so much determination, I tilted my head back to keep it from running over. It was trying so fucking hard to get out, stretching my throat, my heart, my skin of armor.

"Kat…"

A gentle touch grazed my shoulder, and my body rippled with shock. Goosebumps erupted where he touched me so thoughtfully. So *carefully*.

Like he knew I was crashing.

His touch was too much. Too delicate and too kind, and I couldn't take it. Blake had to feel the weakness shaking my body, had to feel the breakdown ripping from beneath my skin and trying to explode out.

Tears gathered in the corners of my eyes, and an unwitting blink set them free. Wetness rolled down the sides of my face in the darkness, and I nearly gasped back in frustration that they'd disobeyed me.

More leaked out when Blake's fingers kept on their unhurried trail down my arm, running the back of his knuckles in a slow graze past my elbow.

Pain was gathering in the hollow of my throat as I held back sobs that were pushing to be free. My chin was shaking so badly, so I rolled my lips together to force it to stop. I was fine. I was fine. I was fucking *fine*.

The warmth of Blake's hand encircled the small of my wrist, capturing it entirely, and a silent sob jerked my shoulders forward.

No. No, no, no, no.

I wanted to tell him to stop, to scream at him to leave me alone, but I couldn't open my mouth to talk. If I opened my mouth, it would set off a detonation of heartbroken wails and mindless tears.

Then, Blake thumbed a tender caress over the center of my palm, and it all came out anyway.

It broke free like the explosion it intended to be, a pitiable sob wrought with despair obliterating my stronghold.

Pressure locked around my wrist, Blake tugging me around to him. "Come here."

Without wasting another second in denial, I went where he pulled me and fell into him with zero reservations and thousands of tears.

"I'm sorry." I pressed myself into his chest, burying my face and my shame in his shirt. "Fuck, I'm *so* sorry."

"I know." His cheek came to rest on the top of my head, his strong arms tightening around me as I lost it.

"I wasn't thinking-I," I hiccuped. "I didn't mean to-to-"

"I know you didn't." He silenced my guilt with a stroke of his fingers up my spine. Then back down. He played the same placating move over and over.

"I just hate this place so *fucking* much, and I-I thought I would be gone by now." Rivers of tears soaked my cheeks and his shirt as I wept. "I thought I would find a way out and-and—"

Thoughts ambushed about how I wasn't gone yet and might never be gone, and that was too much *not* to cry over. Not once in the time I'd been stuck here did I ever think I wouldn't be leaving. I wasn't supposed to be here. I wasn't supposed to be crying in a bedroom with a man I met a week ago.

I was supposed to be *home* with Charlotte and Dominic and Maya.

I was supposed to be talking to Dominic *right now*.

"I miss my sister. She's only five, and I told her I would be coming home," I sighed on a sob. "I *promised*."

Blake only held me harder as my tears came faster. "I hate it here, too."

"We could j-just leave, you know. We could find a way." I sniffled and strangled his shirt in my grasp, wishing I could melt into him and become the smoke in his lungs. "Between the two of us, we could find a way out."

A sigh blew down my back, warm and doused in disappointment. "I've dreamt of getting out of here so much, I eventually had to realize that dreaming only exists in our head for a reason. Reality is too harsh and damaging to support the kind of beauty our dreams can create. Dreams are safer tucked away in our minds where the savagery of humanity can't deteriorate them."

I lifted my head up to rest my chin on his sternum, connecting my watery stare to his.

"More John Keats?"

Blake looked between my lines of tears as if they were familiar to him, brushing them off of my cheeks with that same intimacy. He shook his head.

"That's just me."

TWENTY-NINE

DOM

"Reed, I need to see you in my office for a sec."

My stiff neck jerked at the Chief calling my name. He was leaned around the corner down where the hallway back to this section of the precinct let out, eyes with heavy-hanging bags pinned on me.

He didn't stick around long enough to get a good sense of what he wanted to see me about. Sighing, I pushed my hands against my desk to roll back in my chair enough to stand. There were only three other officers back here with me today.

Ryan wasn't one of them.

Today was Saturday. Exactly one week since Kat went missing.

Seven days of goddamn torture.

My steps were lagging and my posture was wound tight as I made it to Chief Thomas' office. I gave a rasp of my knuckles on the frame of his open door, signaling I was present.

Chief sat back in his chair as I entered, rocking in it a few turns while he did something with his mouth that made his dirty blond mustache twitch.

"Sir?"

He had both hands resting on the arms of his chair, thumbs bouncing up and down on the plastic. He still hadn't made eye contact yet.

An uncomfortable feeling curled in my gut.

Chief cleared his throat several times before speaking. "There was a call to 911 last night."

A typically mundane statement.

However, something about the energy coming off of Chief Thomas said this call in particular *wasn't* mundane.

Nerves joined the twisting sensation in my stomach.

Chief peered up at me from where he slouched in his chair, subtle anticipation making his dull eyes glow. "It was a female who identified herself as Katerina Sanders."

Her name shot through me, a fire-hot arrow of hope. My whole chest was so unexpectedly overwhelmed by her wildfire, I almost couldn't get my words out.

"She called?"

His nod was extremely pleased. "The call was cut off at eleven seconds so it couldn't be tracked. But before the call was cut, the female on the line asked for someone specific."

The implication he was leading to and the fixed look in his stare held all of my sudden hope on a bated breath. Using his head, he nodded in my direction.

"You."

I sucked back all that impatiently hopeful air at once, slapping my hand over my chest in relief.

It was her.

She was okay. She was *alive*.

She was calling for me. After seven days of nothing to go on to find her, she found a way to kick my ass in the right direction.

She was brilliant. She was strong. She was so goddamn phenomenal.

"We need you to listen to the call and give a positive voice I.D., but I'm pretty darn sure it's your nanny."

"Let me hear it." The quiver of excitement was impossible to keep from my voice, even as I spotted the Chief grimace at my eagerness in place of professionalism.

"All right. All right." He reached his hand over to the mouse near his computer. "Keep it in your pants, Reed."

I let the comment slide, not having enough room inside my head right now to think about his soured opinion of me or of my relationship with Kat. All I had room for was her.

Chief Thomas pressed down on his mouse, and the voice of the temptress I'd lost my world to flooded the room.

"Um, my name is Katerina Sanders. I need-I need someone to come get me. Now."

My heart spasmed.

Her voice. It was *her* voice. Hushed and urgent.

"What's your current address?" the dispatcher asked.

"I don't know. I don't know where I am. Listen, you have to get Dominic Reed for me. He's—"

Hearing my name on her tongue sent a thrill of euphoria up the base of my spine.

The horrific gasp from her that came next snuffed that thrill right out.

"Blake, no!" Her voice cracked with panic before it was gone, and the line went dead.

I stared at the Chief's computer screen, my blood heating up enough to produce steam rising from my pores.

Who the *fuck* was Blake?

"It's her, isn't it?" Chief asked to confirm.

"Absolutely."

"The call pinged off of a tower in Atlanta, Georgia, so she's still in the states, which is a true and honest to God shocker. Good for us, though."

Good didn't even begin to describe it.

Finally, after a week of nothing, I had more than just the breadcrumb I'd been turning over files for. I had a location. I had her voice. I had another name to add to my 'suckerpunch' list. *Blake.*

Knowing even the city she was in made me feel closer to her by miles.

"This is incredible. Ryan and I can be down there by late afternoon. We can optimize—"

"Woah, pull back on the reins, son." The Chief chuckled, though there wasn't a damn thing about the current moment I found amusing. "Her case isn't in our jurisdiction anymore. It's out of our hands."

Between my ears, a high-pitch ringing faded in.

I misheard him due to the ringing. I was sure of it.

"Sir," I began low and acutely aware of the shrill anthem in my head. "We've been working these missing girl cases for months."

"Yes, and those cases are still open and need your focus. She's in somebody else's state. They'll handle her case, and you can get back to the ones that have been pilin' up on your desk."

"With all due respect, sir, that's suicide for Ms. Sanders, and you know it." The words felt strange as they formed around my mouth and continued to openly defy my authority figure. "The caseload in such a massive jurisdiction is mountainous. I've seen it firsthand how backlogged they can get at APD. Given the nature of the area, I can be almost positive saying her case will be brushed under the rug and forgotten, and *she* will be forgotten."

He waved off my concerns—literally. "Have some faith in our boys down there, Reed. You know them, they're good men. Besides, this will be good for you." He spared me a look as he gathered some loose papers on his desk. "You've been wound tighter than a Jack-in-the-box this whole last week. You're bound to pop if you don't take a breather from that nanny's case."

As he'd been talking, I discovered a fist had formed at my side. Discreetly, I stretched it out and shoved both hands in my pockets so they wouldn't find their way into a nearby wall.

"Sir, a breather won't help find and save Ms. Sanders' life. She—"

"Is not your responsibility anymore." He leveled me a look as close to a glare as I'd ever seen him come. My jaw set, ticked, *cracked*. "I think being involved with this nanny of yours has fogged your head. You're a good detective and, despite this indiscretion, a good man. I happen to think your nanny showing up in Georgia might be a blessing for you in the long haul."

The only blessing was that I hadn't launched across his desk and tackled him to the floor. People needed to stop suggesting my affection for Kat was a phase that would fade as easily as rolling fog.

She was not a phase. She was not temporary.

She was lifelong and everything after.

"Chief, I am fully aware that her case is out of jurisdiction, but at the end of the day, that's nothing more than a technicality."

"It's the *law*, Detective." He abandoned the papers in his hands, authority pitching the tilt of his head low. "And it's your job to follow it the same as you've been doing your entire career."

Heat prickled the back of my neck, our stares fastened.

He was right.

I'd always done my job exactly as I was hired to. There had never been a time in my career on the force where I'd felt stifled by the rules. I loved rules. I admired the structure they imposed and chaos they prevented. Order was necessary. Laws helped the good stay good and weeded out the structural damage of society.

The rules had always made *sense* to me.

Until recently.

Until the woman who loved to hate rules so passionately blazed into my life.

Order and law were in my core, and for the first time ever, I felt them stabbing in my back.

"That'll be all, Reed. Close the door on your way out." Chief Thomas dismissed me with a curt gesture but stopped to hold me in place with a warning finger. "And I better not catch you working the Sanders case. That's a direct order."

Biting my tongue, I offered him a tight nod and turned to leave before the grip I had on my rage slipped and his desk garnered a new hole in it the shape of his head.

I barrelled down the hallway and through the precinct, past officers I'd normally greet and worried looks I'd ignore and deal with later. That wildfire of Kat's was roaring in my chest, building to a quick implosion, and I needed to let it out somewhere private.

The door to the men's bathroom slammed the wall as I burst inside, satisfied in the verbal *slap* to accompany my explosion. I went right over to the line of sinks against the far wall, slumping over one.

Breathing heavily, my hands cupped the sides of the sink and squeezed the porcelain, picturing it crumbling beneath my grip.

I had her.

I *had* Kat. I knew where she was, I heard her voice. I heard her say my name and then scream someone else's.

The muscles in my neck strained as I lifted my head to find myself in the mirror above the sink. God, I looked tired. I *was* tired—tired of wasting my time at my desk, tired of not having her back by my side, tired of feeling like my hands were strapped.

Kat needed me.

She called and asked for me because she *needed* me, and I loved few things more than being needed by that woman. I had everything I needed to save her. I'd break down every fucking door in Atlanta until I found her if that's what it took.

But I couldn't do that. I wasn't allowed to.

My love for the job was sabotaging the love of my life. The conflict didn't make sense in my head. Rules and law were meant to do good, but what good was letting her sit and rot when I *knew* where she was?

Staring myself down in the mirror, all I could think about was Kat and how we got to be.

We'd broken a lot of rules to love each other.

My marital vows. My moral agency. My self-discipline.

They'd all taken a hit when I found myself more and more enamored by the green-eyed, sharp-tongued goddess I'd hired. They'd all crumbled when I fell in love with her.

Such core facets to who I was as a man kissed goodbye by a pair of strawberry lips.

And I was undeniably happier for it.

Kat proved that sometimes, breaking the rules in the pursuit of something grander might still be wrong, but the result was worth it.

And she was worth it.

My little lightning was worth almost anything.

Perhaps it was time to take a page out of her playbook and do a bit of wrong.

For her, I'd break a hell of a lot more than rules.

THIRTY

KAT

Awareness stirred slower than usual the next morning.

My head felt all dense and my body heavier than usual. As I rolled around on the sheets, realization stirred just as slowly—it wasn't heaviness I was feeling in my muscles.

It was a *lack* of tension.

I was… relaxed.

Weird.

Pressing my palms into my dry eyes, a yawn reached up my throat and stretched my mouth wide, a tiny mewl pouring out. Sighing in this bizarre state of mellow calm, I shifted to lie on my side in my bed.

Except…

This wasn't my bed.

And I wasn't alone.

Cue the reinstatement of all tension in my body.

I stiffened on the pillow I was lying on that wasn't mine and in the sheets I'd tangled my legs in that were also not mine. I'd only given a momentary flutter of my sleepy eyes as I was shifting in place, but now they were *wide* open.

Blake's sleeping face crowded my vision, laying on the pillow directly next to mine.

Well…

Shit.

We must have fallen asleep like this last night after all the crying and talking and more crying.

He talked. I cried. A lot.

Like an embarrassing amount.

I just couldn't stop. It was like the Niagara Falls of breakdowns. The tears kept flowing, and the sobs were fucking *vicious*, and Blake held me through it all. He only left my side twice.

Both times to grab me toilet paper to wipe my tears and snot.

My eyes traced his face, noting that wrinkle he got between his eyebrows when he was miffed had smoothed as he slept. He was only about a foot away, laying on his back with his head dropped towards me. Deep breathing orchestrated an even rhythm through his slightly parted lips.

I swore, even now, there was a tint of fire to his breath.

Last night, I was… unhinged in every imaginable way—hysterical like I'd never quite been before. I mean, maybe when my mom died, but I didn't remember much of that breakdown. I was in and out of consciousness too fast to register just how off my rocker I was then.

I remembered everything about last night.

The weeping, the out of control hyperventilating, the weakness devastating this fearless sham performance I'd been putting on for everyone here, myself included.

That all washed away in the overflow of tears, and all that was left was me.

Frightened, exposed, pitiful me.

Blake had every right to judge and mock me last night. Hell, *I* was judging the fuck outta myself for all of it. All that nasty vulnerability coming right on out for him to use against me or make fun of.

Blake didn't make fun of me though.

He didn't do anything at all except hold me.

I'd put his *life* at risk last night when I made that call, and not once did he bring it up or make me feel guilty for it. I *did* feel guilty. Holy fuck, did I feel guilty. Not because Blake made me though.

For a man of such temper and intensity, he'd been the epitome of solace last night.

Like a total creeper, I kept watching him sleep. Yeah, I knew I was breaking my rule about being too close to him, but having an epic breakdown had to give me some sort of pass, right?

It wasn't my *intention* to fall asleep next to him. I'd just crawled on his bed when the storm crashing through me became too harsh to stay standing, and he'd settled in next to me to keep his arms around me. A funny sort of feeling tingled in my chest as I remembered how he comforted me and how unabashed I became in letting him do it.

Staring at Blake now… something was different.

The cut of his jaw was sharper than it was before, and the clean shave he gave it made him look all… strong. Masculine. His skin was so perfectly sun-kissed and smooth, and I was immediately jealous of the time he was allowed outside. Those cheekbones of his were glorious—chiseled out of marble, I tell ya.

Even those impossibly long lashes of his were something to envy, and how they laid across his high cheeks as he slept was like art. I mean, come on.

Somehow, I'd never noticed how rugged and almost sort of… beautiful Blake was.

Suddenly, a realization hit me that made my stomach *whoosh*.

Holy shit, was Blake hot?

The way I kind of couldn't stop staring at him blared a definitive, *'fuck yeah.'*

How had I never noticed that before?

I'd looked at him tons of times before this up-close moment, so how had I missed it? His beauty was so *glaringly* obvious now. Maybe all those tears I'd cried out last night washed away some film that blocked how I saw him.

With that gone, he was like a sunbeam dazzling through a black leaden sky.

"Are you still staring at me?"

A husky voice, still thick with sleep, jumped my heart rate up double-time.

Practically holding my breath, I denied, "I wasn't staring."

"Yes, you were."

Dammit. "How'd you even know?"

Eyes still shut, his lips pulled up into a soft grin. "Because you just admitted it."

I blinked at his sleepy smile, one of my own twitching to life. My eyes carried back with a playful roll. "Oh my god." *I'm so dumb.* "It's too early for this. I can't be expected to be smart at six in the morning."

He lifted his arm to his face, twisting around a black watch on his wrist. "It's eight o'clock."

"Still too early. Plus, I have a headache."

"That'll happen when you cry for three hours straight."

A scoff hit the air, and I flipped to my stomach and buried my face in the pillow. "Don't remind me. I fucking hate crying."

"I know. You mentioned it about fifty times."

Face stuffed into the fluff of the pillow, my defiance came out all muffled. "'Cause I do. It's stupid. Emotions are stupid."

"People are stupid," he bullishly corrected. "Emotions are what we paint with, but we decide what to create with them."

Dragging my head to the side to lay on my cheek, I grabbed his stare. "Okay, Mr. Poetry."

There went his signature eye roll, and up popped that dab of a smile that always seemed to accompany it lately. With a low grunt, he propped himself up on his elbows and made a move to reach over me.

I inched away and stabbed him with a wary squint. "What're you doing?"

He paused, arm hovering above me and heavy-lidded eyes falling to mine. "Grabbing a smoke."

"You just woke up."

"And?"

"Nothing. Just… you haven't even brushed your teeth."

"I'll brush them after."

The springs of the mattress whined under my weight as I rotated onto my back again and reached towards his nightstand where his stack of Marlboro Reds sat.

"You must have shit morning breath," I mumbled, grabbing an open pack.

My body wobbled on the bed as I situated myself back in place, head against the pillow and his smokes and lighter in hand.

"What are *you* doing?"

I plucked one slender stick of tar free. "Seeing what all the fuss is about."

For a second, I expected him to stop me. To snatch the cigarette right out of my fingers with a scalding look. No such look came. Instead, I could feel him watching me closely as my thumb kicked down on the back of his Zippo, fire erupting into our early morning.

I held the cigarette up to the ceiling, staring at it between my two fingers and wondering which was deadlier. My two fingers or the stick they held. Both were small—such tiny little deaths.

It was astounding how so many of life's deadliest creations were small.

Bullets, insects, viruses, a finger on a trigger, a few around a throat.

As I put the rounded paper between my lips, I realized I hadn't thought about death this much since my mom died. I wondered if she was watching me now as I drove the lit flame closer to the end of the poised cigarette and if she knew why I at least wanted to try it.

My eyes crossed as I covered the back end of the stick in fire, mesmerized as white charred to orange and orange perished to black.

I prepped my virgin lungs as much as I could before dragging an inhale…

Tangy smoke unfurled in my mouth, down my throat and—

Brutal coughing plagued the bedroom the very next second—all coming from me.

"Oh *fuck*," I wheezed, holding the burning cigarette as far away from me as possible as I turned my face over the edge of the bed to hack up the lungs I'd betrayed. "*Shit.*"

In the midst of sucking down strangled gulps of clean oxygen, Blake plucked the death stick from my fingers so I could use both hands to stabilize myself and all my coughing.

"Poison," I rasped. "Fucking *poison.*"

A heated hand found my back, rubbing circles. "It's an acquired poison."

"Oh god." I smacked my tongue to the roof of my mouth, lips pulling back at the soured taste of soot and ash. "How do you do that every day? Your mouth must taste like *ass*."

"Eloquent," he mumbled as I slumped back to my pillow, heaving and cutting a fast look up at him as he sat against the headboard. "I use mouthwash throughout the day."

Then, he oh-so-casually placed the end of the cigarette that had just been inside my mouth in his. His dusty pink lips pursed around the stick of white, pulling back a puff of the same toxins I'd just lost half a lung over, and he did so with *such* suave ease.

Fuck, is that what they mean when they say smoking looks cool?

Huffing, I pushed myself up to face him and sit cross-legged on the bed. "Still, I can't imagine making out with you is a flavor treat."

He pulled the cigarette from his mouth, talking around the smoke funneling out.

"I don't make out with anyone."

I put my hand to my chest, coughing just once more. "Seriously? You're surrounded by hot sex-workers."

"Not interested."

"What, are they not your *type*?" I asked with a teasing bite.

With parting lips, he neared his hand to his mouth and readied for another puff, a skeptical gleam running through his far-off stare. "I'm almost sure I don't have a type."

"Didn't you say Abby was sweet and shy?"

Still not looking at me, he gave a slow nod. "I did."

"So who else have you dated?"

"I don't date."

A scoff took my head back and my eyes around in a roll. "Okay, so you don't date, you don't hook up with anyone here, so how do you know you don't have a type?"

Almost as if he was unwilling, dark eyes slid a slow pace over to land on me.

In the week I'd known Blake, I'd started to learn the different degrees of burn to his stare. There was his simmer of intensity, his outright scorch of fury, and even his pleasant warmth when he dared to be something less than grumpy.

The degree he was heating me up with now was a *fresh* burn though. I'd never encountered it or the humid warmth making my shirt stick to my skin just a little as he dragged those hot eyes down my face and back up again.

Lips parting, he rumbled, "Just trust me."

"You told me not to," I fired back, a subtle tweak to the side of my mouth.

Blake dropped his attention to that curve, staring at it like he was dead positive he could send the impish smirk up in flames. He looked like he wanted to set me and my smile on fire. Like, really *really* badly.

He didn't reply. Just slipped the Marlboro Red back between his lips, bringing all of my focus to his mouth.

It was a nice mouth. Two soft pink petals for lips, supple and smooth.

Perfectly good for kissing.

Staring at it, curiosity to know just how many women he'd kissed with that mouth began to prickle. Just because he didn't date didn't mean he didn't kiss. Or more.

The curious sensation started in my head and traveled down to my chest, ruminating there and asking for the *more*. It wanted to know more than just who he'd kissed or how many there had been. It wanted the intimate details.

How many women he'd bedded, if he'd fucked them in the bed I was sitting in right now, how he even met women to date when he worked *here*?

"You're staring at me again."

His low-timbered statement lifted my gaze back to his eyes.

They were waiting. Watching. *Burning.*

"So?"

Normally, I'd care that he caught me. Normally, I'd deny it or lie and say he had something stuck in his teeth and that was the cause for my staring.

Normal reaction didn't apply to Blake though.

I didn't care that he caught me, and I didn't care to stop either.

Especially with him staring at me just the same.

Thin trails of smoke mingling through his concentrated eye contact, he eased the cigarette towards his parted lips.

"Just pointing it out."

He closed his mouth around the end, giving me his full attention as I imagined whirls of gray smoke filling his starved lungs. It should have felt weird staring at one another for so long, but the only thing weird about it was how it *didn't* feel weird.

Each breath I took with his eyes on me felt heavier, his intensity and dark-eyed focus pushing down on my chest, but I couldn't look away. The air crackled and warmth rose within every crevice, our concentration on one another a thriving, electric fire smoking up the room.

"I was thinking about how many women you've kissed or how you even met them," I said without knowing why I was admitting it.

He pulled the smoke away from his lips, a brilliant cone of ivory blowing out. His head angled in a gesture almost threatening, the narrowing of his stare a damn near *certain* warning.

"Why are you thinking about who I've kissed?"

For the first time in however long this trance had been going, I was able to break it. I stole my focus, my breathing, my thoughts back to myself to ponder about why.

Why was I thinking about who he'd kissed?

On a normal day, my curiosity already bordered on dangerous, but with Blake, it went totally haywire. To know him was an addiction boiling in my veins, and it had been there since the first time he saved me.

Since then, it'd just been burning hotter with each rescue, each kind touch, each unexpected thing I learned about him.

He completely and thoroughly entranced me, and I had no idea why.

Eyebrows lugging together, I met his eye. "I don't know."

Blake breathed deep, his exhale audible from the lowest part of his throat. The backs of his jaw were working hard, pulsing and shifting as he kept his tight focus on me. My stare dropped to his nose where there was a subtle twitch—his telltale sign.

Holy shit, was he angry?

"You shouldn't be thinking about that."

"I can think whatever I wanna think," I casually shot back, but not in defense. Just a simple statement.

What looked like a snarl curved his upper lip, and he popped the burning cigarette back in his mouth. "Not about me."

Then the bed was moving as he tossed the sheets off his legs and moved off the end of it. I tracked his movements through the bedroom with lightning awakening in my bloodstream as he came around to the nightstand.

"It's not like *I'm* thinking about kissing you. Calm your tits. I was thinking about how many women you've kissed since we were talking about making out."

He stabbed out the still-blazing embers on his smoke on a silver ashtray but left the flames in his eyes on full blast.

"Well *stop*."

"Why are you getting so touchy about this?" I shifted to face him, still cross-legged on his bed. "What, have you never kissed anyone before?"

My head craned back as Blake swerved his height over me, blistering my skin with the heat in his pointed glare.

"I've kissed. And I've fucked. Are you *satisfied*?"

The word 'fucked' hit me harder than I expected, wobbling my breath as I shook my head. "No. That's not what I asked."

"You ask too many questions."

"Or you just have too many secrets."

"I like my privacy."

I cocked my head at him. "What else do you like?"

At that, a dangerous smolder darkened every sharp and handsome curve of his face, and all the oxygen got sucked from my lungs.

An uncomfortable mass of nerves bunched up in its place, squeezing tight.

Aside from the nerves, all that was left was… sweat.

It was tickling in the baby hairs at the back of my neck and slicking between my breasts. My lips grew parched from the lack of air flowing between them, but I wouldn't *dare* swipe my tongue out to wet them.

Not when black eyes were already drifting from mine down to said lips all on their own.

Holy shit, okay. So something *definitely* changed between us since last night, and whatever it was, Blake was feeling it too.

And then some.

He and I had always had *tension*. A thick, mucked up, malleable thing, but this was different.

This was… hot.

All heat and no signs of sense.

How did it make *any* sense to be body and tongue tied by the presence of someone other than Dominic? Answer? It didn't. It didn't make any sense for Blake to be looking down at me how he was or for me to be allowing him to.

This moment of senseless staring had gone on too long.

My heart agreed, scolding me with painful rams against my rib cage in punishment for feeling the *heat*. For feeling all breathless and heady for anyone other than Dominic.

My body was just confused after last night and this whole last week. Yeah, that's what it was. I'd been so distraught and amped up on too many manic emotions with only Blake to sink them into, and now my body was reacting out of innate confusion.

That's all this moment was.

I loved Dominic with every beat of my heart, and there was nothing in the entire world that could make me fuck that up.

Three knocks on Blake's bedroom door sliced through the heat of the moment.

Panic shackled up my spine, and Blake went on full alert.

"Who is it?" I whispered.

"No idea." Acting fast, he cupped a hand under my elbow and urged me off the bed. "Bathroom. Go."

He jerked a nod towards the open bathroom door, and I bolted on quiet feet towards it. I slipped inside with a pounding heart, leaving just a sliver cracked so I could watch Blake stride up to his bedroom door before disappearing to the sound of it opening.

"Why the hell haven't you been answering your phone, asshole?"

Sergio. That grating voice *definitely* belonged to Sergio.

"I broke it last night. Something up?"

"Claudia wants to see you about yesterday."

My panic tightened up my throat as Blake cursed softly under his breath. "Okay. I'll be right there."

The second the bedroom door clicked, I came pouring out of the bathroom and right in front of Blake. His broad shoulders had gone stiff, and he'd steered all his glowering to the floor.

"That's bad, isn't it?"

"I don't know what it is, but I'll go find out."

Oh god. Anxiety immediately terrorized my heart, spinning my head and dropping it towards the ground to try and catch my breath that was suddenly missing.

Claudia could kill me today. Now.

I'd been so wrapped up in Blake this morning and feeling cared for and protected by him that I'd forgotten to feel dreadful. Of my future. Of Claudia's repercussions.

Of death.

A thumb dug into the hollow space beneath my chin, lifting my heavy head up. A shaking breath chattered my teeth, and I clamped them together to make it stop as I met Blake and his resolute stare.

"I can tell you're worrying, but we don't know what it is yet." When that didn't do a damn thing to ease back the knife of terror gouged in my chest, he allowed his eyes to warm for me. "She might just wanna compliment me on my stellar right hook."

That did it.

A teeny tiny, barely-even-there curve found the end of my lips. Only on one side, but it was there. Blake looked at it, the warmth of his gaze resting on my little smile, and I watched as even the sharpest points of his black ice stare melted.

His thumb still hooked beneath my chin grazed up until he was touching my smile. Just the corner of it.

The rough pad of his thumb sat over the inspired dent, and we stayed like that for a moment.

Him, absorbing my dimple of happiness that he'd caused, and me watching him do it.

He left a few seconds later, ordering me to stay in the bathroom until he got back. It felt like hours stuck in that bathroom, but in reality, all I had time for was a quick pee and to throw back some mouthwash before I heard the bedroom door open and shut.

A soft knock rattled the bathroom door, and I threw it open to find him.

Blake was still dressed in what he slept in, a white undershirt and black sweats, and I couldn't imagine Claudia was too pleased that he hadn't dressed for her. Or maybe she was a bit of a hypocrite and didn't mind it so much when handsome young men trotted into her office with their tanned muscles bare.

For the longest time, Blake didn't say anything. He simply watched me with those fire-inspired eyes of his.

The longer he went speechless, the quicker I went breathless.

I was an anxious, lightheaded ball staring up at him with my eyes as rounded and worried as they could go. My lips had once again gone dry from the lack of breathing, but I just rolled them in between my teeth to keep from wetting them.

Finally, he spoke.

"You're being taken out of daily Line Ups."

Dropping that shock bomb, he moved around me into the bathroom.

I followed where he went in a spin, my jaw practically touching the floor. *"Really?"*

He gave a nod, rearing back a drawer and pulling out his toothbrush and paste. "She doesn't want any more incidents, and she doesn't want the other girls seeing you or interacting with you anymore. I think she's hoping for an out of sight, out of mind scenario."

I gave my thirsty lips a celebratory swipe from my tongue and sighed.

Well, *that* was some unexpected good news.

"What about you?" I asked, leaning my shoulder to the doorframe.

We both watched as he squeezed white toothpaste with a streak of blue onto his toothbrush. "Got off with a warning."

"What kind of warning?"

Midnight eyes flashed up in the mirror, catching my reflection.

"To stay away from you."

That stupid organ in my chest did a flip flop sort of move at how *profound* that declaration sounded coming from him. We'd been made, and our forbidden kinship had just been leveled up to potentially deadly.

For him. For both of us.

"She's suspicious after yesterday. Told me to keep you locked in your room for the next three weeks and only drop by every few days to feed you. She basically wants you in isolation until the auction."

"Holy shit," I breathed, my memory unfogging. "I completely forgot about the auction."

All of my attention had been on escaping, surviving Line Ups, and surviving Mr. Smith. I hadn't even given a second thought to where I was supposed to end up if I *did* manage to survive this place first.

Blake shoved his toothbrush into his mouth, making fast, angry strokes. The mention of the auction deteriorated any lasting warmth that he'd left here with. His eyes that had simmered for me minutes ago hardened back to coal with the loss of warmth, cracks of rage and self-loathing breaking open in his stare.

A careful step eased me closer. "Have you ever been to one?"

In the midst of all his furious brushing, his nose wrinkled in something *more* than just an angry twitch.

"Once." He leaned over to spit in the sink. One hand cranked on the faucet while the other cupped a palm full of water. Droplets dripped down his sculpted chin as he took back a mouthful, swished it around and spit. His hand rubbed down his mouth, wiping it clean like he was wiping off a stain.

"Came about one shot away from alcohol poisoning after I got back from it."

Dark memories tortured his gaze as he cast it off to the side, not sparing me or the mirror a glance. All I wanted was to stare at him though. His pain was so fucking vivid, and it might be mine to own in three weeks time.

I had to know.

"Tell me about it."

Blake sniffed hard, twisting his mouth as he nabbed a hand towel from where it laid over the sink and swiped it down his face. He threw it down, soft fabric making a slap he probably didn't intend. Both of his hands came to support his weight against the rim of the sink as he leaned on it, his head sagging over as he pulled a deep breath.

He didn't want to talk about it, but he would. For me.

"There's a whole separate division that handles the auctions. They have their own security team, but about two years ago, someone dropped out day-of. Ray picked me to stand in."

My feet worked for me because my brain was too absorbed to make commands. They brought me right up next to him at the sink, our arms brushing. My eyes were glued on him in the mirror.

His were on the grout.

"What did you have to do?"

"Be a fucking *bodyguard* to the prick Ray sent in to auction off his product."

Product. Humans. Innocent women, mothers, children.

"How many?" I asked, not at all surprised to find my voice had vanished to a whisper.

Blake's jaw set *hard*. "Twelve."

Without permission, twelve tear-stained faces crowded in my head, all of them bound and gagged and dressed in tatters of clothing. All with the look of promised death screaming from their watery eyes.

The images swept in and winded me in seconds, stealing air and leaving shadows of bruises over my chest and my head swimming.

I hadn't realized I'd started breathing all that hard until my flighty gaze found its way back to the mirror. Blake was finally looking back at me, that little wrinkle chiseled between his eyebrows and a story of sorrow in his eyes.

That look didn't help calm the overzealous vibration of my heart one goddamn bit.

"I can't stay here," I breathed, shaking my head. "That can't be me."

"Kat…" A weighted sigh cut him off, and then I did it next.

"Do you want that to be me?" I snapped to face him, jutting my chin up to hold his electric stare as he rounded on me. "Do you want me shackled and sold and *raped* like those women?"

"You *know* I don't."

"So then *help* me."

"I don't know *how*."

"So we'll find a way," I explained, determination hitting each syllable. "Between the two of us, there has *got* to be something we haven't thought of."

Blake internalized some vexing noise, the severe bite force being demonstrated in the backs of his jaw giving him away. "Even if that were true, how are we supposed to come up with a plan when I'm not allowed to be seen with you?"

My gasp erupted as quickly as the idea sprung to mind.

"Let me stay in here!"

My hands sliced up in the air, as excited as I was and tapping a pat over Blake's hard sternum as I beamed up at him. "Oh, that's actually perfect! That way, we wouldn't have to work around the cameras or anything."

For how ingenious an idea as it was, Blake didn't seem sold.

His lips parted to protest, casting his stare over my head as heavy thoughts flurried through. A snowstorm of apprehension.

"I don't know if that's a good idea."

"Oh, come on. I'm a hoot! You'll love rooming with me."

He grunted, unconvinced.

"I'll make your bed every day."

"I already make my bed every day."

"So then I'll mess it up and then remake it."

For whatever reason, doubt still painted a unique shade of coloring through his stare. One I hadn't seen yet. He focused that newfound shade on me, idling it over my face, eyes, nose, and lingered it a hair longer on my mouth.

The center of my chest tingled as he held such brazen concentration on me as he thought it over.

We would be in each other's space morning and night. It was a lot to ask, but it was also the only way we could make this work. And I *needed* us to make this work.

"Fine," he gruffly conceded.

A cheer went to rip out of my chest but stalled out as he nailed me with a non-negotiable glare. "But we have to set *boundaries*."

Brightly, I nodded.

"You got it, roomie."

THIRTY-ONE

DOM

Ryan and I were standing on opposite sides of the broad island in the middle of Heather's kitchen.

Even in my head, I was getting into the habit of calling this *her* place. I never was fond of the gargantuan lie to hide our failing marriage inside of to begin with, and she knew it.

All conversation had dragged to a halt about twenty seconds ago when I let Ryan in on my plan and asked him to be a part of it. I needed him to make it work, and considering all the back bending and late nights I'd pulled to help him over the last year, one would think he would jump at the chance to repay me.

However, jumping he was not.

He just stood there, lips a tight line across and eyes dazed in thought.

Why he needed to think about this so hard was putting a crack in my sore jaw.

"Who even is this guy we're supposed to meet with?" he asked, features narrowing.

"Archie Miller. He was Sergeant of Atlanta PD Zone 5 when I was there."

"And when's this all supposed to happen?"

"Two days. He's meeting us at the halfway point between here and Atlanta.

I've requested the day off already."

Ryan was the last piece of the puzzle I needed to get on board. Archie had been easy to convince even though we hadn't spoken much since I'd taken the job up here. Over the years he and I worked together, we'd gotten to know each other outside of the job. He was a damn fine superior, and before I left, someone I had considered a prominent friend.

I was there for him when he and his wife, Annie, went through a rough patch, and he was the kind of man to repay his debts.

I had hoped that Ryan would be the same.

But he continued to argue the proposal.

"Man, you know this is insane, right? This goes *beyond* insubordination. We're talking going to another state, infiltrating their investigation, and trying to hijack it. Meanwhile, keeping all our fingers crossed that, by some *grace of God,* Chief Thomas doesn't find out?"

"You're dramatizing it quite a bit." Heat rolled up and down the length of my body, angry sweat rising beneath my clothes. I'd been fighting like hell since yesterday to keep my wrath at bay. It was *barely* working. "All we're doing right now is meeting with Archie to see what he can find out about Kat's case or if he has any insight on the area. Then we go from there."

"We could lose our *jobs,* Dominic."

More heat. More sweat. The combination roughed up my voice enough to make it lethal. "I would say that Kat's life is worth a hell of a lot more than a job, wouldn't you?"

He had the gall to appear incredulous. "Of *course* it is, but we're going in with next to nothing. A phone call in a massive city doesn't help much."

"And a name." Fucking *Blake.* "Did you ask Layla if the name Blake sparked anything for her?"

Ryan took a swig of his beer, shaking his head. "Nothing. She did start describing this vague memory she has of seeing the guy who brought her food one night, but she said it was dark. Maybe it's the same dude."

"Do you think she could describe him to a sketch artist?"

"Worth a shot."

Yes, it certainly was.

A hollow clatter as Ryan set his beer back down cued me up to grab him another from the fridge. Holding in a heavy sigh, I played the part of a good host and fetched him his second beer in less than thirty minutes. It was still relatively early on a Sunday, and he told me when he got here he didn't have long to stay.

Layla had her second therapy session today, and he wanted to pick her up afterwards.

In any other situation, it was a thoughtful gesture.

Given the fact that he'd been blowing off work to be with her and now couldn't even spare me more than an hour today?

Another layer of sweat slid down my back despite the frigid air pouring out of the fridge.

The bottle cap clinked against the countertop, and I scooped it up and brought it over to the recycle bin on the other end of the kitchen.

Tossing the cap away, my eyes did a scan of the counter display merely out of habit or boredom.

My habitual survey came to a stop when I spotted something out of place.

Or, in this case, something *in* place.

I reached up to touch it, gliding the curve of my finger over its smooth handle.

I could have *sworn* this knife went missing the same day Kat did.

In her letter, she wrote that she'd taken weapons with her. When I got back, I did an inventory of every possible weapon we had in the house, and this kitchen knife in particular had come up missing.

Though, perhaps it was in the dishwasher. I honestly couldn't remember if I'd checked in there or not that day. Everything was pure chaos the day she went missing. Everything down to my head and heart, and it was probable in the mania of them both that I'd forgotten to check the dishwasher for it before writing it off as missing.

I abandoned the now stale theory, heading back to Ryan and setting his beer in front of him.

He grabbed it right away. "Tell me what the plan is if this Archie guy does have intel on her case. What then?"

"Then we go down there and we find her."

"And how long could that take?"

"My parents have agreed to come and stay as long as a week to watch the girls."

"Man, I—" He cut himself off with a weathered sigh, setting his beer with a clink on the hard marble. "I don't think I can take that time away from Layla right now. You saw her. She's a wreck."

"And don't you think she'd feel better if Kat were rescued?" I nailed him with an inarguable glare.

Giving another heavy exhale, Ryan passed a hand over his short hair and stole his beer back up for a healthy swig. I watched him drink, tapping my middle finger over the thinning paper getting drenched in condensation around my own as it went untouched.

I'd grabbed myself one to be polite, but I wasn't interested in drinking.

All I wanted was to hit the road and go get Kat.

After several pulls, Ryan finally set his beer back down with a doubting question ready to spew. "Do you *need* me to go with you to meet with your Atlanta guy? That would probably take up half the day, and I'm running out of vacation time to use."

"Because you've been with Layla *every* day."

Quick-acting defense recolored his eyes. "She needs me."

"And I need you to give Kat's case even a quarter of the attention you gave Layla's when it was her missing," I shot back, feeling my heat rising and my temper slipping.

As if he was candidly shocked, he blanched. "I *am*. How can you say that?"

"I can say it because it's *true*." My hand tightened around the base of my beer. Perhaps I would need a drink today if we were getting into this. "I just need you to be my partner. I need you to *be* there and step up. Maybe show up to work when you're supposed to."

Irritation scratched a perfect visual over his face as he rolled his eyes to the side and heaved a half-sigh. "I can probably start doing half-days again soon, but I really don't think I can promise you a *week* of my time to go off searching on some hunch and risk my job for it."

Staring at him hard across the counter, I peeled my hand from around my beer.

I didn't need to add picking glass shards out of my palm on my list of things to do today.

"What about when it was Layla?" I questioned, pissed to hell that I even had to make the comparison for him. "If we'd found out where she was being held before Kat made the trade, would you have risked your job then? Done whatever you could to save her?"

For this reply, he kept his ashamed gaze on his beer. "You know I would have."

"Then you can't expect any different of me."

"*But* I would have done it myself. I wouldn't have asked you to put yourself on the line for me like that."

His argument sat on my chest, a burden of disappointment that weighed heavy.

"You wouldn't have had to ask me," I offered somberly. "I would have just done it."

From the day I'd transferred here and Ryan and I became partners, not a moment had gone by in our working relationship where I felt we didn't have each other's back. A working relationship had turned to a friendship and friendship had turned to brothers. He was my drinking buddy, my only confidante when it came to my divorce and feelings for Kat, a truly unjudging sounding board when I needed one.

He'd become family. He was even Uncle Ryan to my daughter.

I'd have done anything for that man, and at one point, he'd have done anything for me. Putting your life in another man's hands on a daily basis would do that to a person. Our loyalty was unconditional.

Or it used to be.

"You don't understand," he started, his features thoughtful as he shook his head. "What Layla went through is *unreal*. Watching her go through it is... I don't know. It hurts *me*. I just never want to leave her side now that she's back."

I stopped breathing. I definitely stopped processing.

Ringing. It was back. The same shrill noise rising to high-tide between my ears as I stared at Ryan. There was only the ringing and the *heat*. The build of warmth had actually gotten so hot by now, it'd turned to a cold sweat beneath my shirt.

I'd always prided myself on being a level-headed man, but this week had tested me, and Ryan just shoved me over the goddamn edge.

I couldn't believe he'd just said those words.

My throat stretched to accommodate how deep my voice dug as I growled, "Get out."

He blinked a film of shock over his stare. "What?"

"You heard. *Out.*"

Ryan flinched at the bite of my tone, his face screwing up like he really didn't know what he'd just been cruel enough to say right to my face. Right to my fucking face.

"*Dominic*—hey!"

I swiped up his keys on the counter too fast for him to catch, pivoting and making a beeline down the hallway. Shouts of protest trailed behind me, but I ignored him and rampaged towards the front door with betrayal stinging my chest.

To lose Ryan would be the equivalent of cutting off a limb, but his friendship was dead weight if he wasn't going to help me find her. And it sure as hell sounded like he wasn't. In fact, he just proved to be outrageously tone deaf, singing a song that made him sound like a complete jackass.

If he didn't understand how crucial Kat's survival was to my own, then I would do this without him. I would find and save my girl all on my own because there simply was no other choice.

Survival without her would be trivial and excruciating, and I had no interest in it.

The floor shook beneath my steps as I stomped up to the front doors and jarred one open, stepping aside and widening the exit for Ryan.

"Dominic, hey—" He came to a skidding stop next to me, his feet planted firmly on the side of the house I told him to leave. "Man, talk to me."

"You and I have nothing to talk about."

"What the hell just happened? We were just talking!"

"And now we're done," I clipped.

To make sure of it, I reared my arm back and lobbed his keys as far across the road as I could get them. Metal and his childish holster of key chains soared through the fall chilled air, landing with a plop in the far neighbor's yard.

Ryan looked after where his keys had flown, mouth hanging ajar. "Why would you throw my fucking keys? I don't get why you're being so irrational!"

Irrational. My jaw fucking cracked, knuckles in my tightening fists sounding off next.

"I said *get out,* Ryan."

"No, we're not done talking about whatever the hell just happened."

A humorless exhale sharpened from my lungs. "Oh, now you have time to talk to me?"

He was stupid enough to plant himself dead center in front of me, showing me the breakable slant of his jaw. "I don't understand—"

"No, that's what you just told me," I cut him off, crowding his space. "That *I* don't understand." His eyes switched back and forth between mine; I was too up close and in his face for him to focus on all of me. At this point, I was *vibrating* with too much rage, and I was sure he could feel it as I spelled out his stupidity for him.

"You just told me that I couldn't possibly understand what it's like to watch someone you love be in pain—and you're right. Do you want to know why you're right?"

"Dom—"

"Because the person I love *isn't* here. She's *gone.* She's gone so I can't hold her while she cries or be there when she needs me or beat the fucking shit out of some guy who makes her scream for me on the other end of a phone call. I can't do any of that, because the woman I've been waiting for all my goddamn life might have just given hers up to save your flavor of the month, and you can't seem to be bothered to remember that."

"*Hey.*" Ryan sliced me a glare as ice cold as the breeze that rolled in behind him from outside. "Layla is not a 'flavor of the month'. I'm *serious* about her."

"And I'm seriously about to hit you, so I suggest you get out of my face."

"Because I don't wanna go on some hopeless trip?"

"Because you're calling it *hopeless*," I erupted, my poorly-lidded wrath breaking free. "Because when I asked you to come along, all you could talk about was your *job* as if it's more important than her life. Because you've barely done anything to help me get her back this week when you *know* I will fall apart without her. Because all you seem to give a fuck about is what *you* want to do."

"That is *not* true."

"Then why haven't you been around all *week* to help me? You've been absent and seriously fucking single-minded."

Apparently, I'd hit a sore spot as upset rearranged his face.

"Fuck you!"

My feet worked fast to catch my fall as Ryan shoved me back a few steps into the house. I righted myself and pulled my shoulders back, finding Ryan only a few feet away standing in the silhouette of the open front door.

He also must have felt the shift in the air for what was about to happen as his eyes widened, and he lifted his hands to guard his target-red face.

"Dom, no—"

My fist cut off the rest of whatever he was going to say.

He stumbled back, nearly tripping and falling as he toppled outside. I stayed my ground, standing tall and stiff as I watched him cup the side of his face and curse.

For several seconds, nothing was said. He huffed aloud as he grappled with the punch, and I stretched my fingers at my side and waited for him to recover.

Eventually, he stood to his full height, working his jaw back and forth. His focus was on the front of the house, and the wind was quiet. After another moment, he dropped his hand from his face.

"I deserved that."

"Yeah," I gruffed. "You did."

He widened his jaw, stretching out the ache that was likely growing. He flashed me an apologetic look.

"You're right. I've been an ass, and I did a shit job at balancing my loyalties. If Layla found out you asked me to help and I said no, she'd have my balls for it."

I afforded him a soft nod. "That's true."

Heavy footfall tracked the few steps he took to stand in front of me, putting his stare to mine.

"I'll do anything you need me to do to get her back, and I'm sorry I didn't say that first."

My chest swelled as I breathed in those words, feeling them loosen the knot the last twenty-four hours had tied around my rib cage. I took my gaze over his head and back out to where I'd chucked his keys.

"Do you want to come back in and finish your beer?" I asked.

He sniffed and nodded, and I moved my stance to let him through the door. "Yeah, I think I'll use it to ice my face."

Rumblings of a smile tried to lift the corner of my mouth as he passed by me. I shut the door behind him, falling in step with his paces back towards the kitchen.

"I feel better actually. I think I just needed to hit something."

"Yeah, but did it have to be my *face*?"

A quiet beat sat. I nodded.

"Yeah. I think it did."

THIRTY-TWO

DOM

The halfway point between Lexington, South Carolina and Atlanta, Georgia was roughly an hour and a half away at a diner off I-20 outside of Greensboro.

Ryan and I grabbed a booth and ordered a couple waters, and by the time the server set them down in front of us, the front door of the establishment let out a chime, and my old Sergeant, Archie Miller walked through.

Both Ryan and I stood to greet him, an assertive handshake for Ryan and a quick hug and slap on the back for me.

"Good to see you, Reed." He pulled back, the deepening seams of his face showing wistful. "Wish it were under different circumstances, but still good to see you."

I gave him a curt nod, silently agreeing to both. We three moved around the booth, Ryan and I sitting on one side and Archie on the other. He'd gathered a few extra crows feet and laugh lines since the last time I saw him, not to mention the half a gut he'd dropped since then too.

"Congrats on the new job," I offered, leaning my forearms on the lip of the table. Archie tweaked a side grin and held up his left hand.

"Cost me a wife."

It wasn't until then I noticed the grin he was pulling didn't quite meet his aging eyes. My posture fell out of place in respect for his loss.

"I'm sorry to hear that. I really am."

He and his wife, Annie, had been married for thirteen years. Same length of time Heather and I had been together now that I thought about it.

He waved me off and waved over our server instead, ordering himself a sweet tea. Just as the pen left the paper pad and our server left with Archie's order, Ryan decided it was his turn to jump into the conversation.

"Dominic here is going through a divorce too. Seems *rough*."

Disbelief twisted my neck in his direction, Ryan's eyes doubling as he caught my glare.

"What? It's something you guys have in common. I thought it was okay to say," he defended poorly with a shrug, snatching up his water. Hopefully to drown back any more spilling secrets.

My reply was dry and straight-faced. "Do you want us to start a club or something?"

His focus side-lined for a moment to ponder, coming back *way* too serious. "You could."

Impatient oxygen inflated my lungs, but Archie beat me to a response.

"So you and Heather are calling it quits? Can't say I'm surprised, but I am sorry."

All the frustrated air I'd just taken in came out on a heavy exhale. I hadn't told him about Heather and I on the phone. I hadn't told him who Kat was to me either. There was a risk, however small it might have been, that if he knew the extent of my relationship with her, he'd refuse to let me work on her case.

"We are, yeah," I confirmed, smoothing my hand down my chest. "Thank you."

My old Sarge lifted his empty hand as if he was holding a drink in a salute. "Guess neither of us have had the most stellar last few months, huh?"

I tilted my head in agreement, raising my water to take a drink in solidarity.

Then, fucking *Ryan* opened his mouth again.

"I'm sure hooking up with your super hot nanny helped dull the pain a bit." My body swayed on the booth as Ryan bumped his shoulder to mine, chuckling like a goddamn school boy.

All his childish laughter burned out in the fire I could feel backlighting my enraged glare.

"What? Oh *come on*, was that a secret too?" He snapped back to Archie, attempting recon. "It's not just, like, hooking up though. They're in love and shit. It's the real deal, I swear. He never stops talking about her—*ow!*"

My elbow jabbed into Ryan's side and effectively morphed his words into groans. He winced and jerked back, keeping his sorry eyes on mine as my jaw fucking sawed my teeth down to rubble.

Goddam*mit.*

Well, there went that secret.

The cushion of the booth rustled as Archie shifted around on his side. "This is some kind of a Tom and Jerry partnership you've got yourself, ain't it, Reed?"

The question was posed to me. Ryan butt in to answer it.

"He loves me most days."

Archie raised a finger at Ryan's face. "That love how you got that nice shiner there?"

"Eh, I had it coming."

Curious eyes shifted to me for confirmation. I gave a slow nod.

"He did."

Shaking his balding head, he leaned back in the booth. "I've never known you to even raise your *voice* let alone your fist." All three of us cocked our heads at the server as they flew back in and dropped off Archie's tea before vanishing again. He picked up a straw, jamming it against the table to break through the paper around it.

Eyes on me, Archie observed, "This case must have you all sorts of strung up."

Like you have no idea.

"And give me some credit, Reed. I've been in law enforcement over two decades and've known you for a quarter of that time. I had my suspicions about your relationship with this girl when you called. You couldn't keep your damn heart outta your voice when you spoke about her."

"Oh, he's been like that since the beginning," Ryan added in. "He's so lovesick it makes *me* sick."

"I think my feelings for her have been established." I handed them both a restless look.

Any other day, and I would have loved to go on and on about how much my heart bled for that wild woman, but today wasn't for that. Today was about saving her.

Focusing on Archie, I asked, "Did you read over her file?"

His clear straw sunk beneath the sweet amber drink as he jabbed it around the ice.

"I did."

Ryan and I shared a look when he neglected to say more.

"And?" I pressed.

"And you're not gonna like what I have to say."

A mass of waiting tension pinched inside my chest. "So then say it fast."

He did the opposite, drinking through his straw until his glass was more than half empty. I waited, leg bouncing underneath the table. By the time he finished, I'd imagined flipping the table over and punching a hole through the light-wooden wall beside us in two full successions to keep from combusting.

He set his tea down on the same ring of condensation he'd picked it up from, eyeing me with difficult significance.

"You know what goes on in that city. You know why she's here."

My nostrils broadened even though I'd stopped breathing.

I held his stare as I held my breath, counting backwards from ten in my head to allow the sweltering murder that had skyrocketed my blood pressure to dwindle back down.

I knew what he was implying, and yes. I'd thought about it. Before Kat was even taken, I'd thought about it in relation to our cases and the girls that had gone missing. I'd pitched the theory of human trafficking to the chief, but he was right to shoot it down given the lack of pattern or evidence.

When Kat's call came in from Georgia, my *home* state, the theory came haunting back.

Next to me, Ryan proved his innocence. "What goes on in Atlanta?"

Archie slid his burdened stare over to him.

"Human trafficking. It's a hotspot. Second only to D.C. in the number of reports."

Ryan blustered while I quietly boiled. "What? I thought, like, California and Florida were the highest for that kind of activity?"

"Yes and yes. Human trafficking is everywhere, but if we're talking stats for cities in the U.S., Atlanta is rolling in some of the highest numbers."

I knew this. I knew all of this, but still, something didn't make *sense,* and it was the only thing keeping me from smashing every dish in this quaint southern diner.

"Kat was targeted," I reminded him. "She was tracked, baited, and taken. Normal trafficking victims aren't targeted like she was, so her case is automatically unique."

"I'm not saying it's not unique." Both his hands went up in mock surrender. "I'm saying you know firsthand how sluggish these kinds of cases can be. A missing girl is a dime a dozen here."

I leaned into the table, persistence coursing my veins. "I can assure you, Kat Sanders is as far from a dime a dozen as a person gets." She was my extra in a world of ordinary. "As of four days ago, she was still alive and had access enough to her surroundings to find and use a phone. She called one of her captors by his first name. Normal rules clearly do *not* apply to her."

They never had.

"And I'm not disagreeing with you. I'm just saying I don't know exactly what you want me to do about it."

"Escalate her case," I replied with pre-loaded confidence.

A disappreciative laugh rolled out of him and knocked against each ridge in my stiff spine. My hands vanished under the table, concealing the fists they were turning into.

"I've been working for the FBI only six months now. You really think I have that kind of authority?"

Ryan took over, pitching his suggestion. "Sell her case to them. This is *clearly* personal for whoever took her."

Unconvinced, Archie shook his head slowly, wrapping his hand around his glass and bringing the straw to his mouth.

"And you've got no leads back home?"

"Our main suspect has a solid alibi. So does her dirtbag ex. The only person we couldn't find to question was her father," I told him.

For whatever reason, that set off a spark of intrigue in Archie.

"You couldn't locate him?"

"Yeah, he fell off the map four years ago," Ryan added. "No work history, no credit reports, nothing."

"Do you have a name?"

I nodded. "Saul Sanders."

"And he just… vanished?"

Anticipatory goosebumps beaded over my forearms as he kept questioning. "Seems that way."

"We just assumed the guy's dead." Ryan shared our joint conclusion, but keeping my tightening focus on the wheels rotating behind Archie's far-off stare, I suddenly wasn't feeling so conclusive about it at all.

He threw an arm over the back of the booth, slurping on nothing but sweetened ice at this point. Pulling the straw away, he said, "He could be. That's the most likely theory. His name's not ringing any bells, but that's not saying much."

The booth whined beneath my size as I listed forward. "What are you getting at?"

"I'm not *getting* at anything." He nailed a hard look my way, attempting to keep any swelling hope in check. "I'm just hypothesizing over here about the likelihood that you wrote him off as dead too quickly."

"You think he's involved?" asked Ryan.

"I think there's enough left unanswered about him to wonder. Like I said, his name's not familiar, but most of the big players in the sex trade don't give out real names."

Ryan nearly came out of his seat. "You think her *dad* could be some sex-ring bigwig?"

"I'm not *saying* that. Don't get ahead of yourself, boys."

It was too late for me.

I was already ahead of myself and racing past any sense of caution to find my way to her.

To find *her*.

My heart began to pound with intensity, with excitement, with *hope* as he kept talking. "I'm thinking it would explain how personal her abduction was and why she's not dead or sold yet. Most victims are immigrants or tourist types. Not girls with interconnected relationships. Especially one with someone in law enforcement. It's only a theory, but—"

"It works," I cut in, exhilaration circulating my veins and overworking my brain. "It would explain where he's been, why he's pretty much a ghost to the system, why he wanted *her* so specifically. It makes sense. It's the *only* thing that makes any sense, in fact."

We had a lead.

A *suspect*.

Someone tangible to sink my fists into.

If her father was behind all of this, my record of remarkable first-impressions with parents was about to take a hit to the face. His face.

"But we can't find him." Ryan leaned closer into the table, running a hacksaw through my blip of optimism. "If it is him, all we know is he's hiding somewhere in the middle of one of the largest cities in the U.S."

"Do you have a photo I.D. of him?"

Ryan shrugged a nod to my old boss. "It's an older photo, but yeah. Why?"

Archie filled his chest wide, wide enough to the point he looked as rounded as before he lost the weight. He let out his big breath of air and nodded us in with a brusque jerk of his head, his gaze shifting over every patron in the diner.

"I shouldn't be telling you this but," he leaned in over the table, quieting his voice. "One of our guys picked up on rumblings of an auction coming up in a few weeks. Location TBD."

Ryan drew my attention as he jerked his head back. "An auction?"

Archie explained with a grimace. "Sometimes we get wind of auctions going on around town. Most times, it's a bust because the operations change the location so often, but on rare occasions we've gotten solid intel and been able to bust a few up and nab some nasty folk and save the girls."

"And there's a chance Kat might be at this one," I breathed out, a question and confirmation in an exhale.

For the first time in the ten days she'd been gone, I *felt* her. I felt her in that sixth sense way that was only explained by divine intervention.

"The chance is slim," Archie reasoned. "*Microscopic* slim."

I met his reasoning with a threatening pitch change and bull-headed determination. "And I'll go at it with everything I have."

"*Well*, you'll give us a photo of her father, and I've already got one of Ms. Sanders from her file. I'll hand them out to every agent going in on the bust, and we'll keep an eye out on the day of."

Bullshit.

"We're coming with you," I told him the same way I'd tell someone the ocean was blue.

He let off an exasperated scoff I'd heard him direct at others plenty when he was Sergeant. Never at me though. Not before today.

"Dominic, you know I can't—"

"Sir," I stopped him with a raised hand and not a single inch to budge. "With all due respect, there is no debating this. There is nothing you could say to make it so I won't be there when we find her, and we *will* find her. I'll be there whether you approve it or not. If I have to tail you from the moment we leave this diner until the day of the auction, I am fully prepared to do that."

"Reed, it's *unlawful* to let you two in on something like this. I could lose my job."

"And I could lose the woman I plan to spend the rest of my life with. A five-year-old girl could lose her big sister and her only family left. A young woman in grief could lose her best friend."

Begrudgingly, he fixed his gaze to me. I could tell he was waning, the list of lives that would be destroyed if anything happened to Kat doing his resilience in.

"No one on your team will be as laser-focused on finding her as Ryan and I will, and your men can point their attention to helping others. So either you and I work together, or you spend the whole auction trying to keep me from getting inside and risk losing not only Kat's life, but countless other victims."

He swiped his hand over his mouth, crumbling resistance illustrated in his stare that was trapped on the table.

He needed just one more push.

"We joined the force to protect the ones that couldn't protect themselves. We wanted to help and save and do *good*, and that's what this opportunity is. It may go against the rules of our jobs, but this week has taught me something. A job is just a title, and a title does not dictate what I do with my life. My job doesn't tell me who I can save. It doesn't tell me who I can love. Regret is acidic. It'll eat away at you until you're nothing but the thing you regret. What I know for a *fact* is that I would never regret saving Kat's life. The only thing I would regret is letting her die because I was too afraid to break some rules."

Archie blew out a sigh, dropping his hand to the table with a flat smack.

"Goddammit, *fine*." He pointed a finger across the table and eyed both Ryan and I. "But if I lose my job over this, I'm coming to bunk with one of you two when I'm homeless, deal?"

Victory went off like fireworks inside my chest as I cracked a grin.

"Deal."

THIRTY-THREE

⚬⚬⚬

KAT

The comforting divots of the bed cushioned my curves as I wandered in and out of a lazy slumber.

I wasn't sure how long I'd been sleeping. Time felt ambiguous floating in such a dense state.

Behind my ear, gentle strokes of lips stirred the sleepy haze hovering my head, the sensations pulling a smile up my cheeks. Taking that smile with me, I let my head lull to the side on the pillow, finding the culprit waiting for me with half-lidded eyes.

"Good morning, Ms. Sanders."

Oxygen tasted sweeter as I drank it in when it was all doused with the flavor of his husky voice.

"And a good morning it is."

Any morning waking up next to this man was a blessed and beautiful day.

Scooching closer to where he was laying, I squinted up at his peaceful face. "Has anyone ever told you that you're so stupidly handsome, you should be labeled as a walking safety hazard?"

Dominic's mouth grew into that lopsided grin I loved to see.

"That would be a first."

"Well, it's true. Any time I trip and fall in the future, I'm blaming it on this dimple right here." The tip of my pinky sunk into the dent of his happiness, the handsome curve deepening.

God, I never stood a chance against this face. It was too perfect. He was too perfect.

"You know I love it when you fall so I have an excuse to catch you." Warmth cupped my cheek, silver-struck eyes following his thumb as he caressed it down my face. "Hold you." His wayward thumb reached out and pet along the pout of my bottom lip, his early-morning voice digging deeper. "Kiss you."

The mattress squished as he rolled closer.

My head jerked back and away from his incoming kiss.

"Ew, wait! I have morning breath."

His gaze grew spirited above me, his perfect mouth curving up. "You could have a mouth full of bees, and I'd still want to kiss you."

I blinked, eyebrows flitting halfway up my forehead.

"Wow, what a truly vivid and horrifying image."

I watched as the mirthful sky of gray above me rolled behind a flurry of dark lashes. In the next second, I was being pushed onto my back. Heat and power dominated my body while rumbling thunder covered my lips.

"Shut up and kiss me good morning."

If I had wanted to reply, it wouldn't have made it through. A soft mouth pressed over mine, shutting up any comebacks and turning off my brain in one go.

That was all it took. One brush with heaven, and I was at full surrender.

A breathless whimper signaled my submission, and my lips melted beneath his, moving where he guided them, giving him absolute control.

Like I had any fucking choice to begin with.

My born-again heart emphatically agreed that I'd never stood a chance, and I was always destined to be the sand getting swept up and remolded in the masterful waves of Dominic Reed.

His mouth worked over mine like the slow push and pull of the tide, taking his time as if he had hundreds of years to drift with me in this kiss. He parted the seam of my lips with his tongue, drawing a final gasp of life into my lungs before he drowned me completely.

This was all part of that magnificent death I'd been so afraid of. Dominic deepened the kiss, filling me up with so much of his love, I wasn't sure how my heart hadn't exploded yet. It was so swollen with our love, so doped up on the high our chemistry brewed. I actually stopped to think for a second if it was possible to have a heart attack from too much affection.

This was the kiss of death I would so happily perish for.

In that mere second I'd taken to think about if too much love could medically fuck up my heart, a memory triggered.

The suddenness of it took my head back, parting our lips so I could gasp.

Dominic's handsome features drew immediate concern.

"What's wrong?"

The worry weaved around his bass deep voice fanned an ache across my chest as my brain reminded just how out of reach that worry over me was in this memory.

In this dream.

"Nothing's wrong, I just..." I stuttered as bits of the dream blinked across my mind. "I just had this dream last night. Or a nightmare, I guess."

"What about?"

My mouth parted, but it took some time for the words to come out as I thought about just how horrible they were. "I was kidnapped and... they took me to this awful place where I couldn't get to you and you couldn't get to me. They were gonna kill me, and I couldn't find you in time to say goodbye."

I steered my eyes up to him as the realness of the nightmare crashed through and my heart squeezed with the loss of him, even though the proof of him was laying right against me.

Heart to heart.

"I remember thinking that I was about to die, and you had no idea, and I hated that you didn't know because I knew you were probably going crazy looking for me. I—" How visceral the dream felt tied up a knot in my throat, making it hard to talk as I moved my eyes between his. "I thought I would never see you again."

Which sounded so fucking pathetic now that I said it out loud.

Dominic didn't call me on how sappy or pitiful I was. He simply laid his forehead over mine and let the rough of his thumb caress my cheek.

"That sounds terrible, and I'm sorry you had such a bad dream. I wish I could have been inside this head of yours to make it all go away."

"You wanna save me even in my dreams," I huffed, trying to splice some lighthearted humor into the tension.

His dimples almost peeked from hiding. *"What else is a hero meant to do?"*

"All you're missing is your noble white steed."

This time, his eyes did the smiling for him, crinkling adorably on the sides. He brushed our noses together, going all serious and profound on me again. *"No one would ever be stupid enough to take you away from me, I hope you know. And if they were, I would find you. No matter how long it took or where I had to go, I would find you, I would slay your monsters, and I would never let you out of my arms again."*

"Dominic," I whispered in strain, trying to make him stop.

All those romantic words had gripped my heart, squeezing pools of water from the backs of my eyes, and I wanted to keep them there. That plan went to shit when he brushed his mouth against mine and whispered straight to my heart.

"I waited my entire life to fall in love with you. I'm not losing you now."

A whimper went from my tongue into his mouth as I closed the distance between us before any tears could fall. Dominic knew though. He knew my weakness, and that should have made me furious.

Instead, it made me kiss him harder.

I wrapped my arms around his neck and my legs around his hips, locking him into me. Dominic groaned into my mouth as I put all our intimate parts together, his cock thickening between our sealed stomachs.

The feel of him hardening for me, wanting to be inside of me, burned all other emotions up until I was riding on fumes of lust and need and devotion.

A moan tangled between our kisses as I pushed my hips up into his, grinding against and encouraging his primal need. I wanted it. I wanted him to sink into me and bury himself so deep, I'd never know what it was like to be without him again.

I'd always feel him, his touch, his mark inside of me.

"Aw, fuck," I cried out as he returned the favor, rocking his pelvis into mine to build me up slow and fucking torturous like he loved to do. My clit was beginning to hum at the sensation, crescendoing to that epic final note I was already dying to hit.

"You respond so easily to me, Ms. Sanders." His carnal voice dropped next to my

ear. "You're like a piano. I push down on the right key," a moan belted from my chest as he tweaked my right nipple, "and you sing just for me."

His satisfied rumble down my neck only made more needy noises spill from my parted lips as I arched to press my tits against him, telling him exactly what needed more attention next.

A seductive chuckle melted through my skin, dark and deeply amused.

"Impatient, impatient, impatient..."

I nodded and panted against the pillow. "Yeah, I'm reliable like that."

My eyes fell shut as the weight of Dominic lifted from mine, and I waited to feel him exactly where I told him I wanted him.

Except, nothing happened.

He was just gone, and I was not in the mood to play the waiting game.

Blindly, I reached next to me until I found his arm and pulled him back over.

Or at least, I tried to.

He put in some resistance, the muscles in his bicep tensing and sharpening beneath my fingers as he jerked his arm back. Impatience—yeah, who's shocked—dragged a grumble through my throat.

Frustrated and groaning, I shimmied my way closer to him until I felt the curve of his large body next to mine. Between my legs was still aching with that throbbing need only he could put out, so I skipped going in for a kiss and went straight to backing my ass up into his crotch.

I moved until my back was flush with his front and I could so perfectly feel the outline of his cock stiffen against my grinding hips.

Dominic sucked air back between his teeth, and pride went soaring all the way down to my curling toes. Which is partly why it was so hard to catch up to the change of emotions as two hands found the dips of my waist and forcibly stopped what I was doing.

"Kat," Dominic practically fucking growled.

"What?" My hands overlapped his and tried to brush them off. "I'm so wet. Come on," I whined, trying to rotate my hips in his hold.

Except his grip around them compressed so tight, not only couldn't I move, but I also couldn't wait to see the bruises he was making now show up later. I loved when he left little marks all over me; I loved knowing I could make him lose control of his *perfect self enough to do it.*

"Jesus, fuck."

His curse was as strained as it was out of place for him, but I didn't care. My lust was in the driver's seat, and all other thoughts were roadkill in comparison.

Instead of thinking, I let my body do the work and tangled my fingers with his, bringing his hand across my body. Together, I laid our hands over one of my tits, cupping and squeezing just how I wanted until he ripped his hand from beneath mine.

This second rejection clouded my mind with hurt and confusion and a healthy dose of pissed off. I was gearing up to whip around and lacerate him for the lady boner he'd given me that he suddenly refused to take care of when hot breath kissed the back of my neck and blew all my words away.

"Kat, you don't know what you're doing."

His lips cusped the base of my ear as he spoke, and I almost didn't register just how thinly threaded the restraint in his dark voice was over the whimper I let out. He was holding himself back. Which made no sense. We'd been over this.

He never needed to hold himself back with me, and I would show him just that.

"I know exactly what I'm doing just like I know exactly where I want you."

Before he could protest again, I nabbed his hand from my hip again and sunk both our arms down between my legs, putting him exactly where I meant. The press of friction down there tore an unabashedly loud moan from between my lips, sensations sparking and climbing.

A curse blew out beneath Dominic's heavy breathing, and his other hand that was still on my waist found a new home clamped over my mouth.

"So fucking loud."

His rough voice dripped down the arch of my neck, and I nodded frantically, hoping he'd be tempted enough to do something about my volume. I was completely and thoroughly trapped against him with his hand wrapped around my mouth and our arms strapped across my front and gripped between my legs.

Needing more than just the touch, I began to move our hands as one in circles over the front of my sleeping shorts. Quick, small circles that made my legs twitch and tiny mewls of pleasure seep between the cracks of his fingers over my mouth.

Another strained groan washed down my back, and his hot voice rasped in my ear. "Kat, you have to st—"

The rest of his sentence morphed into one sexy-as-fuck moan as I pushed my ass against him harder than before, servicing his steel-hard length until he finally pushed back.

My core flooded as he thrust back, digging his cock into the small of my back so hard, I saw stars behind my eyes. I panted into his palm, moving our hands together over my covered clit until those stars behind my eyes turned supernova.

He wasn't moving his hand one fucking bit to help out though. Just letting me do all the work while his labored breathing stuck to the baby hairs on the back of my neck. In fact, all his muscles were strung so taut, the rest of his body felt almost as hard as his erection he'd stopped pressing against me.

He'd given that one fantastic thrust, and then turned to fucking stone.

"What, are you already close?" I breathed, shaking his hand from my mouth.

Sounding like he was one second away from breaking his own jaw, he buried his face in the crook of my neck. "Kat, I swear to fucking god you—"

"I'm close," I cut him off, narrowing my focus to the tightening in my walls. "I'm so so close. Please?"

I begged for him, for the release, for him to let go and give that sinfully filthy side of himself over to me.

"I—" He paused, warring with himself as he slid his hand that was over my mouth to cup above my collarbone. All five fingers primed around my tiny little neck, his thumb being the one to pet the skin sweetly. "Fuck."

For the first time since I'd put his hand there, there was motion in his fingers over my core and a waver in his breath.

"This is a bad idea..."

But I threw my head back and cried out a soft moan, and so he did it anyway.

He moved his fingers again, all on their own, applying pressure over my clit and giving a testing circle. In a test of my own, I lifted my hand that had kept his against me to see what he'd do.

His hand stayed right where it was, cupping my heat and starting to move faster.

"Fuck, yes," I sighed, pushing my now free arm behind me and reaching for him. Dominic hissed between his teeth as I fisted his cock through his underwear, my need for him tripling as I remembered his size.

Thick and so goddamn long and—fuck, I needed him inside of me. Now.

"Kat," he growled against my neck, more gruff than I'd ever heard him before as he buried my name against my skin in punishment, sinking his teeth around it to seal in the conviction.

"Oh my god," I whimpered, my oncoming orgasm inspired by the hungry bite he'd carved into my flesh. I was so close. So fucking close. My eyes pinched, legs twitching, his name falling out on a breathy sigh.

"Dominic…"

The hand over me, the mouth against my neck, the body behind me—it all stilled. The only thing I felt from him was the brush of breath over the back of my neck.

"Not quite."

Then he was gone completely. A protest split my lips as his hand vanished from between my legs, and I jerked around to bring him back to finish what he started. My hands flashed out to grab him, but he dodged my reach, swatting at me instead.

"What the fu—"

"Kat, stop." Anger remolded his beautiful voice, and I didn't get why the fuck he was so mad all of a sudden. It was making me a little mad too.

Wrinkling my nose up, I latched my hands over the globes of his shoulders and pulled him closer, vying for a kiss from the mouth that was grunting at me to stop. Dominic was beginning to sound less and less like himself with every octave higher his frustration reached.

Our legs wrestled as I tried to fit him between mine. He kept fucking dodging my hands as I reached for him, and finally—

"Hey!"

A breath shocked my eyes wide open, expanding my lungs with surprise as I blinked wildly up at the ceiling. Or what should have been the ceiling.

Instead, I bustled back as burning eyes were the first thing I saw, a concentrated dose of irritation like I'd never quite seen sizzling in them. Blake was on top of me—*completely* on top of me and between my spread legs—his hands holding my arms hostage above my head.

He was breathing heavily too. Too heavy for having just woken up.

"*Fuck*, you're horny in the mornings," he exclaimed, annoyance wrinkling his forehead.

Shock rattled inside my head, my eyebrows slicing together. *"What?* Why the hell are you on top of me?"

A look of steam fogged over his darkening face.

Then...

Memories slid into place.

Splices of touching, kissing, Dominic—

My jaw fucking dropped with a sharp gasp.

Oh. My. God.

My dream.

Heat attacked my cheeks as replays of what happened flashed through my spiraling mind, my eyes jumping back and forth between Blake's.

"Was I—"

"Yes."

"And we—"

"Some."

"I was *dreaming.* I-I didn't know!"

"I tried stopping you *plenty.*"

Movement around my wrists brought my attention up, Blake resecuring his grip around them. Shame sickened my stomach that I had to ask why.

"Did you seriously have to restrain me?"

The severity that crossed his face told me everything. "You are a very persistent woman, Kat."

"Oh my God."

Humiliation drenched from the crown of my head to my toes, and I wanted to cry. Nope. Scratch that. I wanted to *die.* To climb into the mattress, curl up, and just die in the suffocation of foam before the embarrassment could kill me first.

Scenes from the wet dream rushed through my head, each one multiplying the heat fanning up my face and intensifying the nerves twisting in my gut. Blake watched me with hooded eyes as I recalled each word spoken, each kiss given, each grope made and wondered which were with Dominic in my dream and which were with him.

Those sensations in my stomach were restless as my stare dropped to his lips. They were a little red. A little flushed. A little incriminating.

"Did we kiss?"

He held the answer back for a beat, the wait agonizing.

"No," he answered, voice hard-edged. "We didn't."

The relief that swept in was swift and short lasting as that restless feeling in my stomach wouldn't leave me alone. Was it guilt? Shame? Self-loathing?

Probably a morbid cocktail of all of it.

I squirmed beneath Blake because of it, twisting and moving my hips to find some relief until...

Until I realized *exactly* what that unsatisfied fist of nerves in my stomach was.

Oh shit.

Blake shifted his weight between my legs, sliding his pelvis over mine in what I was sure was intended as an innocent brush to readjust his stance. It was anything *but* innocent however as the move pressed his still hard cock *right* against my tightly wound bundle of nerves.

Electric tingles shot right up my lower stomach, and I stifled a desperate gasp.

"Oh my god, don't move," I breathed, *begged*, barely holding onto the air in my lungs or the orgasm teetering over the edge that had been so close to crashing through in my dream. I couldn't come. Not here. Not now. "Don't move, don't move, don't move."

Fuck, I'd never wanted to *not* orgasm so badly.

This couldn't happen. This *wasn't* happening.

"What?" Concern upended the frustration in his voice. "Are you hurt?"

And then, he did *exactly* as I pleaded with him not to.

The move was so slight, but it was all it took.

His erection grazed my pulsing clit, and a groan with his name carved into it peeled up my throat. The unintentional friction dragged my awaiting orgasm the rest of the way across the finish line, and I tossed my head back into the pillow to pretend it wasn't happening.

Pleasure tore through me, up and down my legs, and exploded through my core. My eyes screwed shut all on their own, but thank fucking god they did.

Even mid-climax, I was totally aware Blake was watching me come undone, seeing me pant, hearing me moan, feeling me spasm against him as I rode it out.

I swore it felt like it went on for fucking ever, sweat breaking along my hairline as the ecstasy worked my chest in labored breaths. The peaceful wash of warmth that usually blanketed your muscles post-orgasm didn't even get a chance to settle in before humiliation shoved in its place.

The final pulsing sensations hadn't even fully died out yet before I was claiming denial.

"That didn't happen. Fuck, that didn't happen," I panted, hiding my face against the pillow.

Blake's grip was still locked around my wrists, holding my arms against the pillow. In his tight hold, it felt like he'd gone paralyzed, and I was too chicken to crack an eye open to confirm.

"Did you just—"

"*No.*"

But my concealed face, fast breathing, and *palpable* embarrassment said otherwise. Blake could have lied too and claimed he didn't know what'd just happened, but his body gave him away just like mine did.

The pressure around my wrists condensed, his grip sinking his bruising frustration into my deserving arms at the very same time his cock twitched against my heat.

His head dropped low, a predatory rumble vibrating up his chest.

"*Fuck.*"

Breaking the internal battle I had with myself not to look at him, I snapped my head back to glare at him straight on. "I told you not to move! I was too close from the dream and..." My head threw back into the pillow with a vexing groan. "This is *your* fault."

His dark head of hair snapped back up. "My fault?"

"I told you not to move!" I complained like a goddamn five-year-old. Pretty sure I was pouting too.

Clouds of black rolled in from all sides of his stare, darkening every shadow on his slanted face.

"I'm not the one who started this."

The reminder that this *was* my fault attacked my flailing heart just like I knew it would. Guilt was such a reliable son of a bitch.

It was me who grabbed him. It was me who *kept* grabbing him after he pulled back and said no. It was me who put his hand between my legs and made him touch me.

The only thing he did was keep it there.

The feel of his fingers moving against me kept my eyes on his even though they scorched hot enough to replace the oxygen in my lungs with smoke.

"You touched me," I breathed, the fact tasting hot riding out on smoke.

That knowledge smoldered across his stare. "You put my hand there."

I nodded without blinking. "I did."

We'd crossed a line. Unintentional on both parts, but we'd done it. Touched each other intimately, gasped, moaned, rode our mutual pleasures out in the same bed. It'd been two weeks since I started staying in Blake's room, and yeah, those 'boundaries' he demanded we set?

They went to shit almost immediately.

The floor was like sleeping on a slat of rock, and the only other rules he'd set for me were to not talk much and to stay out of his stuff. Those lasted a whole of one night before I was in his bed, yapping about a book of his I'd borrowed and read during the day while he worked.

I convinced my way into his sheets, promising that there wouldn't be any issue, and for the two weeks we'd been sharing a bed, there hadn't once been an incident.

Close encounters? Sure. Waking up closer than we fell asleep? Oh yeah.

But nothing like this, and now… we were in trouble.

See, Blake and I had always had this *energy*. It'd been there since our first encounter, and I knew right away it was dangerous. I'd assumed the hum of electricity was dangerous because *he* was dangerous. But the danger wasn't in him.

It was in us.

There was something about *us* that enchanted the forces and hypnotized the air in whatever room we were in. And now, we'd gone ahead and touched each other. He touched me and I touched him, and now we were fucked.

Because now we *knew*.

We knew what the other side of the line with each other looked and felt like, and that prowling energy that vibrated in the silence between us wouldn't let us forget it. His mouth on my neck was a shadow imprinted and unforgettable just like I was sure the taste of my skin was an addiction permanently saturated in his taste buds.

Which was wrong. This was all so fucking wrong.

Did it count as cheating? I sure as hell hoped not. I loved Dominic. I was *dreaming* of Dominic. But that didn't mean the burn of guilt wasn't still present.

It would be best to act like it never happened…

Which would require Blake to stop looking at me like I was a garden he'd love to set ablaze with his fire so he could get high off of the burnt perfume our essences would create.

"I think you're probably safe to let go of me now," I suggested, forcing a laugh that came out breathier than intended. *Dammit.* "I'm awake. I promise I'll be good."

His grip around my wrists loosened, but he didn't move back. His head ticked, eyes smoking.

"Now that's a broken promise waiting to happen if I've ever heard one."

My lips popped apart.

I couldn't tell if he was teasing or still being all broody and serious and sexy. *Fuck.* Not sexy. Just broody and serious.

If I couldn't tell which he was being, I'd just have to be *extra* ridiculous to pull us as far back to the right side of that line wedged between us as possible.

For sanity's sake.

I puffed another laugh, retracting my arms back down. "I'm a saint," I touted, beginning the move from out beneath him. I only made it what I wanna say was a couple inches before the feel of *several* inches trapped against my stomach interrupted me.

"What the—" My focus snapped down between us, and all the words I shouldn't have said came tumbling out. "Do you have a footlong or something stashed down there?"

I looked back up just in time to see Blake's nostrils flare and his chin dip in warning. "Saying shit like that is the *opposite* of being good."

"Sorry, I just... *damn.*"

Astonishment kept my perverted gaze where it was, competing for a totally inappropriate glance of the outline of his cock through his sweatpants. He was right. I wasn't helping *or* being good. But holy fuck, that was one big dick.

My head flattened back against the pillow, blinking up at him.

"Mazel tov to the last girl you fucked."

"You're incorrigible."

"What? You can't expect me to *not* comment on a dick that size. It would be sacrilegious."

The tip of his angry nose twitched at the same time his cock did. Before I could make the rest of the move out from beneath him, Blake was up off the bed and trudging towards the bathroom.

Grumbling, he said, "I've got to take a shower."

I perked up on both hands, calling after him. "What? Why?"

"Why do you think?" he shouted over his shoulder.

Oh.

Just before the door slammed shut, I yelled back. "I'm sorry!"

And then he was gone, locking himself behind closed doors so he could beat off this morning's frustration as I tried *really* hard not to think about him doing it.

I slumped back onto the bed, huffing a loud exhale that tickled my lips.

What a fucking start to the day.

Today marked just over three weeks trapped in this hellhole. The last two, admittedly, weren't so bad. Hopefully I didn't just fuck all that up.

Blake and I had gotten into a nice routine living in the same room. He got up every morning for work and let me hog his bed all to myself. He came back after Line Up with whatever food he could grab from the buffet.

Every night, I gave him a fresh order of what I wanted to eat throughout the day. He *mostly* delivered. Most of what I ate were fruits and pastries and easy to transport foods, and *god* I was getting tired of it. One night, I told Blake I wanted a batch of fresh chocolate cupcakes. He rolled his eyes.

I did not get my cupcakes.

Usually after he brought me food, he disappeared for the majority of the day while I stayed stashed away in his room with the promise that I wouldn't do anything stupid to escape. After all my failed attempts, I'd learned my lesson.

Plus, I didn't need to fashion some desperate escape all on my own given what Blake and I did with the rest of our evenings whenever he got in for the day.

We planned.

We pitched ideas for possible escapes, going over them out loud to listen for any inevitable kinks. We did this for nights on end, coming up with a lot of half-assed, not plausible, definitely death-wish kind of plans until one of us got too worked up and we called it a night.

If it was me who got too upset, I usually found my way to the floor so I could lie back and stare at the ceiling. Blake would join me on the floor and wait until I was ready to talk again. Then we'd move to his bed and he'd pick out a book of poetry to read to me out loud until I fell asleep.

If it was him who got too upset, I'd crack out his busted laptop he kept stashed under his bed and pick one of the old Hollywood DVDs he had around his room. I'd barely seen any of them, and after a while, he'd join me on the bed and we'd watch his favorite movies until one of us fell asleep.

Which was always me.

It was after one of these movie nights that he and I had our first slip up. Somewhere during Gone with the Wind, I passed out and when I woke up, realized I'd passed out on Blake.

What was almost *worse* was that he didn't move me. Instead, he fell asleep sitting up against the headboard so he didn't wake me. I watched him sleep for a bit that night after I'd woken up. Not really sure why.

Luckily, during one of those mellow-down movie nights was where we finally came up with a plan.

A *really* good plan.

It was simple too. All this escape hindered on was Blake being put on the morning job of driving me to the auction. If he could swing that, then we were golden.

The auction was six days away.

I only needed to make it six more days, and then I was home free. Away from Heather's fucked up family. Away from the constant threat of being violated or killed.

Away from the man of mystery and fire walking back out of the bathroom, a white towel clutched around his trim waist.

"Feeling better?" The smile riding my lips was a total tease, and he—as expected—rolled his eyes at it.

I watched him move through the room from his bed, pulling out a pair of black briefs and dark wash jeans from his closet. He showed me his bare back as he slipped into the bathroom to put them on, and my wayward mind took a dip in the gutter as I heard the drop of his towel and wondered how he looked naked.

Goddammit. I needed to get back to Dominic and get fucked. Like yesterday.

As if I'd put my horndog thoughts on a projector, Blake sauntered back into the room shirtless, doing up the button on his jeans and asked, "So who's Dominic?"

My stomach flipped at the sound of Dominic's name on Blake's rough voice, and I wasn't sure why. I suppose I should have anticipated the question after I moaned another man's name while getting off in his bed.

Stupid *dream.*

Sitting up, I tucked an unruly strand of hair behind my ear. "Someone from back home."

Black eyes flashed up at me, knowing streaking an accusing line across them both.

"*Just* someone?"

My posture shifted, confidence aligning my spine with my pride.

"My someone."

Blake dropped his focus to the floor, nodding while he digested the new information. The idea to tell Blake about Dominic never really fit into the scene we were living here. Blake and I were some warped version of friends out of forced circumstance, and talking about *love* with even the people I was closest to wasn't anything I did willingly.

So talking about it with Blake wasn't even on my radar.

Stare still on the floor, he passed a hand back over his shower damp hair. "Is he the reason Heather put you here?"

I gave a slow nod even though he wasn't staring at me.

"She's about to be his ex-wife."

I watched that well-worn frown deepen between his swarthy brows before he looked up at me. When he finally did, the explicit judgement coating his stare stung a hell of a lot more than I wanted it to.

"So they're still married?"

"Only on paper."

He leaned his bare back against the far wall casually; as if there was anything casual about this conversation at all. Or where it was headed.

"So, he's leaving her for you?"

"*No.* He's doing it for himself because he's miserable with her and has been for years. Plus, Heather's a shit mother to their little girl who's—"

"They have a kid together?" he interrupted, those midnight eyes thinning to a barely breaking horizon over black waters.

Apprehension twisted up my once confident spine. "Yes."

The air—the *energy*—between us started shifting, whirling just a little faster, heating just a little hotter. Goosebumps lifted to life on my arms as my slumbering lightning got a whiff of the thickening tension in this bedroom.

I didn't get a good feeling about where this was going. Not at all.

Blake smoothed a hand over his mouth, scratching at the cut of his jawline. "Seems like breaking up a family maybe wasn't the smartest choice."

Offense slapped across my face, all my features dropping wide. Those words brought me right up off the bed to stand my fucking ground with fire propelling my movements.

"I don't know when this became judgement hour, but you're not really in a position to talk. By the way, how *is* the crime business going these days?"

Razored eyes sliced back up to me as he pushed his weight off the wall. "I'm not saying I'm any better than you. I'm just saying maybe try dating someone who's available."

"And I'd say you're talking about something that is *none* of your business. You don't know my relationship with him or anything about him."

"All I need to know is that he's married and has a kid, and dating him came pretty fucking close to ruining your life," he lectured, sparks firing across his stare as he dared to close in. "So you might want to consider backing off before any other lives get ruined in the crossfire."

Electric light blinded my vision, heat fucking sweating from every pore in my vibrating body. "Who the hell do you think you are telling me *I* could ruin someone's life? Do you even know how fucking hypocritical you sound right now?"

"Kat—"

"No! You're a part of a business that helps destroy lives on a *daily*. You have *no* right to judge me for my life choices when your entire *life* is a choice to ruin others."

"That is not my *choice,* and you know that. You chose to fuck a married guy."

Something in my chest caved in and *crashed,* the collapse damn near excruciating. The pain spurred me on and right over the edge.

"And you chose to stand by while countless women got raped and *murdered,*" I seethed back, getting right up in his face. "You wanna play who's the lesser of two evils with me? Because I fucking guarantee you'll lose."

His stare became something other than black, eclipsing every patch of light within reach. Turning on his heel, he charged towards his bedroom door and ripped the thing open, shouting for Sergio.

Then he snapped back to me.

"Get out."

"Gladly," I snarled back, stomping towards his open door and shoulder checking him on the way out. The second I passed the perimeter of his door frame, I rounded back to deliver a scathing last word.

But the door slammed in front of my face before I could.

I jerked back at the slap of wood, staring wide-eyed at the door. Standing there, the rush of rage warped for just a split second to allow everything that just happened to slam into my chest, knocking the air from my lungs.

Holy fuck.

What just happened?

That fight came out of nowhere and brought such *vicious* winds with it. It happened so fast and was so ugly. I was as exhausted by it as I was overwhelmed.

Blake and I went from nothing to clawing at each other's throats in the time it took a car to crash.

Our collision had been explosive. No survivors left.

Before I could stare at the door too long and wonder if Blake could *feel* my glare through it, Sergio showed up, cursed at my presence, and dragged me back upstairs to the room I hadn't stepped foot in for weeks.

And he locked me in.

Just how I was supposed to be.

A good little prisoner locked away with no food, nothing to do, and no one to rescue her.

Turned out, you could pass hours by in minutes if you were pissed off enough, and *boy* was I ever. I paced the carpeted floors for long enough that I think the tops started to char beneath my fast-footed rage.

I couldn't stop thinking about Blake.

What he'd said to me, how he'd said it to me, *why* he'd said it to me.

There was this angry *pinch* in my chest ever since he'd looked at me how he did. Like I wasn't who he thought I was. Like I was such a messy disappointment.

It took the first few hours of pacing to wear off my temper enough to realize exactly what that pinch was.

Hurt.

He'd hurt me.

Somehow, in the short span of three weeks, Blake had gotten close enough to take a swing past all my walls and armored skin and land a blow. Three weeks. That was nothing. Chump change. And yet, this fight, this *hurt,* was deep enough to throb for hours on end.

As the hours prolonged, the throbbing only got worse. By the time I was sure the sky outside had turned dark, my entire body was pulsing in pain over the fight.

I hated to admit it, but I didn't like that we'd fought. I didn't like that I'd yelled and said nasty things too. *Really* nasty things.

Things that I wanted to take back so I could be in his room again, surrounded by his pages of dead poets and walls of dead celebrities and the knowledge that he'd be coming through the door at any moment.

In these four walls, I didn't have any of that.

I didn't have *him*.

Somewhere in the latest hours of the day, the revelation needled in that it was him I missed the most. As delusional as it was, I missed so much about him that I'd come to rely on to get me through the days.

I missed the smell of his dwindling cigarette's sticking to my clothes. I missed the fresh burn of his gaze heating my skin when I said something ridiculous. I missed how he tried not to smile when I said something we both knew was hilarious.

I missed our late night talks about the world and about nothing.

Strangest of all, I missed our silence and how it was anything but.

Truth was, Blake and I were more alike than I cared to admit. We were disastrous as individuals and cataclysmic when we converged. Our tempers were electric and set off by the smallest spark.

Maybe he had his own touch of lightning.

A time came and passed where I expected him to come get me. Then more time passed, and still, not a single rattle on the other side of my door. It was *way* past the time he'd normally be done with work. It had to be.

I waited, and I waited, and I waited. More hours passed. There came a point where I thought about sleeping, but by the time I should have, the worry in my gut was too painful to ignore as was the possibility staring me in the face.

Was he not coming back?

Was he so pissed after our fight that he'd given up on the idea of saving me altogether and decided to let me rot instead?

Or…

What if something happened to him? Had Claudia found out he was helping me and protecting me all this time and punished him for it? Oh my god, was he in trouble? Was he hurt? Was he something worse than both?

By the time I was sure dawn had already cracked, all my worries and terror found me curled up on the bed, clutching Dominic's necklace that I'd hidden in the nightstand up here with a ball of tears ready to explode waiting in my throat.

One of those two things had definitely happened. I was sure of it.

I was so sure of it, I was in the middle of imagining how my funeral would look after they found my body when the door into the room unlocked.

I jolted up in bed even though I didn't have the energy for it, my throbbing head snapping forward to see who'd come here to mock me or beat me.

My heart shot up my throat when I saw him, clogging it so I couldn't speak or breathe.

We both just stared.

He looked a little worse for wear, and I probably was no better. The slight curl to his dark hair was upended in places it shouldn't have been, illustrating a past of hours spent with anxious hands driving through it. His shoulders were so tight, and I could see that tension went to his clenched jaw.

His eyes…

They were such a refined concoction of relief and regret, I practically fell off the bed running up to stand beneath their black-stained beauty.

I skidded to a stop right before I would have collided with him. I needed to hold on to *some* dignity, right?

"Hi," I wisped.

His dark and tired eyes tracked between mine, taking a slow and unapologetic peruse down my face.

"You should be sleeping."

God, his voice was pure gravel. Even so, hearing it again, hearing *him* again, warmed my chest that had been so cold for so many hours.

"If I'm supposed to be sleeping, why're you here?" I tilted my chin at him, hoping he'd say he was here because he missed me just as much as I missed him. Hoping he would say he was sorry first so I could say it next.

Instead, all I got was the corner of his mouth to curve up. "To see if you got yourself into any trouble since I've been gone."

I rolled my lips together, nodding at the ground.

"Where'd you go?"

"I got pulled to an overnight at Reeves to cover for someone. I couldn't find a chance to tell you before I left."

My head continued bobbing at the floor, not knowing what else to do or say. Suddenly, I wished I had on a hoodie jacket so I'd have somewhere to stick my hands. I never knew what the fuck to do with my hands when I was stuck in an awkward situation.

And *this* was awkward.

He wasn't dead or in trouble or so ticked at me that he decided to abandon me. He was just working, and I'd practically lost my damn mind over it. God, my emotions were so fucked.

"You thought I wasn't coming back, didn't you?" Blake asked, his voice a knowing rumble that pulled my head up until it was hanging beneath his.

"Or that something bad happened to you," I admitted.

God, when did I start being so honest? I was never this way back home, bottling up what I felt and why instead.

Blake's thick brows strung together, that little perfect crinkle happening between them. The pads of my fingers itched to smooth it out, but before I could do such a silly and inadvisable thing, he did it first.

The rough of his thumb brushed my cheek, his knuckles caressing down.

"Nothing happened to me," he whispered like a sweet song.

His touch… it was a flame holding to ice, and I melted into him in that helpless way water bent to the elements. I sunk my head and defenses into his awaiting hand, my eyes closing all on their own to relish in the relief.

I didn't know this was what I'd been waiting for all day, but it was. One touch, and all my hurt was healed. He cupped my cheek as if he knew, smoothing another stroke down my face that shouldn't have felt as good as it did.

"You shouldn't worry about me," he murmured, the words sounding strange on his tongue. As if he wasn't used to someone caring about him.

I peeked up at him, the corner of my mouth moving against his palm.

"Don't get used to it."

His lips closed together, that thin line pressing into a barely perceptible smile. Then, just as slowly as it formed, it faded out of existence and that mouth turned so serious. His thumb on my cheek took another slow drag down, shadowed eyes watching his skin touch mine before he dropped all contact.

He stuffed his hands in his pockets instead, bowing his focus to our feet.

"I'm sorry about earlier," he offered in a low pitch.

My stomach dropped, relief sweeping in. *Oh thank fuck he said it first.*

I might have been taking a crack at the honesty policy with my feelings, but I was still shit at apologies.

I inhaled all the way down to my belly button, breathing out, "Same."

There. We were both sorry and both to blame. All apologies should be that easy.

Blake still didn't look totally comfortable though, his Adam's apple dipping as he swallowed hard. He lifted his gaze back up, passing it over my head and into the room.

"Do you want to stay in here or…?"

He cut himself off, trailing out awkwardly.

A broke a grin halfway up my face.

He wanted me back in his room, didn't he? That's what this awkward dance was all about. *Which* meant he totally missed me today as much as I missed him, and that brought a particular kind of relief flooding in.

Crossing my arms with a wry grin, I goaded him. "Are you asking me to come back to your room?"

His chest widened as he filled it with a slow inhale, his eyes finding their way back down to me beneath him. They went scanning between mine, burning in that sweet-fire way of his.

"Yes."

In all my history, I'd never heard a word spoken in such candor. No bullshit. No flair. Just the truth.

"All right, no need to beg." I stepped into the doorframe, placing my back against it, hands behind my back and a devilish twist to my lips as I eyed him. "Who else are you going to *bore* to sleep with your ancient movies?"

Mirth sprinkled through his expression as he lingered over me. "I think you mean who else is going to try and fuck me in their sleep."

My mouth ripped open, a breath of a laugh escaping through. "You'd be so lucky."

"I've told some guys on my team we're fucking anyway," he relayed with a casual shrug. "They started asking questions about us. How else do you think I'm here right now not worrying about the cameras?"

The revelation jerked my head back, blinking up at him.

"Oh." I didn't know how I felt about that. It also wasn't the first time he'd lied to people about us sleeping together. "Am I still an unimaginative fuck?" I asked with a cock of my head.

A lazy half-grin took his head back, and his teeth peeked out and grabbed his bottom lip.

"You're all right."

"Wrong." I pushed off of the doorframe, leaving him behind with the truth rolling out and over my shoulder. "I'd rock your entire fucking world."

I heard him suck in a slow breath before catching up to me, mumbling something under his breath that sounded distinctly like, "too late."

THIRTY-FOUR

⊱═❁═⊰

<u>KAT</u>

It was two days until the auction.

Things were all in place for the morning of. Blake and Sergio had been assigned to drive me to the auction which was all we needed for the rest of the plan to fall into place.

Blake and I found out they'd approved him to be my driver a couple days ago. Ever since then, that live wire energy between us had been… heightened.

We were both aware our days together were numbered. We just weren't talking about it.

The idea of leaving him here…

It didn't sit well, to say the fucking least. It made me sick, in fact. I *hated* the thought of him here and me out in the world, free like he deserved to be.

I'd never met a soul so intricately beautiful with no hope of ever sharing that magnetism with the world. He'd somehow become so stunning enshrouded in so much darkness.

He was a single white lily who'd grown bright and bold in the capture of shadows.

Every night, he still read his favorite poetry to me, so my thoughts were feeling… prettier? Could thoughts even be pretty? I wasn't sure, but even though I didn't understand much about the words he was painting out loud with his graveled voice, I loved listening to them.

He could talk about a rock, and I'd be drooling.

Tonight was our last night together.

We got the day tomorrow, but I'd have to spend the night in my room upstairs so the plan set off on the right foot when he and Sergio came to get me that morning.

So, this was pretty much it for us. Four weeks all boiled down to one night.

Currently, Blake was sneaking me through the sleeping hallways of the house, keeping it a secret to where we were going. Normally, surprises could suck it, but as he led me by the hand deeper into the quiet midnight of the house, the giddiness in my blood was undeniable.

We made it to the kitchen where he pulled to a stop.

"It's so fucking dark. I feel like a *mime*," I whispered, holding my hands flat out in front of me.

"Wait two goddamn seconds." Blake's hushed voice cut through the darkness and made my shoulders drag to a slump. So *bossy*.

A little *more* than two seconds later, neon white light spilled from some large crack in the middle of the kitchen, Blake rearing open the refrigerator door. His arm ducked inside, and he craned his neck back to me and jerked his head.

"Get the light above the stove."

I obeyed, scurrying over to the stove and flicking on the overhead light. A dull wash of yellow just barely lit five feet in front of it, but I guess that's all Blake needed because he pulled his arm out and let the fridge close shut.

He crossed to me in slow strides, holding something in one of his hands. His other hand pushed through his hair, helping distract from the fact that his eyes were busy on the floor instead of me.

Finally, he made it to my little bubble of yellow light and set the thing in his hand on the stretch of counter.

I blinked down at it and the plastic casing it was in.

Like whenever he read his favorite poems to me, my stomach did a little flip flop.

"Is that a chocolate cupcake?" I asked on a quiet breath.

"You said you wanted one."

Steering my gaze up from the cupcake to him, I nodded just barely. My muscles weren't really cooperating all of a sudden, all frozen in shock like I was.

"And you went out and got it for me?"

The glint from the overhead light made his dark eyes shine as they went between mine. "Do you want it?"

"Yeah…"

The intense focus he had over me transfixed my tongue from saying any more. Asking if I wanted the cupcake sounded like so much… *more* when paired with his smokey voice.

The longer we stared, awareness prickled the hairs on my forearms, tickling on the back of my neck. Next went my breathing, struggling to make my chest rise and fall how it was supposed to.

I knew this feeling. I knew exactly what was happening.

Our energy was attacking.

It didn't take much these days, especially after the dream episode. It was always waiting, prowling for even the most insignificant incident to strike. This unexpected gesture was more than enough to enliven it, to brew the humming over my skin and probably his too, creating a wind of its own around us.

Blake and I were a tornado effect waiting to happen.

And it never ever would.

I shook myself from the tension, glancing back down at the cupcake. "Why is there only one?"

"I don't like sweets."

"Oh. Oh, so you *are* a monster."

The eye roll he gave was practically audible, and I hoisted myself up to sit on the countertop with a smile because of it. Cold seeped into my legs as the underneath of my thighs met the marble of the counter. I fought off a shiver, tugging down the shorts Zoey had lent me to keep in some of the warmth.

"There are chairs right on the other side."

I slid my fingers along the plastic seam of the cupcake's container to the baritone rhythm of Blake's disapproval. "And I'm also going to eat the frosting with my fingers like a *heathen*. That bother you too?"

My smug brow popped up in suspense for his reply, opening up the lid over the dessert. The flames in his eyes had such a concentrated burn on me tonight.

"A lot of things about you bother me."

Curiosity speaking when it shouldn't, I asked back, "Like what?"

His signature black shirt stretched over his chest as he breathed in. I tried to distract my lungs with the sweet flavor of frosting instead of the smokey fire filling the air as he sighed.

"Like how you make every surface something to sit on *except* for chairs."

"The world is my chair."

Another eye roll dotted by a tiny smirk. God, I was going to miss that.

Such an inconsequential thing that I was going to miss like I'd missed seeing the sun these last four weeks. Blake's rare smiles were the sunrise and sunset in here.

He put his arms on either side of me on the counter, daggering me from up close with a look of spirited amusement.

"How you're a total fucking bed hog."

Only because I could see a reason to waiting below, I let my stare drop to his mouth.

"If it bothers you, then why are you smiling?"

The curves of his mouth deepened, his losing battle against happiness so fucking breathtaking. I loved watching him find his smile. Even though he'd never admit it, he loved finding it too. His focus had visibly stepped inwards, and I was pretty sure he was absorbing the memory of how it felt to smile into his muscles.

Sighing in delight, I swiped the tip of my pointer finger through the top swirl of frosting and plopped it between my lips.

If I didn't have to be quiet, I would have totally let a moan rip.

Toffee and vanilla flavors poured around my mouth, and I settled for a quiet sigh as my eyes fell shut. When I opened them back up to dive in for another scoop, Blake was watching me.

Well, my lips.

"That mouth bothers me the most," he rumbled, still close enough that his breath nipped at the part of my lips. "Drives me right up the fucking wall."

I swallowed, my throat suddenly sort of thick.

"It kind of has that reputation."

My heartbeat kicked in my neck as he kept all his dark-eyed attention on my mouth. Whereas Blake's emotions were like a picture book to me, his thoughts were encrypted like anyone else's. Right now, they were crawling all over his stoic face and through his stare, making my mind race.

Every natural instinct in my body was screaming at me to ask him what he was thinking, but my rationale, something that didn't usually get a lot of screen time, told my instincts to pipe the fuck down.

I didn't need to know what he was thinking or what was making his black diamond eyes sharpen like they were.

What we needed to do was change the focus.

"So how'd you manage to pull this off?" I asked, stuffing my smart mouth with a bite of cupcake so I didn't screw it up and say anything dumb.

He pulled an unhurried breath through his nose and leaned back so he wasn't caging me in anymore. "Just told Brett not to freak out if he heard us in the kitchen."

"Being Head of Security has its perks, hm?"

"Theresa doesn't care about my position." He jutted his rugged chin at the sweet in my hands. "She only let me keep that in the main fridge because she doesn't completely hate me."

I nearly snorted. "I thought she hated everyone. She never talks."

"Her English is pretty limited."

Mulling over whether I really wanted to know or not, I *obviously* ended up asking anyway. "What's her story?"

Blake sniffed aloud, pivoting towards the fridge and pulling out a bottle of water. "All I know is her and her daughter immigrated here and were promised 'jobs' working for Ray. They were separated almost immediately."

A pang for my own mother went off unexpectedly in my chest. My fingers twitched to rub over where the pain of her loss dug deepest, but she and I weren't separated like Theresa and her daughter were.

Theresa didn't choose drugs over her daughter.

No. That was me and my sob story.

I broke off another bite of the chocolate cake, popping it in my mouth. "How long has she been here?"

"About a year after me."

Nodding, my gaze tracked a crumb that missed my lips and fell to my lap where the dessert's container was. There was a grocery store label on it that I didn't recognize and even a price tag.

He paid $3.59 for this midnight treat.

"It's so weird for me to think about you standing in line at a grocery store to get this," I started, swiping my tongue over the front of my teeth. "I can't picture it."

"It's because you've only known me here." He uncapped the water bottle and set it beside my thigh. "Hard to picture someone outside of the only four walls you've known them in."

He had a point…

And it got me thinking.

"Do you ever wonder how it'd be if we met anywhere else?"

He gave a confident shake of his head, staring at the counter. "I don't think that's our story."

My breath caught, heart squeezing.

Our story.

We had a story.

And it ended tomorrow.

Flurries of feelings attacked behind my rib cage, and I didn't know exactly why. I buried them behind a deep breath, trying to catch his eye.

"You think we were supposed to meet like this?"

His thickly-shaped brows wrinkled just a bit, severity running its course through his cast-off gaze. "I don't think it would have been the same any other way. If I wasn't here, I wouldn't be who I am now, and you and I wouldn't have anything in common."

Trapped in his words, I asked on a weak breath, "What do we have in common?"

His long eyelashes drew up, fixing his black flames on me.

"Pain."

As he said it, I *felt* that pain seize up, thrilled to be acknowledged as something other than bad. "How we grew up, our parents, the people we chose to love. It all brought us pain," he went on, watching me closely as I came to understand.

"Pain is our nexus," I whispered.

He taught me that word just the other day from one of his poetry books. I made him pause and demanded he tell me what it meant. When he finished defining it, I burrowed myself deeper into his bed of smoke and dreams with an unexplainable crease curving up my cheeks.

Warmth melted the hard edges of his stare, and he nodded. "It's because we're made of darkness that we're able to see the little bit of light in each other."

My jaw practically hit the counter, my breath all but disappearing in his magic words.

"Do you have all of these profound statements just locked and loaded all the time?"

A gentle laugh brought his head down, and I immediately missed the connection with his eyes. I didn't have very long left to look into them. Every second counted.

I used the break in conversation to toss back a swish of water, figuring out in my head how I wanted to word my next question. This conversation was provoking my addiction to him, to *know* everything there was to know about him from prologue to epilogue.

In the end, I asked exactly what I wanted the blatant answer to.

"So you don't think we'd be friends if we met on the outside?"

Instead of giving me the answer, he threw a question back.

"You think we're friends now?"

The narrowing of his eyes brought my shoulders back, protective walls ready to slide down over my heart. "Yes..."

Sure, we weren't your typical Mary and Sue best friends forever kind of relationship, and our origin story was totally fucked up, but we were still friends.

Friends helped each other. Friends laughed together. Friends shared meals together.

Maybe friends didn't lay in bed together and wax poetic until they fell asleep, but *still*.

Blake and I were friends, and I didn't appreciate the challenge glossing over his gaze about the fact of it.

Without breaking eye contact, he picked up the bottle of water I drank out of, bringing it to his lips. "There's no telling what we'd be on the outside."

His Adam's apple moved as he drank, and I watched it like a pocket watch being swung back and forth to hypnotize.

"Maybe mortal enemies," I mumbled.

Breaking the bottle from his lips, my eyes cut back up to find him studying me.

His lips parted. "Maybe the opposite."

That funny, flip-flopping sensation bustled around my chest again, and I struggled not to let it show in my expression. Blake was watching me *so* closely for a reaction, and I was beginning to lose all my oxygen in the burn of his stifling attention.

It was just a maybe. A silly hypothesis. It shouldn't have overwhelmed me so much for Blake to suggest that, in another life, we could've been lovers.

The necklace sitting over my heart grew heavier, and I so badly wanted to reach up and grab it so I could feel like I was grabbing Dominic. He would stabilize me right now. He'd take my frantic heart and remind me that everything was okay.

But I didn't want to draw any attention away from Blake and I on our last night together.

I had forever with Dominic. I only had now with Blake.

"You wouldn't wanna be anything more than enemies with me," I said, ducking my stare to my half-eaten cupcake. "Promise."

"Why's that?"

A humorless laugh tumbled off my lips. "Because I'm all fucked in the head."

A lengthy beat sat between us. I broke off a section of cake to stuff in my mouth even though I wasn't really hungry anymore. I just wanted something to do during the pause.

After crafting such a profound silence, he spoke. "Have you ever considered that could be a magnetic trait?"

I blinked back up at him, swallowing my bite of dessert. "Only to people just as fucked in the head as me."

At that, his radiant fleck of light flashed an appearance in his eyes. "Touché."

That little light of his had been showing up more and more over the weeks. Sometimes because of something I said. Sometimes I said nothing at all. I'd just catch him staring at me with eyes not so coffee black and bitter, a sprinkle of brilliance aimed right at me.

I finished off the cupcake and crumpled its wrapper in my fist. Blake plucked it out and threw it away while I downed a few gulps of water, trying and failing to keep my mind from wandering down anymore addiction-inspired paths.

I'd been with him and only him for almost a month, and I *still* didn't feel as if I knew enough about him to sate my curiosity. All we had was tonight and nothing after.

I didn't see any harm in indulging an addiction when I was going cold turkey tomorrow.

"Have you ever been on a date?"

He tweaked his head at me, dark brows furrowing. "Not really the setting for romance," he answered, pointing his chin at me. "You?"

"No. Not a real one. I've been in, like, group setting dates but never on a real one."

Stupid Daren and all the stupid boys before him.

I'd never really cared about going on dates before, but admitting out loud that, at twenty-one, I'd never been on a date felt kind of embarrassing. Though, Blake admitted the same thing, and he had a couple years on me.

He nodded slowly, digesting my reply as he nabbed the water and blurted out, "What about your guy back home?"

Then he sealed the bottle against his lips, showing me his silhouetted profile. Even in the mere brush of light, the tension strung through his strong neck and up his face was impossible to shadow.

My curiosity clocked the tension, and my mind wrote it off because tonight was difficult.

For both of us.

I shrugged at his question. "Can't exactly go on dates with a married man."

I *hated* saying that because I knew it had to bother Dominic too.

Knowing him, the first thing he'd do when I got home and Heather went to jail was whisk me out for a proper date. He'd bring me to some fancy restaurant I'd probably make a fool of myself at, which he would find *totally* endearing. Then, he'd end the night with something spectacular surrounded by as many people as possible and kiss me in front of them all because he was finally allowed to.

Blake broke me of my thoughts of Dominic, recapping the now empty plastic bottle and setting it beside me. Both his arms went on either side of me again, my posture straightening out to level our stares.

"Where would you want to go if you could choose your perfect date?"

I breathed in his question and accidentally a bit of his burnt scent too. It singed the tip of my tongue, sending a shiver down to my toes as they curled hanging in mid-air.

A hum vibrated my lips as I wondered. I'd never been asked a question like that.

Classic Kat would blow it off as stupid, touting how dates and romance were pointless. However, I wasn't that Kat anymore. I'd been infected. Sick as a person could get.

Plus, something about the way the overhead light backlit Blake's burning gaze seared the words right out of me.

"I wouldn't want anyone else around." I paused, finding the words slowly. "So maybe a… midnight picnic, dinner thing at the beach."

I was too easily pissed off by people, and I didn't want to be mad on my perfect date. I wanted a chance to just *be* with my date. No frills or extra people to please. "Just the two of us. The waves. The stars. Probably a bottle of cheap wine that would be gone by the end of the night."

I topped my fantasy date off with an easy laugh, but it died out when Blake didn't join me.

You know those varying levels of burn Blake's eyes could have?

Right now, they were hitting them all at once.

This intensity was unmatched by any flame struck within him before, and all its heat was aimed at me. Even against the cold of the counter, beneath my bare thighs began to sweat. My heart was climbing up my throat as we stared unspeaking, throbbing in the hollow of my throat and readying to break out and scream at him.

What my heart would scream, I hadn't a clue.

Blake was an unexpected side effect of this place that reworked my wiring so it didn't even make sense to me.

The space between us pressed against my chest, compressing tighter when Blake lingered *just* a hair closer. "When I was younger, I used to live by the water. On the weekends, I'd stay up all night by myself just to watch the sunrise the next day."

The heavy feeling in the air told me I shouldn't, but I asked anyway. "Why?"

It probably was just some shadow trick, but I swore the distance between his face and mine lost a few inches as he spoke deep and so fucking pretty.

"I liked watching a pitch black sky bleed with light. It gave me hope that darkness wasn't forever. That maybe something out there was waiting to lighten my world."

By that point, I knew it wasn't some trick of light. My neck had craned back to allot for the space we'd lost between us so I could keep holding his stare. It was right above me now, closer than it had ever been and taking up my whole view just as the night sky should.

Blake owned the air above me and even the air inside my lungs. It all sizzled with his pitch black severity, conducting a vibration to run beneath my skin that felt like my veins were induced with electricity.

My lightning prickled.

Stirred.

It recognized the feeling.

It moved towards it, curling up against the familiar sensation coursing around my body.

The pout of my bottom lip dried of moisture in the sweltering energy that boiled between us.

Seconds ago, I would have called this an attack of our tension.

But that kindred electricity channeling between his chest and mine like a brewing bolt of lightning made me wonder if it was something else. Something even more dangerous than I assumed.

"We should probably go to sleep," I muttered, trying to swallow past the desert in my mouth. "Big day tomorrow."

Not moving back just yet, Blake switched his eyes between mine. "Probably."

After only a few more moments, he backed up so I could jump off the counter and took me back to his room. We moved through the mansion of lurking shadows for my very last time, Blake leading me deeper into the dark where we belonged.

We were the darkness, he'd said.

I couldn't stop thinking about that as we prepared for bed.

About light and dark.

I thought about it as we slipped beneath the covers, teeth brushed and all the lights out, blanketing us in the sheet of black. Just like a night at the beach.

There was me, captured in the bliss of seclusion with only one other, and there was Blake, waiting patiently for his sunrise to break the streak of night.

As I closed my eyes next to him that night, we were on that beach together.

We were passing ships; we each wanted something just out of reach when timed with the other's wish. I wanted the serenity and stars. He wanted the break of day.

There was only a coveted fraction of time where both journeys could co-exist, right before the stars faded to the rising sun, and that's what these last four weeks had been.

We'd stolen our slice of twilight.

And tomorrow…

My ship went home.

And Blake's kept sailing in search of his sunrise.

THIRTY-FIVE

❧❧❧

DOM

"Did you pack socks?"

"Yes, Mom."

"What about your phone charger?"

"Honey." I glanced up from folding a work shirt to see my father put his hand on my mother's shoulder, rubbing it softly. "He's fine. You wanna wait downstairs?"

"No," she blustered, but reached for and grabbed his hand on her arm and squeezed. "My son is going to another *state* to put his life on the line. I'm not leaving his side until he forces me."

"Mom, I am not putting my life on the line," I corrected, zipping up my overnight bag. I slung it over my shoulder, the weight landing light with only two days worth of items. Tonight before the auction and tomorrow after I had Kat back.

Bag in place, I strode over to my parents who stood in the doorway of the master bedroom. "I'll be back with her before you know it."

"Oh, I know, sweetie. I know." My mother put her fingers to my chest, smiling sweetly at the contact. "It's just my job to worry about you."

I wrapped my hand around hers, holding her fingers that were always so

473

cold. She batted her eyes up, and I gave her a small reassuring smile. I knew what it was like to worry as a parent, but I also knew this mission would be cut and dry, and the only injury I could come back with was in my hand after I broke it on Kat's father's face.

"Do you two need anything else before I head out? Heather volunteered to stay at a hotel while you're both here, but if Maya wants to talk to her or you two need something, you have her number."

My father pulled a face, his mouth driving into an exaggerated frown as he shook his thinning head of hair. "I think we'll be just fine without her, son."

I met his toffee-colored eyes with performance disapproval.

He and Heather never quite got along. She minded him and he minded her, neither ever talking unless necessary. It used to bother me. My father and I had words over it once or twice, but the two never got on.

After a few years of marriage, I sadly understood why.

"Do the girls know why you're going?" My mother reworked a button going up my shirt as she asked the question, fussing with anything to distract her.

"All I told them was I had to go for work."

Maya had accepted it easily enough. Charlotte was the one who cocked her little head at me and didn't say a word. She was so much like her sister in way of her curiosity. There was more to my cover story than I was giving up, and even at her tender age, she'd picked up on it.

"And you're positive Kat will be at this, oh, where'd you say, a *mall*?"

"It's an abandoned shopping center on the outskirts of the city. It closed down right before we moved."

That's where Archie's intel said the auction was happening: Walford Plaza Mall. I'd been there a handful of times when I was on patrol in my earlier years on the force. Even back then, it was a sketchy location, well-known for gang violence and the drugs that were trafficked through its walls.

Now, apparently the place had risen its stakes from drugs to humans.

And that's where I was going to find Kat.

My mother nodded fast, taking a deep breath through her nose. "Okay, sweetheart. Don't you worry about us while you're gone. We'll hold down the fort here as long as you need us to."

She forced a smile up her plump cheeks at me, and I brought her into my side for a hug, pressing a kiss to the top of her head. "I promise to send you to a spa or resort when all of this is done to say thank you for everything you've done, Mom."

"What about Dad? Where am I being whisked away to?"

He chuckled as my mother playfully swatted at his arm. Warmth filled my chest as I watched my parents interact as they always had. With love and laughter.

That was all I'd ever wanted.

I'd finally found it in the form of my employee. My daughter's nanny. The spitfire love of my life.

Today, I was going to get her back.

I moved out of the bedroom and down the stairs with my parents in tow, my work shoes falling flat against the hardwood floors as I made it to the bottom.

"Girls, come say goodbye," I bellowed, doing a last minute pat-down for my keys, phone, and wallet. My gun and badge were tucked safely in my bag. Ryan was already waiting for me outside in his car.

Two pairs of little feet came running down the hallway, one strapped in pure white socks and one barefoot.

Maya slid up to me on her socks, hitting my waist with a squeal and wrapping her arms around me. Feigning a groan, I heaved her up to sit at my side.

"Daddy, can me and Charlotte have ice cream when you're gone?"

"I don't think anything I say could stop Grandma from feeding you bowls of ice cream if you asked."

My mother piped up from the background. "It's what a grandma is supposed to do!"

A toothy grin pinked the round of my daughter's cheeks, and she threw her arms around my neck. She squeezed so tight, she nearly choked me, but I didn't mind. I wrapped both arms around her and held her close, silently swearing as her curls tickled my face that I would be back in two days time for another one of these famous hugs.

A tiny voice from just below split the silence.

"Are you going to get Katty back?"

If it was quiet before, you could hear a pin drop now.

Maya pulled back from our hug, her stare on my face as I looked down to Charlotte. She was staring up at me, eyes glossed with a clarity beyond her years. She was so damn intuitive. For the thousandth time in the last four weeks, I wished Kat was here so she could see how impressive a sister she raised. She'd be so proud.

Keeping Maya on my waist, I lowered to my knees to be on Charlotte's level. She didn't want a bullshit answer, and I wasn't going to disservice her with one either.

"Yes."

Her brown doe eyes searched between mine.

"You're bringing her home?"

I nodded just once. "Yes, I am."

Others might have thought it dangerous to tell a child something with so much confidence when there was room left for error, but bringing Kat home wasn't a gamble.

It was fact. It was the only scenario that existed.

I would find her. I would rescue her. I would bring her home and never let her go again.

Gloom drooped Charlotte's eyelids to the floor, a pout protruding from her bottom lip.

"I miss her," she mumbled, trampling my heart in every sad note uttered.

Before I could reply, Maya was scrambling out of my hold and stepping up to Charlotte.

"Don't worry, Daddy's gonna get her," she told her, landing both her hands on Charlotte's shoulders. "He's a hero."

Maya closed the distance with a hug, both girls clinging to each other as I knelt on the ground with that word pinching in my sternum.

A hero.

Everyone who mattered most to me had called me that at some point. Whether it was because I was on the force or a way I conducted myself, I didn't know. Could be both.

Could be because a father is always his daughter's hero or because a good son comes to his mother's aid whenever she asks. Whatever the reason they viewed me as a hero, I needed to uphold it. A hero fought. A hero conquered.

A hero saved the girl right in the nick of time.

My little lightning thought I was a hero too. Now more than ever, she needed me to prove her right.

I'd swoop in and save her, defeat her villains, and then listen with a smile as she told me she could have done it herself.

I planted a kiss goodbye on both girls' heads, hugged my mom, and shook my father's hand before heading out the front door with his blessing.

He said he couldn't wait to meet the woman who'd turned me on my head like this. He said she must be special, and I replied that she was.

More than could be put into words.

And I was bringing her home.

Tomorrow.

Hold on just a little longer, Kitten. I'm on my way.

THIRTY-SIX

KAT

Today was my final day at the brothel.

It was also my final day with Blake.

We'd gone over the plan for tomorrow morning as many times as we could by now, and it seemed at this point there was nothing left for us to do other than say goodbye.

The very thought made me breathless.

Never seeing him again didn't seem possible. In just four weeks, we'd managed to create what felt like a lifetime alignment. Going back to a moment in my life where he wasn't a part of it didn't feel real. It felt like a bad dream.

But the real bad dream was here and now and there was no sleeping through it. Blake and I had found each other through a twist of fate, and now that bitch Fate was back to collect her blessing.

Tomorrow, everything went back to how it was. I went back to my life, and Blake went back to his.

We'd built a life within four walls that would cease to exist, and letting go of it would be a break heard throughout the world.

Our world.

There wasn't any other choice though.

Still, neither of us had brought any attention to the fact that today was it for us. We were both avoiding and ignoring our feelings about it, which was totally on brand for us but *super* annoying as the countdown dwindled.

Blake felt his feelings like a lightning storm, but he spoke about them like a raindrop in a drought.

In so many ways, Blake reminded me of a fathomless lake. A still stretch of dark and pristine water, too breathtaking not to lure unwitting souls closer. His beauty was so obvious—*now*—and I was one who couldn't help but want to get close enough to see below his smooth surface.

I wanted a glimpse at all the mysteries tucked away in his deep pockets and to know what happened when you swam deep enough to get past the point absolved of light.

Except now I knew if you got too close, you could fall.

And if you fell, you could drown.

I'd already drowned when I fell in love with Dominic.

I didn't have the capacity to do it again.

On the morning of my last day, I found myself alone in his room, sitting on his bed counting the teeth in my mouth with my tongue and staring at the ceiling. The days were always pretty boring alone in here. Usually, I picked a book from his shelves to read until I either devoured it in that one sitting or fell asleep and drooled on his precious pages.

There was *one* leather bound book in his room that I had yet to read.

But oh, was the temptation there.

His black notebook was sitting on his nightstand where it always was and had been whispering my name all day like it always did. He wrote in that thing every night after he thought I fell asleep. I'd never once taken a peek.

Not even *sniffed* it.

I'd been so good when all the loudest parts of me were screaming to be so bad.

But since today was my last day here and all…

That curious voice was *extra* loud and persuasive. It was saying things like, 'what's the harm' and 'this is your last chance to sneak a peek.' Honestly, the voice was making some pretty valid points.

I didn't see why I couldn't award myself with just a *tiny* peep.

Like a sentence.

Or maybe half a page.

Or just one poem.

Or maybe two. Two couldn't hurt.

Oh who am I kidding?

I was reading the whole damn thing and everyone knew it.

I snatched it off the nightstand and dove into the first page, smoothing the soft corners of the poem between my fingers and feeling the words seep through. The first one was something about Heaven and Hell. Real morbid kind of shit.

The next few, I think, were about his mother.

The pages of the well-worn notebook were overflowing, his beautiful cursive engraved into every line. Each swoop at the end of a letter was so romantic. Every sharp slice to cross a T was impassioned. Emotion didn't just bleed from his written words, but from *how* he wrote them.

There had to have been over forty poems etched between the cover and back, none of which I really understood. Parts of lines made sense, and I was usually good at picking out themes or whatever it was called.

By the time I got to the last poem in the notebook, my head was so stuffed full of complex prose and impossible to decipher metaphors, I felt like I was going to explode the world's next greatest sonnet all over the walls.

But I couldn't stop reading.

Not when they were *his* words.

And certainly not when I glanced at the top of the page and saw the date this last poem was completed on.

Three days ago.

I began reading.

My rose

A scarlet beauty
Lips sweet as sin, passion red as fire
Thorns armed to strike

Satin on her surface
Coarse as rot in her core

A damaged beauty
Wilted leaves and teardrops of rain
Vicious elements bend her at the stem
Winds tarnish, heat scalds, hail beats
Animals feast from her what they want

A tenacious beauty
Rooted deeply in the soil
Only Death may befall her
She sheds petals of the past
Armor rising anew as she stands tall

An unattainable beauty
My rose dances with the Sun
A mighty and unyielding force
Feeding her soul, warming her skin
Filling her heart - envy rings through me

My rose is to be admired from afar
Revered in secret
She dazzles unaware
I'd fall to my knees
If she left the sun for the dark moon

She'd thrive in my darkness
Bloom in my light
She is a sweet summer dream
Who will vanish by the end of night

Deep in my veins

My wretched love flows
When dawn comes to rise
I'll kiss goodbye
To my damned scarlet rose

My back sank against his headboard, breath hardly able to escape.

Woah.

Images of sun-kissed roses and lonely overhanging moons cluttered my whirling head. His magnificent words practically jumped off the page and beat over my chest, thwacking the heartbreak of these lines into my own.

This had to be about Abigail. She was his rose: beautiful, ruined by this place, and unobtainable in her death.

Oh god, and he wrote this only *days* ago.

Guilt joined in on the attack over my chest at this confirmation that everything about me and my being here reminded him of his Abby. His anguish was reawakened. His memories of her demise so fresh.

I couldn't stop reading the poem. My addiction to it was voracious, eyes scanning over each and every verse, consuming and memorizing until I'd lost myself so thoroughly between his lines of heartache, I didn't even realize I wasn't alone until someone cleared their throat.

My head shot up with a gasp, the notebook slapping shut in my guilty red hands.

Blake stood tall in the doorway, arms folded across his chest and every bit of his tight focus wrapped around me.

Busted.

My eyes were so wide, I could feel them taking up most of my face. The criminal notebook grew slick between my palms as I took on the full brunt of his unblinking intensity.

His lips barely moved as he murmured, "You have zero sense of boundaries."

I took a smart few seconds to breathe back his voice and digest the tinge of amusement flavoring it.

Holy shit, was he *not* mad?

I did a quick check down his body, noting the relaxed posture and the lack of twitch in the tip of his normally angry nose. My eyes came back up, sweeping over the accentuated muscles in his forearms thanks to his crossed arms, and found his face again.

It wasn't smoldering. The black of his eyes wasn't burning like the seventh circle of hell. In fact, the color of his stare was unburdened of its usual shade of black, shadows lifting to reveal something sweeter below.

Something that looked like melted dark chocolate.

I clutched his notebook harder, waiting for that candied look to turn bitter.

"I would say I'm sorry for reading it…" I paused, giving a thoughtful second. "But I'm not."

He puffed a laugh. A short one that barely moved his shoulders, but it still counted coming from him. "Of course you're not. I should have known better." The bedroom door shut with a click behind him. "Leaving you unsupervised anywhere is a risk."

"So…" I bounced my head back and forth, wondering how far I could push my luck in this humored mood of his. "What you're saying is that this is pretty much *your* fault? Because I can get on board with that."

Riding on light air, Blake strolled over to me with a ghost of a smile twisting the ends of his mouth. The nearer he got, the tighter my chest felt until I realized I was holding my breath. Even as the realization triggered, I didn't let it go as Blake towered over where I sat on the bed, mirth ringing a radiant circle around his eyes.

"You're wearing one of my shirts."

And it smelled just like him.

"I picked out my own going-away present."

He didn't seem to mind that I planned to steal something of his. Not one goddamn bit.

"Why my shirt?"

Holding his stare, I didn't miss a beat. "It looks better on me."

Light dashed in sprinkles across his eyes, and I swore a window sprouted along one of these walls to let the sun in for his eyes to shine so much. Sunshine was even in his roguish grin as his lips spread wide.

"You're so full of shit, Kitten."

Something in my lower stomach clenched violently, rolled over, and straight up *died*. All my oxygen died with it. I bustled back against the headboard, eyes stretching wide.

"Woah, woah, woah," I forced out, the words riding on stale fumes. "What did you just call me?"

Blake batted a heavy blink of his long lashes, totally unaffected by my flustering.

"Kitten."

"*Why?*"

"Because it suits you. Your curiosity, your claws, your soft fucking snoring."

"It's *cliche*."

He cocked his head at me, dark eyes flashing. "Does anyone else call you that?"

Yes. Once.

Right before he fucked my brains out all night long.

"Only once," I answered, wary of admitting the truth.

And for good reason.

"Then it's mine to call you," he decided, claiming the name so confidently.

"But you-but…" The words wouldn't come. All that came was stuttering and blood rushing to my cheeks. It was weird enough to hear *that* name come from between his lips, but it felt even weirder to reveal it was strange for me because the man I love back home called me it first.

"But what?" Challenge narrowed his eyes. "Does it bother you?"

Puffing my chest out and my shoulders back, I nodded. "Yes."

My resistant reply did the exact opposite of what it intended.

Instead of backing away, Blake got even closer. He moved right through my defiance and reached both hands behind me to grip the headboard, caging me between his arms. The unexpected move brought my lips to part and craned my head back as he edged in until his face hung over mine.

Somewhere in the back of my mind, I acknowledged Blake was in a particular mood this morning—a *surprising* mood given the significance of today, but the mental capacity to wonder about his good mood got sucked up into the boundless eyes above me.

Weakness untethered every single muscle I had and unleashed my brain from my mouth as he hovered over me. I went limp beneath him and all the power he was exuding, my helpless eyes falling to his pink lips as they moved, and he spoke way too fucking seductive for either of our sakes.

"Tough shit," He held a pause, loading up the silence with tension before he flashed a wicked smile. "Kitten."

Fuck.

Well, that was that. Dominic could never use that nickname for me again, because there was no way I would ever hear it any other way than rolling out of Blake like a sin dripping in temptation.

He was a candy-coated poisoned apple, and I was trying so fucking hard not to take a bite.

To know him was an addiction. To consume him would be death.

I still didn't quite understand this... *momentum* always circulating between us, but I at least knew it was disastrous. Worse than, in fact, and I needed to veer the course of this conversation ASAP.

"I never liked poetry until I came here," I breathed, still staring up at him.

His dark brow hooked up subtly. "No?"

"No. I didn't get it. I still don't get most of it."

"But you like it now?"

"I like when you read it to me."

The words tumbled out, thoughtless and irresponsible.

But then that diamond snowflake winked in his smiling eyes, and I forgot to regret saying it. Oh well. I couldn't say any more stupid things to him after today. Maybe I was just getting them all out now.

His gaze drifted down my face in thoughtful examination, tying my stomach up in knots. "So all those nights you fell asleep in the middle of me reading to you were all for show?"

"Oh no. A lot of it was boring as fuck." He cracked *another* spectacular half grin. There was a part of me that considered never moving out from beneath him if he was going to keep letting those rare sunbeams fly.

"But I did find a poem of yours that wasn't *totally* boring," I mused to keep words flowing and our unique brand of silence from setting in.

A soft chuckle washed over my face, and before I could stop myself, I inhaled his smoky laughter and held it in my lungs.

"Oh yeah? Which one?"

"The last one."

The second I said it, Blake's suave confidence stumbled. The sparkle in his eyes vanished as did he from where he'd so decisively held a spot over me. He straightened, regarding me with alarm down the bridge of his nose.

"You read all the way to the end?"

Oh no.

Aw *shit*.

Here was that wave of wrath coming crashing in that I first expected.

"Yeah. Yes." *Quick. Damage control.* "And it was *really* good. Like, I was so moved, I couldn't stop reading it, and I *am* not easily moved. Emotions are my blockade, trust me." I tossed in a fake laugh. An anxious laugh. "You're actually not a half-bad poet."

The longer I word-vomited my poor recovery attempt, the deeper the lines in Blake's forehead chiseled. His alarm had morphed into such a severe confusion, and his confusion was making sweat sprout on the back of my neck.

"It was about Abigail, right?" I asked, my tone hopeful.

Every muscle in his face froze, a gloss sweeping over his vivid stare. The air melded with tension as we stared and said nothing. Then he ducked his head to the floor, hanging his hands on his waist.

He nodded without looking up. "Yeah. Yeah, it's about her."

God, I'd really fucked up, hadn't I? He and I were doing so *good* just now— maybe too good—and then I had to go and open up my loud mouth about that poem.

Stupid, stupid, stupid.

"You clearly loved her a lot to write about her so beautifully."

Hesitance softened my tone as I tiptoed further over the line I'd already crossed by reading her poem. It *was* beautiful, and my sincerity in meaning it was what drew his gaze back from the floor to me.

In all four weeks that I'd known him, lived with him, survived because of him, you'd think I'd be used to whatever degree of fire Blake could deliver with just a look. Except right then, when he dragged his fan of dark lashes up and pinned those eyes on me, my naïve lungs suffocated like the very first time Blake and I met.

A colorstorm of too many emotions smattered his eyes *pure* black, his pupils like embered coals. My oxygen went up in smoke in the invariable blaze of Blake's fixed stare, and a triggered reaction of just how much I was going to miss suffocating for him took me by surprise.

The flames in his eyes licked at my thumping heart, charring each layer to blacken and burn.

"Yeah." He swallowed hard, boring his gaze into me. "She was a really special woman."

The way he was staring at me… something in his eyes was screaming, and I wanted to scream back, but I didn't know what to say. I didn't even know what *he* was trying to say with that blistering look.

All I knew was it was overwhelming and confusing and our last day together should be neither of those things.

I needed to change the subject. Again.

"Do you wanna go over the plan for tomorrow one more time?" I asked, setting the notebook back where it belonged. "For good luck?"

I perched my fists next to me on the bed to sit straighter, blinking my full attention back to Blake. He was still holding his jaw tight, a flare in his nostrils saying he knew I was trying to veer the conversation.

"Why? We've already talked it to death."

"I *said* why. For good luck!"

And there went his infamous eye roll. "Nothing's changed."

"Humor me." *Please.*

No, I wasn't being subtle about trying to lift the tension in the room, but Blake wasn't subtle about his irritation with it either. He locked his jaw, a vexing rumble resonating in his chest before he listed out the events of tomorrow morning at mundane, rapid speed.

"Sergio and I get to your room, grab you, you struggle when I put the rag over your face that Sergio thinks has chloroform on it—"

"I'll give my Oscar worthy performance of pretending to pass out," I tagged on with a dramatic hand frill.

"Sure. I'll put you in the back of the van that's separated from the front seats, turn up the radio, and when we get far enough away… you leave out the back whenever you want."

"Preferably when the car's not moving," I joked.

He didn't laugh.

Instead, he snatched a pack of cigarettes off his nightstand and plucked one free. It was lit and burning between his lips in seconds.

I watched with a sigh filling my chest as the orange end flamed molten bright as he dragged a thick inhale.

He had to be nervous about the plan. We were being smart about it though. Well, *he* was. He'd already told me I had to struggle for a good two or three minutes before giving up and pretending to pass out since apparently chloroform isn't an instantaneous thing like in the movies.

Plus, he was going to have a second rag prepped and ready to go that *was* doused in chloroform in case anyone got suspicious of him when they came back without me. Blake said that they'd have their doubts, especially Claudia, but there'd be no proof to tie him to my escape.

His alibi would be set between the second rag and Sergio to vouch for him, and I would be free.

Blake's cigarette was already half ashes, the heavy pulls he was giving while staring off at nothing dwindled the cancer stick at double his normal speed. He wasn't savoring the smoke and slow taste of death.

He was treating it like the real addiction it was. Like he just couldn't get enough.

Even as smoke layered a haze and the scent of fire through the room, it couldn't do anything to mask the tension. It was… *festering*.

Blake himself was festering too, shoulders taut and ravenous thoughts eating away at the pupils of his eyes. That predatory energy of ours and something else entirely were practically visible as they swamped him, riding over his golden skin like a hot glow.

He was cooking from the inside out, and my own body was feeling the heat, blood simmering, sweat building. My lightning moved in my veins, encouraged by the anticipated boil between him and I.

This was *not* how our last day was meant to go.

It was supposed to be meaningful and memorable, not one lit match away from volcanic explosion.

Nope. This was *not* how our last day would play out. I would salvage today if it was the last fucking thing I did in this godforsaken house.

"So," My hands clapped, jolting the bullish tension. "Do you have any special plans for our last day? You know, breaking out the champagne or—"

"I have to take you back now," Blake cut me off.

Every single muscle in my body froze, my fire-hot blood running ice cold. *"What?"*

Abruptly, Blake stamped out the end of his Marlboro and stalked fast towards the open bathroom door. "Yeah. There's a lot to do between now and then. I won't have time to bring you back tonight."

He wasn't serious. He *couldn't* be serious.

"Can't you *find* time?"

He slapped on the bathroom light, already making a grab for his mouthwash sitting on the counter before fluorescence reached all the corners of the room. He put his mouth to the head of the bottle and threw it back, spearmint drowning out the remnants of smoke.

He swished it around his cheeks before spitting, swiping his hand over his fresh-mint mouth.

"No. It's gotta be now."

Blake made busy work with his hands, wringing them around a towel while my jaw hit the fucking floor. He wasn't looking at me or at anything long enough for me to see what the hell he was feeling. He was just moving inside the bathroom, finding needless reasons to keep moving and avoiding me at all costs.

Something was clearly wrong, but I hadn't the faintest fucking clue what.

The absurdity of what he was trying to make happen picked me up off the bed to go meet him in front of the bathroom and *make* him face me. I planted my feet flat and sturdy at the doorframe, a phantom hammer hanging above my chest, ready to swing down and clobber my heart if Blake didn't look at me soon.

Why wasn't he looking at me?

"Are you shitting me right now?" I heard myself ask, disbelief cleverly shrouding the hurt thriving beneath.

Hunched and rigid over the bathroom counter, Blake snapped just his head towards me.

"No, I'm not *shitting* you."

That phantom hammer hanging in wait over my chest was released, cracking my chest in two right down the middle. The brutal truth in his eyes fertilized the break in my heart, blossoming a pain so magnificent from within, Blake could have penned a soulful ode to it.

This wasn't some poor attempt at a joke.

He was serious.

Our time together was ending. *Now.*

We were supposed to have time left. *Hours.* Not mere minutes.

My brain was scrambling, my heart trembling, and I didn't know what to say. I was supposed to have hours to myself while he worked to figure out exactly how I wanted to say goodbye to him, but he was stealing those hours and that privilege from me.

He was *stealing* our goodbye.

And I wanted to know why. I wanted to scream and shove and demand to tell me why he was doing this to us when it was all about to be over. I wanted to shake his stiff shoulders and that decided look from his eyes until it all fell away and who he was when he first walked into the bedroom came rushing back. I'd throw my arms around that man and bury my weak truths of how much I was going to miss him into the smoke infused crook of his neck, and I'd do it without caring how pathetic I sounded.

Because I knew his truths were just as weak and his ache for me would be just as strong when I left.

But I didn't do any of that.

Instead, my pride sealed my lips shut and left my temper to seep between my clenched teeth.

"Fine."

I didn't wait for him to respond. My pride led me around his room, ignoring the memories that berated at every step of the hours of my life I'd spent in here, laughing, crying, dreaming, evolving. I grabbed my necklace from his bookshelf where I put it while I slept and hooked it around my neck, walking straight past Blake to his bedroom door.

I yanked it open and pushed down the hallway for the very last time, taking the path I knew well back up to that wretched room upstairs.

Blake followed the whole way, silent and totally fucking maddening.

By the time we made it upstairs, my temper was vibrating. My whole *body* was a chasm of restrained electricity just dying to rip free. Without saying a damn word, Blake unlocked the door, letting it slowly drift open to welcome me inside for my last night of lonely torture.

My feet went numb on the spot.

Reluctance consumed me in one gulp.

I didn't want to go.

I didn't want this to be it for us.

I wanted there to be more to our story, an epilogue, a bonus chapter, *something*. Our story was unfinished and painfully so. I could feel that unfinished *something* like I could feel my own breathing shake as I tried to control the pain radiating in my chest.

There was more for us than this. There *had* to be.

After all we'd been through, Blake and I deserved more than this measly and unsatisfying ending.

Blake knew it too. He felt that unfinished *something* sitting between us just as I did.

The lovely planes of his face were stained with the knowledge of *more* and that he was the one denying it to us. I'd never seen him as tightly coiled as he was now, and I would bet everything it was because he wanted that different ending for us as badly as I did.

Everything we'd been through up to this point amounted to it, and it was *owed* to us. All the tears, all the shared baggage, all the nights spent learning about each other like we were galaxies with endless constellations to be discovered. That deserved more than this.

We deserved more than pretending our ending meant nothing.

We deserved a spectacular ending, one that lit up the sky with explosions and a parade of fireworks, colors splashing across the black canvas of night just how they did in his ever-radiant eyes.

Our ending should have been something like in the movies, spilling tears from the crowd in a combination of sheer awe and insurmountable sadness that it was over.

Our story together was *over*.

And for some reason that broke my fucking heart.

I forced my feet to shuffle the three steps it took to put me just barely inside the room. I felt my thumping heartbeat all the way down to the arch of my feet as I turned to face him. The separation between us now that I was on this side of the room somehow felt so much worse than just the few inches it was.

It was an invisible line drawn between us that would extend into forever after he closed that door.

My tongue swept out to where dryness had thickened at the corners of my mouth, trying to put words in front of my tongue to get the ball rolling. Words I'd never thought I'd be giving to him when we first met.

"I guess I never said thank you... did I?"

He shook his head at the floor with his hands stuffed in his front pockets. "You don't have to."

An ache pinched my throat, but I tried not to let it bleed into my voice.

"Normally I'd take you up on that offer, but... I think when someone repeatedly saves your life, you should probably thank them. Or bake them muffins, but I'm a shit baker."

That didn't even get a crack of a smile. Not even a quiver.

This was ridiculous. *He* was being ridiculous.

I wanted my spectacular fucking ending with misty eyes and proper sorrow, and *dammit*, I was going to get it.

"Could I, uh, maybe call you once I get to a phone?" I asked, my nerves digging my toes into the carpet. "Just so you know I made it somewhere."

Blake was shaking his head before I finished with his stare still stuck on the ground.

"No. They'll be all over our phone history once you're gone. If they see I got a call from an unknown number, they'll know it was you."

That blistering pain in my chest doubled down as he denied me something as simple as a ten second phone call. At this point, my chest felt downright bruised. Then, his raven eyes flickered up to me for the first time since we arrived upstairs, and that agony in my heart fucking exploded.

"We won't be able to speak to each other ever again after this."

Turned out I was wrong before. *Now* my chest felt bruised. All the way down to my black and burnt heart.

"What about tomorrow? When you put me in the back of the van? We can probably steal a few words." I sounded desperate at this point, and I knew it. I just didn't care.

Blake shook his head and dropped it, reaching up and grabbing the sides of the doorframe in both hands.

"There will be too much going on," he muttered, voice garbled like nails had gone through it.

The sound of it collapsed my breathing in on itself, watching with devastated confusion as his knuckles broke white against the frame of the door. His head was hanging low so I couldn't *see* whatever he was experiencing, but I could feel it.

Our shared energy let me feel goddamn everything.

His anguish pushed out of him and dove headfirst beneath my skin, pouring through and twisting around my bones. His restraint dug its claws deep down to the base of my spine as a threat to keep from moving against it. I could *feel* everything he was, and it was how I knew he was just a shoestring snap away from losing it.

He was trying *so* hard not to give into our goodbye, and it didn't make sense *why*. His emotions had unapologetically ruled him from day one.

I didn't see why he was trying to hide them now.

"Blake…" I tried.

He sucked in a sharp breath and ignored me.

Balling my fists up at my sides, I kept pushing. "Will you look at me?"

"*Why?*" he growled, the word slicing between his clenched teeth.

"Because I want to see you before I can't anymore."

The wood of the doorframe whined beneath Blake's grip as he squeezed down, his knuckles bleeding as white as the wood itself. A mangled noise tore through his throat, and his head snapped up suddenly, a tiny gasp getting caught in my throat as our eyes fastened.

Pain. So fucking much of it.

It was everywhere over him, a hurt like I'd never seen him wear before radiating from deep black pits. My own pain wrestled up my windpipe, trying to break out in a whimper so his pain knew it wasn't alone.

Misery loved company, and pain was no different.

We shared in our suffering and for once in my stubborn life, I had no problem admitting exactly what I was feeling. All this fucking sadness. The longing. The overwhelming, gnawing sense of something *more*.

Blake felt it all too, the evidence writhing in his torrid eyes.

God, everything inside of me was screaming to reach out and touch him and absorb his hurt. I could handle the extra dosage if it meant lessening his. He'd done that for me while I was here more times than I could count, and in our last moments, I thought how fitting it would be that I could do that for him.

The only problem being I didn't know *why* he'd suddenly decided to shut me out.

We had just *minutes* left before we were nothing but memories of a time. Our ending was now, our final words being scribbled on the last page, and even though it hurt like a bitch, he needed to woman the fuck up and deal with it.

"Is this really how you want to end it?" I asked, an unavoidable thickness to my trembling voice. "When I don't come back tomorrow, is this *really* how you want to remember leaving things between us?"

An ache cracked up the front of his expression, breath that tasted like suffering blowing through his lips. "I don't…"

But then he stopped himself, and I could have dropped to my knees and sobbed.

"You don't what?" I pleaded on a frail breath.

He said nothing. Just stared down at me like I was a knife he was waiting to fall on.

In a last ditch effort, I gave into that voice screaming inside of me to touch him and lifted my arms to lay my hands over his on the frame. Heat melted through my fingertips as they tingled; they were so *relieved* to touch him in some small way.

At the same time a lump of euphoria jumped up my throat at the contact, a strangled groan tore through Blake's.

Any joy left in the muscles of my face got dragged down by devastation.

It was just a touch. My hands on his, but he reacted like I'd scorched him. A cry of helplessness hitched in my chest because I didn't know what else to do.

I didn't know what was happening or why everything I did or said seemed to make it worse. In the past few weeks, it'd been *proven* that sometimes all either of us needed was the feel of the other to calm down. There was something in our skin that acted as a balm to our nerves whenever we came in contact.

I didn't understand it. I understood very little about our connection actually, but I knew what I felt when his skin touched mine, and I could read in his eyes that he felt the same whenever I touched him back.

Peace. Unconditional peace in the palm of our hands.

Until now. Until right at our very last minute when peace was impossible and Blake was resisting it with everything he had. He sliced his stare over to my hand on his, a boil of emotions fighting to bubble over.

He scrutinized our hands together with fire roaring in his eyes, but I couldn't tell if he wanted to use that fire to burn my hand off or fuse our fingers together so we could never let go.

My breathing was a mess. A total fucking mess as I stood in patience for whatever he wanted to do next.

Slowly, his thumb rose off of the frame and into the air, waiting there with no clear intentions. I watched it harder than I'd ever watched anything in my whole life, waiting to see if he'd peel the rest of his fingers away and slam the door in my face without any of our deserved last words.

I'd break if he did that. Just shatter and scream until my screams were a part of this house, haunting the walls and him for eternity.

Instead of a scream, the most crippling whimper I'd made left my mouth as warm fingers threaded through mine and Blake enveloped my hands in his wholly.

In a rush of quick motions, he used our hands as life rafts to each other and brought us toe to toe, face to face.

Another whimper fell out as my head dropped beneath his that hung so close over mine. Our energy burst in a song of celebration, pulsing around us and humming a tune of anticipation in the air. Blake squeezed my hands in his, staring down at me like I was still that awaiting knife, but now he was ready to be pierced.

I squeezed his hands right back, an ache of tears burning in my throat.

All I knew was him around and above me, a fresh mix of fire and spearmint brushing the tip of my nose as he lowered himself closer. My head fell back inch by inch as he neared, surrendering in that weakness I wasn't afraid to show him.

"What do you want me to say…?" His whisper danced across my face, stealing my own voice away to nothing.

"Anything," I breathed.

Say you'll miss me.

Say you'll think about me.

Say you wish you didn't have to say goodbye.

There were so many things I wanted him to say before he couldn't say anything to me ever again. My breathing was labored and shallow with the thoughts of it all while his was calm and heavy. The space between us was an electrified field that was only getting smaller as Blake lingered in.

A wash of hot breath fanned my parted lips right before black eyes dropped to them.

Realization clenched in my stomach, the heat holding in his stare simmering a line of anticipation across my bottom lip.

The bottom lip he was so boldly captivated on.

Nerves rolled through my stomach… but I didn't back away.

Not if this was what he wanted. Not if this was what he wanted for our spectacular ending.

His stare jumped back up and latched onto mine in those final seconds, burning this moment between us as we both silently acknowledged what was between us and had always been sitting just beneath the surface.

A passion, scorching and undiluted and absolutely lethal.

"You're right," he murmured over my lips. His eyes never left mine. "You really don't get poetry."

A tidal wave of confusion crashed in as Blake suddenly unlinked our fingers and backed up, giving me one last blistering look before reaching for the knob and slamming the door shut in my face.

I stumbled away from the door as if the slap of it shutting were a gust of wind blowing me back.

I blinked at the wood, muscles frozen and eyes retched wide.

I couldn't speak. I couldn't move.

'You really don't get poetry.'

What the actual fuck was that supposed to mean? How was *that* the sendoff he wanted to leave me with? After everything? I couldn't do anything with those words. They were meaningless final words, which meant he'd just stained our entire four week friendship as just the same. *Meaningless.*

We were *so* close. So fucking close to our spectacular ending, and now all I had was an insult to go home with.

I laid in bed all day and all night festering about his last words. My brain kept splicing between them and Dominic. When I reached a phone tomorrow and called 911, I had no doubt he'd be the first one to come and get me. I knew I was in Georgia instead of South Carolina, but the drive wasn't far, and Dominic would drop everything to come rescue me.

My hero of thunder and inexplicable love.

My ignorant fucking hope tingled in my stomach at the very thought of seeing him as soon as tomorrow.

I spent so long in that bed imagining my reunion with Dominic and being pissed at Blake, I didn't even realize I'd passed the night away and it was morning until there was a jiggle at my bedroom door.

Quickly, I twisted over in bed and pretended to be asleep for when the lock unclicked.

Behind my closed eyes, I pictured Blake walking in with Sergio and wondered if I could get a nice crotch shot in during all of my pretend struggling.

The door slowly crept open across the room, and I took that as my cue to start the show. I gave a wriggle under the sheets, an early morning groan through my chest as I rubbed my fingers in my 'sleepy' eyes.

I heard one of them shush the other, and I assumed that was probably enough to 'wake me up'. Tapping into every ounce of dramatic flare born in my blood, I snapped up to sitting with a gasp widening up my throat.

Every muscle tightened with faux panic slacked as I looked at the two men.

My eyes went back and forth between them both.

Authentic panic snuck into place right where it belonged.

Because it wasn't Blake. It wasn't Sergio.

I didn't know who these men were.

Something was wrong.

Run, my mind whispered.

Now.

Everything in the next few moments happened in slow motion.

My heart dropped into my stomach as I scrambled to get out of bed and make a run for it. My screams scraped down the walls of the room, ringing out long and hard as one of the men caught me before my feet could touch the carpet.

My legs kicked out as he lifted me up by the waist, shoving a fat hand over my open mouth.

A prick stabbed at my neck, terror pricking at the back of my eyes.

Coldness ran down the sides of my face as darkness faded in at shocking speed. All the fight in my muscles went loose without my permission and a tortured cry muffled beneath the intruder's hand.

The curtains were being pulled on my tragic story, blackness consuming all the light and swallowing my happy ending up whole.

As I fell into total darkness, one man's name fell down the back of my fading mind with me, an echo of help following me down, down, down as I swan dove into the abyss.

499

END OF BOOK TWO.

Kissing Death: The Final Book

⚜

Read the conclusion to Kat and Dom's story NOW!
Link: http://hyperurl.co/gwwi5s

A rose is nothing without its thorns.

Death was such a funny thing.
It was a fickle *biatch*, if I was being honest.
When I met Dominic Reed, I got my first taste of death and became addicted
to its flavor. Its *potency*. I died when I fell in love with him and his thunder.
Now, the death staring me down wasn't the pretty metaphorical kind, but
the kind that chased you down until your heart gave out.
And all because of love.
Stupid love that I didn't even understand or want, but feelings were
nonconsensual little devils. Dominic had started that revelation.
Blake confirmed it.
In all the fairytale love stories I'd been fed growing up, the princess never had
two suitors waiting for her hand. The only choice she had to make was how
many woodland creatures to invite to their white wedding. Not whether to
stay with the light or drift back towards the darkness she was born into.
Those stories always ended in sparkling smiles and true love's first kiss.
For me…

My story would end in blood.

501

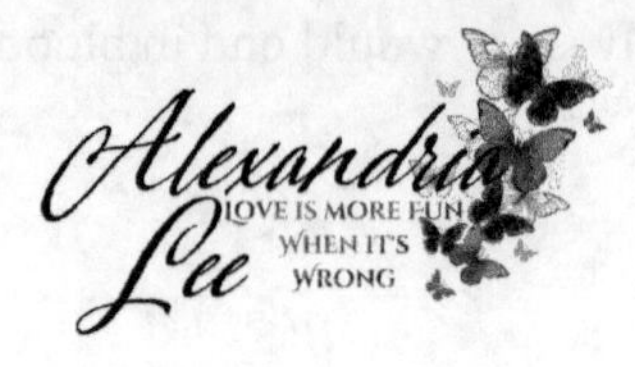

About the Author

I'm an author who loves chatting with my readers! Join my exclusive Facebook reader group for exclusive content, games, and giveaways!

You can connect with me on:

 https://linktr.ee/AuthorAlexandriaLee

 https://www.facebook.com/groups/1155988098182494

Subscribe to my newsletter:

 https://mailchi.mp/d47a710b9325/author-alexandria-lee-books

Pre-Order Kissing Death, the final book in The Star-Crossed Series below!

Kissing Death: Star-Crossed Series (3 of 3)

The epic conclusion is here...

There's Venom in Her Kiss

As a boy, I'd developed a likeness for control.

As a man, that likeness had corrupted into an obsession. Scarlett Avery was the twenty-one-year-old *brat* committed to setting my obsession on fire and dancing in the flames. Literally.

I was an FBI agent, and she was only meant to be a quick assignment. My orders were to chauffeur Little Miss Loud Mouth across the country to deliver to her father—my boss—after her not-so-minor brush with arson.

Now, I was trapped in small confines with a woman that made my hands itch to wrap around her pretty neck and squeeze—and what's worse?

She wanted me to do it.

In fact, she begged me to break her.

Scarlett Avery was a woman of secrets and sins packaged in a body twelve years too young for me and completely off-limits.

She's my boss's daughter, and I shouldn't think about her wicked smirk or fantasize about ways I could rearrange the pouty curves of it. I definitely shouldn't give into the dare always written into the green of her eyes, baiting me to hunt her.

Destroy her. Punish her.

Scarlett wanted a depraved monster.

But she had no idea how nightmarish I could be.

Dancing with Sin: A Standalone Forbidden Love Story

Alice Monroe is a good person who is about to do a very bad thing.

All my life, I had worked tirelessly to achieve perfection. Perfection was in my blood, and so was the art of dance. All that hard work had earned me my dream job as a professional dancer, the perfect boyfriend, and the naïve belief that perfection was built to last.

All it took was one night.

One night to tear down everything I had built until I was left single, jobless, and my heart stained with betrayal.

With my tail tucked between my legs, I drove me and my broken heart to Chicago to move in with my older sister until I was back on my feet.

Little did I know that this was just the beginning of my twist of fate nightmare. E

than Black was waiting for me in Chicago as a perfect stranger. A handsome, effortlessly charming, makes-my-heart-beat-out-of-my-chest stranger. I didn't subscribe to the idea of soulmates before him, but now I'm convinced.

The only problem?

Ethan's engaged to be wed to my sister.